AT WAR

Milly Adams lives in Buckinghamshire with her husband, dog and cat. Her children live nearby. Her grandchildren are fun, and lead her astray. She insists that it is that way round. She is also the author of *Above Us The Sky*.

Also by Milly Adams

Above Us The Sky

Milly Adams
SISTERS AT WAR

arrow books

1 3 5 7 9 10 8 6 4 2

Arrow Books
20 Vauxhall Bridge Road
London SW1V 2SA

Arrow Books is part of the Penguin Random House
group of companies whose addresses can be found at
global.penguinrandomhouse.com.

Penguin
Random House
UK

Copyright © Milly Adams 2016

Milly Adams has asserted her right to be identified as
the author of this Work in accordance with the
Copyright, Designs and Patents Act 1988.

First published in Great Britain by Arrow Books in 2016

www.penguin.co.uk

A CIP catalogue record for this book
is available from the British Library.

ISBN 9781784751050

Typeset in 11.5/14.5 pt Palatino by
Jouve (UK), Milton Keynes
Printed and bound by Clays Ltd, St Ives plc

MIX
Paper from
responsible sources
FSC
www.fsc.org FSC® C018179

Penguin Random House is committed to a
sustainable future for our business, our readers
and our planet. This book is made from
Forest Stewardship Council® certified paper.

For those who served on trawlers in the Second World War, especially James William Rudder Meadows who died on 9 April 1941.

For all the Air Transport Auxiliary men and women, especially Maureen, my cousin.

And of course my mum, who served during the war in Queen Alexandra's Imperial Military Nursing Service (QAIMNS) as a nurse and Dad, who was a fighter pilot in the RAF.

May the wind always be beneath their wings.

Acknowledgements

I am old enough to have grown up hearing anecdotes and family history of the Second World War, throughout which my father was a RAF pilot. Somehow our parents' memories become ours. His admiration for the ATA pilots was immense, and also his knowledge of the work of the ATA men and women. Add to that the fact that another family member, a woman, my cousin Maureen, flew with the Air Transport Auxiliary and you have a reason for me to write this book.

I flew a Spitfire simulator in the ATA Museum section of the Maidenhead Heritage Centre. My father always said it was a woman's aeroplane, and it did feel so. I am not a natural. I crashed through a barn on landing, but it was fascinating to see the memorabilia and generally bone up on the subject. I read around the subject, obviously, and enjoyed *Spreading My Wings* by Diana Barnato Walker, *The Female Few* by Jacky Hyams, *Spitfire Women of World War II* by Giles Whittell, and *Spitfire Girl* by Jackie Moggridge

As for Jersey: a beautiful island, and again I was steered by a friend of a friend's memories and experiences of the war and found *A Doctor's Occupation* by Dr John Lewis amusing and interesting. Charles Cruickshank's *The German Occupation of the Channel Islands* kept me on the straight and narrow.

Trawlermen are a race apart, their courage often ignored if indeed it is known. They should have an honourable and enduring place in our wartime history. I am indebted to a little book I found – *Terriers of the Fleet: The Fighting Trawlers* by 'First Lieutenant' written during the war, which gave me a close-up view of their world. Him indoors, my husband, an ex-submariner, has an understanding of things maritime which far surpasses my own and he led me through the tumultuous seas with aplomb.

Thank you all. You have my immense admiration and gratitude for your pluck and sacrifices.

All mistakes are my own.

Chapter One

Early May 1940

A bird, that's what I should have been, a bird, Bryony Miller thought as she sat at the controls of Combe Lodge Airline's de Havilland Dragon Rapide, high above the white-capped sea. She was outbound from her home, Combe Lodge, near Exmouth, heading for Jersey, her leather jacket undone, overalls stained with engine oil. She loved the sense of escaping the earth, and the soft purr of this particular twin-engine biplane, though her business partner, Uncle Eddie, called it an infernal drumming, and said she was not to be such a silly sod.

She laughed out loud, hearing his voice as though he was next to her, and she patted the control panel. 'Purr away, my little Dragonette. Uncle's a nasty horrid man who's left me running our little airline and home, while he prances about in a wartime uniform. Quite frankly, he's more than old enough to know better.'

That too would have made him groan. She searched the early summer sky wondering if he or any other Air Transport Auxiliary pilots were flying replacement aircraft towards the French coast where British forces were fighting the Nazis. Usually the Ancient and Tattered Airmen, as the civilian ATA force was commonly called, flew military aircraft from factories to maintenance units for arming. But perhaps they were now replacing lost planes on the front line?

Certainly things must be desperate, because they had started to admit a thimbleful of women, but only a tiny few. Bryony searched the sky again. There was only one other aircraft and that was heading north, probably bound for Exeter Airport.

She peered down, seeing what looked like a mass of toy boats heading to and from the Channel Islands. They would be carrying holidaymakers, or returning islanders, and of course potatoes to the mainland of France or Britain. There were some fishing smacks too that would return to harbour at day's end.

She continued and before long Jersey was in sight. It was then that she turned her head, raising her voice, calling to the six passengers sitting behind her in the three rows of double seats separated by a narrow aisle, 'If you peer out of the left-hand windows, you can see in the distance the coast of France and ahead is Jersey. But stay seated please, and no dancing in the aisle or you'll tip us, and we'll head down to Jersey, all in a spin, literally. What's worse, Old Davy who's sitting next to Adam Cottrall won't get back to tend his pigs. The pigs, however, won't go short, because if we hit the deck someone will just feed us to them.'

Above the laughter, and just behind her, a hand shifted her leather helmet, and Adam, leaning forward, said, 'You could land us whatever the conditions, Bee. Uncle Eddie taught you well.'

Adam was the man she loved, but having grown up with Bryony he treated her as some sort of scruffy little brother in overalls, just as all her male friends did. Well, hardly surprising, as she was usually bum up and head down deep in the bowels of an aircraft engine. Or so her mother seldom failed to remind her, in *that* voice.

Old Davy called, 'I can hear you buttering up our Bee, young Adam. Ain't she looking after you proper while you're home at Combe Lodge on sick leave? Tell you what, our Bee's not getting any younger you know, twenty-three if she's a day, and you're the right age for her, twenty-six, ain't you? It's time someone took her off the shelf. You could call her Eve and the two of you could walk off into the sunset.' He paused, then said slowly and loudly as though the other passengers were deaf, daft or just asleep, 'Adam and Eve, got it?'

Bee knew, as she drew ever closer to the coast, that Old Davy would be looking round the cabin for appreciation, and receiving it, more's the pity. Not getting any younger, indeed. All the time she was thinking these thoughts she was alert to the wind, to the engine sounds, to the Dragonette's feel:

to be complacent could mean disaster. She looked around, up and down, then glanced at the control panel. All was well.

Buoyed by the laughter, Old Davy continued with gusto behind her. 'Well Adam, my old lad, you with the fishing smack, or is it a pleasure boat, never know which . . .'

'The *Sunflower* serves as both,' Adam said.

'Well, whatever it is, what with your boat and Bee's half share of the airline, the pair of you could have a right good business when this darned war is over and you could call it . . .' He paused as though waiting for someone to guess, but no one did. Please, please, thought Bryony, let them have gone to sleep. She crossed from sea to land and followed the road leading to her Uncle Thomas's farm and the landing strip

'You could call it Adam and Eve's Juicy Apple.' His cackle almost choked him but didn't.

Lieutenant Manders laughed, but without amusement. 'Lord knows when it *will* be over. Our expeditionary force to Norway couldn't do a thing to help when the Germans occupied them, we just got our bottoms smacked.'

His wife hushed him. 'We're here for a holiday darling, just as that nice Mr Churchill advised us all to do. Besides, it will help your leg. Well, your non-existent leg.' Her voice held breathtaking bitterness. 'Some people call this the phoney war, but we know different.' The bitterness had deepened.

Adam muttered in Bryony's ear, 'The lifting of

some air travel restrictions got us back in the air and earning a few pounds but Manders is right, I doubt it will last. The Nazis are just steamrolling over everyone, and . . .'

She looked around again, then up and down. In Jersey, as in the countryside near Exmouth, the trees were in full leaf, the daffodils long finished, the potatoes being transported in trucks to the port of St Helier. She had knotted the daffodil leaves at home, and her dianthus were blooming, the digitalis too. What's more, the box hedges she and April, Adam's mother, the housekeeper at Combe Lodge, had planted had all survived the winter. It was easier to think of things growing, of nature continuing unabated, than the uncertain state of their world. Adam was waiting for a reply. She said, 'Quite the little ray of sunshine aren't you, Adam Cottrall. You're clearly getting better and back to your positive self.'

He touched her shoulder. 'Indigestion, I expect, thanks to your revolting hard-boiled eggs for our breakfast this morning. But I have to say, the toast was good.'

Soon he'd be telling her she had earned a trip to the pub for a quick one with the rest of the lads. She made herself laugh. 'I know you'd rather have your mum's fluffy scrambled eggs but she's too busy cooking meals for the hotel to pander to hypochondriacs like you. Just be grateful I keep some sort of an eye on you and let's not pretend I enjoy it.'

What else could she say, with Old Davy's idiocy

hanging in the air? Well, she could say: yes, let's stick together, not for the sake of the company but because I'm a woman and adore the earth you walk upon, and always have.

She glanced all around and below, then at her instruments, and gradually eased back on her speed and height once they passed Haven Farm Bridge, which marked the extent of her Uncle Thomas's land. She called, 'Make sure you're all strapped in, please, as we'll be landing very shortly. Adam, I can hear you wheezing even over the Dragonette's purring, so keep that jacket on when we land, or I'll have your guts for garters.'

Adam groaned, 'Ever the lady.'

The Dragonette's shadow flashed over fields. 'Everyone – Adam will have a quick look around to check your straps.' Behind her, Adam coughed, and then again and again. Soon he was gasping for breath. When at last he could speak his voice was weaker and she could hear the strain in it as he checked the straps and kept up small talk.

He returned to his seat and squeezed her shoulder once more before settling back. She straightened her helmet, descending into the wind, checking and rechecking her instruments, her height, her speed, easing the yoke, gently, gently. She saw Uncle Thomas and Aunt Olive arrive at the field, with Rosie, Hannah's mongrel. The doc's Land Rover skidded in through the gate. He always came if there was a landing, just in case of trouble.

Hannah, her seventeen-year-old sister, was not amongst the welcoming party and Bryony felt thankful, though relaxed when she remembered that there would be no histrionics just for once. After all, it was Hannah who had telephoned her, requesting a return flight to Combe Lodge, so she could start at art college.

The Dragonette landed, feather-light, holding steady as it rumbled along the grass with no yawing until it finally stopped. Bryony switched off, and eased her shoulders in the silence. It was always a relief to be safely down. She stretched and removed her helmet, her dark auburn hair falling free. Sweat had dampened her temples. She returned the waves of the doc, and her aunt and uncle before hanging up her helmet. Only then did she slip back through the cabin, where the passengers were undoing their straps.

Adam had the cabin door open. He slipped on to the wing and then the ground, settling the footstool he'd been carrying firmly on the mown grass. Bryony followed, feeling the warm breeze and the soft Jersey air. She held up a hand to Lieutenant Manders, who was sitting on the wing. He slid down, and his wife followed with his crutches, then Old Davy, and finally the last passengers, Mr and Mrs Devonshire. Adam handed Bryony a couple of suitcases while he took the rest. Old Davy toted his own carpet bag.

Lieutenant Manders and his wife struggled over the grass towards the welcoming party with Bryony alongside. Adam had been in Norway too, or almost. A shell had landed near his armed trawler just off the coast and blasted him off the deck into the cold sea, hence the double pneumonia and sick leave.

Bryony heard the doc drive off, saluting her with a couple of hoots. Aunt Olive met them, hugging Mrs Manders as though she was an old friend, patting her shoulder. 'There there, this week will build you both up.' She smiled at Bryony, took the cases, whispering, 'Darling Bee, I'll take over here, you wait for Mr and Mrs Devonshire.'

Rosie was sitting at Bryony's feet, her tongue lolling to one side, her tail wagging. Bryony laughed, and squatted to stroke her while Aunt Olive led the Manders to the gate where Clive, the conscientious objector, was waiting with the trap. He had been sent to Jersey with the other COs to work the potato fields, and earned unofficial pocket money by acting as a taxi service for Uncle Thomas's holiday cottages.

Old Davy caught up. He lived in a cottage not far from Haven Farm and would walk. He pulled Rosie's ears, and as Bryony rose, Adam called, 'You walk on, Bee.' She and Old Davy reached the gate, where he gave her a smacking kiss and slapped her bum. 'You're a great girl, Bryony. If I was younger . . .'

Bryony grinned. 'Or if I was even older and more dusty from the shelf . . .' He cackled and left.

Mrs Devonshire reached her, holding on to her hat to prevent it reaching St Helier ahead of them. She and her husband were heading for a hotel there.

Mr Devonshire arrived, and took his case from Adam saying, 'Thank you, Miss Miller, we will use you again, if, please God, things go well in France. I gather that's our taxi?' He pointed to Jack Blanchet's Morris parked on the side of the road.

Bryony nodded. 'Now remember, I'll be here this time next week to return you to the mainland. Have a lovely holiday.' The couple hurried away. Adam stood with her, waving until the transport was out of sight. She could hear that his chest was worse, and wished she hadn't agreed to let him come. They began to tramp back to the landing strip, where Uncle Thomas was chocking the Dragonette's wheels. Though the wind was strong the sun was hot and halfway there Bryony stopped, lifting her face. 'You need to sit on Aunt Olive's terrace, Adam. It's sheltered and you can breathe in the clean air. You're not even half recovered. Your chest is still bad, and your arm's not healed from the shrapnel.'

He said, 'Never mind me, you need to brace yourself. Hannah's just slouched in the gate and looks as though she has something on her mind.'

'What? But we're doing her bidding.'

Uncle Thomas finished chocking and came to them, hugging Bryony. 'Bee, my lovely lass, all well? Good to see you, Adam – feeling more the ticket, are you? Don't look it, I have to say, but brace for a choppy landing, both of you. Hannah's attacking from the rear. Been in a foul mood these last two days, but what's new?' He grimaced and fled back to the aircraft to lock the doors and check this, that and the other; clearly anything to avoid his youngest niece.

Bryony sighed, raising her eyebrows at Adam. 'I'm getting too old for this.'

Adam laughed. 'Old Davy would agree.'

Bryony wagged a finger. He laughed again, saying, 'It's her age, I imagine, though she does seem to summon up a storm with monotonous regularity. Remember when you shipped her and your mother out here in the first place?'

Bryony snapped, 'Mum needed to spend some time here with Aunt Olive, for her health and—'

'I know,' he soothed her. 'You thought it would put distance between Hannah and Sid the Spiv if she accompanied her. Now you're bringing her home, just as she wanted, so what's the problem with her now?'

'Exactly. On the telephone she sounded cheerful, and just look at her, for heaven's sake.'

Adam whispered, 'Would you have said yes if she'd said she was returning to Sid?'

Bryony glared at him. 'Shut up.'

He nodded. 'Exactly. So do you really think she's going to college, or have you been manipulated and reeled in like a gasping fish?'

'Shut up,' Bryony snapped again.

She watched Hannah approaching. Her sister slopped along, kicking at tufts of grass, then stopped, scowled and examined the sole of her sandal, probably because she'd trodden in sheep poo. Hannah wore a suitably arty dress she would have made herself, and a long striped cardigan with a vivid red shawl, and was so beautiful she could have walked out of a painting. Too beautiful, too clever and talented to be wasting her time on the Sids of this world.

Bryony touched her jacket pocket. Yes, the present Sid had given her for Hannah last evening when he arrived at Combe Lodge was still there. It was a welcome-home gift, he had told Bryony, smirking.

'I don't want to give it to her, Adam.'

'But you must, Bee.' He had turned to her, a light sheen of sweat coating his forehead, his pallor deeper.

She said, 'Look at you. I should never have agreed to you coming. Let's get you to the terrace and you can have a doze or you'll never be a hundred per cent and your mum will chase me round the kitchen with a frying pan.'

He shrugged, 'Maybe, just maybe I have a mind of my own and I decided to come. But now we have other things to deal with.' Hannah had run out of tufts to murder and had halted on the edge of the runway, looking at them, her long dark hair streaming out behind her.

Bryony buttoned up her leather jacket against the wind, but also against her sister. Adam murmured, 'Don't worry, I'm here beside you.'

She wished he meant that in another way.

Chapter Two

Bryony straightened her flying jacket and looked at Adam, who smiled at her. 'Go on, scaredy cat. You can throw an aircraft around the sky, so what's so difficult about a sulky sister who's been kicking hell out of a few tussocks. And let's face it, you've had a lifetime to get used to it.'

Bryony held out her arms to Hannah, who was walking towards them again with Aunt Olive a few yards behind. 'Hello, Hannah, it's such good news about art college.'

Her sister stopped a yard from her, her arms akimbo, her chin in the air, saying, 'Where's the lightweight easel? You know I wanted to paint on the spot.'

Bryony let her arms drop. Aunt Olive had skirted them, eyes to the ground, and was with Uncle Thomas by the aeroplane in no time at all. She helped him fiddle with something that did not need attention. Rosie bounded over to Hannah, who waved her off so the dog came to Bryony and Adam again.

Bryony said, 'Well, I'm very well, Hannah, thank you for not asking, and hope you are, too . . .' Then she cursed herself, knowing she'd just stoked whatever fire was burning today.

She took a deep breath and tried again, smiling at her sister. 'I thought that, as you telephoned to say you were coming back to build up a portfolio for art college, you would want the easel at Combe Lodge.' She stooped and pulled Rosie's ears, while the dog whined her pleasure.

Hannah sighed and looked at Adam. 'Well, Adam, you're looking better. I would have thought you'd be back doing your bit, not joyriding.'

Adam flushed. 'I'm almost there, Hannah. Won't be long.' His eyes were cold.

Aunt Olive had joined them, and Uncle Thomas was approaching, dusting off his hands. His farm overalls were even dirtier than Bryony's.

'Time for lunch, I think,' he said into the silence.

Aunt Olive said, 'Not so fast, Tommy m'lad. We girls will head for the kitchen and sort out the final bits, but Clive will be carting in the potatoes, vegetables, some salad and onions any minute now. You can help Adam load them on to the Dragonette. The onions will smell, Bee, but what's a bit of a pong amongst passengers? Bribe them with a few, and all will be well.'

She put an arm around both sisters, and headed for the gateway, calling over her shoulder, 'You boys take Rosie with you.'

'Yes, sir,' shouted Adam, saluting.

Aunt Olive laughed, 'That's enough of your cheek, Adam Cottrall.' She shook Bryony slightly. 'Oh Bee, how pleased your mother will be to see you. She's torn to think that Hannah is going home, but thrilled she's off to college. She will miss you both, but wants to stay here for longer. The doctor is pleased her consumption seems to be responding to rest and sunshine, and is still in remission.'

Hannah made Bryony jump, as she shouted, 'She's not just in remission, she's completely better, whatever you or that old fuddy-duddy Doctor Clements think. And anyway, I didn't actually promise I was going to college. Why does everyone keep on about it?'

Bryony stared at her, but Aunt Olive's desperate chatter built a bulwark between the two sisters, and for now, that was a blessing. Bryony was aghast. So, it was a lie to get back to Sid, was it? What on earth was she going to do about this girl? She'd refused to go back to school to matriculate, she refused to understand that their mother had TB, she chose boyfriends who were no good. She had said she wanted to come back, but now she wanted her easel here, so was she going to rush off a few sketches within the next couple of hours?

She touched Sid's present. Should she chuck it into the hedge they were passing? Was it some sort of message between the two of them? What the hell was going on?

They turned into Haven Farmhouse, using the

front path rather than tiptoeing around the edge of the farmyard muck to the back door. Bryony said, 'How posh, the front door.'

'I wanted you to see and smell the garden. Isn't it glorious? I've been trying to persuade Hannah to paint it for me. I could hang her picture on the wall, but she prefers to go out and find "intriguing views", don't you, darling, which is probably much better for her portfolio.'

Either side of the crazy-paving path the lavender was getting into its stride, and despite the wind the bees were collecting pollen. As Bryony watched, one almost staggered on take-off because it carried so much baggage on its legs. The pinks were flowering, a few tulips were hanging on, and the groups of poly-anthus were doing well. Forget-me-nots cascaded down a bank. 'Glorious,' Bryony murmured, running her hand along the tops of the lavender, releasing the scent. Aunt Olive led the way into the house, and Bryony turned to Hannah. 'I don't understand. Why do you still need the easel if you're coming home?'

'Oh stop going on and on all the time, Bryony. You're not my mother. Just let me alone.' She stalked up the stairs. 'Call me when lunch is ready, Aunt Olive.'

Bryony called after her. 'That's no way to talk to your aunt, and what's more, you haven't answered my question.'

Hannah yelled, 'All right, all right, *please, please, please*, Aunt Olive.'

There was the slam of a bedroom door. As Bryony started up the stairs in hot pursuit her mother called from the sitting room, 'Bryony, stop thundering about and come and say hello. You do wind poor Hannah up so.' Bryony stopped and slowly returned to the hall. At the doorway to the kitchen Aunt Olive raised her eyebrows, and shook her head.

Bryony mouthed, I'm sorry.

Aunt Olive hurried to hug her, saying into her hair, 'You have nothing to be sorry for. One day Hannah will grow up, and my sister, your poor fragile mother, will see sense. She feels sorry for the girl for losing her father so young, and for being there when he fell off that damned horse and died. She puts all this behavioural nonsense of Hannah's down to that, and perhaps it is partly that, along with a dollop of spoiling from an early age. I wonder sometimes if Hannah is frightened because one parent has already died and the other is fragile and there is the prospect that she could be alone.'

'But she wouldn't be alone, I've always been here for her, and would continue to be.' For a moment Bryony let herself be held by this lovely woman, who smelt of the rosemary she had used on the roast potatoes. 'If only she'd let me.'

Her aunt kissed her cheek. 'Perhaps she sees you as providing stability so she has to test you, again and again, to prove that you will in fact never let her down. Oh, I don't know. I've not had children, so what do I know? I just nurture beasts, and then eat them.'

Both women laughed, loud and long. Aunt Olive dusted her apron down. 'I think you need to prepare yourself for the fact that she might not return after all. She met Peter Andrews a few days ago. He paints too, I gather, but only as a hobby. His dad owns Netherby Farm and he's very handsome. A nice, wholesome lad.'

The two women looked at one another. Bryony sighed. Yet another man, but at least it wasn't Sid – at least it was someone her aunt knew.

Bryony's mother called from the sitting room, 'Come and give me a hug, Bryony. For all I know you've had your hair shaped and you've smartened yourself up since I saw you last week. Miracles do happen.'

Aunt Olive whispered, 'She doesn't mean to be like this. She loves you.' She led the way into the beamed room. Bryony knew that indeed her mother loved her, but also that she did mean what she'd said. There was a glowing fire in the grate, even in this weather. 'Your mother feels the cold, my dear. Don't you, Mary?' Aunt Olive left.

Sitting to the right of the fireplace, her mother smiled and lifted her hand in a wave, then grew serious. 'Oh dear, Bryony, must you always look such a scruff? Just look at those overalls. Is that oil?'

Bryony smiled. 'Yes, as it so often is, and has been, and always will be, I fear. Uncle Eddie's away,

Adam isn't well enough to help with the aircraft maintenance, his friend Eric is working on a boat engine for someone so can't, therefore I have to in order to earn a crust for us all. It will be even worse soon, because I have to paint the hangar roof with camouflage. Just imagine me then, with spots of paint to add to the picture.' She thought her mother would faint. Bryony crossed the threadbare carpet and kissed her mother's upturned face, then knelt by her chair, taking her hand. 'How are you, Mum? I wanted to talk to the doc but he scooted off.'

'I'm fine, just tired. He seems pleased, and I am absolutely no worse. Jersey is good for me. How is April? And what about Eddie?'

From the kitchen Aunt Olive called, 'Get her to eat more, please, Bee. Doctor Clements says she needs butter, milk and all good things, and rest, all of which we should be able to manage, even when the rationing bites more deeply.'

Her mother's skin was almost translucent, and Bryony felt fear clutch at her as it usually did where this woman was concerned. Her mother said, 'The doctor left you a note. I've read it, and he says what he always says, and what Olive has just said: rest, food and fresh air are the ticket. So I'm obeying. After lunch I will sit out on the terrace in the sun. It's what my mother used to do. I can see her sitting there now. Sometimes your father did too, when we came on holidays and before he . . .' She laughed.

'Well, obviously before he died, or it would be daft, wouldn't it? A corpse sitting there, enjoying the sun.'

Bryony had heard all this before. It was her mother's way of showing that she was over her husband's death. She wasn't. Her mother said, stroking Bryony's hair back behind her ears, 'There, that's more tidy. Now, my dear, listen to the good news. Hannah *might* be staying here with us after all. She has found herself a nice young man, the son of Tommy's farmer friend. He so much better than that Sid, who was too old of course, but on the other hand, Sid has money, which is in his favour, don't you think?'

Bryony did not, but said nothing and neither did she sigh, though she ached to do so.

During lunch Hannah was silent, and no one brought up the return journey; not even Bryony's mother, who wasn't known for her tact. Instead she picked at her gammon. The talk was desultory, with Adam seemingly struggling to stay awake. There was an apple pie for pudding, and cream. Aunt Olive poured some on Mary's plate despite her protestations and she ate a little.

After lunch, Adam took Mary's arm. 'Let the two of us pale and interesting beings totter to the terrace and sleep off this feast, shall we, Mrs Miller?'

She laughed slightly. 'Indeed, why not.'

Uncle Thomas beckoned to Bryony. 'Come and

see Jemima. She's done us proud with a grand litter of piglets.'

Hannah followed Aunt Olive into the kitchen to help with the washing up, smiling slightly at Bryony. 'Mum told you that my plans might have changed?'

Again Bryony stopped herself from sighing and smiled instead. 'Yes. Just let me know before we take off. Well, obviously.'

Uncle Thomas left the house almost at a run, and ploughed through the middle of the farmyard, though Bryony made her way around on the concrete slabs which ran around the edge, mindful of treading muck into the cockpit. At the old and worn out sty within the barn, which housed piglets scuttling about, Uncle Thomas hustled her past without a sideways glance and only stopped when he reached the far end. Bryony said, 'I thought you'd have her out in the pig area on the other side of the house?'

He just stared ahead. She followed his line of sight. There appeared to be a new wall smeared with cow dung behind a pile of hay bales. 'You see, the dung ages brickwork, makes it look as though it's been here for bloody years,' he said, looking around. 'I'll brush it off in due course, when it's done its job.' He found a niche in one of the bricks and pulled. It opened and proved to be a brick facing on a door leading into a large area. She hadn't noticed that the barn had lost some space, and said so.

Uncle Thomas grinned. 'Good, that's as it should be.' He looked round again, then pulled her into the new space, which was lit by a skylight. There was a sty and a grazing area. 'It's to pop in a pig in case things go wrong in France. We're so close, the Nazis might come here, and if they do, rationing will tighten, and I want to be able to feed friends and family. Not to make money, you understand. I can hide a young 'un when authorities nose about. Now, don't you be telling anyone, not even young Hannah. She blabs, you see. Don't mean anything by it, but she does.'

He was pulling her out again, and shutting the door. Bryony thought of Sid the Spiv, but then shook her head. Her uncle was not a black marketeer – he would share his bounty with those in need.

He was hurrying out now, and back into the rear porch while she took the path around the yard. He flopped off his boots, while she wiped hers on the doormat. Without waiting for her he trotted down the corridor into his study, his stockinged feet leaving sweaty footprints on the tiles.

The study was cool. He rushed to the inglenook, where he stooped, peering up the chimney and calling her over. 'See here.'

She joined him and looked up. There was a patch of deeper darkness on the left-hand side. 'It's a hidey-hole for the wireless. If the Nazis come there'll be a time when they won't want us knowing what's going on in the world. I'll put a wireless up there, brick it up part way, and leave room for the leads. I can listen on my headset. Now, tell no one, you understand. It's safer that way.'

They withdrew and stood, looking at one another. She saw the determination in her uncle's eyes, and the fear. Bryony's mouth was dry, her heart was dithering, her back ran with cold sweat. 'Do you think they will come? Really? Should you come back with me, all of you? Now, this minute? I can make another run when I take the passengers home.'

Her uncle shook his head. 'No, I think our lads will fight and beat 'em back so it's just in case. You know how I like to think ahead. Either way, there'll be time for you to fetch your mother and Hannah, but your aunt and I will never be chased out of Jersey, you mark my words. They can come and tear it down, but when they're gone – and they will go – we'll just build it back up.'

They smiled at one another, though Bryony felt sure the smile hadn't reached her eyes. Hannah said from the doorway, 'I've come to tell you, Bee, that I won't be coming back with you. Sorry to mess you about, so next time you come, bring the easel, would you? Please.'

Beside her, Uncle Thomas tensed. Bryony asked the question he didn't. 'Have you been there long? You should have joined us. There's a bird's nest in the chimney and we think it's in use. So no one should light a fire.'

Hannah shrugged. 'All right. But I never set the

fires, do I? Uncle Thomas likes to do it. So, just bring the easel, would you? You're taking people back in a week, aren't you, and I can manage until then.'

They were over the coast of Devon by four that afternoon, and by now the smell of onions was so pungent the cabin had fallen silent. The Smiths and Bennetts who had holidayed together in the second of Uncle Thomas's holiday houses were on their way home, pleased at the thought of a couple of pounds of onions each and some potatoes. Her Aunt Olive was a wise woman.

Adam was quiet, exhausted, but he had insisted the day had saved him from terminal boredom. Bryony kept rigidly on course so that the ack-ack on the coast at Exmouth wouldn't think she was hostile, but they were so used to her Dragonette on its regular route that they waved. She waggled her wings. Soon she was on the approach to the Combe Lodge landing strip and yet again she felt her helmet being lifted, and Adam saying, 'I'm not sure I will be able to face onions ever again.'

Those in the cabin laughed. 'You're not the only one, mate,' called Mr Smith. Bryony instructed them: 'Straps on please, Adam will check.' He did and gave her the thumbs up. She adjusted her helmet and brought the Dragonette into the wind to begin her approach, easing down. The wind was buffeting but not too much. Gently now, gently – but as she was about to touch down she saw a child, a girl, rushing from the bushes to the left, across the strip, her hair streaming out like Hannah's. Adam saw too. 'Christ, Bee. Yank the nose up.'

Ignoring him, she pushed the throttle levers forward and pulled steadily back on the yoke. Climbing out she eased back the throttle, banked left to go round again, checking the runway, which was now clear. 'Sorry about that, everyone, bit of a problem on the landing strip.'

She focused, although her whole body longed to go into shock. She came round into the wind again, always looking, but the child had completely disappeared, almost as though she had been an apparition. Gently gently, and down we go, and again it was a feather-light landing. Her hands were shaking, and as she removed her helmet and hung it up, she said quietly to Adam, 'If I'd yanked the nose up immediately we could have stalled, and then what would have happened to the blessed onions?'

He squeezed her shoulder. 'I wasn't thinking, too tired. Sorry, Bee, and thank God for you.'

'How did she get in the field? Is the fence broken somewhere? Everyone knows not to come on to the airfield, for heaven's sake. I'll check it.' She undid her straps with shaking fingers.

Adam said, '*We'll* check the fence, and what's more, find the little idiot. She's got to be told off, Bee, and afterwards we'll go down to the pub with the rest of the lads. Someone might know who she is, but I didn't recognise her, did you?'

Bryony shook her head, 'No. Perhaps she's an evacuee?' She raised her voice. 'Let's get your straps undone, everyone, and your bags off. Your holidays are over, and to make up for that, in a moment Adam will open the door and you can escape the onion fumes.'

A cheer greeted the announcement, and Adam squeezed her shoulder again.

In Jersey, Hannah strolled along the lane towards Netherby Farm, her sketch pad under her arm. She had watched the Dragon Rapide lifting into the sky, hating to see Bee go but glad too. Bee was always pushing her to make something of herself, and yes, college might be nice, but Peter was nicer, so she wasn't going to go anywhere without him.

She hurried. Bee had said she'd have the money for art college after next week's runs, so if Peter went to England to sign up, as he had muttered yesterday, she'd say she was going to college but instead use it to find digs near him. But why on earth Bryony had to make such a martyr of herself and work so hard was stupid. She should just ask Eddie, like Mum said. After all, he thought the sun shone out of Bee's backside and it was nonsense to say there was no cash, because they could just sell a plane. Dad had been his friend in the Royal Flying Corps in the war, and they had been partners and Eddie had bought into Combe Lodge, so why shouldn't

Eddie support them all? If he did, then Bee would have more time for her.

Hannah climbed over the stile, and took the footpath leading across the sheep field and into the bluebell woods, which she had painted in oils in the spring. She had hung it in the local art gallery but no one had bought it. Once in the woods it was more sheltered from the wind and out of the glare of the sun. She remembered Sid's present, and sat on the fallen tree that was slowly rotting, with fungi growing out of it. Was that what smelt so acrid?

She took the present from her pocket, smiling because he had even wrapped it. If it didn't work out with Peter there was always Sid as a fallback. She could go to England and to college, and he could visit on his motorbike.

She unwrapped the gift. It was a jewellery box and inside was a brooch. She took it out, and examined the back. There was no hallmark, and it was light to hold. It was clearly tin. Hannah threw it into the undergrowth where it belonged. How cheap. He could have done better, for God's sake. She'd keep the jewellery box, though. It was pretty.

The branches above rustled and a magpie headed for the light. She remembered Uncle Thomas and Bee looking up the chimney. She had heard what Uncle Thomas said, so why did Bryony tell a stupid story about a bird's nest? Probably because Uncle Thomas liked Bryony more than her, and it wasn't fair.

Chapter Three

27 May 1940

Bryony was in the midst of a recurring dream in which a child ran across the landing strip. She had just reached the point where the aircraft crashed instead of powering out of danger. She could feel the heat of the flames, hear the scream which rocked her body, the screams too, of the passengers, and of the child, when she jerked awake. For a moment she didn't know where she was, and then, as she stared around her bedroom in the darkness of the night, feeling her sheets, the weight of the blankets, she relaxed and drifted off again.

Now she was chasing the girl, who was always just ahead and whose face she never saw until she reached the woods and then she turned, and it was Hannah. She started awake again, alarmed, but not at the dream – it was something else, as though . . . She sat up, but there was no one there. She checked the alarm clock: it was only three in the morning. Her heart was beating in her throat, too fast.

She heard the cry then, 'Adam!'

It was more a shriek than a cry. It was April

Cottrall. 'Adam!' she was calling. 'For God's sake, will *someone* wake up?' Bryony heard the panic, the utter terror. She threw off her bedclothes.

'Bryony, Eddie, someone.' April was panting through the words. She must have run from Combe Cottage, seventy yards from the Lodge. There was light streaming in beneath Bryony's bedroom door from the landing.

'Morgan's on the telephone at the cottage, oh, it's awful. Quick, quick.' Bryony heard the Blue Room door slam open and Adam call, 'Mum?' His voice was confused. He called again, 'Mu—?' but ended on a hacking cough.

Bryony hurtled from her room to the landing. 'What? What?'

She yanked up her pyjama trousers, and met April at the top of the stairs. The woman was in her nightgown, with bare feet, hair dishevelled, panting. Now Uncle Eddie, who had arrived home for his regular two-day leave from the ATA, was in his doorway, hopping on one foot, struggling to put on a slipper, his threadbare red tartan dressing gown undone, his belt dragging on the floorboards. Adam was still coughing at the entrance to his bedroom door.

April gripped Bryony. 'It's Morgan.' She was panting so fast she could hardly speak.

Adam hurried to them now, wiping his mouth, his coughing fit subsiding. 'What, my Morgan?'

'Of course your bloody Morgan, who else would I mean?'

Adam gripped his mother's arm. 'Is he hurt, has his trawler gone down?' he asked.

'The *Sunflower* is needed in Weymouth, he says. We've lost, you see.' April, on the verge of tears, stopped abruptly. Eddie took her hands. 'It's all right, April, love. Just tell us slowly. Come along.' He led her to the sofa below the landing window. It was overstuffed, and had burst its seams, but it had been like this for as long as Bryony could remember. Adam coughed again and stood with Bryony as April and Uncle Eddie sat. 'Now,' Eddie said. 'Someone is lost? Or has Morgan broken down somewhere? Was he on his way here? Why does he need the *Sunflower*?'

April glared at them all. 'Oh, for goodness' sake, why don't you listen? Not Morgan, we – I mean *Britain* has lost. Morgan says we need shallow boats to take the troops from the beaches of France to the big ships to save as much of the army as we can. Perhaps then we can fight another day. Perhaps. The Germans are nearly at Dunkirk, you see. The bloody Germans have beaten us.'

Bryony felt everything slow. It was almost as though she was floating, as though the floorboards were no longer cool beneath her bare feet. She had seen the coast of France when she had collected the holidaymakers, and all had seemed as usual. Had there been the faint sound of guns? It had been such a quick turnaround, and none of the passengers had mentioned anything, neither had her family, but the

Channel Islands were miles from Dunkirk. All she had read recently was that Holland was in peril, and the British forces were busy in France . . . She'd been more interested to hear that Churchill had taken the place of Chamberlain.

Eddie was gripping April's hand in both of his, his dressing gown still gaping open, his striped pyjamas faded. His dressing gown was torn beneath the arm. His belt was collecting dust balls from the floor now. 'Tell me again, dearest April, just what Morgan said. Then Adam can phone him back. He obviously thought Adam had moved in with you at the cottage.'

April reached her free hand to Adam and pulled him down on her other side. 'No, he tried here, but you were all asleep.'

Though her eyes were full, April was clearly not about to cry, and her look dared Bryony to do so. Her lips were quivering though, and her voice was high as she said, 'He telephoned because his trawler skipper is setting off from Weymouth, with some others to help. Most are embarking from Ramsgate but everyone who can do something is needed.'

'What, he's going in his armed trawler?' Adam's voice was incredulous, 'But that's up in—'

'No.' April's voice was almost a wail. 'His own trawler, the *Maid of Torin*, the one he has a share in. Morgan is on leave and they're setting off for Dunkirk, that's where the troops are. Fuel is being sorted, he says, and he'll tow you there to save yours, but only if you're well enough. He says to bring the dinghy too, because someone can take that in to the beach and transport a few back to the *Sunflower* and from there to the big ships.'

Before she had finished, Adam was rushing down the stairs. 'I'll telephone him back.'

April called after him, 'He's at the skipper's house.'

Eddie was on his feet. 'Don't go to the cottage, lad. Call from the study. We can't waste time. April, can you get some sandwiches sorted, and you too, Bee. Adam and I will need them. I'll go to Weymouth with the lad, but then he's on his own. I have to get back on duty.'

He hurried to his bedroom. April was already heading down to the kitchen. Bryony looked from one to the other, and thought – sandwiches, you must be joking. She washed, dressed in her overalls, flinging on a jumper and tying another around her waist. She grabbed her waterproofs then took the stairs two at a time. Halfway down, Adam came from the study and began to climb towards her. She shouted, 'No, go back. It's bad luck to cross on the stairs and we're going to need every bit we can find.'

He backed down, staring up at her. His pyjamas were checked and old, and his feet were bare. He could catch his death on the flagstones. She half smiled: well, they'd be facing more than cold floors soon. He shouted up, 'We? Oh no, there's no we about this, Bee. Morgan's just told me what to expect, and it's too bloody dangerous.' He began to cough again, bending over. She continued down, sweeping past him. 'You think I don't realise that? I'm not a fool. I'll be in the kitchen. Hurry up or we'll go without you, which might not be a bad idea. This is bound to set you back.'

Uncle Eddie was following on behind her, fully dressed, and as she swept into the kitchen she heard him laughing quietly. 'Now, why am I not surprised, Bryony Miller, that not only are you coming but that you've taken over. You are indeed your father's daughter.'

April was banging about on the hotplates, frying bacon that Uncle Thomas had included in his produce. Now April threw in some mushrooms she and Bryony had picked yesterday. There was fried bread, fried potatoes, sausage. Adam came in behind them as Bryony started to cut bread for sandwiches. 'I hope you've written your will, Bee,' he said. 'If Dunkirk doesn't get you, the fry-up will.'

His mother swung round. 'Don't you joke about it, ever, do you hear?'

Adam slipped past Bryony to his mum, putting his arms around her as she stood in her nightgown. 'We have to, Mum. It's how we did it on the trawlers around Norway. Don't worry, we'll come back, no shell would dare hit Bee.'

April's eyes met Bryony's. What was unsaid was that one had most certainly hit Adam's father, at

32

Ypres. 'Of course I've written a will,' Bryony said. 'Everyone who flies does, if they have a grain of sense.'

Bryony had inherited her share of Combe Lodge and the airline along with her mother and sister. She had nothing else except the art college money she had saved. In her will everything she had was left to her sister.

Down at the harbour they stripped out all that was superfluous in the *Sunflower*, to allow as many men as possible to be taken off the beach. They even removed the mast to give them a few extra inches of space. April, standing on the dock, said she'd make sure the benches, table and cupboards were kept safely in the boathouse for their return. They hitched up the dinghy, and loaded the *Sunflower* with containers full of water and tin mugs April had somehow found. Morgan had said the troops that made it through would be gagging with thirst.

They worked alongside another smack, *The Saucy Lass*, belonging to Barry Maudsley and his son Eric, who had been a classmate of Adam and Morgan's and often helped with the maintenance of the aircraft. They too had received a telephone call. *The Saucy Lass* was used, as was Adam's, as a pleasure-boat-cum-fishing smack. It too had been stripped, made mastless and loaded with water in double-quick time. April put down her basket, took packets from it and threw them to Bryony. 'They're cheese, they should keep you going.' Finally she threw a haversack. 'Put them in here. When they're finished, throw the haversack overboard. Every inch is needed, Morgan said.'

Bryony muttered, 'He was always a bossyboots.'

The men laughed and Eric called from the nearby boat, 'Disruptive influence, an' all, according to Miss Staines. D'you remember that, Adam?'

Adam waved, nodding, then he and Eddie yanked out the last cupboard. Eddie asked, 'Got a half share in the *Maid*, has he? It was a quarter, wasn't it?'

Adam carried the cupboard to the edge of the *Sunflower* and Timmie, who ran the nearby paint shop, took it from him. It was all hands to the pump this morning. 'Yes, he's done well and had the sense to keep his share. Bright lad. Exmouth was always too small for him, and the armed trawlers are just right, not too many fuddy-duddy rules, he said. That's why I chose 'em, on his recommendation.'

Above them the gulls were wheeling, and the sun was hotting up.

At last they were done. They'd worked through the dawn, and now it was 9 a.m. April waved them off, calling after them, 'I'll look out for that child while you're gone, Bee. Just because you're not here, doesn't mean we give up.'

There was no word about being safe. Just about life going on, life that would be picked up on their return. Bryony blew her a kiss. 'I love you, April.

34

We'll see you very soon. Look after Dragonette for me, and Hannah if . . .'

With Adam at the controls, Eddie and she stood and waved as they left the calm of the harbour for the choppy waters of the sea, and Eddie put his arm around her. 'Dragonette, indeed. It's a Dragon, little Bee, a ruddy dragon that drums infernally.'

She leaned into her uncle who wasn't an uncle but her father's dearest friend, one who acted like a parent to them all. 'No, she purrs.' He had slipped into his dark blue ATA uniform so he could hurry to Weymouth Station and pick up a train to his ferry pool. The argument continued as the wind tore at her hair and they watched the redness of the cliffs of Devon fade and become the yellow of west Dorset, and then the grey of east Dorset. 'Where will the buggers go now,' she murmured. 'The Channel Islands or us? Jersey's only fifteen miles from France.'

Eddie hugged her, 'One problem at a time, Bee. Let's just get through the moment, shall we?'

She knew he was right. As he left the boat in Weymouth harbour he called, 'I'm setting you up with a test for the ATA. We'll need all the help we can get, because we will fight on. So you get back here, Bryony Miller. You're needed, darling, darling girl.' His voice broke, and he hurried away.

Chapter Four

28 May 1940

From Weymouth the *Sunflower* was towed like a camp follower through what was left of the evening, and then the night. Bryony and Adam had done two-hour shifts at the wheel ever since they'd left Exmouth. Once at Weymouth they hitched up the towline and continued the shifts. Who knew if they'd come adrift as they were towed through the waves?

During the journey they said little to begin with, for what was there to talk about – life, death, the universe? None of that, so it came down to the smell of fish which permeated the boat and drew a laugh from Adam, who told Bryony that if he took people mackerel fishing for a living, what did she expect, and before he took trippers for a pleasure cruise he scrubbed it out, good and proper. Not content to leave it at that, he'd said the smell of fuel in her cockpit was nothing to write home about either. He'd added that Eddie was right, the Dragon engines made an infernal drumming. They bickered and laughed over a packet of April's cheese sandwiches, then a drink of water, and then a perusal of the sea, the horizon, and the *Maid of Torin*, whose wash was visible and, what's more, rocked the *Sunflower*.

By the time they were halfway to Dunkirk, the argument had moved on to who was to take the dinghy forward. It had to be her, of course, because Adam was the best at managing the *Sunflower*. He thought it too dangerous for Bryony because she'd be dealing with desperate men, quite apart from bearding the elements, and he'd wagged his finger. 'You'll be in an open boat and could be strafed and your hair will be a mess and what will your mum say about that?'

She won that one because he started coughing, and while it racked his body she dragged out the rolled-up old rug thrown in at the last minute by April, who'd told them to sit on it because it would keep their backsides out of the slop. She'd added that they could throw it overboard when they arrived.

'Sleep on here,' Bryony insisted. 'I'll wake you in two hours or you're going to be good for nothing. We must keep to two-hourly watches.'

She took her turn at the wheel, he sat on the rug and rested, his head lolling against the side of the cabin. She longed to reach out, and stroke his dark blond hair.

The *Sunflower* churned through the waves until dawn broke, with Adam awake now, and cursing the slow speed.

'If you want fast,' she said, 'you should learn to fly an aircraft that purrs instead of being towed behind a trawler.' He laughed. They had no need of a signpost as they at last drew near Dunkirk, for dark oily smoke hung like a blanket over the town, and the noise of gunfire coiled and writhed around them. But it was more than gunfire: there were explosions, and the smell of burning oil, and cordite. Bryony's hands were fists as she thought of Uncle Thomas and her family on Jersey.

What did they make of the news? Were they frightened, did they want to return to Combe Lodge, were they even now telephoning April? What if she died, here in Dunkirk? Who would look after Hannah and her mother?

She felt her control slipping. She was sweating. Is this what had gone through her dad's head when he was dying in Hannah's arms, after his fall? But he'd had the comfort of telling Hannah with his dying breath that Bryony would, and must, look after her. If she died, who could she ask to do the same?

Adam shouted, as a Stuka dive bomber screamed and raged out of the clouds, drowning the gunfire, the explosions as it passed over the *Sunflower* and the *Maid of Torin*, and then there was another, heading towards their area. He too passed, screaming so that she wanted to crouch beneath the sound. Bryony stared after them, shoulders hunched, struggling to process it all: the noise, the smoke, the awfulness, the strangeness. All these machines so busy killing but the *Sunflower* continued to be towed, as both planes dived on Dunkirk harbour and released their bombs. As they drew closer, the noise increased, and almost shuddered in its ferocity. Again she wanted to whimper but forced herself instead to stand straight, beside Adam, taking a turn at the wheel as though nothing untoward was happening.

Adam said, his eyes on the emerging shore, 'Poor buggers. It's as well we lot are here.' He didn't move a muscle, just took over the wheel and steadied the *Sunflower* as it rode the wake of the *Maid of Torin* just as it had done for so many hours. Well, he'd been in conflict before, hadn't he? Norway.

She hadn't understood.

She remained at his side as the *Maid* headed for the eye of the storm and she nudged him, shouting, 'To our left, a Stuka.' She could hardly breathe as the dive bomber screamed down towards a large trawler, whose captain must have seen but was doing nothing. Then, at the last moment he turned his trawler to starboard. The bomb fell to port, water gushed, the trawler leaned over in the surge and then righted. Adam muttered, 'Something to copy. Keep a sharp watch, Bee, and yell out.'

She did, and one now seemed to be streaking down at them, but it was targeting the *Maid*, who turned smartly, straining the tow rope. It held. The surge of the explosion caught them, tipped them, but they righted. Bryony steadied herself against the swell, before heading to the stern to check that the dinghy was still with them. It was.

From the shore they heard and saw the French cruisers lying off the harbour, letting fly with their pom-poms. The land-based anti-aircraft fire was going mad. Bryony put her hands to her ears, and then stopped. 'Don't be so ridiculous,' she told herself, secure in the knowledge that Adam couldn't hear above the chaos.

Adam replied, however, grinning. 'You're not ridiculous, it's a bloody racket. Just like that cow of your Uncle Thomas's when her calf was taken? Do you remember?' She heard the shake in his voice, saw the tremble in his hands as he held the wheel, the lift of his shoulders. He was as stressed as she, and now, suddenly, she relaxed. No, she wasn't ridiculous. This was what it seemed, a nightmare. It was war.

They drew closer to the shore and now the *Maid* jettisoned the tow rope, and Morgan bellowed through his tannoy. They could just hear him above the noise. 'We're standing off, and you should head for the beaches to take off those you can. Transport them to whichever big ships are also standing off. The men should queue, but then the British always bloody queue. Don't let them panic, they'll swamp you. There'll be one or two that lose it. Hit them with an oar, or whatever you've got to hand. Grab their balls if you have to, Bee.'

He waved them off and moved back, while they joined other shallower draughts and drove in with the tide. As they drew closer they saw what looked like swarms of ... well, what? Swarms of men, beneath a sky clouded with oily smoke. On the beaches explosions hurled sand and God knows what into the air. German aircraft were strafing everywhere, everything and everyone. Stukas were raining bombs on boats. Bryony's throat thickened as Adam said, 'God help us, it looks like the whole bloody army is waiting to be saved. We'll never take them all home.'

Men were queuing out into the sea, lurching with the surf, which pulled and pushed at them. But they held the line as the enemy came in again, and again, and then again. Bryony squeezed Adam's shoulder. 'I'm getting into the dinghy now and I'll bring 'em back to offload onto the *Sunflower*. There are longer queues over there, Adam, that you can take straight on board.' Adam nodded, easing back on the throttle, closing in on a line of men. 'Yes, I've got them in sight now, Bee.'

A sergeant was yelling at Adam's queue, 'Straighten up now, my lads, into that boat, and there are another two tubs coming up alongside who will take you. Now, in you get, in an orderly fashion, and you'll be home to Blighty for a bun and tea in next to no time.' Bryony saw that there were another two pleasure boats on the other side of the *Sunflower*.

She was unhitching the dinghy at the stern when

Adam shouted, 'You be careful, you hear me. You be bloody careful, Bee, or I'll have your guts for garters.'

She was lowering the oars into the dinghy, holding it in tight, clambering down the ladder, and rowing now, heading for a shorter queue to the left of the sergeant's.

Another flight of Stukas came over. It must be like shooting ducks in a barrel she thought. She ignored them, and the shouts and screams from the beach as the machine-gunner had a field day. The line she was heading for held, but of course it would. She called to the lead soldier, 'I can take five, that's all, five out to the *Sunflower*. In you get, one by one. No baggage. I'll come straight back.'

One young man three from the head of the queue, and who looked as though he should still be at school, held a dog in his arms. He lifted it. The corporal yelled, 'You can get rid of that now, sunshine. What part of no baggage do you not understand, you bloody fool.'

Bryony called, as the older man at the head of the queue clambered in, careful not to tip the boat. 'That's not baggage, sergeant, that's an ally. Get in, lad, you're not going to get a printed invitation.' The boy did, once the second in line had clambered on board. They were all shivering and frozen, their hands white, but the lad still clutched the drenched and yelping dog. Another two edged in, and she rowed hard back to the *Sunflower*. They clambered up while she clung to the rope and kept it alongside.

Again and again she went back, while others swam and waded out to Adam, who had moved along to allow a larger pleasure craft to take precedence at the head of the queue. Once full, Adam then edged back from the shore, and headed for the *Maid*.

As he did so, there was a great roar and crash, and the large pleasure craft was bombed. It keeled over, smoke and steam streaming into the sky, with the sea too shallow to allow it to sink. Troops screamed, debris was hurled into the air, and as Bryony watched the sea turned red. She merely moved further down the beach, as the queues were doing, and rowed in to shore, with hands that had blisters the size of halfpennies. Then she picked up another five, promising to return.

As she rowed back she peered over her shoulder to where Adam would return. She saw that he was transferring his passengers to the larger ship. They were clambering up the nets hung over the sides, and as she watched she spied the lad holding on to the dog, climbing one-handed and using his teeth too. He had almost reached the top, when he fell. She waited, straining to see through the smoke, and there he was, climbing, one-handed again, and now the man next to him helped, hauling him up, step by step until they made it to the top.

One of the men in the dinghy muttered, 'I'm

taking that as a sign you know, Miss, that we'll win through. It will take blood and guts, but we'll get there and we better bloody had, because I'm not having me local serving bloody Kraut beer.'

The soldier next to him grinned. He had very few teeth. 'As long as they're not my blood and guts, sunshine.' Everyone laughed. She looked at their grimy exhausted faces and marvelled that anyone could laugh here, but then found that she was doing so too.

They waited as the *Sunflower* came about and headed towards them. The sea was crinkly, one of her men was vomiting over the side. Once the large ship was full, it would head for Dover, taking man and dog with it. It all made sense, she thought, and blessed whoever had thought up the plan. Adam was diverting to another sinking passenger vessel and taking on survivors. The bombed pleasure craft was burning, with the men who had escaped lining up further along.

Bryony saw a corvette at anchor and instead of waiting for the *Sunflower* she rowed to it, ignoring the pain of her hands and the screaming ache in her shoulders. Her passengers scrabbled up the nets, and back she went to the beach, but the queue she'd left there was gone, its sergeant too. Instead there were only helmets floating on the red-stained sea, and for a moment all she could do was stare, but then a roaring anger took her over, and pride. Because, even as she looked, another queue was walking out into the sea, almost alongside the remains of the first, led by another corporal, and somewhere, honest to God, she thought, someone was playing a harmonica.

On and on she went, rowing, and now her blood was on the oars: how bloody stupid of her not to bring gloves went through her mind like a song.

When the tide turned and the *Sunflower* could no longer nudge in close, she saw Adam coming towards her in a dinghy. He shrugged. 'I dropped anchor. This was floating by, so let's make use of it.' He was deathly pale, but was that because the light was leaching from the day?

He threw her some gloves. 'No one will want to hold your hands if you go on like this, so whack these on, you daft thing. Got 'em off a sailor. You look bloody exhausted. We'll have to back off soon and take a break.'

She threw back the gloves, and continued to shore, and the ever-present patient men. She yelled, 'The gloves are yours. Try to keep some part of your anatomy dry, for heaven's sake.' On the breeze the smell of cordite and burning oil was heavier.

He shouted across to her as he caught a crab and fell backwards. 'No, they're bloody not. They were a gift from a sailor, and all the girls love a sailor, you daft idiot, so you'd better love his gloves too. Bit damp, but better than nothing.' He gathered himself together and chased after her.

He threw the gloves to one of the soldiers who

was scrambling into her dinghy, calling, 'Make her put them on, for the love of God. Stubborn bloody woman.'

The soldier caught them, and handed them to her. He was shaking. Cold or fear? What did it matter? She said, 'At least I've been promoted from a bloke.'

He stared at her, and then yelled to Adam. 'She says at least she's promoted from a bloke.'

Two other soldiers had clambered aboard in time to hear this. They looked at Adam. 'Well?' one of them shouted.

Adam was dragging in a soldier, who flopped half in and half out, too exhausted to do anything more than lie there. His mate heaved him up and over, and sat him against the side. The dinghy rocked dangerously. Adam sat still, then looked across. 'Bloke? With hair like that, and a face like that? What the hell's she talking about?'

Her boatload complete, Bryony rowed away from the shore. The man who'd passed on the gloves said, 'Well, what the hell are you talking about?'

The pain in her gloved hands felt easier, and the surf seemed almost fluorescent. Another soldier, a lad, said, 'Yes, what the hell *are* you talking about?'

'Oh, for goodness' sake,' she bellowed, with what was left of her energy. 'Your noses are much too long. Keep them out of my business.' But in the gloom she saw that they were pinned to the subject because it was normal, better than the hell of the beaches, and the turmoil of the surf and sea.

She shouted, as she hauled the oars through the water. 'He said, not so long ago, that we'd go for a drink with the other lads. It's what he always says.'

They looked at one another. 'When?'

'The last time was when I was piloting a Dragon Rapide back from Jersey. You see, he and Uncle Eddie taught me how to strip an engine, and so I do. There's now no one else who's around to do it so it's as well I can. That's why he thinks of me as a lad. Well, actually, I think he's always thought that since we were tots.'

They looked at one another as they headed for the *Sunflower* tugging at her anchor. She said, 'The old girl stinks of fish, but it will get you to a bigger one, and home.' She rested the oars on the rowlocks as they scrambled up the ladder at the stern.

As Bryony pushed away, one called after her, 'I reckon he thinks of you as a woman, lass. He just doesn't know how to say it. You wait, it'll happen. You pilot a Rapide? Strip engines? Bloody Nora, I've got to tell the missus.'

When she returned from a further trip, having had to swipe a hysteric over the head with the oar, and then haul him on board before he drowned, Adam was on board the *Sunflower* watching her. 'You look as tired as I feel. Let's deliver the lads onwards, then take the *Sunflower* out a bit and try to get some sleep or we're not going to last.' She unloaded the soldiers, tied up the dinghy and hauled herself on board. The *Maid of Torin* was back in the vicinity and Adam shouted his intentions to Morgan, who gave him the thumbs up. 'There are enough of us to take it turn and turn about, but you two can't. Get your heads down.'

They delivered their load, and stood off about half a mile, flopping on the base of the cabin like stranded fish, because the rug had been chucked overboard. They fell asleep immediately in spite of the canopy of pom-poms, screams, crashes and bombs, waking curled up against one another for warmth. They sat by the wheel and crammed sandwiches into their mouths, and slurped water. Several water cans were empty, but not all by any means, and the job wasn't finished. Morgan would tell them when they could withdraw, but that wouldn't be until the end was in sight. They looked at each other. 'Up and at 'em?' Adam asked as the dawn came up on 30 May.

'Yes.' They levered themselves upright. 'Getting old,' she murmured.

'Ah well, you've a way to go. Come on.' He slapped her on the back. In a minute she felt he'd say, be a man. She checked the dinghies they towed as he headed the *Sunflower* back to the beaches , and then scanned the sky for planes. There were still too many Germans having fun, and only a few RAF aircraft able to fight back. She thought of Uncle Eddie delivering planes frantically from factory to maintenance units to make good the shortfall.

Soon, many more ferry pilots would be needed, and she wanted to be one of them.

They were nearly there and searched for Morgan and the *Maid of Torin*, but Eric, who was taking passengers on board *The Saucy Lass*, called across, his voice breaking, 'The *Maid* was hit. She's gone down. None survived,'

On Jersey, Hannah sat on the top of the cliff, which had a path leading to a cove she and Bryony used to run down to. Once on the beach, they'd search the rock pools for crabs. Bryony had said that it was the sort of cove where warriors would come on a rescue mission.

She lay back on the grass thinking of Peter, who was staring at the sky as he lay next to her. She could still taste the beer from his lips, just as he would have tasted hers. The empty bottle they had shared lay on its side between them. She picked it up and tucked it back in the basket. Her uncle would never know he was missing one. He had a whole stack in the cellar because he'd bought up practically the whole shop when war was declared. He'd also bought crates of wine off a French skipper as 1939 turned to 1940.

When Aunt Olive had protested, he'd held up his hand and said, 'Just in case, Ollie dear. One never knows.'

The stub of the cigarette she and Peter had shared was ground almost to nothing at her side. She tossed it away, watching the wind take it.

'Dunkirk sounds exciting,' she said.

'No, it's not exciting, it's serious and we still don't know how many they can get off, so I want to join up. We'll need reinforcements.' He lifted himself on one elbow and kissed her again.

She jerked away. 'What? But what about me?'

'It's war. Like I said, they'll need every man or the Nazis will come.'

She looked up at the sky. He was just talking the talk, silly beggar.

Rosie whined beside Hannah and licked her face. She pushed her away. 'For heaven's sake, Rosie, stop fussing. I hate being licked. A lot of people have had their dogs killed, so you behave yourself, stupid animal.'

Hannah sat up and looked around. Perhaps she should have gone to Devon after all. If she had, Sid might have given her a gold or silver brooch, and he definitely wouldn't leave her. She glanced at Peter. But she didn't love Sid, she loved this boy. She reached out and stroked his face.

'It's because of Bryony and Adam, isn't it, showing off and rushing across to Dunkirk to be heroes. I wish April hadn't rung us, I wish I hadn't told you. You've been restless ever since.'

He kissed her again, and lay back down, pulling her to him. 'It's nothing to do with that. It's my duty.'

Above them larks flew. She sighed. Could she bear to go back to April and Bryony and the garden, and what if they had evacuees again? Last time they'd wrecked the attic. Well, not wrecked it, but one of them had wet the bed, for heaven's sake.

They'd gone home though, back to London, when nothing happened. That's it, nothing *had* happened, and after Dunkirk it would be like that again. So it was nothing. He wouldn't go. The Germans would stop in France, of course they would.

'What does your dad say, anyway? He'll need you on the farm,' she murmured.

'Dad said I couldn't sign up, but I will, one day. You just wait and see.'

She kissed him again and again. She'd just have to make sure he wanted to stay because if Peter went . . . She kissed him once more, wanting to ask him why people always left her, and to beg him not to go, but she now decided that if he did set off, she'd follow and stick to him like glue. That was all there was to it.

Chapter Five

3 June
Dunkirk

At midday on 3 June, Bryony rowed another boatload of exhausted and bandaged soldiers to the *Sunflower*. They were still embarking evacuees off the beach, day and night, alongside Eric and Barry Maudsley. As she knocked against the boat and grabbed for the rope to hold the dinghy steady, Adam came aft, yelling something. Bryony held up a hand, unable to hear over the noise of shouts, gunfire, ack-ack, strafing, bombs, shells. He leaned over, cupping his mouth. 'We're almost out of fuel. When I transfer this lot I'm reporting to the skipper of the *Wind of the North*. He'll tell us what he said before – head for Dover with as many as we dare when we know our time is up. The old girl's had one near miss too many, been battered once too often, the engine's failing. So just one final time, Bee.'

Bryony nodded, feeling momentary relief, but then nothing. She was too tired. Adam shouted, steadying himself as the waves tossed and turned. 'Nearly home and dry, Bee.' He smiled, coughing.

He was pale, dirty, and soaking wet. Not quite the thing when you were trying to get 100 per cent fit. She took up the oars and rowed on back as the *Sunflower* chugged to the trawler. She could hear the engine, even over the noise. Adam was right, the old girl was protesting.

She hauled back on the oars, digging deep, letting the tide help, and the waves. A helmet floated past, and debris. She heard the Stuka begin its dive but as usual didn't even flinch. How could you? You'd go mad. She kept rowing. The bomb blasted a river cruiser to the left, and shrapnel, or shards of metal, or something else, who the hell cared what, holed the dinghy, scorching past her legs and out of the other side. 'Thank you,' she murmured, and meant it, because her legs were intact, but the dinghy was beginning to disintegrate beneath her. She ought to do something, but she suddenly couldn't think.

The wash hit and she was thrown into the water, and it wasn't for the first time. It was cold, salty, stained with blood, oil and heaven knew whats, though she did know what, that was the trouble. Another wave swamped her and she sank, then fought to rise, her mouth full. She surfaced, choking, spitting and thrashing. She struggled to find her feet, but was too far out. She swam. A damaged oar crashed into her, catching her shoulder. Adam was shouting, or was it Adam? No, he was on the *Sunflower*. She saw her own blood now, spreading out, and then someone grabbed her by the hair, dragging her towards the shallows. She found her feet at last, and heard the voice. 'You all right, Miss?' It was a young sub-lieutenant.

'I needed a bath,' she said.

He laughed, patted her shoulder. She screamed. He swung her round. 'Just a splinter but that's your dinghy gone.' While she looked back she felt a great sharp pain, and sagged. He held her up, showing her the shard of wood. 'Came out like a dose of salts.' He tossed it aside. 'Might have a few tiddlers of splinters left, but nothing to vex you. Shall we take a walk, Miss?' He was pointing behind her. 'Your chariot awaits.'

It was the *Sunflower*, which Adam had brought close in, and now he was embarking the men surging through the surf. One carried a rifle above his head. Bryony and the young sub joined them. Once at the *Sunflower* the sub hoisted her up, and over the side. She in her turn reached out a hand to help him up. He shook his head. 'No, I'm in charge of the queue.'

He turned, then swung back. 'Tell them at home how far I got, would you . . . just in case. And tell them I love them.' He gave her a telephone number. She repeated it to a soldier slumped on the deck. 'Don't let me forget it,' she shouted above the cacophony as another Stuka came over. She turned back to the sub-lieutenant but he was ploughing through the surf, back to his role of directing his queue. This time Eric was bringing in his dinghy.

He yelled that it was *The Saucy Lass*'s last run. She shouted to the sub-lieutenant, 'I promise.' He waved his hand but didn't look. He was too busy sending the queue forward. She repeated the number again to the young soldier who sat, half asleep. 'Please, please remember it, in case I forget.'

An older man, a corporal, reached the *Sunflower*, holding his rifle above his head, well free of the water. He clambered up beside Bryony. 'We'll need this, because I've had enough of the buggers. Let 'em try to set foot on any of our beaches and I'll shoot 'em dead, and when I've no more bullets, I'll ram it up their arses. Begging your pardon, Miss.'

He then sank to his knees, and passed out. Bryony hauled him to one side, propping him up against another soldier, making sure his rifle was there, with him. She charged the men either side with keeping it dry, because 'If he wakes and it isn't, he won't use a bullet, he'll shove it you know where'.

For a moment she touched the rifle. It was shiny, and seemed to be the only thing in the whole damn world that was. At last the *Sunflower* had as many as could be carried. Adam held up the last can of water towards the men. 'I can chuck this and take one more, or we can keep it in case we need it on the way back to Dover. What do you think?'

They thought they'd each take a drink now, then chuck it. They did. Adam tossed it overboard to take its place with all the other debris drifting on the sea and piling up on the beach. Then they took one more passenger before they chugged slowly away from the oily smoke, refusing to look back at the beach and the queues of men they were leaving. Add to them the rearguard who were still fighting and the young sub-lieutenant who was still standing alongside his queue and it didn't bear thinking of.

It wasn't until 6 June that Bryony and Adam finally reached Exmouth, having dropped their charges at Dover, grabbed an excuse for a nap, and nursed the *Sunflower* along the coast. They hailed the bus, and asked Dan, the driver, for the stop near Combe Lodge. People shrank from them, firmly placing shopping bags on the seat next to them. Bryony and Adam knew they smelt, because it reached even them, not to mention that their clothes were stiff with dirt, blood and salt.

One woman complained. Dan said, 'Dunkirk.' It was enough. The shopping bags were lifted, the seats patted. They had no money to pay the fare. Dan waived it. 'You must be bloody joking.'

They sat, then walked from the bus stop, swaying on the steady ground as their sea legs struggled to adjust. It was so quiet, and the hedgerows were in full leaf, with dog roses blooming. Above them birds flew, and they felt the breeze, and the sun, and heard the bees. It was unreal. Where were the Stukas, the ack-ack, the screams, groans, debris, smoke, gunfi—? Bryony shut off her mind.

Entering Combe Lodge Drive, Adam stumbled. She caught him, and pulled his arm over her shoulder, taking his weight as he coughed. He was too hot, too clammy. She forced herself on, heedless of her shoulder, feeling the blood seeping. It was nothing. Adam had similar wounds, and a heaving chest, but that was nothing either compared to the men they had left, and those they had brought back, men who would fight again for them, for all of this. She looked around.

Combe Lodge seemed a long way up the drive. They struggled on, kicking the gravel, Adam coughing and apologising. They reached the front door, opened it and stumbled through into the kitchen. There was April, drinking tea at the kitchen table.

Bryony said, 'We're home.'

Bryony slept solidly for three days, and woke to blue sky, to a bed that didn't sway and lurch in time with the waves, to silence, and to the knowledge that she could not remember the sub-lieutenant's telephone number. Adam was in bed with a recurrence of double pneumonia, so it was Bryony who went with April to Exmouth to see Morgan's parents. There was nothing the two of them could say really, except that he had saved so many lives, and perhaps that helped. Perhaps, but as they walked away neither could forget the devastation in their eyes, and knew it was a replica of April's grief when her husband was killed, and Bryony's when her father died. She said quietly, as they walked along the lane, 'But Dad was older. These men are so young.'

For Bryony the following days were quiet and she seemed to be elsewhere. Nothing was real, and the hours were pierced with flashes of sounds, and sights which didn't upset her, didn't do anything to her. She sat with Adam and bathed his forehead, but it didn't matter that he muttered and twisted and turned. April said, as they sat together in the sitting room, 'It's all right, Bryony, the doctor says he won't die. He's just poorly, and tired. You're tired too, you know. Your Aunt Olive telephoned again.'

'Right, I will telephone her back.' She didn't.

She stared at the phone. She still couldn't remember the sub-lieutenant's number, only his face, and the way he had waved when she had called, 'I promise.'

There were no flights arranged to Jersey, to anywhere. Eddie had cancelled them all, he said when he telephoned her from his ferry pool. 'Commercial flights are no longer allowed. It's sea power from now on. Besides, you need to rest, darling girl.'

'I am resting, Eddie.'

She replaced the receiver and passed through the kitchen to the garden. She passed the washing line where the overalls she had worn to Dunkirk were billowing in the breeze. April had said everything was worth saving in these days of rationing, and had boiled them three times to remove all odour and besides, they were worthy of their full span of years, in repayment for the valour with which they had weathered the storm. Bryony took up a hand fork and weeded the herbaceous bed. The lavender was full, the bees busy as they would be at Haven Farm in Jersey. The digitalis created some height in the bed, and the hollyhocks were in bud. The roses bloomed, and she deadheaded a few, stuffing the spent blooms into her overall pockets. She clipped the young box hedging, or some of it.

April called her in for lunch. It was an egg sandwich and they sat together at the kitchen table. 'How kind,' Bryony said. 'But it's too much.' April smiled at her. 'That's all right. Your appetite will return once your body and mind have processed and absorbed.' Bryony could barely hear her as she chewed just the one mouthful she could manage, but could not taste.

'Hannah telephoned this morning, just to tell us that one pair of holidaymakers remain, and that they have British troops still in Jersey to defend them. Aunt Olive came on and said that your mum insists she wants to stay for as long as she can, because it's where her history is. She and Hannah have moved into Haven Cottage, you know, the one on the edge of South Field. It's better for everyone, or so she says.' April paused, her eyes on Bryony. With a start Bryony realised she should say something.

'Yes, Hannah can be a little trying,' she murmured. 'But she's young. She'll learn.' She'd heard her mother's words and it was so much easier to repeat the thoughts of others rather than to form one's own.

April smiled, and reached across to grip Bryony's hand. 'The doctor came as usual this morning, and says it will be a while before Adam's out of bed, let alone signed off. You haven't been in to see him this morning?'

Bryony stared at the hand that gripped hers, scarcely feeling it. 'Haven't I?' She was drifting again, floating. She rose. 'I will, later, but I think I must get on with camouflaging our hangar. The Luftwaffe might come, you see, and bomb it, or strafe it, and then the house, and the cottage because they might think it's an RAF airfield.'

April insisted, 'It doesn't need doing today, Bryony, and besides, Tony Wallis from the village did the roof in your absence.'

'Yes, today, because the walls need painting too, not just the roof. He didn't do those?'

April shook her head, sighing.

Bryony left, walking out into the sun, hearing April calling after her. She found the paint in the shed near the hanger. She lifted it. It dragged on her shoulder and hurt the healing sores on her hands, but it was good to feel something. She left it on the ground on the shady side of the hangar. She returned for the ladder, because Eddie had taught her to start at the top to allow the drips to be smoothed on the way down. But as she hoisted it on to her good shoulder and dragged it along the ground, her burden eased, as someone else took some of the weight.

It was April who said, 'There's no way either of us is going up the ladder without the other at the bottom. We will take it in turns.' When they arrived at the hangar, Bryony saw that April had changed into the Dunkirk overalls. April smiled. 'There's no voodoo about them, so I will break them in for you. Now, you first, madam, up the ladder with you, and no stretching over to reach just that little bit further. Instead, you must scoot on down and we'll move it along together. Incidentally, you've received a letter from the Air Transport Auxiliary. You applied, if you remember, or agreed that Eddie should do it for you.' Bryony remembered but so what? She started up the ladder with the paint.

April called, 'But the ATA is for another day, darling. There's no hurry.'

They worked all afternoon, taking turns and were a quarter of the way down one side when they finished for the day, but that was better than nothing. They left the ladder and the paint, but washed out the brushes in the scullery. Only then did Bryony lie down in her room. She slept.

She woke, and saw the sub-lieutenant's face, saw Morgan's parents' faces, saw the sub-lieutenant's mouth working, but couldn't hear him, couldn't remember. She heard Morgan's mother saying, 'At least we know what happened, and where.' She couldn't tell the sub-lieutenant's parents that, and she had promised.

By the end of the week she and April had finished one side. Both pairs of overalls were stained, and on the Saturday, April boiled them unmercifully.

Bryony opened the letter from the ATA. She was invited to a flying test on 21 June. 'The longest day,' she said, pushing the letter into a drawer and forgetting it. She had seven days.

She and April began on the second side, in spite of the baking heat. They were nut brown beneath the paint and Adam, improving daily now, struggled from the Lodge to call, 'You missed a bit, Bee.' She waved her hand, but ignored him. April told him to go back to bed and stop trying to be funny. He did.

The sun on her back soothed her shoulder, but burned the back of her hand. April called up from the base of the ladder, 'We're doing a splendid job, Bee, even if we do say it ourselves.' Bryony peered down. Had she answered? She couldn't remember. She'd been trying to read the sub-lieutenant's lips, tracing them in her mind.

April continued, 'Eddie telephoned while you slept yesterday evening, wondering if you were attending the flying test. He said that even if you pass, which you will, you might not be called up. There are very few women yet, but you never know what's going to happen, especially now. I lie awake at night wondering if we'll be invaded or will Hitler be content with the Continent?'

Bryony didn't want to think about what might happen, and neither did she want to think about what had happened. For a moment she heard the blasts, the shouts and screams but then she floated away, seeing the sub-lieutenant's lips. She made herself grip the ladder, made herself dip the brush into the can which hung from the hook on the ladder. She brushed on the paint. 'So, Bee, what shall I tell him when he telephones again?'

'Who?'

'Eddie.'

'Tell him I'll reply.'

The paint was running down the brush, on to her wrist. She watched it, and remembered the raindrops on her bedroom window when she was eighteen and her dad had just died. Late that night Hannah came to her room, because their mother couldn't bear other people's tears on top of her own. Bryony had held her until she slept, and then she let herself cry, but only for that first night, because Hannah had woken and shaken her, and said, 'Don't, you mustn't cry, never, ever. It frightens me and Daddy said you must be responsible for me. He said I must ask you to promise you will always look after me. Then he died, in my arms. I keep telling you that.' So today, yesterday and it seemed every other day as far back as she could remember she had not cried, and she had looked after Hannah.

Three days later she and April had almost finished the end of the hangar too. In the evening, April cleared the kitchen table, heaving Mary Miller's sewing machine from the bottom of the big dresser, together with two pairs of Eddie's almost new overalls. Bryony just looked. April said, 'The paint has ruined the ones we've been wearing and Eddie said I could alter these. You'll need them when things get back to normal and you are quite well. We will keep these for dirty jobs.'

'I am well.'

April threaded the machine, then turned the handle, settling into a steady pace. There was a comfort to the ticketty-tick. Bryony moved from the table to the armchair set by the kitchen window. She slept until the sound of the doorbell woke her. She checked her watch and April said, 'Who on earth?'

Bryony rose, and walked to the front door. She opened it. Gerry the local policeman was standing with a middle-aged man in a cap. He was a stranger. 'Hello Bryony,' Constable Heath said.

'Is it Eddie?' Bryony was floating and drifting again. April ran to stand with her now, gripping her hand.

'Oh no, nothing like that,' Gerry Heath said.

April relaxed her grip. 'Would you like to come in?'

The man with Constable Heath was checking his watch. Gerry Heath shook his head. 'Look, Bryony, and you, April. This is Mr Templer. He is the uncle of a lad who was on the *Sunflower*.'

Mr Templer butted in. 'My nephew says that you asked 'im to remind you of a telephone number, and he didn't. It's been weighing heavy on his mind. He's in hospital, not too well, but will be all right. Bit of a do, weren't it, as I hear tell, but you all brought the army home. Many more than anyone thought. A good do, it was. He remembered the name of your boat, and his dad, the wife's brother, wrote to me to see if I could find you. You see, I'm here with me lorry from time to time. I brought a load down today, and thought I'd ask a copper. That's what our mums say, isn't it? Ask a copper, they'll always see you right.'

Bryony was hardly breathing as she listened; she was seeing the sub-lieutenant, turning away and heading back to his duty, and the wave of his hand. The man said, 'So I asked at the Police House, and the constable brought me here, or I brought him, should I say.' He laughed for a moment. 'So 'ere is the number. He writ it down, d'you see? First thing he did when you set course for Dover. Just forgot to give it to you.' He handed a tattered, water-stained piece of paper to Bryony.

She took it, gripping it. The man tipped his cap. 'Thank you for bringing our lad back. He said it was bloody murder and he doesn't know how you kept on rowing that little dinghy day and night. They watched you from the beach, and you just kept doing it, you and that young man of yours. The wife sent some goose grease for your hands 'cause 'e said they was bleed . . . .' His voice failed him. He coughed, handed her a pot wrapped in newspaper, then turned abruptly, coughed again, and said quietly, 'I have to get back, hate driving on them little slits of light.'

He walked away, and Gerry Heath tapped her

hand. 'You take care now, Bryony Miller, and that young man too.' He followed Mr Templer down the drive. Bryony ran after them, 'Stop, what's your nephew's name?'

Mr Templer called back. 'Stan Jones.' His voice was stronger now.

Bryony said, 'Tell Stan Jones to get better.'

'I will.'

Bryony returned to the house. April held her hand, and they moved into the hall. 'Did it get too wet or can you read it? Is it important, will it matter if you can't?'

Bryony nodded. 'Yes, it will matter.' She unfolded the sheet. It was readable. Now she moved to the telephone, lifted the receiver, and asked the telephonist to connect her. A woman answered, 'This is the Rowan residence, can I help you.'

Bryony swallowed, gripping the receiver tightly. She said, 'This is Bryony Miller. I was at Dunkirk. Your son gave me your telephone number. He wanted me to let you know how far he'd got, and for me to tell you he loved you. But I couldn't remember the telephone number. I'm so sorry, but I just couldn't remember it but I wanted you to know he was so brave, making sure his men got on the—'

Mrs Rowan interrupted, her voice very quiet. 'The *Sunflower*. Yes, we know. I'm sure you'd like to know that our son, Ben, is safe. He returned on a destroyer. He knew you'd call if you could but he will be so relieved to know that you are safe. It has so worried and upset him that you might not have made it home.'

Bryony couldn't speak, because though no tears were falling, her shoulders were shaking. April took the receiver from her. 'Yes, they made it home,' she said. 'They're both home and now Bee will get better. She's very tired.'

Bryony was climbing the stairs. She walked into Adam's room, her nose running, her heart breaking, the sounds and sights of the days off Dunkirk vivid, noisy and terrifying. He was propped up on pillows and leaned forward, 'Bee? What is it?'

'I'd forgotten it, you see, the telephone number but someone came and gave it to me. Stan Jones is safe. Ben Rowan is safe. They made it home.' She sat on the edge of the bed, and now she was sobbing, almost howling. Adam pulled her to him and held her, rocking her. 'Slow down, tell me what you mean.'

She told him, and as she did so Dunkirk came back, and the horror, and the sadness, the exhaustion of it all. As the day wore on into evening, and then night, the pair of them talked, and slept, and talked, and shared, as they always had.

April looked in at four in the morning, and smiled. They were asleep, clinging together like the two kids they'd once been. Bee would be all right now and perhaps Adam would realise that he was indeed 'her young man'. He'd better, or Eddie and she would give him a good whack across the backside.

Chapter Six

21 June 1940

Bryony leaned back against the Combe Lodge kitchen dresser eating her toast, watching April, who had moved from the cottage into the Lodge last week. Bryony and Adam had helped her transport her belongings, to make space for two pregnant women who had been evacuated from Jersey the previous week.

April no longer helped with meals at the hotel, as holidaymakers were practically non-existent, and instead was helping at the school. She grinned at Bryony as she put lettuce into a string bag for the school lunches. 'You're a noisy chewer, just like your father. I can hear you crunching from here.'

'Well, thank you for that, not that you haven't said it a million times before.'

April laughed, and now it was the potatoes that she and Bryony had dug early this morning that she heaved into a string bag. She said, 'I suppose, Bee darling, your Uncle Thomas's phone call last night wasn't, by some miraculous chance, about Hannah and your mother's intentions?'

Bryony finished the last of her toast, smelling onion on her hands. Perhaps she shouldn't have cut up the wretched things for the stew that April was to leave slow-cooking for their evening meal. But who on earth was going to notice while she did her three test circuits at Hatfield for the ATA? Eddie had said it would be in an open Tiger Moth, so the breeze would blow all smells away.

April was saying, 'For heaven's sake girl, your nails are dirty from the digging. Make sure you clean them before you head off for the train. Can't have you turning up showing a lack of respect. Let me see your shoes.'

Bryony sighed as April checked and nodded her approval. 'They'll do. Now, you haven't answered me. Did Thomas say whether Hannah is any nearer to agreeing to come home?'

April shoved more carrots into a rucksack. Bryony flicked a look at the wall clock. Six forty-five a.m. She would have scrubbed her nails anyway, and April knew that of course, but she was agitated, and seemed more nervous than Bryony about the test for the ATA. Perhaps she was frightened Bryony would actually be taken on, and therefore put herself in danger – again. Dunkirk had upset her, and Bryony thought it was this that had really hastened her move into the Lodge. She wanted to be in the midst of them, almost touching Adam and Bryony whenever she passed to prove to herself that they were whole.

Bryony moved to the sink, turned on the tap, and water gushed and splashed on to her pristine white blouse. She reduced the pressure and scrubbed her nails, feeling that it didn't matter where any of the British were, or what they were doing, because from now on bombs and danger were coming to everyone. So who was to say that Hannah and her mother weren't the sensible ones if they opted to stay out of harm's way? If indeed it was. That was the trouble; no one knew what was the right way to jump any more.

Bryony said as she scrubbed, 'Hannah won't budge while she and Peter are in love, and Uncle Thomas said that though people are registering for evacuation, and our troops are leaving, there's no sense of urgency and many think the Germans don't want to bother with little potato-growing islands.'

She turned off the tap and dried her hands. 'Let me see,' April commanded. Bryony grinned and held out her hands. 'I'm twenty-three, not three.'

'Well, sometimes I have trouble remembering.' April began to heave the bags out through the back door, while Bryony took the rucksack. They dropped them into the cart that Adam had made to fit on to the back of his mother's bicycle.

'Where is Adam?' Bryony asked, looking towards the shed where the bikes were kept.

'Down at the *Sunflower*. He's had to re-strip her because she's still not right. Dunkirk wore out the old girl, I think, but he wants to get her engine running as smooth as a baby's bum in case your mum and Hannah need to come home in a rush. I do wish he'd take it a bit easy but he's insisting he's well enough to be signed ready for action any day now.' April's voice was tense.

Bryony followed her back into the kitchen. 'He shouldn't work so hard. He must have been down there before it was light. I can always take the Tiger Moth, now I've got the Dragonette's engine in bits.'

'Rubbish, Bryony Miller.' She didn't see Eddie until he spoke. He was standing in the hall doorway in his dressing gown, yawning, his thinning hair dishevelled. 'Don't even think of it. It's too dangerous. I gather the Germans are overflying the Channel Islands.'

'I'll avoid them.' She grabbed her jacket.

Eddie muttered, leaning forward and waving his finger. 'Do not be flippant, Bee. I forbid you to fly to Jersey, do you hear? Who knows what might come out of the clouds at you.'

Bryony raised an eyebrow. 'So says the man who delivers aircraft from suppliers to maintenance units, or airbases, in practically all weathers.'

'That's necessary. A flight to Jersey is not. Promise me.'

April looked from one to the other, and slipped her arm through Bryony's. 'You had better do so, or you won't get through the door.'

Bryony recognised the set of his jaw, and knew

that he was deadly serious. 'I promise. Really I do, Uncle Eddie, so relax.'

Eddie nodded, and moved aside. April smiled at Bryony. 'Now, Miss Contentious, you need to run for the bus or you'll miss it, and then the train. Fly well, darling girl.' She kissed Bryony and they walked past Eddie, down the hall to the front door. As she opened it, Bryony looked back as she always did before she left for a flight, loving the wide staircase, lit from the tall window halfway up, the ancient flagstones of the hall, the old runner of a carpet, the paintings Hannah had done, and which she insisted hang here, out of direct light.

There was also the evocative smell of the place: a slight hint of dog, even though Rosie was not here at the moment, the scent of polish, and of something indefinable but which was the essence of Combe Lodge. Perhaps, she thought, it is the sum of all those who have ever lived here, which meant Uncle Eddie, and her dad's ancestors, the Millers.

Eddie came along the hall, a mug of tea in his hand, the steam rising, to join them at the door. His slippers were shabby and frayed. Well, everything in the house was shabby and frayed. As always, they were just managing to limp from one year to the next, doing what they all loved, and she would fight to the death to protect it. She laughed aloud at her histrionics. Obviously it was in the Miller genes, and it wasn't just Hannah who had a dose. Eddie said, 'I might be a laughing stock, my dear girl, but I love you. Fly well today, if it's what you want. There's no pressure on you.'

'I love you too, Uncle Eddie. I think I do want, because we've got to stop this madness. But am I good enough?' Eddie shared a look with April. He groaned, and said, 'I do despair sometimes, don't you, April? You've a commercial licence so of course you're good enough, silly sod.'

Bryony smiled, but nervousness was dragging at her. 'Tell Adam, when you see him, that he mustn't do too much on the boat today if he wants to go back but must pace himself. I'll see you all later.'

April hugged her, and hoiked her gas mask off the hook. 'You simply must stop forgetting it. Have a good journey. Hurry, now.'

Bryony kissed them both, then ran down the drive, turning to wave. It was then, as she saw the two of them standing close together at ease, waving, that it occurred to her that they loved one another. Of course, how on earth could she have missed the familiarity, the caring, the looks that must have passed between them for years? Why on earth hadn't they done anything about it? Everyone would be so happy for them.

She ran on, the gravel crunching, out on to the narrow road, passing Stubby Baines the milkman who was putting some bottles into the crate April left at the bottom of the drive.

'Fly well, young Bee.'

'I will.' She rushed along the road, following the

bend. The bus was waiting at the bus stop. She checked her watch. She was late. She clambered on. 'Thank you, Dan.'

'Ah well, couldn't have you missing the train, but let's get on, for Gawd's sake or Eddie won't buy me that pint he promised if I got you there on time.'

Mr Hampton, sitting on the front seat, hollered, 'Get the bloody bus in gear, Dan, or you'll have to drive her to Hatfield. Mark you, I could do with a day out.' She sat next to him, laughing as the passengers chanted. 'A day out, a day out.'

Dan got a wriggle on, yelling at embarking passengers to hurry up, or Bryony would miss her train. They reached the station in time and as she joined those waiting on the platform she checked that she had the letter from the ATA. She had. She checked her nails, her shoes, and the time. The train was late. Please, please, not too late.

A voice behind her said, 'Very smart, even if I do say it myself, and you have your gas mask. What a turn up for the books.' It was Adam, flushed and panting. She smiled, speechless. He was here. He had bothered to come when she'd be home this evening anyway.

'I was caught up between a gasket and hard place, so I had to cadge a lift off a delivery van, and I need to get Dan's bus on its return trip, which is due any minute now. Break a leg, make sure they know you have a commercial licence, make sure you bring the Moth in to land like a butterfly, make sure you're safe, then maybe we'll get rid of you at last, and get you obeying orders.'

He was turning on his heel while she shook her head at the speed of it all. She wanted him to say, I love you, I always will. Be careful because I can't live without you. She lifted her hand.

He turned, 'Bee ...' He stopped, looked down. 'Oh, never mind. Give 'em hell.'

He was gone as the train drew in but she watched him until he was out of sight. He walked with much more strength, and fluidity. His shoulders were braced instead of slumped. Yes, he had made a rapid recovery, though still wheezed and coughed. He said he was ready to go again, and she didn't know how she could bear it. But of course she would, just as everyone did.

On the stop–start journey to London and then back out to Hatfield she thought of Eddie and April. Why had they never said anything? Or was she wrong? She checked her letter, the date and time for the hundredth time. She listened to the other passengers. She stared out of the windows. She thought of Hannah, and her mother. Bryony had telephoned Hannah last week and had created a major sulk in her younger sister by asking when Peter was joining up?

Hannah said, 'You just want to spoil my life because you're an old maid in love with your stupid planes.' She did hate it when Hannah hung up on her.

She looked out of the train window as they screeched into the station. She was here. On the platform were young men in RAF uniform. Excitement and a deeper nervousness vied with each other as she stepped down on to the platform.

At Hatfield Aerodrome, Bryony showed her letter to the security guards and the RAF police at the gate. As she followed one who sparkled in his uniform and white blancoed belt towards an administrative block, she breathed in the smell of the place, the aircraft, the noise. The windsock indicated a gentle breeze, the lush grass of the aerodrome stretched before her. It was familiar as all airfields were familiar, a sort of 'home'. Above, yellow Tiger Moths followed a leader round and round in a circuit, then came in to land, most bouncing then settling. Beginners, she thought.

The policeman left her at the door to an office. She knocked.

'Enter.'

Sitting at a desk was a smart and sharp female Air Transport Auxiliary senior officer wearing a navy tunic, on the shoulders of which were two broad gold stripes. Well, a First Officer, then. On her left breast were wings embroidered in gold thread with the letters ATA in the centre. She indicated the chair set up on the opposite side of the desk. Bryony forced herself to sit as though relaxed, and answer questions on flying hours, types of aircraft she had flown, and qualifications. When asked, she admitted that she hadn't flown for at least three weeks. The woman smiled. 'Yes, Eddie Standing has filled us in quite comprehensively, Miss Miller. I gather you were busy elsewhere. Now, let's see how all this translates into fact – or not.'

As the two of them left the office, the woman handed her a leather helmet and goggles. They walked silently across to a two-seater yellow Tiger Moth that had seen better days. The woman climbed into the front seat, plugging in the speaking tube and doing up her straps. Then she sat quite still, waiting. For a moment Bryony hesitated. She never flew without checking her aircraft thoroughly, so instead of climbing straight into the dope and canvas warhorse she carried out a preflight inspection, ignoring the mechanic who tapped his foot and whistled in irritation as he waited to swing the propeller.

Only when she was satisfied did she climb into the seat behind, tucking her gas mask on to her lap.

She drew on the helmet and goggles, and waited. 'Shall we proceed, Miss Miller? Three circuits and three landings, if you please,' the woman said through the earpiece. It wasn't a question, but an order.

Bryony took a deep breath and switched on. The mechanic swung the propeller. Nothing. They tried again and the engine burst into life. She eased the throttle to control the flow of petrol, and signalled to the mechanic to remove the chocks. In his place she saw Uncle Thomas in charge of the Dragonette's chocks and it settled her. Opening the throttle, she taxied to the downwind boundary. Again she heard the voice through her earpiece. 'Three circuits, three landings, and be aware this is an RAF training school, and of course there is also de Havilland's air traffic, Miss Miller. Let's all get down in one piece, please, and not be "ill met by beginner", if I may paraphrase badly.'

Bryony acknowledged this, saying down the speaking tube, 'Yes, thank you, Miss . . .' She petered out. Should she say Ma'am? But she wasn't in the ATA yet, and wouldn't be, unless she shut up and got a move on.

She stopped at right angles to the take-off path, and now she was calm, now she knew her business. She checked that the petrol was sufficient for the flight, the throttle friction nut adjusted to prevent the throttle slipping back during take-off. The trim-tabs were set, both magneto switches were on, the mixture control fully rich. She looked up and round the sky, the yellow chicks were all down, and the runway was all clear.

Finally she turned into the wind, opened the throttle, easing the control column forward to increase her speed and lift up the tail until at sixty miles per hour they had lift-off. The old dear climbed steadily, and because she was old and had been round the block a few times, she could probably fly herself. Bryony's heart was singing, as it always did when the earth fell away. She checked all around, and saw nothing but thermals, clouds, and empty sky – all of which amounted to heaven. Were there angels sitting on the few fluffy clouds? She often waggled her wings once she reached cruising height and speed, but today common sense prevailed.

She flew the first circuit, and landed perfectly. There were no comments in her earpiece. She taxied back to the take-off point examining the sky and the landing strips. All clear. She took flight again, climbing to one thousand feet and throttling to cruising power, watching the altimeter, then turning, banking on to the crosswind leg. Slowly she closed the throttle, trimming for the glide, keeping the speed steady as she came in for the landing, checking the sky, and peering at the ground from the cockpit. She saw movement. It was not all clear.

A yellow Tiger Moth had appeared, and heedless of possible traffic had begun its take-off. Seamlessly Bryony aborted, easing away, and only when all was clear did she come round again, landing lightly. Immediately she taxied back to the take-off point and began her final circuit, thinking of the child who had run across the Combe Lodge landing strip. They were still searching but it was a mystery. She had even stood outside the school gates but had recognised no one, and the school had no child of that vague description attending. The billeting officer had shaken her head, asking how on earth she could be held to account for every strange child who ran across a field and, instead of fussing other people, Bryony should check her boundary fences.

Perhaps she was a visitor who had gone home? If not, would she do it again? Well, it didn't matter for now, because there were to be no more flights, unless Hannah phoned. She heard again Eddie's orders, but . . .

She was by now completing her final circuit. All was clear, the wind had freshened, it was drying the skin on her face, and her hands were cold but completely healed. It was amazing how forgiving one's body was. She thought of the gloves Adam had tossed her; today, she should have worn gauntlets. Slowly, slowly she reduced speed as she approached the runway. She checked all around, and peered down from the cockpit. Steady, steady, there was the fence, level out, back on the control column, and they sank to the earth, feather-light, the grass skimming beneath the wheels, the tail settling.

Nothing was said as they unstrapped, and undid the voice gadgetry. The First Officer climbed down first, and then Bryony. The mechanic strolled across and chocked the wheels, whistling. He looked at Bryony and winked. She raised an eyebrow. He shrugged, so she was none the wiser. Had she done enough?

Together they walked back across the grass to the pathway. To the right it led to the administration block, to the left were the main gates. The First

Officer stopped, and her smiled reached her eyes. 'Eddie taught you well, but then you have your father's genes. I know him by reputation. A great loss. He checked his aircraft, too. It's a professional practice. Your anticipation is excellent; there could have been a difficulty with the training aircraft taking off. You will hear from us as to whether you have passed but the admission of more women to the ATA is in the lap of the gods, or the higher-ups, but then they think of themselves as gods. We'll just have to wait and see. It's going to be a hard road to acceptance but if the Luftwaffe try to tip the scales, as surely they will, it makes perfect sense to hike our numbers. Have a safe journey home.' She pointed towards the gate.

The journey back was like the journey out, stop and start, and as they passed along the tracks and through stations, the June evening became night and there were no lights shining, courtesy of England's blackout blinds.

An elderly woman in the unlit compartment laid down her knitting for a moment. She smiled at Bryony and said, 'I suppose one shouldn't like anything about being at war, but isn't it wonderful to have such a clear night sky now there is so little ambient light from the streets and houses. Have you noticed, my dear?'

Bryony had, and replied, 'I feel sometimes that I could reach up and touch the stars. And I love it, particularly when the moon is full or, even better, when there's a hunter's moon.'

The woman smiled again. 'Indeed. Soon, of course, we could be bemoaning that very same moon. I remember in the Great War the Zeppelins dropping their bombs "By the light of the silvery moon".' She sang the last bit, her voice heavy with irony.

Bryony caught a bus from the station, though it took a slightly different route and she would have to walk across a few fields to reach the road leading to Combe Lodge. It didn't matter as long as she got home, because she was so hungry she could eat her fist. Neither did it matter that the slow cook was off-ration rabbit, and absolutely the last on her list of likes. It would, however, be inundated with the onions she had chopped and April was bound to have baked some potatoes.

Norman, the night-shift bus driver, asked how it had gone in the flying test. 'I don't know. It seemed to be all right but they'll let me know. How's Tommy now?' It was all she could do to ask, because Tommy had been at Dunkirk and she still didn't like to think about it. The dreams were quite enough to be getting on with.

'Back with his unit,' Norman said. 'Helps when you're with people who were there, he says. Prefers it to his mum's fussing.' He laughed, but the strain of knowing that his son had been in the front line, and would be again, was showing.

Bryony walked along the edge of the woods and was glad that she had brought her torch, though the light could only shine through the slit cut in the paper cover. It was, however, enough to stop her putting her foot into a rabbit hole, which she skirted instead. She strode past Mr Simes's wheat field, hearing the wind rustling the grain heads. The owls were hooting, and she imagined the eyes watching her, not to mention any field mouse foolish enough to show itself.

The thought of the owls made her remember the Stukas seeking their prey at Dunkirk. Stan Jones was right, it was good to be with people who understood. Sometimes she and Adam would exchange a look when thunder clapped, or a door slammed, and they jumped and paled, or when a night had gone by without sleep. It had brought them closer, she thought, but then when had they not been.

She sighed, and refused to go over the same old performance of wishing it was a different closeness, and instead concentrated on picking her way over the rutted ground. She reached the gateway, crossed the road, and was in the field adjoining the landing strip. She could skirt the airfield fence and come out on to the driveway. It was then she heard a rustling over to her left. She hesitated, flashing her torch in that direction. Nothing, except the usual shrubs and birch saplings. It was probably a damned fox heading for Combe Lodge's chickens.

She began to walk on, but heard the rustling again

and thought she caught a movement in the beam, but then it was gone. In its place was the sound of something, or someone, blundering into bushes, and then her torch caught a glimpse, but of what? It wasn't a fox, it was ... hang on, it was a figure, surely. She peered again. There – it burst from the bushes, and was running beside the landing strip fence. 'Hey!' she called.

She began running, because she now realised it was a girl. Was it the one who had run in front of the Dragonette? But then she was gone beneath trees, and Bryony heard a crash, and a cry. She slowed. Suddenly Dunkirk was with her again, the darkness, the cry, the crash. Sweat ran, and nausea swept over her. She swallowed, forcing herself to walk on, making herself stay here, in this moment, because Dunkirk was gone, finished. Instead, she was in Devon, on Combe Lodge land. She gripped the torch so hard that her fingers ached. She shouted, her voice shaky but loud, 'Stop running and stay where you are. This is private land, we own two yards' depth around the perimeter fence, and we have some talking to do.'

There was no movement, no sound but an owl's hoot, then the sound of crying. She drew in a deep breath. Not a bomb, not the filthy seawater, not the horror, but a child's distress. She said, calmly now, 'Stay quite still, I'm coming to you.'

She walked steadily in the direction of the sounds, the torchlight probing all the while. She found the girl and knelt by her side, her torch playing on the girl's face, the smell of unwashed poverty rising to meet her. 'I didn't mean nothing, Miss,' the girl said, her eyes dull.

'Where does it hurt?'

'Just me leg, a bit. Not bad. It's me dress. It's caught, you see, and if I rip it again, she won't like it. She won't, really she won't.'

It was so dark amongst the undergrowth that Bryony's torch took a while to locate the brambles that had captured the skirt. When she did, she laid down the torch, and unsnagged it, thorn by thorn. The girl wriggled free, and rose to her feet. For a moment she stood still, testing her leg, and then, with a swift look at Bryony, she turned and ran. Bryony was ready. She grabbed her, because she had seen the rip that matched a piece of material that had caught on the landing-strip fence on the day of the inbound flight.

'Not so fast. We need to talk, so you're coming with me.' As soon as she touched her, the girl sagged and became compliant. They set off together, Bryony holding her arm, ready for further flight, knowing she could tighten her grip at a moment's notice.

'What are you called, young lady?'

'What's me name, d'yer mean, Miss?'

'Yes, that's what I mean.'

'Celia, Miss.'

They were skirting the landing strip, then they headed down the path towards the back of Combe Lodge. The owls were in full voice, and the cockerel had taken leave of its senses and was crowing. His wives would give him hell for waking them way before the start of the day.

'What did you think I meant when I asked what you were called?' Bryony asked as they walked along the clinker path by the vegetable patch. Now the clouds had cleared, the moon lit up the profusion of potatoes, onions, leeks, and all good things. In amongst them she had planted marigolds, and a few roses and herbs. She felt it kept the pests away from the veggies.

'She calls me other things,' the child said. 'Sometimes I almost forgets me real name.'

Bryony didn't want to pursue the conversation in this calm and beautiful place. Now they were walking along the front of the formal garden, or so it had been called in its days of glory, but she was doing her best with the new box hedging around the herbs. It needed cutting. She knew the herbaceous borders needed more work, and she wasn't keeping up with the deadheading of the roses. She and April had always worked the gardens, but these days it was getting away from them a little, just as this child had got away.

She said gently, unable to stop herself, 'What does she call you?'

'Bitch, cow, stupid idiot, things like that, because I'm naughty, you see. I wets me bed and I don't know what she wants, sometimes. She doesn't tell me, and so I don't know, so I do something and I gets it wrong, so I reckon she's right. I am a cow, or idiot, things like that.'

'Who is this *she*?'

The girl stopped, and pointed to the east. 'The lady the billeting person put me wiv, Mrs Galloway. She's kind to have me, I knows that cos the billeting lady told me. She said, "These kind people have opened their doors to you children from London, so you must behave." But you see, I don't know I'm wetting meself until the morning, and like I said, I don't know what she's thinking. I winds 'er up, she says, and she gives me the strap to make me good.'

They had reached the back door. Was anyone up? It must be about eleven. You couldn't tell if the light was on with the blackout blinds. She reached for the handle, but now Celia pulled back. 'You going to take me in there and hit me, Miss? I know I was naughty to be 'ere, but I wanted to see the plane again. It makes me feel sort of free, just watching it up in the air, or coming down. I'm sorry if I got in the way of that other plane.'

Bryony knelt beside her. 'No, no one is going to hit you. I just want to get you home safely and stop Mrs Galloway worrying.'

'She never checks. I comes out because I think if I do a tiddle in the woods really late, I won't do it in the bed.'

'Right.' Momentarily Bryony was lost for words. 'I was the one flying that day, and I was just worried, and wanted to find you to see why you were there and if you were all right. Now I know. I think perhaps I need to eat, so why don't you have some food with me, then I will walk you home. I could explain to Mrs Galloway that you were caught on brambles, and were stuck and couldn't get home earlier. Is that a good idea?'

They opened the back door, and entered the dark passageway. They walked into the kitchen, which was bathed in light. Adam, April and Eddie were sitting around the table. April was sewing, Eddie was reading, and Adam was leaning over an old newspaper on which was a knobbly bit of the *Sunflower*'s engine. He looked up, an oily rag in his hand.

'The pilot returns.' He stopped. Then continued, 'Returns with a passenger.' Celia pressed hard against Bryony's skirt, trying to hide behind her. Bryony led her to a chair. 'Sit there, Celia, and we'll share my meal. I feel quite full and could do with some help if that's all right with Mrs Cottrall?'

April dropped her sewing on the table, and was up at the oven before Bryony could discard her gas mask and jacket. In the light, Celia was thin and dirty, her nails encrusted, her hair unwashed. Her arms revealed bruises in the shape of a person's fingers. Her cheek was swollen with a yellowing bruise. Eddie raised his eyebrows and nodded towards the door into the hall. Adam was already rising. Bryony said, 'I just need to find my slippers, Celia. Adam and Eddie are coming to help me look.

You stay here, and Mrs Cottrall will dish up the stew. I will be back, and soon I will take you to your billet.'

April said, 'After eating, you and I have somewhere to go, dearest Bryony. Because, late though it is, we need to investigate things further.'

Once in the hall, Bryony repeated pretty much verbatim what Celia had said. The men looked grim. 'We'll all take her home,' Adam said, groping in his pocket for his packet of cigarettes. He hardly ever smoked. He offered one to Eddie. 'I think I will,' Eddie muttered, 'if you don't mind. I'll bring some back on my next leave.'

Bryony looked at Adam. 'She's the one who ran across the landing strip.'

After a moment they returned to the kitchen. Bryony and Celia ate their stew, Celia using her fingers. April whispered to Bryony. 'Thankfully, she let me help wash her hands. She's very hungry, and malnourished.' Eddie drew April to the pantry and Bryony saw him talking urgently, then April laid her head on his shoulder, while he held her tightly. Bryony watched Adam as he smiled at the couple, and then return to his gasket. She longed for someone to hold her.

Celia ran her finger along the bottom of her plate, and licked it.

April emerged from the pantry. 'I think we will have some bread and butter now, how about that? You can use it to soak up the last of your gravy.'

She started to cut a slice of the freshly baked loaf and as she did so, Celia reached out to try and snatch some crumbs. 'Don't!' Bryony shouted. April stopped, mid-slice, The girl flinched, and dropped the crumbs back on the breadboard. 'Sorry, Miss.'

Adam looked from Bryony to Celia. Bryony pointed to the knife. 'I'm sorry to shout, Celia. I just didn't want you to get hurt. That knife is extremely sharp.' April resumed cutting. A slice fell to the board. She lifted the knife clear. Bryony took the bread. 'Here, let me put some on your plate, and then you're quite safe.'

Adam smiled at Celia. 'We call this lady Bee, though her real name is Bryony. You see, bees make really sweet things, like honey. Which means our Bee is really sweet too.'

Celia looked from Adam to Bryony. 'She got the thorns out of my skirt, Mister. One pricked her but she never said nothing, so I think she must be.'

'There you are, then,' Adam said, before whispering to Bryony. 'You can pay me later, and the fact that you have a sting worse than a horsefly's bite is to be left to another day.'

She kicked him beneath the table. He dropped the cleaning cloth.

When they'd all had a cup of tea, weak by this time of night because the leaves had been reused so often, Bryony said she, rather than a posse, would take Celia back. The others should get some sleep. As they were leaving, Eddie asked Celia, 'Why did you run across the landing strip, and why were you there tonight?'

Celia pressed against Bryony again, but Eddie squatted down on her level. 'I'm not cross, just interested,' he told her.

'I like them planes. It must be nice, up there. Quiet, sort of different. Everything must look so small, and you can go just anywhere, miles and miles and never come back, and you can't hear the shouting, not up there.' Her face was animated, her eyes alive for the first time that evening.

Eddie rose, and very gently he stroked Celia's hair. After a moment he said into the silence that had fallen, 'You are right, it is all of those things, and one day, when you're older, we will teach you how to fly. How about that?'

Celia nodded, her face blank, her eyes dead. She didn't believe a word. April handed Bryony her gas mask, and her own to Celia, though it would be too big, but was better than nothing.

Adam said to Celia, as Bryony reached for the door, 'You don't have to go up in the air to get shouting to stop, you know. People can help that happen.'

Again there was no reaction.

Celia led her along the lanes to the next village. April had said before they left that she vaguely recollected a Mrs Galloway but she was not someone who was a member of the WI or the church, or was seen about Exmouth or Combe village very much. April had wanted to come, but Bryony shook her head. 'It's late. You need your sleep.'

Celia led her to a bungalow set apart from all the others on the edge of the woods, the tree branches bowed over the roof. Bryony knocked on the door, easing back off the step. Celia waited, rigid by her side. The door opened, and an elderly woman stood there. 'What's she done now?' Her tone was abrasive.

Bryony's was worse as she said, 'She's done nothing except have a good meal, which must be the first for many a long day. I am sending the billeting officer, Mrs Sanderson, round tomorrow and there had better not be a finger laid on this child ever again, do you understand? Neither will you call her names. She will be treated with care and consideration from this moment on.'

Mrs Galloway stood to one side. 'It's late, she should be in bed. Nips out, she does. Nothing I can do about it. You should try it if you think you can do better, and the bed-wetting . . . what a stink. These city kids; animals, they are.'

Bryony stared at her, and breathed in the smell that oozed from the darkness of the house.

'Get in here, you little . . .' The woman stopped.

Celia left Bryony's side, her head down. 'Sorry, Missus.'

There were no tears. The darkness of the house was the darkness of Bryony's Dunkirk nightmares. Did this child even know how to cry? Did she know a world that was better than this? Where were her family? If they existed, why didn't they bother to find out how she was? Where was the billeting officer? Why did she never check?

Celia was disappearing into that darkness, and now Bryony moved, leaping up and hauling the child to her, lifting her and backing down the step. 'She won't be coming back, Mrs Galloway.' Carefully she lowered her and eased Celia behind her, standing between her and the old hag, for that's what she was: an old hag, a witch, an appalling witch.

The woman just looked at her. 'Good riddance, I say. I only did it for the allowance. You can fetch her ID and ration card in the morning.' She slammed the door.

Together they began their walk back, Bryony holding on to the child in case she ran off. 'We'll find you somewhere better, Celia. Then we can let your mum know.'

'I got a sister, not a mum. She ain't got time to see to me, she's busy with her blokes, really busy now cos of the soldiers, that's why she sent me away. They're coming and going a lot more, and I gets in the way.'

Bryony followed the narrow beam of her torch along the road. No cars passed, which wasn't surprising with the fuel rationing. Blokes always there, doing what? She didn't ask. Enough was enough. She shone the torch on her watch, and then heard hurrying footsteps gaining on them from behind. She pulled Celia to her. 'Hush,' she said, switching her torch off and holding it like a weapon. The footsteps drew nearer. She spun round. 'Stand back!' she shouted.

Adam's voice came out of the darkness. 'Turn the torch on, for heaven's sake, Bee. You didn't really think we'd let you come without backup surely. Who knows what you'd get up to – I've been togging along behind from the start. Let's hurry and we can each tumble into a nice warm bed, at last, because it's been a long day. What do you say, Celia?'

She looked up at him. 'You'll be cross in the morning, when I've wet it.'

'Oh, never mind about that, worse things happen at sea. Tell you what, let's hear about Bee's flying test, because that's where she's been today. Somewhere near London, showing someone if she can fly well enough to help ferry aeroplanes.'

The three of them walked along, following the beam, while Bee talked quietly about the Tiger Moth, how it felt to fly, and then Adam talked about his boat and how it felt to be on the sea, fishing for lobster, or line mackerel, or taking out holidaymakers. When they arrived home, April had already made up a bed. 'I know you too well, dearest Bee,' she murmured as they escorted Celia to a middle bedroom, in which there were twin beds.

'Look, Celia.' April pointed to the waterproof rubber cover over the mattress, then pulled up the sheet to cover it. 'So, it doesn't matter what happens in the night. I think, though, we will pop you in the bath, late as it is. We need to see what nasty scratches those brambles made.'

'Don't have baths, Missus.'

Bryony said, 'Oh yes you do. Mrs Cottrall has some nice smelly stuff that Eddie flew over from Paris for her before the war.' Again Bryony wondered why on earth she hadn't understood earlier about the relationship between these two people.

As a distraction Bryony told Celia about Eddie's flying and how he was away for thirteen days and back for two, and before the child realised they were in the bathroom. The man in question had already run the bath. He left them to it. 'I need to get some sleep, I'm off at dawn to fly more aircraft, Celia. But I will see you again, I'm quite sure.'

The women bathed her, and washed her hair. They did not mention her bruises because that would be dealt with later but they put iodine on her scratches. It stung and turned her skin yellow. April said, 'Ah, but warriors need to keep their wounds clean.'

Celia had nits too, but not many. They helped her out of the bath, wrapped her in a towel and she hung her head over the basin while April worked up a lather with her own shampoo. Bryony rushed down for vinegar. They rinsed Celia's hair free of shampoo, and the lice came with it. They soaked her hair with vinegar, promising her it wouldn't smell, and then ran the steel comb through to remove the nits, while she squirmed and protested. Bryony asked if she'd prefer to have it all cut off instead. That calmed the situation.

April found an old nightie of Hannah's in the 'just in case' drawer while Bryony carried Celia through to the bedroom. They closed the blackout blinds and the flowered curtains before switching on the light and leading her to the mirror. Celia's clean hair was blonde, not the dirty brown it had appeared. 'Vinegar makes blonde hair even blonder, and more beautiful,' Bryony said.

Celia pulled a face. 'The steel comb don't. It just hurts.'

'That it does,' Bryony agreed. 'I had to have it when I was growing up, but I'd rather that than have a shaved head.'

Celia stared at her. 'You've 'ad 'em too, have you?'

'Most children do.'

Celia's relief was palpable. 'I thought I was a bad cow again.'

Bryony felt April's hand on her back. Together they said, 'Your name is Celia. You must never think of yourself as anything else. Your new foster parents won't think you are bad, ever. We'll make sure of that.'

Celia looked from one to another, then moved stiffly to the bed. The bruising must hurt. Again they said nothing but instead tucked her in. It was now nearly one in the morning. 'I'll see Mrs Sanderson tomorrow, it's far too late tonight, and then I will wring her ruddy neck,' Bryony whispered, as they shut the door. 'Bad billeting officer, clearly.'

Celia called, 'Don't shut the door, Miss Bee. Please don't shut it.' Bryony opened it again. 'There, now try to sleep, you're quite safe.'

April said, 'I would like to come with you. I know the old trout, and it's time she took some responsibility. She must find this child somewhere suitable.'

As they spoke, Adam nipped from his room into the bathroom. 'I'm up early for the appointment with the doc. I could be signed off, you never know, and get back into the fight. Get some sleep, Bee, you must be whacked, you've had a long day.'

She was, but there was little sleep for her, because Celia cried out several times in what was left of the night. In the end Bryony gave up, and instead of returning to her room she crawled into the other twin bed and talked of the Dragonette, the clouds, the buffeting wind, and it was for her peace of mind as much as the child's.

They left Celia with the pregnant mothers, Catherine and Anne, in Combe Cottage, though she should have been in school. But it transpired she had not been while in Devon and not a lot in London. She was eight, she said, and her sums and reading weren't very good.

It was of this Bryony and April talked as they

walked to Mrs Sanderson's cottage. 'Best we hurry, before she buffs her badge and bustles off to be important around the place,' April said.

It was a beautiful day. The verges were alive with vetch, cornflowers and even the odd bee orchid. Bees proliferated and midges darted amongst the profusion. Bryony was tired, her eyes felt dry, her head ached. As April stepped out, swinging her arms and humming, Bryony murmured, 'It must be exhausting always being so cheerful.'

'You're one to talk. You always have a spring in your step and ooze energy, young Bee, just like your father, dear old Reggie.'

'Don't you worry about him?'

'Who?' Suddenly April's tone was guarded.

Bryony laughed, and slipped her arm through April's. 'Eddie, of course. It's as plain as a pikestaff you love one another, but why do you both keep it quiet?'

April said nothing until they reached the stile leading to the west end of Combe Village and Miss Sanderson's thatched longhouse. 'Why do you think?'

They clambered over and walked single file along the edge of the potato field, scaring three pheasants into a squawking lift-off, but they were so fat they took ages to achieve height. 'They'll never make old bones – they'll be picked off by the guns if they don't sort out their take-offs,' Bryony muttered. 'And to answer your question, I have no idea why.'

Ahead of her, April shrugged. 'At the moment your mother is away, so we can relax, and not upset her.' She stopped now, and waited for Bryony. 'Your mother is a fragile woman, Bee, you know that, and finds things hard to cope with. The worst day of her life was when she lost Reggie. Eddie and I knew how we felt about each other but how could we say so in front of her? Besides, as I say, we know how we feel, and we have a good life together. Remember I have – well, had – the cottage for privacy.'

Bryony put up her hand. 'Stop right there.'

April laughed. 'Don't worry, you won't be hearing about the details. We're happy, settled, and one day we can be more open, but not yet. It works, and when your mother returns you will say nothing, and things will trot on with discretion, as always.'

They continued walking and soon the back of the longhouse, which was a former cider house, hove into sight. Bryony muttered, 'You're a good woman, and Eddie is a good man.'

'We're a happy man and woman. We're lucky. You will be too, in time.'

April was opening the back gate of the longhouse and Bryony followed. 'Not according to Mum or half the village, and especially Old Dave, who all think I'm on a dusty shelf. I just haven't found the right man, or perhaps it's that he hasn't found me. I suppose my overalls and filthy nails have a limited appeal, but it's my job and without it I can't keep my family.' She gave a laugh but it was hollow.

They traipsed round the house to the front along the crazy paving path. April knocked on the old oak front door, and within seconds it opened. Mrs Sanderson was in the act of pulling on her leather gloves, and wore her usual tweed suit. How hot she must be, Bryony thought, as she prepared to launch into the catechism of Celia's woes, but it was April who said, 'We need to talk to you in your role as billeting officer.'

'I'm just off out on my rounds, Mrs Cottrall. It's best to make an appointment.'

'Appointment be damned,' April almost snarled.

Mrs Sanderson stopped, her foot poised over the lintel, registering shock. April gave her no chance to recover, but loudly and firmly said, 'We have removed Celia Whatshername from Mrs Galloway. How could you even think of letting that awful woman have her? There are other homes in the neighbourhood, surely? What about your own road – not many evacuees here, but oh, let me see, they're friends of yours, I believe. And why haven't you offered us any evacuees? Combe Lodge has an attic that we prepared in readiness when war was declared. Some came, and then went when nothing happened. We have not been asked since.'

Bryony pulled April back, hushing her. 'Mrs Sanderson, Celia is covered in bruises, unwashed, and not attending school. We really feel she must be rehoused.' Though she was as angry as April, somehow she kept her voice level.

It was then that Mrs Sanderson collected herself, stepping back into her hall and adjusting her felt hat, her balance regained in more ways than one. 'I find this all rather disturbing.'

'So you should,' muttered April.

'You ask why I didn't try Combe Lodge. Well, I did, fully aware that you have many bedrooms. It was your mother, and indeed your sister, Hannah, young Bryony, who told me very firmly that there was no room at the inn. Or rather, your mother insisted that she was too unwell to cope with children, and Hannah that she was too preoccupied with caring for your mother. Then they shut the door, much as I am about to do, now.'

Bryony felt rooted to the ground. 'I can't believe that. Where was I?'

'As your sister advised me, Bryony, you were too busy swanning about in your aircraft to involve yourself in the day-to-day running of the house and its inhabitants.'

The walk home was muted, each of the women busy with her own thoughts. They collected Celia from the cottage, thanking Anne and Catherine and hoping that they were well. Anne smiled, touching Celia's head. 'Yes, not long now before we have our own little ones. We'll be lucky if they're as lovely as this young miss.'

Celia lifted her head and smiled. 'Fanks for the biscuit, both of you.'

April and Bryony walked Celia back to the house, stopping to show the roses. Bryony pulled the different blooms down so that Celia could smell them more easily.

It was only when they were sitting around the kitchen table and Bryony was pouring home-made lemonade for the three of them that Celia said, 'When do I go?'

April waited for Bryony, who said, 'Never, Celia. You will be staying here, in that same bedroom, for as long as you wish. But you will be going to school, because we talked to the headmistress, and she is so looking forward to having you. There you will make lots of friends.'

Celia smiled, 'I don't mind about friends, but I like it here. I'm near the aeroplanes, and that man said he'd teach me to fly, when I'm older.'

'Well, that's sorted, then.'

Celia slurped her lemonade, then dragged her hand across her mouth. April winked at Bryony. Changes would have to be made, and what would happen when Hannah and her mother returned? Well, they'd just have to adjust because the house was big enough for even more. There was, after all, the whole of the attic as well as Celia's existing room. It would be filled with those in need, for the duration.

Celia looked at Bryony, creeping her hand along the table to touch hers. 'What happens if you go with that man to help fly them planes? Do I go somewhere else then?'

Bryony shook her head. 'No, you will stay here with April, and between us all we will work it out.'

She and April stared at each other and nodded, because indeed the situation would be worked out. Bryony swallowed her outrage and confusion, because after all, she should have realised that there was something strange about the lack of child evacuees. It wasn't just her mother and Hannah's fault, it was hers, as head of the family, for she had allowed the situation to arise.

April came close, and whispered, 'You're not a mind-reader, and I didn't know Mrs Sanderson had been here, either. We weren't the ones to send her away and, after all, you opened Combe Lodge to Anne and Catherine.

Anne and Catherine were different: they were friends of Uncle Thomas and had come when their husbands had joined up. They had heard a rumour that the Germans took babies away from the mothers, to be brought up as Nazis. No one knew if it was true, but these two weren't going to take the chance.

'Anne and Catherine asked.'

'Exactly,' April said. 'We were asked, and we didn't refuse. We took evacuees in 1939 but they returned home. We will be asked again, and we will accept.'

She went to the sink and banged and crashed the pots.

Chapter Seven

26 June 1940

After tea, when they were sitting around the kitchen table, Bryony watched Eddie playing dominoes with Celia. He had hunted for the game and found it in the bottom of the dresser on the first day of his five-day leave. He had decided that the numbered tiles were one way of helping Celia with the grim business of getting her head around arithmetic. What he hadn't bargained for was her quickness of mind, let alone her competitive spirit. It matched his, and he was being forced to concentrate just as hard as he would if he was bringing a Spitfire in to land. Bryony asked, 'Are women ferry pilots allowed to fly Spitfires yet?'

'Nope, and be quiet, let me concentrate.'

April laughed quietly as she sewed. Bryony returned to her plan for reassembling the Dragon Rapide engine. 'When will they be allowed?'

'Not sure, now *do* be quiet,' he grunted. 'I need to keep on top of my game, for heaven's sake, Bee.'

Celia shouted. 'I've won, again. Again, Bee. I've won.'

Eddie groaned, leaning back in his chair. 'You do know, of course, that even though Celia's schooling has been so skimpy, she's such a quick learner that she'll have no problem. It's her reading that needs help, but trust me, she'll be working her way through the library before we know where we are.'

'Come on, Uncle Eddie. Set 'em up again.'

Over the noise of their laughter, Bryony heard the ringing telephone. She shook her head at Eddie, who was doing as he was told and setting up. 'You keep going with the serious stuff. If you're being recalled, I'll give you a yell.' Celia was studying the tiles, her chin on her hands, her elbows on the table. Bryony pushed back her chair as he groaned, 'You're going to win again, you're just too good, young lady. Now, will you count these dots on the domino tiles for me? I haven't got my glasses on.'

'You don't wear glasses, Uncle Eddie. You just want me to count,' Celia shrieked, laughing.

'Too smart by half,' Eddie said, grinning at April who was altering some dresses her WI friends had given her for Celia.

Bryony reached the telephone and picked up the receiver, wondering if it would be Adam, who was in Portsmouth with Eric, trying to get a piece of the *Sunflower*'s engine re-ground. Or it could be her uncle's ferry pool, needing him. It was neither; it was Uncle Thomas, who sounded as bluff and hearty as ever. 'So, how are you, my darling. Have you heard from the ATA?'

'Yes, Uncle Thomas. I'm through but they don't need me at the moment. Uncle Eddie says they're still not taking on many women, but we're busy enough here, one way or another.' She hadn't yet told them of Celia because the possible reaction of her mother and Hannah would cause total outrage to rise within her. But perhaps they had changed, perhaps they . . .

She shrugged off her meandering. 'What's happening your side, Uncle Thomas? We've heard that the military are leaving. Are there still queues for evacuation at the harbour, and—?'

'Oh, don't start, Bryony,' he interrupted. 'Your aunt and I are not leaving, so no need to go on. Anyway the official evacuation is over. The soldiers have all gone, but life continues as normal. After all, we're still digging up the spuds. I know, I know,' he said, as though she was arguing, but she understood that it was with himself. 'Let those who want to, scarper, but most of us will stay. It's daft to think of a whole population turning tail and leaving. We'll stay, and plant our fields, nurse our sick, man our shops, and deal with it. Anyway, who knows what will happen? They could come straight for you lot, or stay in France stuffing themselves with pâté and wine.' Bryony could almost see him shrugging.

She said, 'I suppose what I'm really asking is what's happening with Mum and Hannah. Are they intent on staying? Can you really cope if they do? They're my responsibility, not yours.'

Uncle Thomas laughed, and lowered his voice. 'Young Hannah's her usual selfless and beguiling self and yes, I am being sarcastic. She won't budge because young Peter is still here. His dad, Keith Andrews, is still saying, no bloody way. It's the potato harvest, you see, and Peter's not that selfish.' She heard the doubt in her uncle's voice. He continued. 'Well if he does bugger off, we'll all pitch in. By the way, Bee, your mum and Hannah are not your responsibility. They're big girls now.'

'Dad told Hannah before he died that I was to look after them.'

'I know all that, lass. But he had no right, and that time has long gone. You need to cast them off and row your own boat.'

She laughed quietly. 'Turning into a sailor in your old age, Uncle Thomas?'

Celia called from the kitchen, 'Bee, are you going to play now? Uncle Eddie says 'e needs a bit of time to relax and recover, cos I beats him all the time.'

'Have you got company?' It was Aunt Olive now, who had taken over the receiver. Briefly Bryony explained, but said nothing about her mother and Hannah's rejection of more evacuees. It was still something so awful in Bryony's mind that she couldn't process it properly.

'Don't tell—' she began, but Aunt Olive was already talking over her. 'An evacuee, oh how wonderful, Bee, darling.' Bryony heard the longing in her voice, because her aunt and uncle had never been able to have children.

She heard Hannah then. 'She's what? Oh, for God's sake.'

She'd clearly snatched the receiver from her aunt, and now Hannah said, 'You've done what? For heaven's sake, Bee, you'll go swanning off to your ATA and we'll have to deal with it – if we come back, that is. But that's one good reason not to. Just make sure it doesn't go near my room, or my stuff. Mum will be furious, she didn't want the noise or the mess. We told—' She stopped.

Bryony asked, her voice steady, 'We told who, and what? Surely you wouldn't reject those in need?'

'You're just so thoughtless, Bee.'

The receiver was slammed down. Into the silence Bryony said, 'One day, madam, I will spank you so hard my hand will hurt.'

She sighed and turned, and there was Celia, looking shocked and backing away before turning and running pell-mell into the kitchen. Bryony shut her eyes. Children were a minefield. She'd rather deal with an aircraft in a spin any day.

The telephone rang again. It was Uncle Thomas. 'I got through again quickly. Didn't think I would, so the cable's working well. Of course if they come, the first thing that will happen is that the cable will be cut, so you won't be hearing from us until it's over. Can't say you'll feel that's a bad thing after young Hannah's tantrum just now. I know I shouldn't say it, Bee, but she could do with a firm hand. She plays on being the orphan, and the poor little girl who needs mothering. You know, of course, she's man mad. Mark you, I was girl mad.' He laughed.

He talked on and she let him, knowing he'd had a few beers and was uncertain about the future, and was trying to find a way through in his own mind. The line was beginning to crackle, which usually meant it was about to fail. He drove on, heedless. 'Just to say, Bee, Sammy's let me know he has a secret cellar full of booze and he wants his boy to join up with some cash in his pocket. I'm going to buy it, and stash it below the barn, along with some of the other bottles. It's wine, more beer, and some baccy. The Italians have been interned, and the German waiters, did I tell you? Yes, I'll hang on to Hannah and Mary. They're in the cottage so we have our space.' The crackling was worse. 'Don't worry, Bee. We'll be all right. Always have been, always will be. You need to look after yourselves you kn—'

The line went dead.

Later that evening, Hannah and Peter sat with their arms around their knees on Col de la Rocque. They watched the whitecaps in the distance. It was Hannah's favourite place, and she loved to be here with him, and adored his strength, his kisses, his humour, his talk of the farm and what he'd do with it when his father and mother retired and it finally became his. Did he mean 'ours'? She thought he did.

He picked and flicked grass. 'I'll turn the main crop into tourists, let them have their own units and look after themselves. I'll keep some goats, chickens, and a donkey for the children. I'll rent out the fields so someone else can look after the ruddy spuds, and the house will be free of boarding tourists, wanting their beds made and their breakfast on time.'

He swung round and kissed her, gripping her tightly. His mouth opened. She broke away as she remembered Bryony. 'Talking of bed and breakfast, guess what Bee's gone and done. I thought we'd scared off Mrs Sanderson, but no, Miss Goody Two-Shoes has opened the door and let in an evacuee. Others will come without a by your leave, you just wait. I should have been consulted. It's as though I never existed. I bet the little brat's got my room by now, and my stuff.'

She threw herself back on the grass. It smelt of the hay in Uncle Thomas's barn. Peter lay down beside her. 'Oh well,' she said, 'I'm happy here, with you, and nothing else matters.' But she wanted to cry, because Bee had sounded so cold and cross.

She felt Peter ease himself to one side. He said nothing for a while, just chewed a piece of grass. Finally he muttered, as a gull chased another high above them, 'I suppose she thinks she has to do her bit because she's not been called up to the ATA yet. Or do you get called up to a civilian organisation?'

She rose on her elbow, tore the grass from his mouth, and kissed him hard, saying against his mouth, 'Who cares, we're here, just the two of us, and there's a party tonight at Cheryl's.' She kissed his lips, then his cheek. 'I have a bottle of wine from Uncle Thomas's hoard. He thinks I don't know about it, but he wants help to move the wine he's buying from Sammy into the barn later today. So that's payment in advance.'

'Don't be mean, Hannah. Leave him his wine. I have some and that'll do. He's looking after you and your mum, for heaven's sake.'

He stroked back her hair, blinking against the brightness of the day. She said, 'It's partly Mum's farm, so it's not being unfair. She inherited it along with Aunt Olive, and though he sends her a share of the profits, it's not half a share.'

Now he was sitting up, shaking himself free of grass, not looking at her for a while, as though deep in thought. At last he stroked her cheek. 'Well, your uncle does do all the work, but hang it all, don't let's argue. It's so hot, so beautiful, and so are you.' He was dragging her to her feet. 'Race you to the bikes, and I bet I get to the pub before you. Let's make this a day to remember.'

His laugh was infectious, and Hannah kissed him again, holding his face in her hands. 'I love you,' she said.

He turned, and started to run. 'Come on, fancy pants, or you're buying the drinks.' As they ran a

German aircraft flew over, low, its shadow chasing them, its engines roaring. They threw themselves to the ground. Sometimes the Luftwaffe did this, but they were only playing games, surely; still, the sound made her mouth go dry, and she buried her face in the grass. Peter raised himself up and bellowed. 'Just you wait, you bugger. Just you damned well wait.'

The following morning, 27 June, Hannah and Rosie were squashed together in the passenger seat of her uncle's lorry as he drove with a load of potatoes to the harbour at St Helier. While he unloaded she took Rosie for a walk, through the milling relatives and friends who were here to see people off. Next stop, Britain.

She had a headache from too much wine, so she walked carefully, turning her head, looking for Peter. He had said to be here. There were plenty of merchant boats being loaded with produce, and another boat was drawing away from the quay with passengers heading for Britain. People seeking mainland sanctuary? Returning holidaymakers? Both, probably. She stroked Rosie and people stopped to do the same because there were far fewer dogs and cats on the island, as so many had been been put down in the war panic.

A man passed, and she asked, 'Have you seen Peter Andrews?'

His eyes were red, his cheeks wet. He replied, 'Peter, you said? I thought I saw him with his parents half an hour ago.' His voice broke. 'Sorry, just seen off my wife and children. They missed the main evacuation, and we've only just decided it might be for the best after all.' He moved on.

Suddenly Rosie started barking and straining at the lead. Hannah could hardly hold her, even using both hands. She shouted at her to behave. It seemed to calm her, and she let herself be dragged back to Hannah's side. 'Sit,' Hannah ordered and yanked on the lead.

Far over, there were people queuing for a boat. Whenever she saw this scene it made her panic a little but then her uncle, who was chatting to the other farmers, a cigarette at the corner of his mouth and scratching his head beneath his cap, made her calm. He was like a rock, so solid, his feet stuck in the soil from which, he declared, it would take more than a load of bloody Nazis to move him. She nodded. What would the Germans want with their little island anyway, when the plum would be mainland Britain?

She looked behind her and around her. Above her the gulls called. Were they the same ones who'd finished the crusts yesterday? They would follow the boats out of the harbour, just as some were following the passenger boat already out at sea. She looked around for Peter, then walked on, watching as *The Susan Gill* cast off.

People were waving to those already on board. She saw Peter's parents on the quayside. Mrs

Andrews was flapping a handkerchief. But where on earth was Peter? He had walked her home last night, hugged her as though he'd never let her go, and ducked away into the farmhouse. The chickens had been fussing, the dogs had slunk out to see him, and then returned to their kennels as he entered the house. He hadn't turned round, just called. 'You take care, lovely girl.'

It was what he always said. She shaded her eyes, searching the quay. She checked behind her again. Her uncle was still chatting, but the cigarette had gone. She looked again at Peter's parents, but he was definitely not with them. Mrs Andrews was standing on tiptoes, waving, and now it was Hannah who was on her toes following the older woman's sight line. As she did so, a heaviness took over, her heartbeat seemed to slow, and her body grew cold, though the sun was hot. Somehow she knew what she would see. There on *The Susan Gill* was Peter, a huge rucksack on his back, waving his hat at his mother. They were easing away from the quay, heading out to choppy waters.

'Peter!' she shrieked. 'Peter!'

Rosie looked at her, and yelped, then lay down, whining. Mr and Mrs Andrews turned at the shout, along with many others. Mrs Andrews forced her way between those bidding farewell. 'Hannah, he left you a letter.' The woman was crying as she handed her an envelope. 'He couldn't bear to tell you, but wanted to know you were here.'

Hannah stared at the envelope, but ignored it, and instead dragged Rosie to where she could see the boat more clearly. 'Come back,' she called. 'Just you come back here. How could you?' But *The Susan Gill* was well under way, chugging out into the choppy sea. Mrs Andrews had followed and stood beside her. 'Hannah, he should have told you, but he couldn't.' She held out the envelope.

Hannah just looked at it, and then at the weeping woman. 'But *you* knew.'

She slapped the envelope to the ground, hitting Mrs Andrews's hand but not caring, though the shock of the slap jolted right up to her own elbow. Then she stamped on the letter. Mrs Andrews recoiled. 'How could he?' Hannah raged. 'Why didn't he tell me yesterday?'

Mrs Andrews just stared at her, her hand reddening, and then said quietly, 'I told you why, and now I can understand. He probably knew you'd behave just as you have done. Listen to me, Hannah Miller, my son is leaving, and you are having a tantrum. Shame on you. It's high time you grew up.'

'Bitch,' Hannah shouted, yanking Rosie to her feet. 'And your son's a coward and a bastard.'

She dragged Rosie through the crowds, not caring that many had heard and were watching, appalled.

Bryony was doing the airline accounts when the telephone rang. She checked her watch. It was three o'clock in the afternoon, Thursday 27 June.

She wasn't expecting anyone and for a moment she paused. Eddie? Late last evening he had heard that his close friend had flown into a mountain in bad weather and he had been recalled. He was at the station first thing this morning. Before he left he had hugged her. 'He knew the risks,' he said, 'and survived the First World War, so has had twenty years many didn't. You, my girl, will not fly into any hills when you join us do you hear me? Because, never fear, you will be needed. And if Hannah changes her mind, yet again, you wait for the *Sunflower*. You promised, remember.'

He had left, saying, 'You can have your turn at being thrashed at dominoes.'

Now she lifted the receiver. 'Yes?'

It was the familiar Jersey crackle. Was Uncle Thomas taking a break from harvesting the spuds?

'Bee?' It was Hannah.

Bryony sighed, recognising the hysterical tone. What now? Celia would be home soon, her satchel banging on her back, her gas mask over her shoulder. She had made a friend, hallelujah, another evacuee, but from north London, not south.

'You must come, now. Today. I need to return. I'm frightened, do you hear? People are leaving.'

'Why exactly are you frightened today, Hannah, when you haven't been before?' She didn't bother to keep the exasperation from her voice.

She heard the back door open, and Celia call, 'I'm 'ome.'

Bryony put her hand over the mouthpiece. 'I'll be with you in a moment, Cissie.' It's what her new friend, Agnes, called her, and Celia preferred it. She had announced she would not answer to anything else because Cissie made her feel new, and not sad, like her old name. 'So be it,' Bryony and April had said.

'What's the matter with you, Bee? You sound in a right old mood. Is that child getting you down? Well, you've only yourself to blame.' Hannah was curt. 'You've been asking me to come home, and now I say I really want to, you're like this.'

Bryony, who had been holding her breath, exhaled into the receiver. 'The Dragonette is in dry dock, and Eddie has embargoed any flights – at all. I promised I wouldn't. The *Sunflower* is being refitted and is not ready yet. Besides, last night Uncle Thomas said you were determined to stay, wh—'

'Peter left this morning. He didn't even say goodbye. I loved him, Bee. I was staying for him. What is there now? I might as well come back and go to art school, so bring the Tiger Moth.'

'I told you, Eddie forbade it.'

'Since when have you listened to people? You don't want me back, do you, now that child's at the Lodge?'

'Of course I do. Uncle Thomas told me the evacuation was over, but why don't you book passage on one of the boats?'

'They're all booked. Look, I could help you with the evacuee, I could help with Mum.'

At this, Bryony was alert. 'Mum wants to come home?'

'Of course she does.' Hannah paused. 'She misses you, and she wants to see the doctor, her own doctor, not Doctor Clements. I really do want to go to art college and I can help with her, as I said, but in the college holidays.'

Bryony stared at the musk roses on the telephone table. They had a scent that took the breath away. She was thinking. Her mother wanted to come. Did she sense her TB was on the prowl again?

She asked. Hannah said, 'It looks that way, and I think she needs to see her own doctor. Do I have to say everything twice?' Then her tone changed. 'I'm sorry, Bee, if I sound rude, I'm just worried.'

Bee touched a rose, a petal fell to the surface of the desk. Soon she would have to cut more. It was a quick flight, after all, just an hour or so, then a rapid turnaround and back again. By the time she returned no one would be able to fuss. She thought of the German planes overflying the island, but that wouldn't be all the time. The line was crackling. She would lose the connection, and her mother wanted to return. Hannah wanted to go to art school and get on with her life. Was everything coming together at last?

'Bryony?'

'Be at the landing strip, with Mum in about two hours. I'll bring the three-seater Tiger Moth and will need someone to swing the propeller for the return.

Either that, or I'll keep the engine going, and you must get into the plane quickly.'

She slammed down the telephone, and dug out her helmet and goggles from the cupboard under the stairs. She scribbled a note, apologising to April, who was at the Women's Institute meeting, and saying she'd be back in no time, and that Cissie was with Anne and Catherine at the cottage. It was an emergency. Her mother needed to see the doctor, and she wasn't to worry.

In the kitchen, Cissie was eating the biscuits and milk Bryony had laid out for her. 'Come along, Cissie. I know I'm rushing you, but I need you to go and spend a bit of time at the cottage.'

Cissie slid off the seat, and followed her out of the back door, past her sheets drying on the line. She said nothing until they arrived at the cottage doorway, and Anne said they'd love to have her. Then Cissie clung to Bryony. 'I heard you on the telephone, and you're bad. Eddie and Adam said you mustn't go. They said she could get a boat like everyone else. They'll get cross, and I'm cross. They said it was dangerous.'

'Of course it's not, sweetheart. If it was you who needed to be flown home, I'd come. So you must understand why I need to do this.'

Cissie cocked her head. 'That doesn't sound real, it sounds pretend.'

Anne took her. 'I haven't a clue what you're talking about, but if you're taking off, get Percy to

119

swing the propeller. He's cleaning our windows, and then he said he was heading for the Lodge to do yours.'

Final problem solved. 'Can you get him to come to the landing strip straightaway. I'm going ahead to the hangar to fuel and do the preflight.'

Within half an hour she was flying over the Devon coast heading for Jersey, waggling her wings above the ack-ack. She held her breath. No one fired. The flight with the wind behind her would take just over an hour. It was a warm day, but at this height it was cold, and the wind dried her skin and lips. Before long she had reached Jersey, and followed the road to the farm. All the time she scanned the skies, ever alert, not knowing what she'd do if she saw a German aircraft. Her hands were sweating. Well, she was sweating all over.

In short order she was coming in to land. She saw her mother and Hannah, and Uncle Thomas. Good, he could swing the propeller, but there were two others. Had they come to see them off? She throttled back, down, down, glad of something to concentrate on instead of the accusatory reaction of the inhabitants of Combe Lodge when next she saw them. Thankfully, Adam and Eric were still in Portsmouth, and Eddie away, so they might never know.

She switched off, watching the elderly couple standing with her mother. Bryony waved Hannah and her mother across, calling, 'Hurry up, I don't want to wait a moment more than I have to.'

Her mother came to the aeroplane, and called up, 'Mr and Mrs Sobell need to come instead of Hannah. Mrs Sobell must go to Southampton, where there's a good hospital. I feel ashamed I wouldn't take the evacuees, Bee. Uncle Thomas told me. I'm so proud that you have, in my place.'

'But your health, Mum? I thought you were worried and wanted to see your own doctor?'

'I'm the same as always. Jersey suits me, it always has. I don't know where you got that idea.'

Hannah was standing with her arms crossed, her brow furrowed, her eyes red. Uncle Thomas came to stand with her mother, who said to Hannah, 'Bryony will come back for you tomorrow, or the next day, won't you, Bee? You can see we have to do this, Hannah. Mrs Sobell is not at all well.'

Uncle Thomas now helped Mrs Sobell into the passenger cockpit just in front of Bryony, and then the old man into the third seat, 'Quick as you like, please, Mr Sobell. Bee needs to hurry. Who knows . . . Oh, well, let's just hurry.'

'I'll try to come back,' she said. 'But Adam hasn't nearly got the *Sunflower* finished so please, Hannah, try to book on a boat first, because we might not be able to get her going and . . . Oh, never mind, just try. Mrs Sobell, tie your scarf around your head. It will be breezy. Mr Sobell, I'd remove your hat if you want it when we land.' Uncle Thomas was checking their straps.

Hannah glowered. 'Just fly in again, for heaven's sake. You could do it today, if you tried.'

There was no way Bryony was going to say in the hearing of Mr and Mrs Sobell that Eddie had quite rightly embargoed any flying.

She just said, 'Take it or leave it, Hannah. If I come at all, I'll come by boat.' Her hand itched to shake this selfish little besom.

Uncle Thomas leaned into her cockpit, whispering harshly. 'For God's sake, you shouldn't have come, you know damned well you shouldn't. Blasted girl, you shouldn't let her manipulate you. I bet she's spun you some story.' He put up his hand. 'I know, I know, your father said to look after them, but I don't want to hear that again.'

She asked, 'Is Mum really just the same?'

Uncle Thomas just looked at her. 'The doc says she's doing well. He's pleased with her. Why?'

Bryony looked past him to Hannah, who met her gaze with tear-filled eyes, before turning away. 'Peter's gone,' she shouted. 'It's not damn well fair.'

Uncle Thomas nodded. 'Yes, and he didn't have the grace to tell her. Bad do, but she will always make such a scene, which is probably why. Doesn't alter the fact that you shouldn't have come, it's dangerous.'

Bryony was searching the sky and called Hannah over. She raised her voice over the engine. 'Tell me the truth,' she said. 'Mum's all right, isn't she, so it's about Peter? If you come back will you promise hand on heart to go to college and stop all of this nonsense. It's time you grew up. I've spoilt you for too long.'

When Hannah shouted back, her tone was different. It was sad, bewildered. She said, 'Why couldn't Peter tell me? I loved him, and he made a fool of me.'

Bryony didn't answer, for there was real pain in her sister's voice and she felt defeated knowing she had helped to create this person that Hannah now was.

'I want to come home, Bee, where I belong. I promise I'll go to college, and do well, if you promise to come back tomorrow, if not tonight. The boats are full, and you can't take a lot of stuff anyway, and I have all my paintings. Dad said you'd always be here for me.'

Her uncle was working his way round to the front, waiting for Bryony's signal. She called to Hannah. 'Be at the cove, we'll come in that way, if not tomorrow, the next day, even the next, if at all possible, or wait at the house. I'll find you. Remember those words, "*if at all possible*". She gave her uncle the signal. He swung the propeller, the engine caught.

She taxied round and into the wind, waved, and built up her speed, then was up in the air. Once up high, she circled, waggled her wings, leaned over and waved. Her mother and Uncle Thomas looked so small, and Hannah too. She flew over the farmhouse, and the potato fields. She waggled her wings at it all.

She flew home.

Hannah watched her go, then walked off, leaving her mother and Uncle Thomas to follow. Slowly she began to feel better because soon she'd be in England. If she found out where Peter was from his parents, it would be easy to track him down once she was on the mainland. She could paint wherever she was, so she wouldn't really be breaking her promise about college, and if she lived with a soldier, it would make her grow up, which, after all, was what everyone was going on about.

Chapter Eight

Bryony approached Combe Lodge landing strip, riding the wind that was buffeting the little biplane. She peered over the edge of the cockpit, and down below saw Adam waiting by the gate leading into the landing area. His arms were akimbo, the tilt of his head indicative of rage. Her hands tightened on the controls. Well, what did she expect? She looked instead at the hangar. Yes, the camouflage had done its job and now it pretty much blended into the trees that edged up to the rear and both sides. She snatched another look at Adam as she came round into the wind.

He still stood at the gate, watching. She forced herself to concentrate on the business in hand, reducing speed, steady, slow, slow. She didn't need to check the instruments, she had grown up with the sounds of the engine, the wind, and knew it as well as she knew herself. Soon, and as always, the ground seemed to be coming up to meet them, rather than the aircraft coming to it, as she touched down.

She bounced, once. Then the Tiger Moth settled. She cursed. It was the hardest thing in the world to bounce a Tiger. She gritted her teeth as she slowed, then turned, trundling over the grass towards the hangar, taking a wide sweep so she could turn again to face away from the opening. She could then shove it backwards into the hangar. Would Adam help her? If not, who?

She stopped. Switched off. Undid her straps, removed her helmet, shook out her hair. The sun was hot, the wind which had roared against her at height was a pussycat of a breeze down here. She did not look anywhere but ahead, because Adam was walking away without a backward glance.

The Sobells unstrapped themselves, and she helped each of them down. Mr Sobell rammed on his hat, put down his small case and hugged her tightly. 'You have probably saved my wife's life, you and your family. How can I ever thank you all?'

Bryony smiled and patted his back. 'Perhaps by letting me go, I'm not sure I can breathe.' They all laughed. She said, 'Now, we have to get you both to Southampton, and I'm not sure how.'

She led them from the field, taking the hundred-yard path to the Lodge. They traipsed through the trees on the cinder path which became claggy in the wet, but today was just crisp. She often wondered if it wouldn't be better to lay gravel instead, but never did anything about it. It was where they had always spread the fire and range ash at her father's suggestion, and so it would always be. It was this she explained to her passengers, anything other than think of Adam. They came out into the wild flower garden, which was at its best, then on past the herbaceous beds. Usually the walk back to the house grounded her, and gave her time to lift a few weeds, and deadhead. But today she had forgotten her secateurs in her haste to head for Jersey.

At the back of the house, Adam waited. He was smiling at Mr and Mrs Sobell. 'I have ordered a taxi for you which will take you to the station in time for the Southampton train. I gather from Thomas that is the final destination. He managed to reach my mother a short while ago. She sent a message to the boatshed. Is this one bag your luggage?'

Mr Sobell said, 'We stay frequently in our holiday home in Jersey, and keep clothes there. My wife has cancer, and we fear . . . Well, we need to see her specialist. Thanks to Hannah and Mrs Miller, we were able to return to England quickly.' He was grey with worry. Adam was urging them along to the front of the house and not once had he looked at Bryony, who returned to the hangar

So that's how they knew. Well, thank you, Uncle Thomas. Now it was Cissie who waited for her hopping from foot to foot at the end of the path. Bryony braced herself for coldness from the child too, but instead Cissie rushed towards her, flinging her arms around her hips, pressing her face into her stomach, saying, as Bryony held her close, 'They're so cross wiv you, but that's because they're scared. I can see it, because I'm cross and scared too.' She was crying, pressing herself closer and closer to Bryony. She pulled away, wiping her face with the back of her hand, and then she kicked Bryony, hard on the shin. 'I hope that hurt, because you hurt us.'

It did hurt. Bryony looked down at her overalls. They were wet where Cissie had cried, and there was an ash print where she'd kicked her. The child was stalking away, towards the Tiger Moth. Bryony called after her, 'It did hurt my shin, and I'm sorry I hurt you, Cissie. Sorry I hurt you all. Come back.'

Cissie reached the Tiger Moth, and kicked one of the wheels. 'That's for you too, you bugger.' She now stood with her arms crossed, shaking her head, her back to Bryony.

Bryony joined her. 'You shouldn't swear.'

'You do.'

Bryony put her arm around the child's shoulders. 'Only when I'm really angry or upset.'

'Well?'

'Look at it another way: this dear old aircraft brought me home safely.'

Adam's voice was loud, and he was right behind her. She did wish he'd stop doing that. 'You were bloody lucky, Bryony, and what's more, you promised you wouldn't. You knew you shouldn't go, but oh no, Hannah crooks her little finger, and because you think you are a knight in shining armour, and no one can look after her but you, you fly to the rescue. You're a bloody fool, Bryony Miller. Now get the other side of the damned plane so we can shove her back in.'

Cissie stared up at Adam, then at Bryony. 'He's really really cross, and he's really really 'urt too. Listen to 'im swearing.'

Adam ruffled her hair. 'Everything will be all right, you run along and ask April to put the kettle on, there's a good girl.'

She did, and together Adam and Bryony pushed in the Tiger Moth, then closed the massive doors. Adam dragged the chain through the handles, and clicked the padlock shut, removing the key. Bryony put out her hand but he shook his head. 'Even April is furious, and she telephoned Eddie about it. His orders are for me to confiscate the key. You've gone too far this time, Bee.'

They walked back to the house. At least he had called her Bee, but that was the best of it, because in the kitchen April said, 'You've let us down. You could have been killed. What's more, you betrayed our trust.' The whole evening the atmosphere was sullen with fury, and shock.

Bryony telephoned Uncle Thomas, thinking that the cable should route them through automatically, so often were they calling one another. She let him know she was home, and he was cool too. 'I didn't know that you were flying behind their backs, and for what? A spoilt child.'

'For my family, Uncle Thomas,' she cried. 'It was for Mum, too. Hannah still wants to come home to get her life sorted, and I promised her I would fetch her.'

'Well, ask Adam to come by boat.' The telephone went dead. He'd hung up. She said into the emptiness, 'But anyway, I've already said it would be by sea, so there.' She felt about five.

She put Cissie to bed, and read her a story. When she finished, Cissie said, 'You can go back to your own room to sleep, Bee, because I don't want you in here with me.' The child turned over, and lay with her back to Bryony, who kissed her head, stroking her hair for a moment. 'Sleep well, and I can stay if you change your mind.'

Cissie murmured, 'Nah, I'd keep waking to see if you were still there because you might go in the night, like you did today. So this way I'll know you're not there and I won't check.'

'I'll come if you call and stay with you,' Bryony said.

'So will April, or Adam, or Anne or Catherine, like they all stayed with me this afternoon.'

In her own room Bryony sat on the bed, staring out at the evening sky, She wanted her father to be alive, so he could look after his family. She wanted to have been here for this troubled child.

The bed sagged as someone sat beside her. She knew it was Adam. He said nothing, and did nothing.

She said, 'I don't know what's the right thing to do any more for Hannah. She wants to come home, and she said Mum did too, but Mum doesn't. I think

Hannah will go to college, I think she'll grow up. I promised her we'd go back for her in the *Sunflower*.'

He sighed. 'For God's sake, Bee, she can get a place on a boat, and anyway, the Nazis won't want the Channel Islands, why would they? They'll come straight for the big peach – us. So why bring her back here, into danger?'

'But we can't know that, and I repeat, she wants to come home, and she says the boats are full, and anyway, she has so much to bring.'

'That's what she says but wake up, Bee. She's always got an answer, whether it's an honest one or not is another matter.'

'But I promised.'

He stood up. 'The *Sunflower* engine refit isn't finished.'

She looked up at him. 'It could be a test run for it.'

Hannah couldn't wait any longer to hear so she telephoned Bryony from the farmhouse at the afternoon on the 28th. She shut the door between the hall and the kitchen, so her aunt and mother wouldn't hear. Bryony answered, and replied to her question, 'Hannah, I just don't know if we can. Please try to get on a passenger boat now, today, leave everything behind. You can produce more paintings, I'll find other easels. Telephone me to say it's sorted. To finish the refit Adam has to work through the night or maybe the next two, and he's just told me he has to report for duty in five days. He's quite better, he says, but he isn't. I can still hear him wheezing, and what's more, the *Sunflower* is an old girl, the engine has taken a bashing, so who knows if she'll make it.'

Hannah felt the irritation rising. She said, 'You promised. The German planes have been really busy today, flying over, some really low. If you don't hear from me, you'll know I'll be at the cove most of the day tomorrow. If the *Sunflower* breaks down, then come again. Dad trusted you.' She put the telephone down. Bryony just had no idea about artists. She couldn't create more paintings, just like that, and what about her clothes, and her easels which bore smudges of paint, and were *hers*, through and through. God, she hoped Bee hurried because she'd discovered from Mrs Andrews that Peter was at Aldershot. She'd surprise him once she was on the mainland.

She hushed Rosie, who was barking as another plane flew over, very low. Its roaring seemed to fill the house. She entered the kitchen. 'I'll take her for a walk,' she told her mother. Her aunt and mother had turned up the volume on the wireless, as they always did to drown out the sound of the planes. They were busy with the jam making and just nodded. Her uncle was down at the harbour so she set off, keeping Rosie on the lead. She cut across fields, thinking of Peter, and the party planned by Sylvia and Cheryl tomorrow. Well, she wouldn't be here and she didn't mind, because Cheryl slept around, which was not quite right, though she wasn't sure if Sylvia did too.

She strolled along the edge of the fields for an hour and then took the path letting Rosie sniff and explore the verge. There were orchids hidden amongst the grass, and she'd see if there were any on the verge. She clambered over the stile and took to the road. The sky looked thunderous, and clouds blocked out the sun and there was a heaviness as though it might rain.

She called Rosie to her and was wondering whether to turn back when she heard an explosion, then another, and another, and she searched the countryside, confused. Explosions? What? The earth seemed to tremble. Fear broke over her like a wave. Rosie wrenched at the lead, barking, whining and cringing, then she leapt forward, the hair lifting up along her spine. Hannah screamed, 'Rosie, stop!'

She clung to the lead, fighting for balance and now, in the distance, she saw the German planes over the harbour, and there were small black things, falling . . . What? Bombs? Yes, that's what they must be. She broke into a sweat, not knowing what to do, where to go. A plane roared across the sky above her, then another, and, yes, there were more bombs falling, near the harbour, where Uncle Thomas had gone to unload the lorry full of potatoes. Ahead of her, she saw smoke billowing, and then heard a roaring behind her. She pulled Rosie close, but it was Old Davy taking a lorry to St Helier for Peter's father.

He stopped, his windows open. She heard him shout, 'What the hell are you doing?'

She reached up, and opened the door. Rosie leapt in, and she followed. 'That's the sodding harbour, ain't it?' he yelled. He rammed the lorry into gear and set off again. She shouted, 'No, don't go towards it. Drive back you old fool.'

He stopped again, looking from Hannah to the smoke. Another bomb fell and again there was the roaring of a plane. She leaned from the window, searching. It was behind them, but Old Davy pulled her back. 'Get down,' he shouted. She did and he threw himself across her. There was a rat-a-tat-a-tat-a-tat, and bits of tar from the road flew up as the bullets tore into it, and then the plane was roaring away. 'Not aiming, just testing his guns,' Old Davy said, his voice shaking. 'We're demilitarised, the bloody troops have gone, so what the 'ell are they playing at, or did Churchill forget to tell 'em?'

The explosions were continuing. Old Davy rammed the lorry into gear and turned, going backwards and forwards in the narrow lane until he was driving like a madman back the way he'd come. He dropped Hannah and Rosie off at the farm, before swinging round the bend towards the Andrews' farm. She rushed indoors, tugged along by Rosie. Her mother and aunt were sitting at the kitchen table, gripping each other's hands. They looked up when she rushed in. 'Thank the Lord, you're home. Oh Hannah, I thought—' her mother said.

Hannah shouted, 'And I'm supposed to get the bloody boat at *that* harbour. Oh, good idea, Bryony.'

She flew to the telephone, but the lines were jammed.

All night she tried, and at two in the morning she finally got through. 'Bee, the harbour's been bombed. They're coming, they must be. You tell that Adam he's got to get the *Sunflower* ready. He must. Nine have died, Bee, and many more on Guernsey. I need to get out, now, or I'll never leave, never find . . .' She stopped and drew breath. 'Mum wants to stay. She won't leave a sinking ship, she says, but she wants me to leave.'

The line crackled. Bryony voice came through, still drugged with sleep. 'All right. Don't go near the harbour. I'll come, even if I have to bring the *Sunflower*, or another boat, by myself. Remember that: I will come for you, if not tomorrow, then later, even if it's much later. I promise I will come, to the cove and if you are not there, I will come to the cottage and bring you home. You are not alone.'

Chapter Nine

Bryony pounded up the stairs. The phoney war was over. Well, it had ended with Dunkirk, but now the Nazis were on the move again, with their bombers pounding the Channel Islands, where her mother's family had lived for generations. She stood on the landing. 'That doesn't mean they will invade,' she whispered to herself. 'They could just be scaring them, playing around. But I need to get her.'

'Did you promise?' Cissie said quietly from the doorway of the twin bedroom, rubbing her eyes, sleep slurring her words. Her nightie was creased, her hairline sweaty from the night-time heat. 'Let's get you back to bed,' Bryony murmured, her finger to her lips. 'Everyone else is asleep.'

'Chance would be a fine thing.' It was Adam, also creased from sleep. 'I suppose that was the little madam on the telephone?'

'I'll talk in a moment, let me get Cissie to bed.' Bryony took the child's hand and led her into her bedroom. She lifted the blind, drew back the curtains and opened the bedroom windows wide. 'Let's get a draught going through here,' she said as Cissie clambered into the bed.

'My bed's dry, Bee.'

'That's so good. You are doing really well, you clever girl. It might not be by the morning, but who cares.' She paused, and together they half sang, 'We don't.'

As the draught came through the open windows she found herself listening for bombers but there were only the owls, and the odd screech of a fox, and somewhere the call of a cow for her calf. There was the smell of the night-time stocks she had planted beneath the window, mingling with the honeysuckle over the old shed. The side gardens were bathed in light from the moon. She remembered her fellow train traveller, and the song 'By the light of the silvery moon'. Now, in Jersey, it would be a bombers' moon and next, would it be troops? Then would it be Britain? 'Don't put the light on, Cissie. Whatever you do, now more than ever, don't.' Suddenly her voice was urgent. Cissie sat up in bed. 'I know that, Bee.' She eased herself back down, and was asleep almost immediately.

It was only after Bryony had tiptoed out on to the landing that she remembered too late that she should have taken Cissie to the bathroom. The landing was empty. She waited a moment, listening to the creaks of the house, which seemed alive to her, enfolding them in its arms as it always had. One of its children wanted to come home, of course she did, so she would bring her.

Adam's door was still open, and she took it as a

signal. She padded over to the doorway. He too had hauled up the blackout blind and drawn back the curtains. A soft breeze cooled them both, and the moonlight was clean and bright, but perhaps soon such gentle light would become their enemy. He sat on the edge of his bed, waiting. She settled herself beside him, wishing she wore a pretty nightgown instead of her old striped boy's pyjamas. No wonder he thought she was a bloke.

'So, what's happened?' he muttered, running his hands through his hair.

'They've bombed Jersey.'

He swung round. 'Really, not just her story?'

'Even she ...' She stopped and shrugged. 'She wouldn't make that up. It will be on the wireless news, I suppose. It's the harbour, and Guernsey, which seems to have caught it worse than Jersey. There are deaths on both islands. She needs to leave.'

Adam was nodding as she spoke. 'Has she by any remote chance got herself a passage?' His voice was heavy with irony.

She sighed. 'With the harbour bombed, I suspect that's no longer an option, so I promised I'd go. But forget the *Sunflower*, I know you're doing your best, but she's still nowhere near ready. I'll hire a boat and do it myself.'

Bryony rose and walked to the door. He said nothing. He was going to let her go alone. Well, she could do that, of course she could. The weather would stay fair and with the moon she could ...

Cissie barred her way, her little bare feet making damp footprints on the polished floorboards. 'You never answered me, Bee. Did you promise 'er?'

Byony nodded. 'Yes I did, and you should be in bed.'

Adam said from the bed, 'Yes, off you go now. It's like Piccadilly round 'ere, I mean here.'

'I fought I'd go to the lav while I was awake, and I heard you two talking. My sister says I 'ear too much, and that's why she sent me away. I can see why Hannah wants to come 'ome to 'ere. So, Adam, I fink if Bee promised, she should go. So should you, because you don't want 'er to get 'urt. I can see it in your bleedin' eyes.'

'Don't swear,' Adam and Bryony said together.

Adam said, 'It's the *Sunflower* I don't want hurt, young lady. Bee is a tough old bird capable of looking after herself, and don't you forget it. Don't stand there hopping from one foot to the other, go to the toilet, for heaven's sake. Bee, we need to get dressed and get down to the *Sunflower* and see if we can't make a silk purse out of a sow's ear in next to no time.'

They didn't leave the harbour in the *Sunflower* until six in the evening of 30 June, even though they'd had Eric's help. He had also offered to come to Jersey, but what was the point. If they were bombed, then why kill more people than necessary? It was still light, and later there should be a moon by which to see, but clouds were drifting as they chugged along, and the air was heavy. 'Could be squalls,' Adam muttered, half to himself.

The sea was crinkly, and they stood full square in the cabin, rocking with the movement. 'Come on, old lady,' Adam said, patting the wheel. Down at the harbour he and Eric had toiled on the engine while Byony refitted the benches and replenished the supplies: water, torches in case they had to clamber up from the cove. She had been unable to reach her family after Uncle Thomas had followed up on Hannah's call, probably because the cable was cut. At least, though, the BBC had announced that the Channel Islands were demilitarised, so that should save them from further bombing.

She moved out of the cabin, searching the seas and sky with binoculars. There were fishing smacks out, without lights, though not many, but no bombers that she could see, or hear. But then, there shouldn't be, unless they were heading for Britain.

She moved back into the cabin. They spoke not at all for the three hours they thrashed through the waves, and when Adam finally did, his tone was cool. 'The *Sunflower*'s heart's tired, Bee, and just like we have dreams and see Dunkirk, and smell and and taste it, so does she. This dear old girl bore the brunt, and now she's at it again, straining herself because someone wouldn't get a bloody boat.'

Bryony said, 'But she said they were full. I've told you that.'

He didn't respond because he was too busy listening to the *Sunflower*'s engine. He said, 'Listen to her. We should go back.'

Bryony stood beside him looking out at the chaotic waves. It was gusty, and growing worse. They laboured on for another hour, sometimes the wind would drop, sometimes gust. They were making little headway, and now it was as though they could hear the separate parts of the engine clicking over, not quite synchronising.

Another gust, and surge, and suddenly the *Sunflower* lurched. Bryony slipped in the seawater that was slopping in the bottom of the cabin. She clutched at Adam but he shrugged her off as the *Sunflower* cork-screwed and he had to fight the wheel, peering out, trying to get a fix. Bryony crashed into the side, keeling back, falling on to the bench, and then the floor. She felt the crack of her arm, and the pain. It took her breath. She lay there, in the salt water. He called, 'Help me get a fix, Bee.'

'Just give me a moment,' she said, as her breath became a thread.

She staggered to her feet, the *Sunflower* misfired, then twice more. She held her arm tightly against her side as she stood next to Adam. 'Sorry, Bee, did I knock you? It's squally, and the cloud is building. Always bloody gusty here.'

'It's fine,' she said, but her voice was still faint. She hadn't enough breath to talk, only to breathe, but she couldn't seem to suck in the air.

'Can she try for a bit longer? Please.' She touched his arm.

'Listen to her, Bee.' He wrenched the wheel again, knocking her. The jolt almost made her scream. She nursed her arm. It was the upper arm, and it was bruised, that was all. 'But what if the Germans come and I can't bring Hannah home?'

'I know how important this is to you, and I'll nurse her on a bit, but if she gets worse, we turn around, and that's that.' He didn't look at her, just at the encroaching darkness as he held the *Sunflower* on course, but she knew that his anger and worry were building. The *Sunflower* was his baby, and he was sure Hannah could have taken a boat, so there was no contest, and through the pain, she felt the stress too. He was heading for Scotland tomorrow. He didn't need this.

She sat on the bench, her legs wobbly. He said, 'Things are conspiring, Bee. It's not our fault, and absolutely not yours. It just *is*.'

'I know.'

The *Sunflower* lurched into a trough. Bryony gasped at the pain.

'So, when do you go?' he said.

'Go where?'

'For your ATA training, you daft dollop. What is it they call you lot, the Attagirls?'

She made herself answer, wishing the sea would calm, and that her arm wouldn't feel as though the bones were grating together. 'I'm not one yet. I've passed but they might never call me, and then I'll have to find something else. Perhaps the Wrens?' She thought for a moment she'd whimpered. She made herself continue. 'No call for more female ATA pilots at the moment.'

'Use the "bins" and sweep the sky would you, have a scan round about. Don't want to bump into an invasion force.' Adam's voice was tense.

She picked them up, her left arm limp, and stumbled outside, propping herself against the back of the cabin and then the side. She scanned as the wind and rain tore at her. Nothing.

She returned. 'All clear. So, now you think they could invade the islands, having said it was rubbish?' She heard the sharpness in her voice.

'For God's sake, Bee, don't be so bloody cheap. How was I to know? How were you?'

The *Sunflower* misfired again, spluttered, and almost died. He turned to her. 'That's it, Bryony. I'm turning her round, she doesn't deserve this.'

'I promised,' she shouted.

He yelled back, 'That's your bloody fault, not mine. I'm not ruining the *Sunflower* and getting us both stuck here in the middle of nowhere, for God knows how many Nazis to come along and clap us in irons, or shoot us out of the water. This isn't a game, Bee, it's war and it's hotting up, and I need to get back on duty. You might think we've done our bit getting a few lads off the beaches, but it's just the beginning, you stupid bloody woman.'

He was turning the *Sunflower*, and now the wind was behind them. She stared at him, her head swimming. 'I promised.'

'Shut up.'

She sagged suddenly, beginning to laugh, though it was strange, high-pitched laughter. He snapped, 'There's nothing funny about this. I've got to get this old boat back. It's . . .' He trailed off as they nose-dived deep into a trough; somewhere distant lightning flashed, and thunder crashed. She leaned forward and heard him mutter, 'Well, if she gets back then we might all get through what's coming.'

But he was talking to himself and still the laughter was coming and going but from a distance, and she was thinking of the soldier at Dunkirk having a second go at climbing the netting to the deck of the bigger ship, refusing to let go of the dog. Was it a corvette? She couldn't remember. Somehow, in his arms, instead of the dog, he had held all their hopes of survival in this war. It wasn't funny but the laughter wouldn't stop, though it must only have been in her head, because Adam took no further notice.

They made better time now they weren't battling the wind, which was actually behind them, helping, and all the time she imagined Hannah lying awake, waiting, or huddled at the cove with no one coming. 'One day I will, because I promised,' she said aloud.

He turned. 'Yes, one day we will get her. I promise, too. Sorry I shouted, Bee.'

'It's not important.' She leaned back against the cabin wall and thought of her lovely Dragonette, now in bits. Would she ever be put back together, would the skies ever be free? Would ... She stopped. She was like a record. He'd said they'd get Hannah, one day, but they had to get home first.

A mile out, as the conditions calmed, they met a fishing smack heading for harbour. It was Eric's father, Barry. 'Good, if the old girl fails, he'll tow us in.' They ran the last hour together, limping into harbour under their own steam, but only just. They docked, Adam chivvying her to hurry and get up the ladder to the quay and tie off the rope. Somehow she did it, and clambered back down the quayside ladder. It was the early hours of the morning, and they still had to unload the *Sunflower*. Bryony tipped the water from the water carrier over the side, and only then did she lug it back up the ladder to the quay, though she didn't know how. They cycled home, and somehow she did that too. The moon was behind clouds, the summer air was heavy, the owls hooted. They said little to one another, because she was beyond speech. As they headed into the drive of the house, Adam said, 'For goodness' sake, don't sulk, Bee. I have to leave by ten in the morning. I've got to be on my ship. I've done my best for you.'

She could barely speak for the pain, and nodded. 'I know. Thank you.' It was all she could manage.

She dropped her bike on the ground when they

arrived at the shed to the side of the house. She let it lie, the front wheel spinning, like her head. 'Getting lazy in your old age, are you, Bryony Miller? Not that I blame you. It was a tough trip.' He picked it up and propped it inside as she headed for the back door. It was unlocked. In the kitchen there was a teapot with a note from April. *Welcome home, Hannah. In celebration we have fresh tea leaves.* Adam looked exhausted but smiled and slung his arm over her shoulders. 'I'm sorry, but we *will* go again.'

She slipped from him, the pain too sharp, the weight of his arm too great. He dropped his arm, and stalked from the kitchen without even looking at her but flinging over his shoulder, 'Well, if you're going to be like that, get on with it. I can't be doing with this, Bryony. You need to get yourself sorted. You're getting as selfish as your sister, and don't worry, I won't wake you when I go, and I'll call on Eric to get him to sort out the *Sunflower*, so you don't need to go down and clean her up. Don't want to put any of the Millers out, do we.' It wasn't a question.

Bryony stared at April's note, but could no longer read the writing. She was shaking, all over. Somehow she climbed the stairs and inched to her room. She lay on the bed, and knew something else was wrong because she couldn't breathe properly, even now, and her rib hurt as well as her arm. She slept, or drifted, and heard Hannah calling, but how, because she knew now that the cable was cut. She heard Adam shouting, you stupid bloody woman. But he had called her woman, and even in her pain she had to laugh, because that seemed to be the best she could achieve from the man she loved.

In Jersey, Hannah sat in the kitchen as the clock ticked through the night, dressed. They had not come on the 29th, or during the day on the 30th but they still might, and at least there had been no more bombing. She waited all night. They never came. But perhaps they would come today, she thought, as 1 July dawned. She slept for a little on her bed, fully clothed, and then came down at lunchtime, when she heard Uncle Thomas come in too early for lunch.

Her uncle brought in the leaflet that the Germans were dropping calling for the surrender of the island and the cessation of any type of resistance. 'We're to fly white sheets, flags, any old white how's your fathers, from the windows, and white crosses painted here, there and every bloody where.'

He sat down suddenly at the kitchen table, quite pale, and growing paler. While her mother watched, Aunt Olive came to him, pulling out a chair and sitting facing him. She took his hands and kissed them. 'Then that is what we shall do, though the how's your father can be a pair of your long johns. We can't do much, but that we *can* do.'

Her mother sat down next to Hannah, and held

out her hand. 'Bee will have tried, but there's no way for her to tell you that they did. You must trust them. They said they would try again, and they will.'

Hannah stared at these old people, who understood nothing. She was stuck here, while Peter was over there. She said, 'I told her Dad said she had to look after me. I told her, and now she's let me down, and I'm stuck here, with the enemy, and with you.'

Aunt Olive gripped her husband's hands so tightly he winced. Her voice was level as she said, 'I never did understand how he could ask that, Hannah. The fall broke his neck, and smashed his skull. How—'

Hannah glared. 'Yes, that's right, the Nazis are on the way, and my sister hasn't come, and now you're calling me a liar.'

She banged from the room, and pounded up the stairs, standing at the window and cursing the Germans, cursing Bryony, and missing Peter with a pain that slashed her. 'For how long?' she cried. 'How long is this going on? I'm seventeen, and what about my life?'

Her mother knocked on the door, and entered. She stood beside her daughter, slipping her arm through hers. 'It won't go on for ever. Britain might capitulate. It could all be over very soon and if it isn't, Bryony will come. You know she will. She keeps her promises, and remember, your dad was the strongest of men, and he loved us all. He would have held on until he made sure we were all looked after.'

They watched her uncle paint a white cross on the hay barn across the road running in front of the farmhouse. 'He's painting it in whitewash, so it washes off,' her mother said. 'He can't bear it to be permanent. His friend tells him the Bailiff of Jersey, who has been made Civil Governor, will be formally handing over when the Germans land.'

Hannah didn't care what he painted it with and who was handing what over to whom. She shrugged free of her mother. 'I'm going to keep my easels and paintings together. I won't unpack, so there. I'm exhausted, so I'll eat and then have a sleep. Wake me if she comes, Mum.' Seeing her mother's face, she added, 'Please. Then I might as well go and meet Sylvia tonight, and we can go to the pub and see what's happening. You could send Bee on to the pub, if she comes. I'll leave my stuff packed. I can't just stop living, though that's how I feel.' She ended on a wail, and her misery was there for all to hear. But who was listening?

Chapter Ten

2 July 1940
Scotland

Adam arrived in Scotland on 2 July. It was a grey day, with a wind chill factor of hell knows what as he finally approached the wharf, lugging his canvas holdall. He sighed, thinking of Dunkirk. Morgan should have been here but instead he was feeding the fish. He hunched his shoulders and set his cap more firmly on his head, hearing the gulls, and the crash and bang of coalers and cranes.

He'd just heard from a gunner he vaguely knew that his last trawler had gone down soon after the Norwegian debacle, though some had survived. He didn't know who and where the survivors were, but maybe some would have been posted to his new draft, the armed trawler, *High Ground.* Either way, the officers would mainly be from the RN Reserve, like him, and the crew from deep-sea trawlers, so it would be like home, sort of. God, he hoped no one thought he'd been swinging the lead.

He coughed, and again, his chest rattling. The cough took hold, and he pounded his chest, though what good that was supposed to do he had no bloody idea. His eyes were streaming as he struggled for breath, swallowing, willing the coughing to stop. He faced the sea, managed to draw a deep breath, and coughed once more, wiped his face, and headed for the sentry who guarded the entrance to the wharf.

He asked where the *High Ground* was lying.

'Inside berth on Number 5 Trot, sir,' the sentry replied in his pronounced Scottish accent. He adjusted the rifle slung over his shoulder. 'Bit of a cough you have there, sir?'

'Had, seaman. Had. What you heard were the dying embers.'

'Aye, Rabbie Burns is your middle name then, is it, sir?'

Adam laughed. 'Yes, that was a bit poncey wasn't it? Sorry about that.'

The sentry saluted again. 'Ah well, Sassenachs know no better.'

'True,' He followed the sentry's hand signal. 'Straight on, sir, and not an ember in your way.'

Adam laughed again, returning the sentry's salute, and strode on to the wharf. It was good to be called sir again, to know that he was back, fit and ready for the fight and that the fleet procedure was as informal as it had always been. Mavericks, they had been called by an upright Royal Naval senior officer. It wasn't intended as a compliment and would have been something even worse if the commander had known that two of the crew of his last trawler had left to join the special forces, who were a great deal more than mavericks. In fact, pirates would cover it nicely. Others had followed.

He walked along, stopping at Number 5 Trot. As the gulls wheeled he looked down on *High Ground*, which was slopping on the ebb tide, knocking against the barnacled wharf. The dinghy deck was spotless, which was not surprising because a seaman was bent over, sweeping some minuscule dust particles over the side, his overalls well used. Adam knew his uniform was shamefully clean and tidy, with a gleaming solitary gold sub-lieutenant's ring. He flushed. Bee would laugh at him. He sighed – or would she?

She'd shrugged him off and let him leave the kitchen without a backward glance last night, after he'd slogged to take the *Sunflower* to sea because it was what she wanted. She'd not even emerged from her room when it was time for him to leave, though he'd banged about to the point where Cissie had crept up the stairs, and peeped round the newel. 'You in a mood?'

'Not me,' he'd said, squatting down to her height. 'I was just reminding myself of the house. I love it, you see. To begin with, my mum and I lived here when she was housekeeper. She was upstairs in the attic, which she preferred, wanting some privacy, but I had the bedroom I have now. Later, she moved to the cottage, and I stayed on. It just seemed right, sort of where I belonged. Eddie's always been like a father to me.'

'Where's your real dad?'

He had looked at Bryony's door, and given up. Well, he deserved the cold shoulder, he supposed, because he'd shouted, but bloody hell, he had every reason, and bugger it, he'd put himself out for that spoilt brat, Hannah. He'd sighed, wanting to burst in and have it out with her but this was new, different. Bryony didn't go in for these women's sulks; she was like a bloke, and gave as good as she got.

He'd stared at her door, then walked down the stairs, following Cissie who bounced in front of him. He guessed she'd skip once she reached the hall, and she did.

'My dad died in the last war,' he said.

'Don't fink I 'ad a dad, but me mum's gone.' Her feet were bare, and it seemed her heart was happy, because for the very first time there'd been a dry sheet this morning. His mother was making a medal for her, and he'd given her sixpence for her money box. She didn't know what a money box was, and hadn't one anyway, so he'd had to explain. In his room he had found his old pig money box, which he gave her. Thankfully it still had its bung in the bottom.

He'd run down the stairs and hurried into the kitchen, placing the pig on the table. 'Here, April will tell you where you can keep this safe. Look after it now, it's special.' The words were out before he could stop them.

He remembered how Cissie had looked at him, as had his mother. 'Why?' Cissie said.

'Well, it was a present.'

'But who gived it to you?'

'*Gave* it to me,' he said.

'But who?'

'Well, it was Bee. She knows I like pigs.'

Cissie had nodded. 'Yes, she's the kindest person I know. Well, so is April too.'

The two of them had waved him off when he started down the gravel drive, his canvas holdall slung over his shoulder. He would catch the bus to the station. Perhaps it would be Dan, who would chat and then he wouldn't think of Bee. What an idiot she was being. He snatched a glance over his shoulder. She was not at her bedroom window, and neither was the blind up, or the curtains. The windows were closed, too. Had she been too tired to open them? He started to call his mother to check that Bee woke by lunchtime, as she'd need some food, but then the bus hooted, stopping at the bottom of the drive instead of driving to the bus stop.

He waved to Cissie and his mother again, and ran.

He felt the same ache now, in his gut, as he stared at *High Ground*, and then up to the gulls, watching them wheel, and he could have sworn he could feel the air move beneath the thrust of their wings. One banked, turning like Bee in her Tiger Moth. He turned away, blocking the image because it hurt, goddammit. He kicked a piece of coal. Damn her.

'Oi, who did that?'

He came to himself, and peered down. The leading seaman who had been sweeping had now taken up residence on a hatch and was pulling the heavy wire he was about to splice on to his lap. The piece of coal lay at his feet. Coal dust had spattered on the immaculate dingy deck. 'Sorry about that … Hey, it's you, Mick. Really glad to see you made it,' Adam called, recognising his old gunnery leading seaman.

Mick grimaced. 'Oh, bloody marvellous, you're our sub-lieutenant then? Just chucking coal at us to make yourself feel better, eh, laddie? Nothing changes with you bloody Sassenachs.' His Grimsby accent was heavy, his years of working on trawlers written deep in the lines on his face.

'As one Sassenach to another, you could say that, Mick Weatherby. How've you been behaving in my absence?'

Mick rested his elbows on his thighs, grinning. 'Badly, obviously, as I've been nice and cosy on this old tub and who turns up but a sprog like you. Five of us are here.'

'Who?'

'Tom, Derek, Andy and Dozey.' Mick voice was emotionless, and now he began splicing. 'Skipper's gone. He was a good 'un, weren't he? And the Number One. They bought it off Norway. Glad you went into the drink before that and were whisked away. Glad you're bloody back too, lad. Don't go swimming again, will yer?'

Adam began to climb down the quayside ladder and called, 'Bloody well hope not. I'm sorry about Mike Todd, and Evans, they were good men. Who's the skipper of the *High Ground* then?'

'Lieutenant Cobham, RNVR as usual. He's a good bloke, been around a bit, just caught the end of the last lot, and has his grey head screwed on. He's learned to get along with us. Well, learned to trust us, I suppose. Or should I say, he lets us be.'

Adam clambered on board over the fo'c'sle head, thinking that, like most converted trawlers, she looked almost top-heavy with the high bridge built on top of her wheelhouse, and the platform perched on the fo'c'sle head which carried the four-inch gun.

'Is the skipper on board?' Adam asked.

'That he is. Right good to see you again, sir.' They grinned at each other.

'Good to be back.' It was. It was easier than putting up with promises that couldn't be met, and sulks.

Mick was pointing to the hooded hatchway on the well deck, in the shadow of the bridge. Adam climbed down the iron ladder from the gun platform.

'Permission to come below?' he called down the wardroom hatch.

'Permission given.'

He heaved his holdall in after him, then stepped down into the gloomy light of the trawler wardroom which smelt of cigarettes mixed with generations of stinking fish. The skipper shook his hand. He was grey-haired and would at any moment, Adam feared, be seconded to a corvette or some such, because the Royal Navy were short of experienced officers. 'Good to meet you, Adam. Tip-top, are you? Well, looking at you I'd say not yet. Still a bit wheezy, if my ears don't deceive, and a bit pale, but we'll not throw you to the fish yet.'

He turned to another sub-lieutenant. 'Here you go, Geordie Gilchrist. Meet Adam Cottrall, your new boot-shiner who took a swim off Norway. Bit bloody cold, I reckon, gave him pneumonia, double, I believe. Probably how he likes his Scotch too. Then he had another dose after some derring-do off Dunkirk, I hear. With a slip of a girl, I also hear. Don't think you two have met, though you will know some of the other brigands, Adam. Have a look around, say your hellos and then come and eat.'

Adam shook hands and dumped his holdall. As Geordie led the way up the ladder, Adam followed. All right, so he was the shoeshiner, the last in the food chain, but it was only what he expected. He just needed to get into the swing of things again and build up some seniority. Out on deck Geordie shouted above the gulls that had clumped together above the boat in a squalling riot: 'We'll be on convoy duty, Adam. Or sub hunting, one or t'other and maybe some minesweeping at some stage. You never know. Mark you, we sub-hunt whatever the hell we're doing but, aye, you know that.'

They were heading past the depth-charge thrower and up a couple of iron ladders to the top bridge, which contained submarine-detecting gear, binnacle, chart table and bell-mouthed speaking tubes through which to communicate to all parts of the ship.

Then down through a trapdoor in the deck of the bridge into the wheelhouse. Off this was the small wireless cabin and Adam remembered now that it was like a Turkish bath when blacked out at sea, tucked as it was behind the steam steering engine. On the other side of the wheelhouse a companionway led down to the skipper's cabin as comfortable as that on his former trawler, the *Mistress of the Seas*.

'They don't do themselves badly do they, these trawler skippers?' Adam grunted.

'Aye, and why the hell not? Tough old life.'

Adam liked the walnut panelling which was a step up from the *Mistress of the Seas'*, and thought that one day he'd like a study like this. The study could have a bathroom off it, like this, too. Be good to have bedrooms with their own bathrooms. There was room at the Lodge. He stopped because it made him think of Bee, of Bryony-bloody-Miller and her moods.

'Old Cobham lets us use the bath, and he stands his watch, so it's four hours on the bridge and eight hours off.' Gilchrist shrugged. 'Some don't, so on the *High Ground* we can even get some sleep.'

They scooted through the petty officers' mess, and

the galley with its old iron cooking range and sink. The way to the stokehold lay through the engine room, then down the ladder into the petty officers' quarters. The coxswain was there, writing a letter. He looked up, and Adam shook his head. It was Mick. 'Well, well, didn't think to share this earlier, then?' Adam looked at Geordie. 'Promoting the troublemakers, eh?'

Geordie looked from one to the other. 'Ah, Norway?'

Both Mick and Adam nodded. The two subs moved on, checking the Carley floats and the lifeboat. All was well. Down in the mess deck the ratings' quarters were spacious, and then they moved on to the gun platform and Adam checked over the four-inch. 'Hope you're going to be a good girl,' he said.

'She could be a he,' objected Geordie.

'Not if I know anything about women,' Adam almost growled.

'Ah well, no more to be said.'

'Quite.'

They moved aft to the machine guns, and then to the bridge to check the machine guns there. Adam murmured, 'Oh, *High Ground*, if only you had known what you would become, you'd have turned tail and hidden somewhere warm and dry so you could fish for cod at a later date.'

'Let me show you the depth charges.' Geordie led him to the charge rails at the stern, and then Adam checked the charge throwers flanking the skipper's cabin.

Geordie came to stand by him as Adam looked at the other armed trawlers lying alongside the wharf. They might look the same, but some had luck, some had heart, and some didn't.

Adam muttered, 'So, is she hearty, lucky, happy, or is she not?' He made it sound like a joke, but it wasn't, because his other trawler had not been and things had gone wrong from the start. Someone on the trawler alongside was smoking a pipe. He could smell it.

Geordie smiled, 'Aye, she has heart and luck, man. It's the same with the coal mines back home. Some are good girls, some are not, with creaking roofs and bad safety.'

'Quite,' Adam said, but then felt guilty. No, Bee wasn't bad, she was just being bloody-minded: first she'd taken the Tiger Moth, then . . . Oh, what was the point. Sometimes people just outgrew one another, even if they'd been mates for a lifetime.

He followed Geordie back towards the wardroom. 'That's all right then,' he said.

'What is?' Geordie asked.

'That's she's lucky.'

That evening the skipper told Adam and Geordie to go and have a drink or two, because they'd be off with the dawn to rendezvous with a convoy. 'Make sure you call home. Let them know you love them. I'll nip out when you get back. Shall we say eleven, no later?'

Later they followed the seamen down the wharf, shoulders hunched against the harsh wind, and the same wind burned down their cigarettes too fast. They all tumbled into The Bannock Bray, a pub where even in July a great fire roared in the grate. The warmth was welcome. Adam and Geordie took a table, flipping beer mats and waiting their turn at the bar, while the seamen jostled and shouted their orders. Geordie said, 'I've learned to wait until the crush has died, or there's no seat for love or money.'

'Nothing changes,' laughed Adam. Mick sent over a couple of pints with a seaman. 'A christening present, sirs,' he bellowed. They grinned their thanks. The seamen drifted over, and soon they were all sitting round the table together, and the beer mats were getting a real going over. The talk was of home, of the sea, of the last convoy. This is what Adam liked about the armed trawlers. Less pomp, more bloody do. Though that wasn't fair, because the bigger ships did plenty, not that Morgan would ever have agreed with that.

Morgan. Adam's heart twisted.

He was expected to stand a round as the new boy, and so he did, and then Geordie did, because, although he wasn't new it was the tradition on *High Ground* that the subs saw off the ship with a good drenching of beer for all concerned. The songs began at ten, and were getting increasingly raucous by the time 10.30 came around, and Geordie nudged him. 'They have till midnight, we have until eleven. I want to get to the telephone box.'

Mick raised his glass. 'Same place as it was last time we berthed. To the left, fifty yards, sir.'

Geordie laughed. 'I think I might just have found my way, but my thanks, Chief.'

The night was cool, the moon was bright as they left the noise and fetid warmth behind and clipped along the cobbles, to the left. It was indeed fifty yards distant. 'You go first,' Adam told Geordie.

'Ah yes, I sniff avoidance. Woman trouble, I'm thinking. She dumped you, eh?'

'No, nothing like that. Family row, well, not really even a row, just things being different, and I don't know why.' Geordie had stepped into the booth, and wasn't listening. He closed the door. Adam stood on the cobbles, staring up at the sky, and then out to sea. When there was no light on land, the stars seemed so bright. 'By the light of the silvery moon'? Who had told him about the old lady on the train? He searched his memory, and then it came. Bee, of course.

Well, he'd telephone his mother, and maybe he'd ask if Bee was over her mood. He felt strange, upset. But then why wouldn't he? Morgan was dead, while he was back here. He just needed to settle in.

'All yours.' Geordie was holding open the door to the telephone box. 'I'll get on, relieve the skipper. See you back on board.'

Geordie strolled off, whistling. Adam entered. Why did telephone boxes always smell of pee, or was it just damp? Adam fed in money, and was put through to Combe Lodge. He hoped his mother wasn't in bed, because he had nothing to say to Bee. It was all too difficult.

He leaned back on the side of the phone box, looking out. Clouds were scudding across the moon. It could be breezy tomorrow. His mother answered, he pressed the button, the money dropped, 'Mum,' he called.

'Oh thank God,' she said. 'I didn't know how to get hold of you. It's Bryony.'

His hand gripped the receiver. 'What do you mean? Oh God, she hasn't gone again, in the Tiger Moth? The Germans are there, for God's sake. What the hell is the matter ...?'

'Oh, do be quiet, you stupid boy. After you'd left she didn't come down, and Cissie crept into her room. She was lying on the floor, there was blood, a lot of it. Cissie screamed, I came. She had fallen, hit her head hard on the corner of her dressing table and cut it open. The rug was wet with it. She was so cold and I don't know how long ...'

He felt sick. 'Mum, Mum,' he was shouting over her now. His mother stopped talking. He said, 'Is she all right?'

'Of course she's not bloody all right, you utter idiot. She told the ambulance crew when she came to for a moment, that she'd already broken her arm.

163

It was on the *Sunflower*, coming back, but she didn't want to say anything because you were so worried about your bloody boat. When she fell again, she made it much worse, and there was a rib broken, and what with her poor cut head . . . Oh, so many stitches. She hasn't woken again, not yet. She still hasn't woken. Eddie's there, now. I called him, and he came straight back, but he might go back on duty tomorrow, but only if she wakes. They might have to operate on her arm . . .I will go to the hospital tonight. The girls in the cottage will move in to look after Cissie.' His mother was crying. She never cried.

'Fell on the boat?'

He remembered now. Yes, he'd shrugged her off. She'd fallen. But she never said anything, not a bloody thing. She'd helped him tidy the boat, she'd cycled home. How quiet she'd been. He rubbed his forehead. Someone was knocking on the glass of the door. It was Dozey.

'Will she make it?'

'Yes, of course she will, she's just exhausted, she's been through a lot recently.' But she said it in that way of hers. Yes, of course the fire will catch, yes of course your homework is wonderful. There was no of course about it. The pips were going.

'I should come home, but I can't. I'm needed. Oh goddammit. Look, I'll telephone you when I come back. Not sure when. Look after her for me.' He put down the receiver, his mouth dry. He forced himself to smile at Dozey. 'All yours.'

'You all right, sir?' Dozey cocked his head. 'Woman trouble I 'ear?'

'God, I'd forgotten what a load of bloody old women you blokes are. No, it's not women trouble, everything's fine.' He mock-punched Dozey's arm and strode along towards the wharf. He had a job to do but he didn't know how, when his best friend could be dying. He turned on his heel, and found the pub. He hurried in and paid the man behind the bar a few bob to lend him a pen, the back of a receipt, an envelope and a stamp.

He wrote. *Bee, Forgive me, I didn't know you were hurt. I'll take you down to the pub when I'm next home, and we can catch up with the lads – get that darts arm up and running. Then we'll fetch Hannah but you need to get better first.* He hesitated. *With love, Adam*

The barman said he'd post it. Mick came up to him. 'He will, if he says he will. What's happened, Adam?'

'Bee's hurt, she came to for a moment, but then she's not regained consciousness again. I don't know what I'll do if . . .' He stopped. 'I just don't know.'

'Did you tell her that, in case she wakes?'

'Sort of.'

Mick sighed. 'Well, sort of will have to do. You have five minutes to get back to the ship.'

Adam flashed a look at the clock over the bar, and ran.

Bryony lay in the hospital bed, her lids too heavy to open, a strange taste in her mouth. She was floating in darkness. Something banged, a strange voice was calling from somewhere far away, 'Bryony, Bryony, dear.'

She was too tired, and drifted again. She was in the water, it tasted foul, a different foul to the seawater. There were bangs, but different bangs to the bombs, and not so many. A different voice was calling her. 'Come on, Bee. I have to go back. I'll be flying. Soon you will be flying too, but you have to wake up. Come on, darling girl.'

Flying? Ah yes, up there, feeling the wind as she flew the Tiger Moth, banking, floating, once the earth had released her, let her go, set her free. She wanted to smile, but she was too tired, and the pain in her head, her ribs, her arm . . . She drifted into the darkness, but for a moment she felt the shudder of the Dragonette engine, and heard the purring, then nothing.

The noises came again. Her head was pounding, her mouth foul and dry. It hurt to breathe. Don't, then. Don't breathe. She slipped again into the darkness, where nothing hurt and she just drifted as though she was gliding on a thermal.

Her hand? She wanted her hand back. It was being gripped, then tapped. A voice was calling, hauling her out of the darkness, out. Out. She gasped. The pain was back, but not the pounding. Her head hurt, but it wasn't making her want to scream. She lay still. She could breathe easier. Her lids weren't so heavy. Someone was pulling her hand, again. Slowly she turned her head. A woman leaned over her. 'Good, you're awake. My word, you've had us worried, my dear. You're going to be rather sore but all should be well.' She had a white hat on. It had a frill.

She disappeared, and Bryony's eyes closed and she was floating away again and she didn't have to breathe, she really didn't. So she stopped, but someone was tugging her hand again. 'Bee, don't go. Bee come back.' It was a child, Hannah? But no, not Hannah, they had turned back instead of going on. Poor *Sunflower*, she did her best. Should she have flown? She should have done something. But she hadn't. She would go. She must go. She struggled, opened her eyes, but they were too dry, the light was too bright, she half closed her lids. Where was she? Where should she be?

Her hand was squeezed. 'Where have you been, my lovely girl?' It was a man. She turned her head slightly. It hurt like her eyes. She stopped, and tried to lift her hand. She couldn't because that hurt. She closed her eyes. The hand and voice wouldn't let her go. Was it Adam, please say it was Adam? Who was Adam? She dragged her lids open, and this time she didn't have to turn because someone was leaning over her. 'Let me make it easy, sweet child. You just lie still.' It was Eddie, her wonderful Uncle Eddie. She loved him, but there was someone else, she . . .

'What's happened?' she asked, her lips stiff and her words slurred.

'You told them when they put you in the ambulance that you fell, once on the boat, once in your . . .' Eddie's voice sounded strange. He stopped. She waited. He half coughed, his voice shaky and strange. 'You came round after Cissie found you in the bedroom.'

Ah, that's who the child was. Yes, she remembered Cissie. Now she remembered the fall on the boat, but was there another, later?

Eddie told her now. He lifted her slightly, and she saw her arm. 'They had to put in a steel pin, because it broke so badly when you fell again, you daft sausage. You broke a rib too, but when? They're not sure whether it was the boat, or the bedroom. Then you hit your head and bled all over the rug, you know, the one you never liked very much. So that's why you did it, isn't it? Just to get rid of the rug. Then you passed out, came to again, ended up in hospital and then had to have an op, and since then, well you've worried us.'

He lowered her. 'You've got to stop this. I'm even more grey, and I must sit down. Holding you up is killing my back.'

'You should be flying.'

'Not while my niece is lying about, being a drama queen, but now you're back, I will be off. A certain young lady, though, is driving us all mad to the extent that the hospital says she can come in again, just for a moment. Not that children are really allowed.'

168

'Hannah?' she breathed. She turned her head, as he sat down. 'Is it Hannah?'

'No, you didn't manage to get to her.'

Oh yes, of course. She had remembered a moment ago.

A young nurse came, her cap pristine white. It was the same face as before. She said, 'Ah, so the princess awakes.'

'Where's my prince?' Bryony asked.

Uncle Eddie and the nurse laughed. The nurse was feeling her pulse. 'Good and steady, but thready. I am a poet, and your mind is back in place so we're a winning team. You have one more visitor, then you rest.'

Was it Adam? Eddie kissed her. 'I must go. Don't worry, you'll fly again by the time you're needed. Things will hot up, especially now Jersey . . .' He stopped.

'Bee!' a child's voice screeched. Hannah? No, no, of course not. Cissie. 'Oh Bee, I found you but I couldn't lift you, and they said it was good I didn't, but I 'ad blood all over me hands, and me dress. It was disgusting.' She sat on the chair that Eddie had just left, and reached for Bryony's hand. 'The Germans have landed on the Channel—'

April's voice cut across her. 'Cissie, hush now.'

Cissie clapped her hand over her mouth. April had entered and now she came to stand the other side of Cissie. She stroked Bryony's cheek. 'They had to cut your lovely hair, and actually—'

Cissie interrupted, 'Yes, they've shaved it where you fell because you had such a long split in your skin. A really long split and they had to sew it up. You're quite bald on that side, but Uncle Eddie said you can wear a hat until it grows. It looks horrid.'

Bryony stared at her, then at April, who was raising her eyebrows at someone on the other side of the bed. Adam?' She turned. The pain made her gasp. No, it was the nurse, who said, 'It really will grow, and quickly, so don't look so sad.'

Bryony felt tiredness sweeping over her. A child said, 'Goodbye, Bee. We'll come tomorrow.'

Bryony murmured, 'Goodbye, Hannah, I'll come for you and Mum soon, I promise. I'm sorry, Daddy. I just couldn't. But I will try ag—'

Then the darkness came again and she let it take her away.

In Jersey, the Germans had arrived, though Bryony had not. Hannah met Cheryl at her rented house. It had been a holiday let until the holidaymakers dried up, and she had managed to get it at a low rent. Together they walked towards St Helier, standing on the verge as a German on a motorbike approached. Bryony had seen one on the day of the invasion. He'd been riding a funny little folding motorbike. Her uncle had said it must have been dropped by parachute along with its rider.

Cheryl waved uncertainly. The soldier ignored her. He wore a leather helmet and goggles. Cheryl

chewed her lip. 'It's all so strange. I'm frightened.'
She had been working at a shop for the holiday
season and was stuck here now, with no job. 'No
tourists, no job,' she said. 'Don't know how I'm
going to pay the rent unless Sylvia moves out of her
flat and we divvy up the rent. What the hell are we
all going to do?'

They reached St Helier, and the sight of soldiers
in their field-grey uniforms made them turn down
side streets to avoid them, feeling clammy and
uncertain. 'I shouldn't be here,' Hannah said. 'She
should have come.'

Cheryl leaned against the side wall of a shop, and
took out her cigarettes. 'Have a ciggy and give it a
rest. That poor sister of yours can't do anything
right, can she? If you'd wanted to go that badly you
could have got on one of the boats.' Hannah took a
cigarette, and cupped the match Cheryl struck and
held out to her. She inhaled. It was her first of the
day, because Doctor Clements had called at the
cottage this morning and given the results of her
mother's examination at the hospital. As he did so
he told her to take her filthy habit outside from
now on. Yes, her mother's TB was still at bay but
why tempt providence, he'd said in that stuffy way
of his.

Bloody Bee had got away lightly, living over
there, away from all these rules: no smoking, no
loud music on the gramophone. She opened her
mouth to say something, but Cheryl was flicking

her ash on to the road, and nudging her. Two German soldiers walked past the end of the street.

Cheryl said, 'What are they going to do to us? You know, it'd be good to go home to England, but it's not home. Not with Mum gone, and Dad at sea.'

Well, Hannah thought, home to England would be different for her. She would have her art college money, and she could find Peter.

'Come on,' Cheryl whispered, flicking the ash off her cigarette, inhaling and then stubbing it out against the wall, and putting it in her pocket for later. Hannah did the same. Together they almost tiptoed to the end of the street, where they looked both ways. The soldiers were marching on. The girls ran across the road and down another street, and did the same once they reached the end, until they were on the way out of town. They set out for home, wishing they had never come into the town, wishing they never had to again.

'But they won't stay just there, you know,' Cheryl said as they hurried through the lanes and fields. 'They'll be everywhere and telling us what to do, and probably shooting us if we don't. You know what the other countries have had to put up with.'

Chapter Eleven

28 July 1940

April put a small case on Bryony's hospital bed. Cissie helped Bryony pack her few personal items and pyjamas, while April gathered up the cards people had brought or sent. They were so numerous Bryony had had to rotate them, keeping the majority in the drawer of the bedside cabinet, and swapping them over when Sister gave her the nod as to who had arrived to visit. Cissie's cards were hand-drawn and painted, and there were many from her as she charted Bryony's recovery.

'Look, Bee,' she said now. ''Ere you are on that Tuesday after your arm had gone wonky and you 'ad to have another operation. Look at the mouth. You weren't 'alf sad.'

'I felt rather sad, you horrible child. It hurt.'

'You made Eddie cry. I don't like it when grown-ups cry. He said he had something in his eye, and he kept saying, "That poor child." I didn't know he meant you, because you're grown up and . . .'

April grinned over Cissie's head at Bryony. 'Would you rather stay in the peace and quiet of hospital?'

Bryony sat down on the bed, exhausted suddenly. 'It begins to look appealing.' She kept an eye on the ward entrance as Sandra, one of the other patients, called, 'If Sister Newsome sees you sitting on that bed, she'll break the other arm.'

The whole ward laughed.

April closed the case and patted it. 'The girls from the cottage are preparing lunch. That should tempt you home. They've been looking after the veggie patch, well, we all have, haven't we, madam? So there'll be fresh salad, and—'

'Scotch eggs,' Cissie interrupted. 'They're like elephants, Anne and Catherine, I mean, not the Scotch eggs. Their blokes are at Catterick now, and they're all just glad they got off Jersey when they did.'

April said, 'I've asked Eric to come to help us dig out the footings and then erect the Anderson shelter. We could need it any minute now, because how can those poor young RAF pilots go on fighting the Luftwaffe? We're losing so many, and it's just so dreadful.' She sounded distraught and despairing.

'I'm such a fool,' Bryony groaned. 'It's exactly what Churchill called it, the Battle of Britain, and while Eddie's lot are racing around delivering replacement aircraft I'm sitting here in a plaster cast. April, if I'm called on, I can't go.'

Cissie turned, and came to her. 'Uncle Eddie said you'd be in a tizz about it.' She took Bryony's good hand in hers. 'He said to tell you you're to keep

174

doing them exercises, and you'll be ready when you're needed. 'E said to tell you that . . .' She stopped and took out a piece of paper. 'I wrote it down, because I can, almost with the right spelling. He helped me just a little. He said, "Our boys will hold".' She looked up, her face puzzled. 'I don't know what they'll 'old, though. Anyway, he said to tell you he'll be *on the case*. But April's got the case, so I ain't a clue what he means.'

April smiled and lifted the case off the bed. 'Right, we can explain that on our way home, but now, come on, you two troublemakers. Have a check around, Bee, in case I've missed anything.'

Bryony checked the cupboard and drawers while the other two waited. April said, 'I think Eric's missing Adam so wanted to do the shelter for us after he heard Eddie telling us he thinks we'll be bombed before long. Eddie thinks they'll possibly target the ports and harbours, the Channel, and certainly the cities, and heaven knows what else.'

Cissie yelled, 'Eric said we must be like the Boy Scouts, prepared.' She laughed and then skipped down the ward, waving at the patients, who called their farewells to her, and to Bryony.

'Fly well,' one of them told her. 'We want to see you in your uniform when it happens.'

'You'll be home before then, but I'll see you all in the pub in six months, and maybe I'll be in uniform. Stranger things have happened.'

Bryony was in a pale blue cotton skirt, a white

blouse, sandals and a dark blue jacket. In one pocket was the note from Adam, the one written on the back of the receipt. He would still be out escorting the convoy, so there'd been nothing else from him. Well, why should there be? They'd had a row, when he'd done his best to help her collect Hannah.

They caught the bus, at Bryony's insistence. 'I don't need a taxi. What I need is to get back to normal.'

Dan tipped his cap as she clambered on. 'And here she is, the wounded warrior. How the hell you carried up the water can with a broken arm, I will never know, Bryony Miller, and your hair will grow. Bit like a boy right now, but don't let that worry you.' The passengers applauded, April grimaced. 'Like a boy indeed, never heard such rubbish.' Bryony laughed and sat down with a thump, her energy expended. Every jolt hurt but she kept her smile in place.

Cissie sat beside her, April behind, with the case next to her. It seemed for ever before the bus approached their stop, which still meant a walk of fifty yards before the entrance to Combe Lodge. Instead, Dan drove right past and drew to a halt at the entrance. 'Special dispensation today,' he said. 'Out you get, carefully now, then toddle off and sit yourself down with a nice cuppa. Always strange when you're first out of hospital, or so the missus says. Says it rather a lot, but then she's in hospital a lot. Tummy trouble, poor soul.'

Bryony kissed him. 'You're a pal. Give Myrtle my love.'

He whispered, 'Take it slow, no one expects miracles. Get it one hundred per cent, or you won't get into the air and do your bit.'

She nodded.

They walked up the drive, the gravel crunching, and the occasional stone being flicked into the beds either side, in which there were asters and stocks still in bloom, and weeds. The couch grass was way out of hand. The roses were doing well, though. 'Anne's been deadheading, and I've clipped the box hedge, but the weeds have taken on a life of their own. Sorry, darling.' April tucked her hand in Bryony's good arm.

'April, you do so much. Don't be daft.' Ahead of her Combe Lodge beckoned, gleaming and white, and dear. She was home.

Cissie gripped her skirt. 'I likes coming up the drive. The Lodge sort of opens its arms, don't it, Bee?'

'Doesn't it,' she corrected automatically.

'Doesn't it, Bee?' Cissie repeated, and leaned into her. 'Now it will feel like home, but it will be more like 'ome, sorry, home, when Uncle Eddie is here, and Adam.' She was off again, skipping ahead.

April walked beside her, 'Welcome home, dearest Bee.'

'I still have to fetch Hannah.'

'Don't let your mind play on that, not yet. Later. You're no good to anyone until you're well.'

After a lunch prepared and shared by Anne and Catherine, who looked as though they would pop at any moment, Bryony sat on a sunbed on the terrace while Cissie played with her new evacuee friend. Agnes had been collected by her mother and carted to Bristol, where she had an aunt, but Pearl had arrived from Luton and, if anything, these two girls were even closer.

Over to the left of the terrace and twenty yards distant Eric Maudsley was digging out the base for the Anderson, the sun gleaming on his blond hair which was longer than her own, but then most people's hair was. He stopped and yanked off his shirt, then began again, his muscles rippling as he dug out the earth. He had situated the shelter on a slight slope. 'Why have you chosen there?' she called.

Eric rested on his spade. 'I'm going to dig a trench, to funnel the run-off around the shelter. If I don't, the inside will get flooded. I also want it on the slope with the rise above it, so it's not so obvious from the air. We can put turf on the corrugated iron roof. It'll be a good disguise.'

She grinned. 'You're wasted, you should be in the Sappers.'

He shrugged. 'I tried, but with my club foot they

turned me down. I'll have another go, though. It doesn't do to give up. How's Adam getting on?'

'He seems to be all right. I haven't heard, which is good news.'

Eric began digging again. 'Yep, that it is.'

She touched the note in her pocket.

By the end of the week the shelter was finished, but Eric came to Combe Lodge anyway, strolling up the drive, whistling, his hands in his pockets as she weeded the bed along the drive. 'Thought you wouldn't be sitting still for long, Bee.'

He squatted beside her as she grinned at him. She was kneeling on a rubber mat, but the gravel still pressed through her overalls into her knees. He said, 'Let me give you a hand.'

'Ah, but do you know the difference between a flower and a weed?'

'Teach me.'

She gave him her hand fork and pointed to the couch grass. 'Its roots are deep and we need every bit out, or it will just keep spreading.'

He laughed softly. 'Could be Hitler you're talking about.'

She shook her head. 'If only it could be solved that easily.'

It was he who shook his head this time, plunging in the fork as Bryony took up a trowel. She had sharpened the edge, because when she gardened, she took no prisoners. 'We had enough rain last night to soften the soil, Eric. It'll be easy.'

He muttered, as he dug out a clump of couch grass. 'This weeding may be, but it'll be a bloody tough battle now the Germans are gunning for us. Thought they might not come and be content with the Continent. What's this, Bee?' He pointed at the remnants of a forget-me-not.

'Dig it up, it will have seeded for next year.'

They dug in silence, except for the birdsong. Sometimes the war didn't seem real to Bryony. It was so calm here, so much as it had always been, like the hub of a wheel with everything else whirling around it.

She pushed down hard on the trowel, levering up the earth and grass, putting it on the pile she was building. She tossed the trowel down and, one handed, shook the soil off the roots she had accumulated, before throwing them in the trug which stood between her and Eric. The ground was friable where they had been working. 'So have you heard any more about the Sappers?'

'It's pointless, so I'm trying for the motor pool. I can mend anything that chugs. But I've more work in the meantime, digging out and erecting shelters. And Tommy Martin wants his old boat overhauling while it's out of the water.' Eric squatted back on his heels, and checked his watch. 'Enough, Bee. April gave orders you were only to slog away for an hour at a time. You must have been at it for far longer.'

He stood, and then leaned down, pulling her up

by her good arm, taking her trowel and dropping it into the trug. It was completely full of couch grass now, and he carried it as he walked alongside her to the terrace, where April had tea ready. On the tray was a cup for Eric. Bryony looked from one to the other. 'Oh I see, Eric, you've been allotted the minder position.'

Eric said, 'Oh stop your mithering. Sit down and behave yourself, for goodness' sake.' It was like having Adam here. She laughed suddenly as he sat alongside her on another sunbed. 'This is the life,' he murmured, leaning back and shutting his eyes.

'Don't you need to do Tommy's boat?'

'Yes, starting tomorrow, so I'll be along later in the day. But your babysitter *will* be here. We must get this garden under control, and look—' He pointed towards the herbaceous beds, and the box hedges around the herb garden. 'Lots to do.'

She shaded her eyes with her hand. 'Not sure we can afford you, Eric.'

He turned his head. 'I like to keep busy, so it's not for money. We're friends, and I'm sure you'd scrape a few barnacles off the bum of a boat for me.' She pulled a face.

He laughed. 'Got to keep you under control, Bryony Miller, or you'll go doing something daft and set yourself back.'

The weather was good and for the next week or so they worked on the garden most afternoons, extending the time daily, and by the evenings

Bryony was too tired to wonder if Adam would telephone. What's more, her good arm was regaining its strength, and so, too, her legs which had spent far too many days up on a bed. She was tanned, and had an increasing appetite.

On Friday 9 August they were clearing elder from the area near the cottage. Bryony was swearing quietly to herself, checking repeatedly that she had every bit of the pernicious white root, even the tiny hairy bits, when Anne came rushing to find her. Eric was digging with the big fork, heaving another load out for her to pick through but leaned on the fork as Anne looked from one to the other, breathing heavily. 'It's Catherine, she's been in labour for a few hours and wouldn't let me get anyone because she said it would take for ever, or so the midwife said. But Bryony, I think . . . Well . . .'

There was a desperate shout from the cottage. 'Anne! . . . Anne!'

Bryony's mind went blank. April? Where was she? She swung round, then remembered she was in Exmouth and Cissie was with Pearl's foster mother. Eric sprang up. 'I'll call the doctor, shall I?'

'I tried the midwife, there was no reply,' Anne said, before waddling back to Catherine, calling, 'I'm coming. For God's sake, Bryony, shift your arse, and come and help me.'

Bryony scrabbled to her feet and, holding her arm, started towards the cottage. She called back to Eric, who was setting out for the Lodge, 'Come back, use the cottage telephone, I've only got one arm so I can't do much.'

He spun, lost balance, regained it. Bryony had forgotten about his built-up boot. 'Sorry,' he said, the panic showing. He headed towards her. She didn't wait but continued, half running in spite of the pain. She entered the cottage, hurrying through the living room and up the wooden stairs, then back down, and into the kitchen, where belatedly she heaved off her wellington boots. 'Clean hands,' she muttered to herself. Eric was in his socks, limping because one leg was shorter than the other. He at least had had the presence of mind to leave his dirty boots outside and was now searching for the telephone. 'Where is the damned thing? I'm going to try the midwife again. We can't deliver a baby, Bee.'

Anne called from upstairs, 'The number is by the telephone, which is on the window seat. Bryony, come *on.*'

Bryony ran the tap, then looked helplessly at her filthy hands. 'Eric, I need you to wash my hands.' She could feel her own panic matching his. A baby? One hand? And what did she know about babies?

Eric dropped the receiver back on the rest. 'No one there. I'll try the doctor in a minute.' He hurried into the kitchen and took her hand, reached for the nail brush, held both under the tap, and scrubbed. Water splashed them both. He flung down the nail brush, turned off the tap, and dried her hand. 'There you go. I'll phone, then wash mine, and don't we boil water or something?'

She yelled over her shoulder as she headed for the stairs, 'I think so, but I don't know what for.'

Anne called from upstairs, 'I've already put the kettle on the hotplate. Bryony, get up here, it's coming.'

Eric and she looked at one another. 'Telephone, then come.'

'I can't.'

'Yes, you have to.'

She rushed upstairs. In the cottage's spare room Catherine was pacing.

Anne muttered, 'Why not get on the bed?'

'Because it bloody hurts, that's why. This is better,' Catherine groaned, leaning over, gripping the end board of the bed.

Bryony shouted, 'Get on the bed now, or how can we catch it?'

She grabbed Catherine's arm, while Anne yanked back the eiderdown. Eric stood in the doorway, appalled. 'Help me. Be my other hand,' Bryony said to him, over Catherine's groans.

To Anne, who was wincing, she said, 'Get towels. We'll need to wrap the baby.' Eric came to hold Catherine's other arm. 'Come on now, lass. Hop on to the bed, there's a good girl.'

Catherine muttered through clenched teeth, 'I'm not bloody hopping anywhere, and I'm never going to be anybody's good girl, ever again. Men. Bloody men. Do you hear me?' The last was shouted, into Eric's face.

'Loud and clear,' he said. 'The whole of Devon's heard you.' His voice was shaking.

They got her on to the bed, she slumped across it, her lower legs hanging over the edge. Anne brought towels, then groaned and bent over herself. 'Oh, God,' Bryony said. 'You too?' The kettle was shrieking.

'Go and turn it off,' Anne ordered Eric, who looked relieved and dashed out.

'Then come back, d'you hear? We'll need everyone.' Bryony was panting as though she'd run a mile while Anne sat in the armchair near the window, blowing in and out.

As Catherine's contractions seemed to pause, Eric returned, and Anne gasped, 'Did you get hold of the midwife?'

'Some woman answered. She's on another case, they both are, so I rang the doctor again too, and he's on his way, his receptionist said.'

Catherine's face was beaded with sweat, Anne was up on her feet. 'It's gone,' she said. 'The pain's gone. It was just backache from hurrying.'

Eric looked at Bryony, but then Catherine groaned, putting her legs up. Eric had to help rip her knickers off, while Anne stood with them. She said, 'We need to look and see what's happening.'

Eric moved to the window. 'I'll keep a look out,

but not sure there's much point. I'd have heard if the doctor had arrived.'

Catherine shrieked, 'Not there, you idiot. *Me.*'

Bee and Anne laughed, while Eric shook his head. 'That's your job, Bee.' He was pale and sweating, and sat down quite suddenly on the dressing-table chair.

She snapped, 'Get up, you're not the one having a baby, these two are. Imagine she's a boat engine and you're trying to get a piston sorted.'

Catherine started laughing. 'Don't tell him that, he'll get a ruddy wrench.'

The sun was streaming in through the window. They heard an aircraft above. Eric said, 'That's all we need, a bomb.'

Catherine gave a deep groan, and Bryony made herself take a long breath in, and then out. Where had she seen this before, the heaving, the moaning? She patted Catherine's knee and it came to her – Uncle Thomas's farm, that's it, the cows, the sheep. 'Don't cut the cord,' she said. 'Whatever we do, we mustn't cut the cord. Anne, it's you and me, with Eric as a last resort.' But Anne had left her and was panting on the easy chair. Bryony said, 'That's all right, Anne. You'll be fine. Really, it's all right, you too, Catherine.'

She was telling herself as much as them. 'So, it'll have to be just us, Eric.'

He nodded, grimly, from the dressing table, and limped across to stand beside her. Bryony said,

'Catherine, I can see the baby's head, or I think it is. When you feel a contraction, you push.'

Catherine muttered, 'What do you mean, you think?'

But then she groaned, and pushed, and the head began to come out, then stalled. There was another contraction almost immediately, and then the head was out, and then there was another long grunt, more than a groan and full of effort, and now the shoulders appeared, and the whole of the body, in a great slurp and gush of water. 'Oh God,' groaned Eric.

'Stop fussing,' Bryony shouted, reaching for towels off the end of the bed and handing him one. 'Be ready to cuddle the baby in this when the afterbirth comes out. Just look at the baby, not at anything else. I can't have you fussing.'

'Crikey, Bee, you're so bossy.'

The baby cried now, and they both stopped and looked. 'Perhaps you should just put the towel over him,' Bryony said, suddenly uncertain. The baby had cried and she knew that was good, and she knew, too, that all this was very real and she actually didn't know what she should do.

'It's a boy,' Eric said, 'And his little feet are perfect. Did you hear that, Catherine? He's perfect, lucky little blighter.'

Catherine groaned again, and this time it was the afterbirth, and the baby was still crying so Eric rubbed him, and Bryony and he stared at one another. Panic was rising again.

Anne was standing by the window, half bent over.

'Oh God, what if Anne...?' Eric almost shouted. Then, 'I'm just going to wrap him up, that's what I'm going to do.' He did so, and sat close, his hand on the baby, staring at him, hushing him, while Bryony used a towel to pat Catherine's forehead, telling her she was so clever, and the baby was very lovely. 'Check for blood,' she told Eric.

He shook his head. 'No, you do that.' His voice was absolutely firm, and she did, and all seemed well. Catherine turned on her side. 'I want to see him.'

Eric and Bryony looked at each other, and then at the afterbirth, the cord, and the baby. 'In a minute, when the doctor comes. You see, we don't quite know what to do with the cord and all that. Just talk to him, let him hear your voice.

'I'm just so tired,' Catherine muttered.

'Is that normal?' Eric asked Bryony.

'I'm not sure. Leave the baby and call the doctor again.'

He started towards the door, and then there was the sound of a car hooting at Combe Lodge and wheels on the gravel leading to the cottage, where it skidded to a halt. Another hoot, and then the crash of the car door, and the front door of the cottage slamming back against the wall. Footsteps pounded up the stairs, then back down again. 'Handwash,' Eric and Bryony said together, grinning at one another. 'Better than weeding?' she asked Eric.

'He's a little belter,' Eric said, touching the baby's face. 'You can hardly feel his skin, it's so soft.'

Catherine called, 'He's my little lad, you know, and I'd like to hold him.'

She eased on to her back as the doctor swung into the room. 'Must be something in the water, because all you pregnant women are at it today. Now let's start to get this sorted, but first, Bee, would you telephone for an ambulance and we'll get this little party off to hospital. Good job. Excellent job, and you didn't cut the cord. My receptionist is new, she didn't know to tell you.'

Bryony said, 'I've a farmer for an uncle. I just thought of the animals.'

Catherine, who was by now holding her son, raised her eyebrows. 'I'm going to call him Eric,' she said.

The ambulance came twenty minutes later and took both the women to hospital. Bryony and Eric tidied the cottage, and locked it, hearing Cissie calling outside the Lodge, 'Where is everyone? Bee ain't gone in the Tiger Moth again, has she?'

'We're here at Anne's. We have some news for you.' Bryony started towards the Lodge, and suddenly her legs felt weak beyond endurance. Eric caught her arm, saying, 'Steady the Buffs.'

She let him take her weight for a moment. He laughed quietly as they stood together on the path while Cissie sped towards them, her plaits flying, her dungarees grass-stained. 'What? What did you say?'

He let Bryony go and caught Cissie as she flew at him. 'What, Bee?' she demanded.

They told her, and her eyes grew large. 'A baby? And I missed it. Oh, please can I tell April? She'll be home soon.'

She scooted off, and Eric took Bryony's arm again. 'Time you settled into a chair, or went to bed.'

Bryony laughed, 'What about you? Quite an education, eh?'

'Makes a change to gutting fish, or refitting an engine, and it so didn't help to compare it with that, Bee. You know, seeing something born is magical. One minute he doesn't exist, and then he's here, living and breathing, and somehow he's already a character. It might make a difference.' He spoke almost as though to himself.

She said nothing for a moment, not sure what he meant. He said, letting go of her arm, 'I haven't slept very well since Dunkirk. Daft, I know. I keep seeing and hearing stuff.'

As they approached the back door, Bryony realised that her sleep had been untroubled since her hospital stay; all she dreamed of was the garden: the scent, the feel of the earth and the plants. Was that wrong?

She said, holding him back, 'Since my operation, my head seems clear of it. I wonder if we need something to shake us out of the pattern? I don't even worry about Hannah so much.'

He asked why Hannah hadn't been evacuated

and she explained, ending, 'I'll fetch her when I'm fit enough. I promised, you see.'

April was opening the back door. 'Are you two going to come inside and tell us all about it, or are you going to stay outside chatting like two old dears?'

'It's a boy, called Eric,' Bryony said, entering. 'After the assistant who helped deliver him.'

Bryony and Eric laughed at April's face, though Eric said, 'Assistant, my Aunt Fanny. A seamless team, April, that's what we were.'

'Well, off you go, on to the terrace, and we'll all have tea there.'

She shooed them out, and as they headed along the path Eric said, 'About Hannah. Why don't we work on the *Sunflower* engine together so that when Adam comes she's all set up? If he can't be here, don't worry, I'll take you, because there's no way you're going on your own, Bryony Miller. The Germans aren't ready for that sort of invasion.'

They settled down on the terrace, where the sun was soft. 'I need to put the tools away,' she said, sitting bolt upright.

'Oh, for goodness' sake, I'll do it, and what's more, we should wet the baby's head. Let's go out this evening, on me.'

He was shading his eyes against the glare. She felt too tired, but restless as well, so why not. 'It's darts night at the pub, isn't it?'

'Yes, but you're not a bloke so let's go to Frank's Restaurant. He caught some mackerel off the point today. They'll be fresh and he does a good salad.'

April came along with Cissie, who said, 'Oh, mackerel, I don't like bones, so I'll stay here.'

Eric and Bee shared a look. 'Yes, you will, young lady. It'll be well past your bedtime,' he said. 'But I'll take you one day. I promise.'

That evening, Adam telephoned Combe Lodge to speak to Bee, but April answered. The first thing he said was, 'How is she?'

'By she you mean Bee, she's busy as per usual even though she's had a second operation. She is home, and should probably be resting but today she was weeding the garden, delivering babies, and now she's out wetting the babe's head.'

There was a pause. 'What did you say? Another operation? Oh my God, poor Bee. But she's all right? I was imagining . . . What was that about babies?'

April could hear shouting and singing in the background. 'Where are you, darling?'

'On the quay, we've just come back but are off again first thing. Never a dull moment in this job, or rather quite a few, in between whiles.' He sounded tired, and stressed.

'What quay?'

'Let's just say, up north, beyond the border. Now, what operation?'

'She had to have a pin put in and there was a fracture of the lower arm that they hadn't noticed, but honestly, you know what she's like. She's been weeding the flower beds along the drive, and then today Catherine went into labour and the midwife wasn't answering the telephone.'

Cissie was hurrying down the stairs in her nightie. She reached the bottom and ran to April. 'Is it Adam, is it, is it?'

April smiled. 'Yes, it is.'

'Adam, they delivered a baby and I haven't wet my bed for ages,' she shouted.

April laughed into the mouthpiece. 'Can you hear our extraordinarily loud-mouthed child who should be asleep?' She held the receiver to Cissie's ear.

'Loud and clear, and that's excellent news, Cissie. A dry bed? I'm really proud of you.' Adam was laughing too. 'But tell me again, Mum, about Bee.' Cissie handed back the receiver to April, who heard the urgency in her son's voice. 'She's really all right? And what's that about the baby?'

Cissie was leaning against April's leg, yawning, as April said, 'Yes, she really is. She's taking it easy and we're helping her to pace herself because she so wants to be ready when the ATA need her. We feel sure they will with the RAF losses and the need for new planes. And Cissie is right, they did deliver a baby. Catherine's little boy.'

'Catherine has called him Eric.' It was Cissie shouting again.

'Hush,' April murmured, 'I can't hear Adam. Say again, Adam?'

'Eric? Why Eric?'

Cissie shouted again, 'He's taken her to Frank's, for mackerel, but I don't like bones, so I said I wouldn't come. He said that was good, because I wasn't invited.'

April said into the silence. 'Are you there?'

'Yes, Mum.'

'Eric sorted out the Anderson shelter and then I suggested he give Bee a hand with the gardening, for which, I might add, he wouldn't take pay. So he was on hand, to give a hand with the baby, if you get my meaning.'

'So they've gone to Frank's? But it's darts night at the pub?'

April sighed. 'As Eric said, our Bee is not a bloke, Adam. She's a woman, rather a beautiful woman, actually. Perhaps he's realised that when you haven't.'

There was another silence. Cissie asked for the receiver, and into it she said, 'I think he should join the new thing, you know, the Home Guard, because he can't be a soldier or sailor with his foot. Then it will be nice, because he won't be going away, like you. He'll be here to help us and he can do his other work too. He said he'd help get the *Sunflower* engine running properly and take Bee to Jersey as you're not here . . . I heard him. What's that noise, Adam?'

April took the receiver back and heard the pips. 'Adam, Adam, be safe, telephone us when you can, and then you can talk to Bee, she misses you so very much.' But she spoke into emptiness. They had been cut off.

Chapter Twelve

Scotland

Adam replaced the receiver, but couldn't somehow release his hand. Eric? Bee?

Of course he knew she was a woman, but he just hadn't been able to find the words, damn it, when he scribbled his note because his heart was being wrenched from his body at the thought that the worst might happen. It was then that the knowledge that Bee was everything in the world to him had burst upon him, together with the realisation that he had shrugged off the person who was his life's breath. He had not slept while away, but had ached to know her fate. As they had gathered up the lost sheep of the convoy he wished he were there at her side, never to leave, making her live, and then keeping her safe for the rest of her life.

And here she was, bloody waltzing off with Eric all the time he'd been half out of his mind with worry and grief.

There was a knock on the glass of the telephone box. 'Setting up shop in there, are you, Adam? Come on, old lad, enough of the sweet talk or I'll be hoying you out and into the harbour.' It was Geordie Gilchrist.

Adam's knuckles showed white. It was as though he needed to unpeel his fingers one by one until the receiver was as virgin as it should be. The damp imprint of a hand remained. Was that all there was of him in Bee's life? Just an imprint? He leaned back on the door, opening it, hearing the gulls, the crash of the coaler, the singing from the pub, and feeling the wind. Well, when didn't he feel the wind on land, or on the deck, or the bridge, as the waves surged and . . .

'Bloody hell, man, what's happened? Not Bryony? She's not worse? Oh hell's bells. You need a drink. She's not dead?' Geordie's lips had thinned, and he shot a look at Mick, who was just behind him in the queue for the telephone. 'Let's get him into the pub, we can make our calls later.' It was an order, but Mick was already slinging an arm over Adam's shoulder.

Adam said, 'No, everything's fine. Sorry lads, just a bit tired.'

And yes, it was fine, because she was alive, Bee was alive. Now the relief drenched him, thank God, thank the Lord, thank the powers that be, she was alive. Then the relief was swept aside with such a wave of regret, pain and jealousy that he felt the ground beneath him shift. He staggered and thought he'd vomit.

'Whoa,' Mick said. 'Steady, lad.'

The men in the queue snaking towards the tele-phone box looked at one another, waiting to know what had happened. It was only then that they'd know what to do. Adam forced himself to grin. 'Come on, let's have that drink, and just stop prop-ping yourself up on me, Mick, if you don't very much mind.'

Mick grunted, and slapped Adam on the back instead. 'First pint's on me, then you can stop the bullshit. We didn't come down in the last shower so we know when someone's telling porkies. Just tell us if she's alive, and all right, *now* and we'll wait for the rest.'

'She's alive, and all right. Very all right.'

He heard his bitterness, and checked it. The queue was getting restless, and he gestured them forward. 'Telephone's free, lads. Sorry, just a bit . . . Oh, you know.'

He walked away, wanting to be alone under the night sky, a northern sky that didn't get dark until very late in the summer months. But being alone wasn't an option, because Mick and Geordie caught up, and marched either side of him until they reached the pub. He was shoved inside, with Mick muttering, 'Now we want to know the ins and outs, and then that's an end to it, or you're going to be a ruddy misery to have on board, and let's face it, I want something to tut about, as my old lady says.'

They were in the beer-heavy warmth, the dim gas lighting, the low beams hung with beer mats signed by trawler crews, and the raucous singing of men just back from patrol. Some clustered around the bar, with others jostling behind the two darts teams, one of whom seemed to be slinging a good hand. Thud, thud. A great cheer rang out as the *Highland Laddie* team won, to groans and curses from *High Ground*.

Darts. His mother was right, Bee wasn't a bloke, but he knew that only too well, so why the hell had he written on the back of the pub receipt that he'd take her to the pub on her recovery, when he'd really been almost sick with fear that she would die. Why the hell hadn't he said what he had been thinking and feeling? What was the matter with him? Why hadn't he written instead: 'Get better and I'll tell you how I worship the ground you walk on and once this is over I will never leave your side again.'

But how did you tell that to your best friend, someone you'd grown up with, someone you couldn't live without, because what if she hadn't felt the same? Then he would have lost even that friendship.

Mick shouted to the barman, his arm back around Adam's shoulders, 'Let's have three beers poured, and a chaser, if rationing allows, and it had better bloody do. Move along, lads, make room for the big boys.' The sailors did, shoving along the bench at the table by the window, taking their dominoes with them.

Was Eddie still playing with Cissie on his leave?

He didn't need to, because she was good with figures, but she liked the game for its own sake. A dry bed, clever little thing, clever Mum and Bee.

Geordie fetched the drinks. 'Beer, no chasers,' he grumbled. 'Get this down you, Adam.'

They drank in silence, and then he told them about her second operation, about Eric, about his note.

Geordie spluttered on his beer. 'You wrote what, you bloody idiot?'

Mick grunted, 'Well, I can see where the girl's coming from. Why wouldn't she choose a bloke who buys her mackerel over a pillock who takes her for a drink with the boys. You might just as well have said, the *other* boys.'

Adam stared at the dregs of his beer. It looked like he felt. 'Well, thanks for that, lads, I feel a lot better now.'

Geordie wiped his mouth. 'I reckon you should write her a proper letter, telling her how you feel, and get shot of this bastard, somehow. What's he doing in civvies anyway? Black market, is he? Got a better deal going?'

Mick was flipping his beer mat again and again. Adam longed to slam his hand down on it and rip it to shreds, just to stop him. Instead he said, 'That's the trouble, he's a grand bloke, got a club foot but it didn't stop him taking his boat to Dunkirk with us. Been my mate since for ever. Pure gold. He's getting the *Sunflower* engine up to speed too, because she needs to fetch her sister from Jersey. I made a bloody balls-up of that too.'

'You said earlier she was up for the ATA,' Geordie said, checking the change in his pocket. 'Time for another, methinks. My shout, then it's you, laddie.' He nodded at Adam. 'Look, don't fret, we'll probably be sunk anyway, so just drink up and forget about it. But if we're not, and if she's fit enough for the ATA, she'll be delivering the training aircraft to Scotland. Where are we? Scotland. So you'll have time to get stuck in while the mackerel king is still in Devon. But there will be no dartboard, no drinks with the lads. Is that a deal?'

The whole table laughed. Adam shook his head. 'Get on with your dominoes and leave me to my mess-up.' But yes, she would be flying up here, and Geordie was right, Eric wouldn't. Suddenly all things seemed possible, just as long as Eric didn't move things along quickly. Adam wouldn't let himself even play with that idea, but joined in with the blokes as they drank themselves into hangovers.

The next day, the coalies humped a never-ending flow of coal on board, and the supplies were ticked off as Adam checked the Oerlikon guns. All along the wharf the trawlers were preparing for sea again. As the day melted into evening the *High Ground* left harbour, one of eight fighting trawlers pitching and tossing into the rising storm. They set course, destined to escort an outbound convoy until it was beyond the normal danger zone for U-boats, not to mention Focke-Wulf Condors, and then they would turn about and rendezvous with an inbound merchant convoy carrying supplies to a beleaguered British public.

They rolled and pitched throughout the night, Adam taking his four-hour watch with Leading Seaman Noddy Thompkins and Seaman Trout, who had never lived down his name. It was cold, wet and Adam's head ached as badly as everyone else's. Why couldn't they drink without paying for it? At the end of his watch he pitched into his bunk and burrowed into the deepest sleep he had ever known, waking to a shake from Geordie. 'Rise and shine.'

The seas were huge, and the wind sounded like an express train. With dawn the wind eased, and somehow the trawlers were all in sight of one another. The hours passed and then a signal was picked up, reporting the torpedoing of a merchant ship fifty miles away. The skipper received orders to head for the position, together with their sister ship, the *Mary Lou*.

They drove through seas that heaved, pulled and tilted the trawler, and rain that roared horizontally and stung like nails for the rest of the day and night. Adam liked the sheer blackness and nothingness of the night in a storm. It made the trawlers seem indomitable, even more singular, and reminded him of the *Sunflower*. For a moment he was glad that Eric was nurturing his beloved boat; she deserved it. But it should have been him. He stopped the thought because after the *Sunflower* would come Bee. And Eric had better bloody well not be nurturing her.

'By the light of the silvery moon' played again and again through his head as he stood his watch, though why it should in this nothingness he had no idea. Where are you now, Bryony Miller – not under some moon with Eric? Do you ever think of me? Can I wait until you come to Scotland in a training aircraft? As he scanned his world of salt spray and upheaval, he knew he couldn't.

He glanced at the charts in the corner, and took a mug of cocoa from Seaman Trout. He sipped it, balancing as they hurtled into a trough, and out at a kilter. He took his bearings from a flashing lighthouse. He darted behind the blackout curtain in order to plot the position on the chart, then back out on to the bridge, his eyes aching from the need to see any looming bulk of shipping before it was too late.

Behind him the Asdic rating was dimly silhouetted in the light from the binnacle, Noddy Thompkins was stirring on lookout on the wing of the bridge, the wheel and steering engine were rattling as the helmsman in the wheelhouse below kept the ship on her course. This was his world, for now. But he would not give up on Bryony. How could he, when life without her would be meaningless?

Dawn eased the blackness and it also eased the storm. As Geordie took over his watch, Adam saw that to port was the *Mary Lou*. He had breakfast in the wardroom while the skipper examined signals. It was then the call went up, that a lifeboat had been seen. 'All hands on deck.'

The lifeboat was empty of men, though a cap floated on the water that slopped in the bottom. They picked it up with the derrick, the water gushing back into the sea, and Adam felt again the cold of the sea off Norway, the terror of being perhaps forgotten and left to drown, the lifeboat that had headed for him, the grappling hook that had saved him.

His eyes met Geordie's. 'Poor bloody buggers,' Geordie muttered.

Adam nodded, reminding himself that this was war, and it was not a priority to know whether or not Bryony loved him. It was life and death that was important, and she was alive. That was enough.

That afternoon, as they set course for the convoy again, having hunted further for survivors, the Asdic picked up something that behaved like a submerged U-boat.

The skipper ordered the *Mary Lou* to be signalled, but she was already on the case. A pattern of depth charges was being dropped following each skipper's grid and each one took with it the anger of the two crews. Oil came up, in quantity. The *Mary Lou* signalled, 'Looks like we've an early catch.'

The Asdic tracked the U-boat as it powered beneath the *Mary Lou* but then both trawlers turned to starboard and followed the trail of oil. The Asdic told the story as he tried to escape but then, with the *Mary Lou* in the charge, they attacked, three times in quick succession.

Adam gripped his hands into fists, wanting the submariners dead, but knowing they were men. Bubbles of air came to the surface. The skipper looked at Adam, who hurried to the gun platform, where the gun crew were readying. 'Keep alert, lads.'

They nodded, watching the bubbles, but then – nothing. Just oil, and death, as the submarine presumably sank to the depths where the hull would be crushed like an eggshell.

Adam looked from the oil to the lifeboat lying on the foredeck. 'It's war,' he murmured. The men nodded. Above the gulls wheeled and called, heedless.

Just to make sure the debris was not a feint, the *Mary Lou* attacked twice more, and twice the sea split with the hammer blows of TNT. On the third attack, a waterspout of destruction shot skywards, bearing oil and debris. It was finally done.

The crew of both trawlers watched as the spout faded, the oil and debris settled. The waves allowed the debris to cling together for a while, and as Adam lit a cigarette, and handed the packet round to the gun crew, the remains of the submarine began to disperse. Soon it would be as though it had never happened. But it had, and a lot of Germans had lost their lives. The men inhaled the last of the cigarettes, which were burning down fast in the wind.

'There'll be the midday rum ration soon.'

The skipper called for their course to be altered to meet up with the convoy, and the engines took on the load again as they forged through the rising wind. 'Does it ever bloody stop?' Geordie muttered before going on watch, leaving Adam in the wardroom. He meant the wind, probably.

The skipper came in, after hanging his waterproofs outside. He was pale with the cold and rubbed his hands together. 'All well with you, Adam? You looked a bit peaky when we sailed. Affairs of the heart have a way of seeping, wouldn't you say?'

'Seeping, sir?'

The skipper slumped down. 'Ah, indeed they do unless we put up a bulwark, for sanity's sake.' He winked at Adam. 'Yes, these old girls seem to be sailed by a load of similar old girls whose gossip gets around faster than this damned gale.'

They braced themselves as the *High Ground* tilted. The skipper, wiping his face as if hoping to remove all traces of tiredness – he failed – said, 'Hope the helmsman's got his wits about him and doesn't let her broach to.'

She skidded back into the trough. 'That's the thing, see, Adam, mustn't let the girls make us broach to. I'd suggest a trip down to Devon when leave allows, no standing about hoping the other bloke fades. Get your oar in, if you get my drift. We'll probably be heading into Portsmouth at some stage, to rendezvous with convoys from the starting gate. Poor buggers'll be having it tougher and tougher getting through once Herr Hitler and his gangsters really start getting into their stride, supposing the RAF hold 'em for now, that is.'

Adam checked his watch. He needed to get to the ratings' wardroom to supervise the rum tot. The skipper closed his eyes. Adam eased himself up, but then Lieutenant Cobham murmured, 'I was on submarines between the wars. Hate to see 'em downed. Needs must, though. Nasty death.'

Adam sat down again. The skipper opened his eyes. 'Off you go, laddie. Give the blokes their rum. They've deserved it. Keep 'em busy, they don't care for dealing in death any more than the rest of us. I'll bear you in mind when we're to sail for our old friend, Portsmouth, or Pompey if you prefer, then you can go across, all guns blazing.'

In the ratings' mess, Mick was waiting, the rum divvy all ready. Adam stayed while it was doled out. The mood was forced. He talked of the weather, of the summer, which seemed to have come and gone, if it had been there at all. That got them grumbling.

A shout came down from the deck entrance, 'Messman's brought dinner from the galley. Dry hash, followed by prunes and egg-substitute custard. Then how about some bread and margarine? Lovely grub, eh?'

There was a universal groan, and now Tom, Derek, Andy and Dozey went to pass the dinner down from the deck. The food would loosen tongues, and get things in their place, especially for the new boys. For a moment Adam was glad he'd been in Norway, and Dunkirk, because that was his blooding, and he could process things more quickly. What's more, it was a further tie with Bee.

He smiled at Mick, who nodded, 'The crew will be all right, sir. It's the new ones who just need a moment to get their minds round it. They're used to fish, see, and can whack the head off one of those without a murmur. The others already take it in their stride. We're in for the long haul, I reckon. I also reckon the skipper will let you off for a couple of days when we call in to Pompey.'

Adam sighed. He'd thought a submarine sinking would take everyone's mind off his love life, or lack of one. Mick winked. 'Know what you're thinking, but it's the little things that turn out to be the life-savers for the crew. There'll be something else tomorrow, don't you worry.'

There was: Seaman Tom Seaton slipped and tore a ligament. His language was imaginative, as the skipper called it, and the remedies suggested were many and varied. Adam breathed a sigh of relief, and shelved the whole bloody business until he could do something about it.

Chapter Thirteen

Early December 1940
Jersey

Hannah pulled up her scarf against the wind that was swirling in her uncle's cobbled farmyard. It carried bits of straw and hay, and the dust caught in her eyes just as her sketch pad slipped from under her arm. It splayed at her feet in the mud, the loose pages flying.

'Damn it!' she shouted, and snatched at them as they took off, gusting higher and higher, this way and that. She caught all but two pages and these soared higher still, heading for heaven knows where.

'What are you doing, girl?' Her uncle was standing in the barn doorway. What did he think she was doing, having a cup of tea?

She picked up the pad and shoved the loose pages back in. They were smeared with mud. Well, she hoped it was mud.

'Coming to find you, Uncle Thomas. I wondered if you had a few potatoes we could have for our tea at the cottage. Mum fancies one baked and stuffed with scrambled egg.'

He had disappeared back into the barn, and was closing the door on her. She sighed, hurried over, caught the door, opened it, and slipped in after him. He spun round. 'Shut the bloody door,' he bellowed.

She did. 'Well, can we, or not? Aunt Olive sa—'

'Oh, never mind that. Help me get this darned weaner back in its sty, girl.'

Her uncle, his arms outstretched, his wellington boots kicking up straw dust, was herding a squealing weaner towards the other end of the barn. Hannah dumped her sketch pad on the step of the pony trap. 'What's he doing here? He should be in the sty with the others round the side.'

'Just you mind your own business and give us a hand.' She pulled a face, and flapped her hands. He barked, 'Take the left hand side of the barn, and be quick about it, lass.' Together they pressed the weaner back towards the hay and straw bales.

It was then that she saw the opening in the brick wall. It was a doorway. The door was brick-faced. She understood after a moment and said, 'Hang on, this must be the piglet you reported to the authorities as having died. Uncle Thomas, what the hell will you do if you're rumbled? You'll be imprisoned or something, and by the Germans probably.'

The weaner darted between them. Her uncle made a grab and it squealed. He said, 'Let's get the little devil behind the wall, and then we can talk.'

The weaner headed for the left of the straw bales.

Just as he lurched after it, they heard a shout from the yard.

'Good morning. Is any person there?'

It was a German. Her uncle paled, spun round and whispered to Hannah, 'For God's sake, go and keep him talking. It's the patrol that Old Davy warned me was on the way, before he went on to Sonny Jim's place.'

She looked from the pig to her uncle, and then to the huge barn door, which was ajar. She was due to start a job at the nursing home tomorrow, where it was warm, and she could eat the leftovers from the patients' plates and maybe food in the kitchen. If her uncle was caught and they were disgraced, that could be the end of that.

Her uncle had grabbed the pig. As he hurried towards the brick doorway, his hand clamped over its muzzle. She ran to the barn doors, picking up her sketch pad on the way, and slipped out, barging straight into a German soldier, whose patrol were gathered on the edge of the yard. The bump shocked them both: she dropped her sketch pad, and he stepped away. She reached behind her and shut the door, then leaned back against it.

She'd never been so close to one of the enemy. His corporal's grey uniform was spotless, he was young, tall, broad-shouldered, and laughing. She'd never seen the soldiers laughing. Well, amongst themselves they had as they strolled in the town and bought up goods like ravening hordes, or so her

Aunt Olive had called them, hate in every word. But they had not smiled or laughed at anyone she knew. But then she remembered how an airman had knocked old Mrs Bertram off the pavement as he strutted along. She fell into the gutter and, oh yes, then he'd laughed.

Hannah heard a squeal from the barn, and coughed. 'My uncle's just trying to catch the rats. We have to grow grain instead of potatoes to feed the islanders, he's been told, so he's . . .' She stopped.

The corporal moved back another step. 'Yes, he kills rats but how strange, that they squeal?' His laugh had died. He was looking from her to the door.

Her mouth dried. 'But they do,' she said. 'You wouldn't know if you haven't spent time on a farm.' She looked at her sketch pad lying on the ground. More loose pages had escaped, and though two were stuck in the mud, others gusted up into the air.

'I was just showing my uncle my sketches.' She daren't move from the door. He made a grab for a page, snatching it. He looked at the view of the hawthorn tree by the cliff, bowed over in the wind. 'Is good. But, how strange again, that you show him as he rats?' He returned it.

The other pages were being wafted towards the patrol. He shouted in German. The soldiers caught them, guffawing as they did so. Hannah used the distraction to leave the door to its own devices and reach for her pad, but the German saw, and did the same. They banged heads. It hurt and she fell back against the door. He reached for her just as her uncle opened the door, pushing her off balance so that she slipped to the side and fell into the mud.

'For God's sake, Hannah, what're you doing down there, girl?' Her uncle stood above her with his shovel over his shoulder and a rat's tail in the other hand. 'Got one of the little buggers.' He waved the tail at the German. 'Pesky little beggers. Get everywhere, they do, spoiling things for ordinary people.' Blood dripped on to the ground.

Lying in the mud, Hannah hardly dared breathe because she knew her Uncle meant the Germans, especially after the order issued in October insisting that Jews register with the authorities, and then the news that wirelesses had to be handed in. He still had his hidden up the chimney, silly old fool.

She started to scramble to her feet, and the German hauled her upright. She wanted to break away, and hide behind her uncle. The German smiled. 'Ah, we all feel the same about rats, I think.'

His eyes were deep blue. He released her.

He turned to her uncle. 'I come to give you this. It is an order that your two cottages are to be used as billets for the German troops. It informs you that you must move the occupants into somewhere else.'

He shouted something to his patrol. One of them strolled across, his rifle slung over his shoulder, Hannah's pages in his hand. He handed them to her. He too was young. He half bowed. His boots were muddy. Her pages were, too. She took them. Her hand was shaking. The pages, and her mac, and hands, stank of foul mud and echoes of cow and sheep dung, and awful pig poo. Her tears began. The German said, 'War is hard. But our bombers do not come again to hurt you, they fly to Britain which still stands against us. Such fools. Perhaps to be muddy is not a bad state, Fräulein, when they are to be very pummelled.'

Her uncle said, 'Stand up straight, and get some self-respect. Stop them tears, for the love of God.'

The German looked from her to her uncle. 'I will leave you to your rat catching and wish you a good hunt. I was in England for a year of my university. I wish that we were friends, and not this.'

He turned on his heel, and walked away, the rest of the patrol following. Her uncle watched until they had left the yard and were on their way along the road again. He muttered, 'But you damn well are "this", and loving every minute.'

Hannah held her sketch pad at arm's length. 'Can I have those potatoes, then, and a few eggs? I want to go and wash, and what's going to happen to Mum and me now?'

'Oh don't start your blessed tears again, girl. You'll come to us, of course. Your mum's here most of the time anyway. Good girl for helping. The pig's not for us; well, a bit is, but when it comes to it there'll be others more in need, like your nursing home, you mark my words. We're cut off right and proper now. Our people are out of work, no tourists, not much call for help in shops, fishing carried out only with a ruddy German on board, and for limited times at that. There's that lot of Nazis to feed too. I bet the Jersey authorities will have to ask for credit from France, which will mean the Boche, because who runs France now? It's a bloody pig's ear, that's what it is.' Uncle Thomas moved to the edge of the barn, checking that the patrol really were long gone. They were. He said, 'They bombed Coventry, you know.'

She shouted at him. 'No, I didn't bloody know, and you shouldn't be saying, because you're not supposed to have a wireless, and someone will tell, and then we'll all be imprisoned or taken away to one of their camps, you stupid old man.'

There was no way she was going to live with a load of old miseries who hid a pig and then were going to give it away. The least they could do was have the gumption to sell the ruddy thing. She was young, eighteen now, and she was covered in mud, and what the hell was going to happen to her, and for how long? And how could someone just come and take your home away, like these Germans were doing? She wept as she walked, wishing Bee were here, wishing she had come for her because . . . Well, because she was Bee.

That afternoon, after feeding the weaner, Thomas took a calf and six pigs to the abattoir to be offered for sale, as decreed by the Germans. While there, he saw the official, a Jersey islander, who had certified as lifeless the dead piglet that Thomas had received from a nearby farm, and which he'd registered as his own, before passing the carcass on to Peter's father to do the same. It had enabled them to secrete a piglet from their litters, and bring on to fill the bellies of family and friends.

He tipped his cap at Thomas, shaking his hand and whispering, 'I'm being replaced. They'll be clipping the dead pig's ears, so that's the end of that. Pass it around.' He hurried on. Thomas sighed. It had been good while it lasted. Now all he had to worry about was the silent killing of the beast when the time came. He dug his hands in his pockets, then drove home, wondering how often he would be able to use the Morris, what with the fuel rationing and all. It would soon be the pony and trap.

He reached the farm and saw two Luftwaffe officers waiting outside. They flagged him down and showed him the requisition form for the Morris. Before they drove it away, the officer asked if it had been checked for rats, the ones that squealed. He laughed as he left. Uncle Thomas was pale with rage and helplessness until Aunt Olive came to stand beside him and said, 'But you've still got the weaner so perhaps it's an honourable exchange. You haven't the petrol to run the blasted thing anyway.'

It didn't help, not really.

*

215

Hannah moved into Sylvia and Cheryl's rented house that very day, after she'd helped Uncle Thomas and Aunt Olive hide the valuables from the holiday cottage in the attic of the farmhouse. Clive, the conscientious objector, who had been stranded on Jersey and still shared his labours between the Andrews and the Charltons, harnessed the pony and trap and collected her mother, as well as the bits and pieces.

Clive was about to set off when he called, 'And you, Hannah. Do you need help? I can take your mother, and come back.'

She shook her head. 'I have my bike, Clive. Bet you wish you were back home.'

He shook his head. 'There are people I would miss.' He looked long and hard at her, and for the first time she realised he was a young man. Had he a woman, is that why he had stayed when he could have gone? And what was it like to say to your friends, no thank you, I would rather be disgraced than fight? She couldn't really be bothered with such questions, and turned away. Clive clicked the reins, her mother called, 'Goodbye, darling, and good luck with the job.'

Hannah waved them off, then cycled with her clothes in her backpack to the girls' cottage on Farmer Morton's land. She was due to start work at the nursing home on the early shift tomorrow, helping in the kitchens. To begin with she'd be washing up and preparing the vegetables for lunch.

It made her think of April, who sliced carrots at a speed of knots, and for a moment she ached for Combe Lodge but, as she cycled alongside the stream and over the bridge, she thought of bombs falling on London and Coventry and all the other cities.

She pulled in to let a German army lorry pass. The soldiers in the back waved. She waved in return, scared not to. At least the Germans weren't likely to bomb their own. So what was a bit of rationing, a bit of fear? That wouldn't kill her. She thought of Thomas's wireless. It was just as well she was moving out.

When she arrived at the house, Sylvia was at work as a nursing assistant at the same nursing home, and it was Cheryl who answered the front door. 'Come in quick, before my nettle tea gets cold. Someone told me it was good for my skin,' she said to Hannah. 'I dry it too, because I reckon I might make a smoke out of it. Why not? Tobacco's just dried leaves, after all.'

Hannah liked coming to the girls' house, because there was no sound of her mother coughing in the room they shared, and there were girls to talk to about Peter, who she was struggling to remember. It made her feel lost.

Cheryl stood to one side, drawing Hannah into the dark hall and hugging her. 'It'll be fun,' she said. She wore old slippers, socks over her stockings, two cardigans and smelt of sweat, but perhaps they all did because there was so little soap around. 'Put your bag down, then come into the kitchen, at least it's warm. I'm making paper chains ready for Christmas. You can help as you're an artist. Have you brought your paints?'

They walked to the kitchen. Hannah shook her head. 'They're at the farmhouse. I'll cycle back for them before it gets dark.'

'You've got your ration book, though?'

She nodded. Cheryl said, 'Off you go then and pick up the paints. We'll have tea when you come back. Make sure you bring your week's rations back with you and whatever else you can get hold of. I think we should have a party. Not tonight but tomorrow, after your first day at work. Go on, then.' Cheryl scooped a key off the table, and threw it to her. 'Hurry up. Bobby has brought us a rabbit, and it's in the pot, with carrots. I'll look like carrots, or a rabbit soon. Keep an eye on me ears, and let me know if they grow furry. He'll bring a bit of booze and cigarettes to the party too, you know what he's like. Fingers in pies, that lad.'

She waved Hannah off into the hall and shut the door. For a moment Hannah stared at it, then turned and headed for the front door, the key cold in her hand. Her mother would have made her a cup of tea first. As she went out, Sylvia came in, bundled in an old coat and two scarves. 'Off so soon, Hannah?'

Hannah explained. Sylvia raised her eyebrows. 'What's she like, for heaven's sake. I'll come with you to help. Wait a minute.'

She dragged Hannah on to the front path, before darting round the side of the house and re-emerging with her bike. 'It's best we hide them round the back, or they might get nicked.'

They rode two abreast along the road, but were flagged down by a two-man German patrol. Sylvia breathed, 'Damn.'

An elderly corporal stood there, his eyes cold. *'Verboten,'* he snapped, pointing to the two bikes.

Sylvia said, 'What?'

'Two abreast.'

Hannah said, 'What?'

The corporal glared, 'Fifty marks, now.'

The girls looked at one another. Hannah said, 'No money.'

He pointed to the bike. 'Bike.'

Sylvia said to Hannah. 'He wants the bike instead.'

Hannah said, 'But that's not fair.'

The private standing alongside the corporal said, 'You go to court, and big fine then. Too many cars. Road little.'

Hannah looked back. 'I don't think there are too many. There are none coming along and I don't think there's a rule about two abreast.'

Sylvia hissed. 'Shut up.'

The corporal looked at Hannah. 'Bike.' It was hers he pointed at now.

They took both bikes in the end, and cycled off. The girls walked back. In the kitchen Cheryl looked up. Sylvia explained. 'Well, have a cuppa instead, but it'll be Shanks's pony for you two from now on. But borrow mine when I'm not using it, which I will be tomorrow, so you'll both have to walk to the nursing home, or maybe the bus is running. Hey, your uncle must have another bike, surely, Hannah? Farmers have everything. Try him after work, why not?'

She was smoking a proper cigarette, and now handed the pack to the others, grinning. 'Take your coats off and have a smoke. Bobby's just popped in with some. We're having a party tomorrow, Sylv. We've decided. Bobby's friends are coming. Got to welcome our Hannah, haven't we?'

Chapter Fourteen

Next morning Hannah and Sylvia caught the bus, which ran infrequently, to the Elms Nursing Home. Sylvia had recommended her for the job, and as she stepped in through the back door she entered a world of clatter, and heat. The kitchens were full of steam from the washing in the laundry, and the cook was bustling, with a smile for her, and instructions on the washing up. 'Soda, I'm afraid, and hot as you can. We have to make sure everything is sparkling clean. There are pregnant and new mothers in the main house, and convalescents in the west wing. Hurry now, Hannah. You come highly recommended by Sylvia, and what a hard worker she is. I just hope you're of the same ilk.'

Hannah sighed. How like Aunt Olive this woman was: a nag. After half an hour her hands felt like raw meat. She said as much, and Mrs Amos dug her out some rubber gloves. 'Take care of them now, and put goose fat on your hands when you get home. I expected you to bring your own.'

After washing up the dishes there were the vegetables to chop. The carrots stained her hands orange. The leeks and onions made them smell, just adding to the awfulness. Somehow she kept up, and then it was lunch, and the plates were returned by Sylvia and two others, but with no leftovers. Hannah's stomach was rumbling as she piled them up for washing. When she was finished, Mrs Amos called her to the table. 'Come along, our turn.' It was breast of lamb stew and fatty, but Hannah was so hungry it didn't matter, and she refused to think of the dishes waiting for her.

Having eaten, she worked on until at last the shift was finished. Mrs Amos waved her off. 'Yes, you'll do. You need to speed up though, but otherwise the plates were clean, the vegetables cut. We'll make a deckhand of you one day.' She laughed. Hannah too, but even to her own ears it sounded false.

She rammed her hands into her coat pockets, to protect them from the cold. All she could think about was her sore feet, and sorer hands, as she and Sylvia travelled by bus to Haven Farm where they picked up potatoes, vegetables, and a cake her aunt had cooked. It was apple and honey, and Aunt Olive wrapped it in muslin. 'Here you are, girls, get this inside you with a cup of tea and you'll grow hairs on your chest.'

Hannah grimaced but Sylvia laughed. 'That's so kind.' She meant it. Hannah smiled, asked after her mother, and wondered if she could have the rest of her week's rations, to take to the house.

Aunt Olive was contrite. 'Of course, I didn't think. I know it's tricky these days.'

'I was just wondering, you see, Sylvia and I were stopped for riding abreast. They took our bikes. Do you have any to spare, or we'll be walking everywhere?'

Aunt Olive put her hands on her hips. 'Whatever next? Sometimes these Germans are reasonable and then one does something like that.'

'Never mind that, what about the bikes?' prompted Hannah, irritation soaring. Sylvia looked at her, her eyebrows raised in surprise, and said gently, 'I agree, Mrs Charlton, you never know where you are with them, but I suppose if they feel they're the conquerors, they'll think they can do anything.'

Hannah snapped. 'It's not just that they think it – they can.'

Aunt Olive flushed, and Uncle Thomas said from the doorway, 'There'll be no bikes for you, young lady, until you start treating your relatives with respect, and learn to say please. How often have I said this? Besides, my car's been requisitioned, so I'll need the only one we have.'

Hannah spun on her heel. 'Fine. Absolutely fine, and never ask me to cover for you and your pigs again, then. I don't remember a please back then.'

She strutted from the kitchen, with Sylvia running to catch her up, snatching at her arm. 'Hannah, they're your aunt and uncle. I don't think that was fair.'

'Oh, shut up, Sylvia. They're not the ones walking back, are they?'

They had reached the bridge when they heard the steady rattle of a tractor. Her uncle pulled in. 'I have the rations you left behind. If you girls want to get up on the bar at the back, I'll drop you off on my way to the field. It's the best I can do.'

Hannah looked up and hesitated but Sylvia said, 'That's really kind. Come on, Hannah.'

They climbed on the bar. Hannah said, 'He'll be going to check the sugar beet, so it's not that kind.'

Sylvia hung on as Thomas started the tractor. 'The sugar beet is over on the top road, he didn't have to come this way. Just be reasonable.'

Hannah shouted above the engine and the rattles. 'Thanks, Uncle Thomas. Sorry about earlier. Tell Aunt Olive, will you, please?'

He nodded. She shrugged. They'd always need extra food at the cottage, so Sylvia was right, it was daft to rub him up the wrong way. They went into a pothole and out again. She lost her train of thought, and began to think about the party. She hadn't been to one for ages, and had thought she was too tired. But perhaps not.

The party started quite early, at 7.30, because they were all working at the crack of dawn the next day. Bobby brought wine, which he had acquired, he said. Hannah thought of her uncle's cellar.

Cheryl had a gramophone, with jazz records, and some old-fashioned waltz music. Bobby's friends were fun. He, and they, reminded her of Sid. She sipped her wine and ate a slice of quiche. They had made two with the eggs her aunt had sent with her uncle. They had also used some awful Camembert, called Tramp's Foot because it was so high and strong, but it gave the quiche a kick.

Bobby and his friend David produced more bottles from a box they had put beside the table in the kitchen. It was red wine, and made Hannah feel happy, and free. David grabbed her as jazz came on. 'Come on, we can dance to this.' She put her wine down, and the cigarette she was smoking. 'I like cigarettes,' she said. 'I didn't think I would but they make me happy.'

David laughed and swung her round. 'Could be the wine that's doing that.'

She laughed along with him. 'It's a shame there's not more. But I know where there's some, just sitting on shelves in the dark, being miserable.'

He swung her again, and caught her, pulling her back against him. 'You're a cutie,' he murmured.

Someone was knocking on the door, but no one took any notice. Then there was further knocking, on the window. Cheryl shouted, 'Someone get that. Hannah, off you go.'

David groaned. 'You heard the boss, Hannah. Better do her bidding.' As she left for the front door he was working his way across to Bobby, holding his cigarette high in the air, to avoid the dancers.

There was another bout of knocking, this time back at the door. She opened it. 'Oh,' she said. It was the German corporal from yesterday, still in uniform. He held up a bottle of wine. There were three more Germans behind him. He said, 'I have wine, I hear music. Well, *we* hear music. *We* have wine. Perhaps we could join in with you as we are your neighbours.'

Cheryl came to the door 'What's going on?' she said, then, 'Oh.'

He addressed Cheryl. 'We have wine. We would like to meet you all, but we understand if you feel it is not to the liking. We do not force you. I know Bobby, if that would influence you.'

The corporal turned to Hannah. 'I did not know that you would be here.'

She said, 'I nearly wasn't. Your lot took our bikes because we couldn't pay fifty marks, and German soldiers took our house.' She walked away, back to the room.

Cheryl laughed. 'Come one, come all. We're all young, and there's some quiche.'

Hannah wound her way through the dancers, all of whom were Cheryl and Sylvia's friends. She felt alone amongst the music, chatter and laughter. Laughter and chatter that faded when the Germans entered but quickly grew loud again when the bottles were raised high and Bobby welcomed the four of them. She longed for Peter, and moved to a corner, where she sat on the arm of the sofa. What was Peter doing? What about Bee, was she flying? Did they still have that child, and had they moved her into her bedroom?

She suddenly felt tired, sipping from a glass of wine which was on the small table. It probably wasn't hers. She examined it. No, it wasn't, there was lipstick on the rim. Well, who cared? She downed it in one. A German stood in front of her. 'Perhaps you would dance?' he asked.

It was the corporal. Well why not?

It was a waltz. He held her closely, but not too close. David was dancing with Sylvia. 'My name is Hans Ader. Yours is . . .?'

She said, 'My name is Hannah Miller, but you must know that because suddenly my cottage was requisitioned, and my uncle's car was also, and I have absolutely no bike. All a bit of a coincidence, don't you think?'

Hans flushed. 'These things happen. Sometimes they cannot be stopped, only minimised. My men talk, they hear of the . . . "rat". There is talk of pigs. Deals are done. Forgive me. I did the best I could.'

She looked up at him. His eyes were so very, very blue, but he looked tired, and strained. He repeated, 'Forgive me. I minimised what could have happened.'

His arm was strong around her, her hand in his felt safe just as her head began to spin. She rested her head on his shoulder. 'Yes,' she said. 'Thank you for the deal. Yes, thank you.'

He said, 'It was wrong to take the bikes. I knew nothing of that. A trick. It is not as it should be. We are not all such people. It is stealing.'

They danced all evening, and she felt less alone,

and resented it when Bobby came along and cut in. 'I hear from David that you're a cutie,' he said. 'It's sad that such a lovely girl hasn't more lovely wine to drink, but a little bird tells me that there are some bottles sitting on shelves. Well, that's a lucky person, that is. He must have done something very good to have that little bit of bounty at times like these.'

He swung Hannah round, and she squealed, almost overbalancing. Bobby held her close. 'We ought to invite him and his wine to the next party,' Bobby laughed.

She saw Hans staring, and could see the jealousy in his eyes. Bobby pulled her towards him, doing some sort of a shuffle with her. 'I'll give him an invite,' he crooned in her ear.

She shook her head. 'If you think my uncle would like a party, you've another think coming, and his wine and beer will stay right where it is, for just as long as he and his mates can make it last.'

'Ah ha, so where would a farmer put it, to be safe? It will be found, and requisitioned, you bet your sweet life.'

She shook her head, then wished she hadn't because she felt so dizzy. ''Course it won't, he's hidden it really well under the barn.' Bobby swung her away again, and this time it was Hans who caught her and swept her away, into some sort of a waltz, and she was glad, because she felt as though she'd been on a swing too long and just wanted to sit still.

*

The next day, when she and Sylvia returned from their shift, having had to walk as no bus arrived, they found their bicycles propped up inside the garden wall. There was a note in Hannah's shopping basket.

I try to be helpful so here are your bikes. Please may I see you this afternoon? I think you say your shift finishes at one, and you are home at two. A walk perhaps? Just wave from your path, towards my house. It is my day to be free.

She waved from the path, though Sylvia said, 'You can't, it will make you a Jerry-bag, a horizontal collaborator.'

'Don't be stupid, I'm just going for a walk, and anyway, we are all collaborators, I suppose, to have them to our party, Sylvia. Don't be so stuffy. I think I could love him, really really love him.'

She waited outside the house. She hoped it wouldn't matter to Hans that she was in her work clothes but there was no time to change. It didn't. He kissed her, as he had kissed her the evening before, and she knew that she could be happy again, and why not. Her life was screaming past, empty and lonely, so – yes, why the hell not?

Chapter Fifteen

**15 December
Combe Lodge**

Cissie was waiting with Bryony at the bus stop, wriggling and pacing. 'What if she's missed it? What if a bomb got her before she left, what if Timmo wouldn't let her come after all? Oh, Bee, she's got to, she said she could stay for a lot of days.'

'Hang on, why ever wouldn't Timmo let your sister come?'

Cissie stopped, peering ahead, tapping her foot. 'Because she's really really busy with her customers at Christmas, silly.'

'Oh, of course.' Bee looked for the bus. What on earth had this child seen? What was Wendy, her sister, thinking of?

'There it is, there, look.'

The bus trundled into view. There was a *toot-tiddly-toot* of its horn. 'It's Dan!' shrieked Cissie. 'That's so good, cos he'll 'ave looked after her.'

The bus pulled up. Wendy teetered off the bus, her peroxided hair up in a pleat, a red hat perched on top, high heels, bare legs red from the cold, tight red shirt beneath a red tartan jacket, and red lipstick. Suddenly Cissie was quiet, as though she felt uncertain. Wendy looked at her, then at Bryony. Dan called, 'Have a good time, lass, and Merry Christmas.'

Wendy turned, and waved to him. 'You look after that wife of yours. Myrtle will like whatever you give her for Christmas, you mark me words.'

Cissie whispered, 'She's like a princess, isn't she, Bee?'

Bryony stroked Cissie's hair, which they'd put in plaits for the occasion. 'Indeed she is.' She looked down at her paint- and oil-spotted overalls. Well, she had to leave the house, all the aircraft and the *Sunflower* as shipshape as possible when she left for the ATA on 3 January. She hadn't told Cissie she was going yet. Somehow she hadn't been able to, as the Blitz hung over them all like a cloud.

Even in Exeter, Exmouth and Teighnmouth bombs had fallen, and people had died, not in any great numbers of course, because they were only lone bombers but nonetheless . . . She'd been travelling on the bus to Exeter to receive some physiotherapy in November, when more bombs had fallen. They were said to be landmines but whatever they were, the shudder, the noise, the fear had been Dunkirk all over again.

Wendy waved the bus on its way, and only then did she turn again to Cissie. It was as though they were both shy. Bryony stepped forward, taking Wendy's little case. 'Wendy, I can't tell you how pleased we are you could spare the time.' She stopped. 'I mean, it's a long way, sometimes the trains are so slow, but we were worried, Cissie especially, what with the bombs. She so longed to see you, to have you safe for a while, though the bombs have fallen here, so is it safe . . .' She petered out. 'I mean, we're just so glad you're here.' She gestured in the direction of Combe Lodge.

Wendy said, 'Kind of you to 'ave me, but more kind to 'ave Celia. I mean Cissie. I'm still getting used to the name, but I like it. I just feels dreadful to think she was with that old witch and I didn't know.' She squatted down, her high heels digging into the verge. 'Give us a kiss, darling. I've missed you.'

At that, Cissie flew into her arms, and the shyness was broken as Wendy lifted her, laughing, and kissing her all over her face and hair, then blowing on her neck until Cissie screamed for her to stop. Wendy set her down, and Bryony led the way along the road, finally reaching the drive, as the two sisters chattered and laughed together.

'Here it is,' Cissie said, pointing to the house at the end of the drive. 'Oh, I forgot, 'ow's Mrs Morton and the sweet shop?'

'Oh, poor old dear snuffed it when the bombs hit our area. Did us a good turn, though, because the dump we were kipping in 'as gone too. Collapsed when they cleared the street, taking the rats with it. Timmo found me and another couple of girls a nice flat. Bit more up west, better sort of punt . . .' She stopped. 'Better sort of neighbour, I mean. I were sorry 'bout Mrs Morton, nice old trout but with the rationing she weren't making much anyway.'

As they walked up the gravel drive, Bryony winced as she saw the stones ripping the heels of Wendy's shoes. 'Please, let's go on the lawn. I'll try and repair your heels when we get to the house. I'm afraid Cissie will want you to help her stick the paper chains she and the new evacuees cut and painted in the week. Cissie was given the afternoon off school to meet you, and the others will be back at three.'

The December cold was getting even to her, and she wasn't the one with bare legs, but instead wore her usual flying boots and a pair of Eddie's socks. She gestured Cissie and Wendy towards a gap in the flower beds and on to the grass. Wendy had a gravy seam running up each leg. Somehow it endeared Wendy to Bryony more than anything else. This girl was so damn 'game'.

April was finishing the baked potatoes, topping them with a little cheese and herbs, and vegetables from the garden. They ate their meal quickly, the talk desultory, and when they finished, Wendy pulled out her cigarettes. 'Who's for a fag?'

Cissie looked down at the table, sliding a glance at Bryony, and then April, flushing. Wendy saw. 'What's the matter?' She was tapping the cigarette on the table and fishing for a match.

April said firmly, 'Nothing's the matter. We're delighted you are here, so you must just relax and enjoy yourself.'

Here, in the warmth of the kitchen. Wendy's heavy make-up was glistening. She wiped her face with her hankerchief, revealing a bruise.

Cissie said, 'Has Timmo 'it you again? You must tell 'im to stop.'

Wendy laughed at her, her hand to her face. ''Course not. He don't hit me. I walked into a door.' Her hand was trembling. 'Now, don't you go worrying yourself, Cissie.'

Cissie stared at her, then smiled. 'I 'spect that in a new flat you forget where the doors are. But in a while you'll be used to it.'

Wendy smiled, so gently that Bryony had to swallow. 'I dare say I will,' Wendy said, leaning back in the chair. April found an ashtray in the bottom of the dresser. She didn't allow smoking in the house, but Bryony could tell from the grim set of her shoulders that from today, and until Wendy left, that rule would be broken.

A little after three, the other evacuees came whooping down the drive, to be met by Cissie who dragged them into the kitchen to meet her sister. 'We started the paper chains,' Cissie told them.

Frankie, from London, stuck his hands in his pockets. 'Bet you ain't left any for us. Miss gave us some glue from the store cupboard.' He looked cross.

Betty shouldered him to one side. 'Open your

eyes, you daft dollop. Look at the strips there, all in a pile, so course they haven't, have they, Sol?'

The three children and Cissie clambered on to the seats that April, Wendy and Bryony vacated, with April pulling a stool forward for Sol, who was only seven. April waved Wendy and Bryony away. 'Go and have a look around the gardens, get some fresh air, then pop in on Catherine and Anne while I find a biscuit for this lot.'

Bryony found Wendy some wellingtons and insisted on socks, and then they were ready.

Cissie called after them, 'Tell her about the babies, Bee.'

As they set off along the path, Bryony explained her and Eric's role in the birth of Eric junior.

Wendy laughed. 'Bet that was enough to put you off for life, weren't it?'

Bryony hesitated. 'It made me think it would have to be someone special, to go through it. What about you?'

Wendy stopped by the Anderson shelter, and fished out her cigarettes again. 'What about me, eh? There are ways to stop it, before or after it's started.'

She looked inexpressively sad. She waved the packet towards Bryony, who shook her head. 'No vices then, Bryony?' Wendy asked.

'Call me Bee, everyone does. Flying's my vice, and April's cakes, and I have a temper. I blamed someone for something, shouted at him when he'd done me a favour. He doesn't telephone much any more. Well, I suppose he can't, he's at sea, but even when he's ashore . . .'

Wendy held her cigarette between her teeth, and struck a match. She inhaled deeply. 'Ah, Eric?'

'No, Adam. He's on the armed trawlers. He phones from time to time, but it's not the same. He's cold, sort of careful, too polite.' She stopped, shrugged. 'Life's difficult.'

Wendy's laugh was harsh. 'Bet your bleedin' life it is.' She inhaled again, lifting her head and exhaling. In the daylight, under another layer of powder applied when the children had arrived, the bruise could be a trick of the light. She pointed to the turf on top of the Anderson shelter. 'Good idea, let's 'ope you don't 'ave to use it.' She studied her cigarette, in no hurry to move on.

'Who's going to look after all them kids when you've gone to the – what do you call it?'

'The ATA. I'll deliver planes from the factories to the maintenance units where they'll be armed. Then another ferry pilot will fly them to the airfield. Unless we're taking trainers up to Scotland, of . . .'

Wendy had crossed her arms, nodding, but Bee knew she was not really listening, because she broke in: 'So what'll happen to the kids? Will they go somewhere else, another bloody witch?' She stared at Bryony, her jaw jutting out. She dropped the stub of her cigarette and ground it into the path.

Bryony linked her arm in the girl's. 'They will stay here with April. I will be back every thirteen days for two days. My uncle Eddie will be back for two days' leave every thirteen days, and then there's Eric. He does odd jobs, but is a friend. They'll be well cared for, trust me. No one is taking them anywhere they don't want to go.'

She pointed towards the lawn. 'Let me show you the herbaceous beds. Did Cissie tell you she helped me deadhead the roses in October, when I was one-handed?'

Wendy shook her head. 'Who's this uncle, then? Is he one of them "uncles" or is he kosher?' Her voice was intense, her hand gripping Bryony's arm.

'Oh, he was my dad's best friend. He and I run the airline together – in peacetime, that is. He and April are a couple. You'll like him. He's just gone back so should be home for Christmas. Why not come down again, and meet him?'

'Maybe, it depends. Got a lot of bombs to get through between now and then.'

Bryony was pointing to the magnolia. 'This is a picture in the spring. Come then too and let Cissie show it to you.'

Wendy stopped at the edge of the flower bed, looking at the magnolia tree. 'Strange, ain't it, how them come up year after year, no matter what bloody mess we're making of the world. You forget that in London. Yes, there are parks, but not this.' She looked along the length of the bed. 'Cissie helps, does she?'

'Oh yes, and don't worry, we're keeping her safe for you, Wendy, never fear. She loves the aircraft too, and is longing for peace so she can come in one with us, and when she is old enough, with your permission, she'd like to learn to fly.'

Even as she said it, Bryony wondered how she would ever be able to send the child she loved back to a world inhabited by Timmo and punters. What hope would there be for her?

They began walking again, still arm in arm. Wendy said, 'You see, Bee, life is difficult, like we said. Mum died. I worked at this and that, but Cissie went hungry and I weren't there in the day. I met Timmo and he said I could make enough, you know, having punters. I can afford her now, but it ain't no life for her.'

They were in the herb garden. The small box hedge was perfectly trimmed, for wielding the shears was good exercise for Bryony's arm and she wasn't about to tell anyone how much it still hurt. She nodded to herself. She said, 'Yes, it is difficult, I really can't imagine.'

'Oh, you shut your eyes and think of England, that's what you say, isn't it?'

They both laughed, but without amusement. Bryony said, 'Come here and stay with us. Just leave London. It's dangerous, you can get work somewhere, or we'll keep you, and just think how Cissie would love it.'

'Yeah. Be nice, but Timmo wouldn't 'ave it, you see. He'd come and get me, or hurt Cissie, or something. He's all right, don't get me wrong, and he looks after me, don't let anyone hurt me.'

'Anyone else, you mean.' Bryony couldn't hold back the words.

'Look, I made me bed but I want a better world for our Celia. I have been saving, Bryony. Me money's wiv a solicitor, who's one of me punters.' She laughed. 'Yes, some of 'em are right smarty pants – when they have 'em on, of course.' The two women laughed, and it was real this time.

'Come on, let's go through here, and we'll work our way round to the cottage,' Bryony said.

Wendy held her back. 'No, wait, listen to me, Bee. She's to have the money if anything happens to me. It's all legal. I'll be adding to it.' She pressed a letter into Bryony's hand. 'If I dies . . .' She trailed off. Then looked at Bryony, her eyes shining. 'Use the money, keep her straight, give her a chance for a good life.'

She was gripping Bryony's hands. 'You goin' to promise me?'

Bryony gripped hers back. 'Listen, give it up, come here, now. Who knows where the bombs will fall, it could be on us, but they won't go on for ever, and here won't be as bad as London, and we'll all be together.'

'You ain't listening. I can't just up and leave, it don't work like that. I'll bring trouble to your door if I do.'

Smoke was rising above the trees. Anne and Catherine had put damp wood on their fire. Cissie and Wendy could have the cottage after the war. Yes, that would be an idea.

Bryony said, 'No, no, I'm not having that. I'll talk to Eric, ask him to make sure his Home Guard mates keep an eye on the place. Police Constable Heath will keep his ear to the ground. You *can* live here, please. Please.'

Wendy smiled at her, her eyes tired. She nodded. 'Keep the letter, I'll try to find a way. But keep that letter safe, and make me the promise.'

Bryony did and as they walked towards the cottage she tried to imagine yet again the life this woman lived, this sister who had assumed the responsibility of caring for Cissie. A woman who Bryony knew would not come unless she was totally sure it would not endanger Cissie, who was probably the only person in the world that she loved. Cissie, who had changed her name from Celia to forget who she had been. How that act must have bitten deep, but still Wendy adjusted, and now Celia was Cissie to Wendy, when this remarkable young woman remembered.

They walked on, Bryony tucking away the letter in her pocket. After they had held the babies, one called Eric, one called Bryony, they returned to the Lodge, and while Wendy rested and the children glued the paper chains, Bryony put the letter in the writing desk. She then shared the conversation with April who said, 'Something must be done.'

'But what? We don't understand Wendy's world, April. We must just try to let her know we are always here, and will do whatever we can. It's up to her, she's made that clear.'

That evening, they all ate around the kitchen table, Eric too. He had been felling a dead tree for logs, and when the children groaned at rabbit again, Eric promised them fish at the weekend. They were talking about the bones when the telephone rang in the hall.

Eric answered it and called through, 'Wendy, it's a man called Timmo for you.'

She smiled, but Cissie held on to her hand. 'Don't go back. That's what he wants, so don't.'

Frankie was staring at her. Bryony said, 'Remember what I said, Wendy.'

Wendy disengaged her hand, and stroked Cissie's cheek. 'You're such a worryguts. It's war, there are things we all got to do. Look at you kids, 'aving to leave your mums and dads. Right little heroes, you are.'

She dropped her napkin on the table. April said, 'There's a bedroom next to Bee's now Cissie is up in the attic rooms with the other children. Timmo can come here. He might like that.'

Wendy was already in the hall, though, and while the children talked, Eric looked from April to Bryony. 'What's going on?'

'Nothing,' they said together, straining to hear the conversation. Wendy was saying, 'He's a friend of Bee's, is all.' Then a pause. 'What, tomorrow? Yes, I know what will happen. Yes, I'll be there, 'course I will. Yes, I know.'

As they heard the click of the receiver being

replaced, April launched into a long story about the latest WI meeting while Eric looked confused. As Wendy sat down, Cissie turned to her, shouting, 'You're going back. You came all this way, and now you're going back. You don't love me.' She rushed from the room.

Wendy slumped in her chair, looking helplessly at Bryony, who said, 'I'll talk to her. Give me a moment.'

The children fell silent, looking from one to another, and then Frankie said, 'What's got 'er rag?'

Betty snapped, 'How do I know?'

Bryony ran through the hall after Cissie. As she passed the telephone it rang. She snatched it up. If it was Timmo . . .

'Bee, it's me, Adam, I need to—'

She said, 'Not now, Adam. April, it's Adam.' She put the receiver down and tore off.

April shouted, 'Eric's taking it, I need to stay with the children. Give him my love, Eric.'

As Bryony pounded up the stairs she wanted to turn back, or at least call, 'Mine too,' But there was no time because she heard Cissie crying – well, more than that, she was sobbing – as she pounded ahead of Bryony up the second flight of stairs. Bryony heard the door to the attic bedroom slam. She tore along the landing, reached the door, knocked and entered.

Cissie was kicking the chest of drawers, and sobbing. Bryony grabbed her from behind, holding her in a hug. 'She loves you. That's why she has to go back. She's the most wonderful sister in the world, and I just wish I had one like that. She loves you.'

The struggling child slowly stopped. 'She's leaving.'

Bryony knelt, and turned her around. 'It's a difficult time, and we all have to do what is necessary. You, me, Frank, Betty, Adam, Eric, Uncle Eddie. Everyone. So, what you have to do is dry your tears, and get yourself back down those stairs and enjoy every moment before your sister goes. She says she will try to come at Christmas. *Try*, Cissie. It's not a promise to come, but a promise to try.'

'But there are bombs falling. She's not safe in London,' Cissie wailed.

'Frankie, Betty and Sol's parents also have those bombs. We all have to be brave, don't we?'

Adam joined Gilchrist in the pub. He shrugged. 'I started straight away like you said. "Bee, I need to . . ." But she rushed off. "Not now," she said. Not now? Cissie was having a tantrum or something, or so Eric said. Eric, for Pete's sake. He might as well bloody live there. So, the script didn't work, Geordie, and I didn't stay on the line for long, there was no point.'

Mick called from the bar, 'From the look on that face I reckon it's definitely a chaser too, so go to your secret store, bartender, and don't spare the horses. But at least it's not heartbreak, I reckon our laddie is cross.'

Adam was more than cross, he wanted to punch a hole in the wall. How the hell was he going to get through to her, when there was never any time? The *High Ground* was off again, and then Bee was joining the ATA, bloody Eric had said, coming on the line while his mum dashed about dealing with the other kids. It was total bedlam.

'Eric said, just before the pips went, that there was going to be a party on the second of January to see her off to the ATA.'

Mick came over, bearing three pints. 'Perfect. Did you have a chance to tell her you might be coming to Pompey? Did you tell any of them? Chasers are on the bar.' He flicked a nod at Gilchrist. 'Chasers are on the bar, I said.'

Mick repeated, 'Did you tell them?'

'Why, when we might not? What's the point – and to tell *him*?'

Gilchrist came back with the chasers. 'For pity's sake, lad, faint heart never won fair lady.'

The sailors around cheered. Gilchrist bowed. Someone said, 'Sir's name's Rabbie Burns under that weak and wobbly exterior.'

Geordie laughed along with them, but for Adam there was just a damn great furious ache. He sipped his beer. No, he hadn't told them he could be coming into Portsmouth, because it had been a possibility before, and never happened. And why bother? It was

Eric, Eric, and more Eric, so he'd only be a spare part, obviously, watching the rest of them have a good time.

'Someone change his face,' Mick groaned, 'or he'll explode.'

Adam laughed, 'No, I'm fine. It'll be OK.'

A seaman called from the doorway. 'Aye, 'course it will. We could all be dead tomorrow.'

Another cheer greeted this, and Adam nodded. *The Dream of Islay* had gone down on the flank of the convoy, along with two merchantmen. He pulled himself together. He was tired, that was all, and he missed Bee with an ache that was deeper than he'd ever thought possible, and now it was mixed with a fury that made him want to pace the wharf until he was tired enough to sleep.

He sat straight. 'Next round on me, lads.'

He was alive. So was she. It was enough and what's more, Cobham said the men were having a great time sorting out his love life. There were bets on it, so best not to sort it too soon. Well, bugger that for a game of marbles, but on the other hand he wondered how much Geordie had on it working out. He asked on the walk back to *High Ground*. Geordie wouldn't say.

Chapter Sixteen

25 December 1940
Jersey

Hannah woke, and stretched. It was Christmas Day, the early morning light was oozing round the edge of the blackout. 'I'll have to sort that, I suppose,' she said aloud.

Hans tightened his arm around her. 'Together we will do it.' His voice was drowsy from sleep. She rolled over, and touched his face. *'Liebchen,'* he murmured.

She said against his naked chest, 'I don't usually do this.'

'Yes, and neither do I. It is fast to be here, in bed with you, but it is war. I have yesterday and today as leave. But how long I remain in Jersey, I do not know. We grab, I think you say, at love.'

He tightened his hold, kissing her hair, cheeks, lips. There was silence in the house, until a yelp from the landing reminded her that Rosie needed to go out, but she'd just have to wait a bit longer. Her aunt had come with the dog a few days ago, because her mother wasn't feeling very well, and

Rosie would whine so. Usually Sylvia, an early riser, put her out but she and Cheryl were spending Christmas with Bobby and his mates. Bobby had secured a goose for their lunch. Perhaps she and Hans would go, perhaps they wouldn't. They might stay here in bed, all day.

Rosie yelped again. Hannah moaned as Hans ran his hands over her body. Rosie barked, Hans opened his eyes, and laughed. 'We need to see to your dog or there will be things to clean up.'

She smiled, but it was hard. Damned dog.

Hans eased himself into a sitting position, and pulled her up too. Hanging on the door was his uniform. Somehow it was a shock. It looked dangerous, frightening, foreign. She turned away from it. A woman had pushed her off the pavement yesterday, and shouted, 'Jerry-bag.'

But she wasn't. She just loved Hans, not the German army. Hans, and it wouldn't have mattered what army he belonged to. The minute he had danced with her at the party it was so nice. He was kind, a gentleman and had said, that first night, 'I think, for some reason, I could love you. It is not what I expected from this war. It is not what I expected when I was at your relative's farm. It is not what I might have wanted, but within minutes of this evening, Miss Miller, I think I could love you.'

He was twenty-two. She was eighteen. If there hadn't been a war no one would have called her a Jerry-bag. It wasn't fair. She reached for her clothes, putting on layers against the chill. He dressed too, in his ordinary trousers and a sweater. As they went downstairs Rosie met them halfway, her tail wagging. 'Oh, stop it, Rosie. Get out of the way, you're such a nuisance,' Hannah muttered, pushing past her.

Hans followed. 'You British and your dogs.'

'At least we've kept her. A lot have had them killed, worrying they couldn't feed them because of the invasion, or because they were evacuating and leaving them. It was terrible.'

In the hall, Hans stopped, swinging round. 'It is war.' His voice was wary, and there was an edge to it.

She nodded, and together they walked to the kitchen and she said, 'Of course, and they didn't have to go, they could have stayed, like me, and seen what you were all really like. Just people.'

'Indeed.'

They walked to the kitchen now. She put out Rosie, and made Hans toast with bread he had brought. For lunch they were to have some steak, again something he had brought. She had vegetables from Haven Farm. As she spread her toast with butter, again from him, he said, 'And now you go to your uncle to take your presents?'

Hannah nodded, her stomach clenching. 'You would wish me to come too?'

She shook her head. 'It will be quicker if I go alone.' How could she tell him that her uncle had said he'd run him through with a pitchfork if he set one foot on his property? She could still hear the edge in Hans's voice when he'd said, 'It is war.'

'They would not like us to eat with them?

Again she shook her head. 'They're old, they like a quiet time.'

He said, 'It is not just that, *Liebchen*. It is who I am, but never fear, because soon we will win this war and they will be proud to have a protector, and people will not dare to call you Jerry-bag, for to do so will mean that they will be dealt with.'

He stretched out his hand, and grasped hers. 'Trust me, I have seen that things change when people see that we are their rulers. They do not dare to behave in this way, so they will settle, they will be proud to know me. And you? You will be a great painter, I will see to that.'

His eyes held hers. He kissed her hand, pressing his lips hard against her skin. 'I love you. It is so strange. I have not ever felt this before. For this reason I am glad that war began.'

She left him in the house and walked along the road to Haven Farm. It was the road that Bee followed when she flew in, and Hannah imagined herself high up, looking down. She swung her arms. It would serve Bryony right to have to face having a sister who was powerful. Then they'd all have to come to her, Hannah Miller, for help. The bag over her shoulder wasn't heavy. She had painted small

249

pictures for her relatives for their presents before her uncle had told her that she and her boyfriend would not be welcome.

She had shouted, 'So, it's all right to be nice to the man I've come to love when he needs diverting from your damned pig.'

He had shouted back, as he cleared the ditch alongside the road, 'You're always bloody in love, but not with them, surely not with them. They're the enemy.'

'He's not a them. He's a man. You don't know him at all.'

'Aye lass, and you don't know him either, not really, but now you'll be known for ever as a Jerry-bag.'

Hannah stopped swinging her arms now, and crossed them, her shoulders slumping. She'd replied, 'But he'll be with me for ever and in charge of you.'

She'd stalked on and his words had followed her. 'He's a soldier, and we're in a war. He might not live, they might lose, then what?'

She was nearly at the farm, and hesitated. Why was she even bothering?

She forced herself to walk up the path. The lavender had been cut down for the winter, the pinks too. She knocked, and waited. Her Aunt Olive answered. Her smile didn't quite reach her eyes, but she hugged Hannah. Her aunt smelt of lavender, as usual, but that was because she collected the flowers, dried them, and placed them into bags for her drawers and it impregnated her clothes.

'Come in.' She was almost whispering. 'Your mother is in the front room.'

She led the way, and opened the door. Hannah's mother was sitting in the easy chair near the roaring inglenook, knitting. She looked up. 'Hannah darling, Happy Christmas. Come in, do.' She held out her hand to Hannah, coughing. Hannah kissed her. Her mother didn't stroke her hair as usual, or hold her close, but picked up her knitting again, mouthing: knit one, purl one.

Aunt Olive stood in the doorway and said nothing.

Hannah withdrew her gifts from the bag. Her aunt approached and unwrapped the one Hannah handed to her. It was a painting of the headland near their farm, above the cove. She said, 'Hannah, how kind, lovely. You had such promise.'

Hannah muttered, 'I still have, I'm not dead.'

Her mother was unwrapping hers. 'Very nice, dear.' It was of Combe Lodge. 'It all seems such a long time ago, a sunny time.' She coughed again as she placed the painting down on the side table to the left of her chair, and continued knitting. The logs were spitting in the grate as silence fell. Her mother slowly put down her knitting and looked at her daughter. Her aunt stood motionless. The front door opened, slamming back against the wall.

Hannah said, 'When Germany wins the war, Hans said I would become a great painter with his help, and I would have thought you'd be more grateful for your presents. What's the matter with you both, you're even crosser than usual and it's not fair.'

Aunt Olive sighed. 'Your uncle's back, and you probably know his wine and beer were stolen from the cellar yesterday. We're all, well, we're all . . .'

Her uncle stood in the front-room doorway now. Aunt Olive held out Hannah's present to him. He ignored it. 'I'm not having her in the house, I told you women I wasn't when I found me wine gone. Go on, sling your hook, Hannah Miller. You're the only one who knew about the wine, apart from the three of us, so what have you got to say about that?' He didn't give her a chance to reply, but powered on. 'Nothing? But what can you say? Take your poxy present with you and sling your hook. We've all had enough of you and your tricky ways, even your mother.'

Hannah heard the words. His booze was stolen? But why was that her fault? 'I didn't take it,' she said.

'I don't want to hear it.'

She looked to her mother for support, but saw only the same distance in her eyes that was in her aunt's.

She reached out. 'Mum, it wasn't me. Why would I? I even helped him with the pig.'

Her uncle said, 'Go back to your soldier, the one who will win the war and make you a great painter. Go on, you've chosen your side, and it isn't us, but that's no surprise to me if there's some gain in it for you.'

Aunt Olive came across and took her arm. 'Come along, Hannah. He'll cool down, but best to leave it for now.'

She escorted her to the door. Hannah said, 'It wasn't me.'

'Maybe not, but perhaps it's the company you keep, and the things you tell them. You're a silly girl, Hannah, and not safe to have around.'

Hannah called, 'I'll come and see you, Mum.'

'If you like, dear, but not for a while.'

The tone of her mother's voice was chilling. She walked down the path, and somehow struggled back along the road, to Hans.

She told him what had happened. He said, 'Bobby must have heard you at the party, just as I heard you. You do say too much, Hannah. It is something you must guard against. I am a German, you are British, so must I also be careful what I say?' There was a real question in his voice.

She almost blurted out the actual truth about the wireless but just in time she caught the words and bit them back. What was the point? Though it might be some news that he would value, it would be further proof that she was indeed loose-tongued.

He kissed her. 'My little love, this will pass and I am proud of you because I have just given you the chance to betray him further, and you have not. There is, after all, much you could say about rats who squeal.' He smiled.

She said nothing for a while, because war was so

difficult, and it really wasn't a game, but a frightening new world. Her uncle had been right, she didn't really know this man, or was it the world in which he lived she didn't know? She asked, 'Can you get the wine back?'

He shook his head. 'Bicycles are one thing but I cannot touch this man, as he will supply others in the German army with produce from France. Don't worry, Hannah. Remember that one day your uncle will be pleased to know you.'

He held and kissed her. Her family faded.

Combe Lodge was shrouded in mist on Christmas morning and though Wendy Jenkins had telephoned the previous day to say that she couldn't come after all, she had promised absolutely to come for a week in the spring, so spirits were high.

These spirits rose even further at teatime when Uncle Eddie telephoned, promising he would be home for the party on New Year's Day. He had decided that he and Bryony could travel to Hatfield together on the 2nd in order to get her settled in her lodgings, so she could report for duty, bright as a button, on 3 January. He had then asked to talk to April, who had shut the kitchen door and spoken quietly into the receiver.

Cissie had muttered, 'Grown-ups and their secrets.'

Bryony leaned forward. 'What secrets?'

Cissie shook her head, as Frankie giggled. 'I don't know.'

Bryony wasn't sure if she believed her.

As December drew to a close, the Blitz of London rose to new heights and as it did so, Cissie, Frank, Betty and Sol grew quieter, worried about their families, and why wouldn't they be? On New Year's Day, however, with the farewell party imminent, the children decided to cheer up, and grinned when Catherine and Anne came knocking on the back door and came in with the chill.

'Shut the door, please,' April said. 'You're bringing in the breeze and letting out the heat. Now what can we do for you two girls?'

Catherine said to the children sitting around the table, colouring some triangular flags, 'We need some pram-pushers urgently, aged from seven to nine. We need free time to help convert the rations for Bee's farewell party into something magnificent.'

Anne said, 'We even have badges. The prams are parked outside with Bee and Eric junior champing at the bit.'

As the children put on coats, hats and scarves the front doorbell rang. April let in Alan Baker and Bill Thomas, Catherine and Anne's husbands who had arrived last night, one from Catterick and one from Aldershot. They carried through a wooden box with mackerel from Barry Maudsley and soft cheese from the farm down the road for which they'd swapped eggs and a chicken.

'Black market?' Alan queried.

'Now, now,' Bryony wagged her finger. 'We've

been saving our stamps, and together they almost covered it. The chicken swap did the rest, and it's for the good of everyone at the party.'

Bryony looked around the kitchen. Cissie waved as she ushered the others out in front of her. She'd assumed the role of older sister by dint of being the longest-serving evacuee, as Eddie put it. Bryony called, 'Hey, Cissie. I have asked Frankie to organise the team to paste and plant the flags you've made along the drive. Are you up to be leader, or would you like a break?'

Cissie smiled, and nodded. ''Course I'm the leader. We'll be back when we've finished the pram pushing.' She started to follow them, then turned and ran to Bryony. 'I'm going miss you. Everyone goes – Eddie, Adam, and now you. But it's you I will miss most of all.'

'I'll always come home.'

Cissie stepped back, shaking her head and not meeting her gaze. 'No one can say that any more.'

The food was prepared by five, and Bryony was sneaking a piece of mackerel pâté on toast when April peered around the kitchen door. 'Hey, madam. Out of those overalls.' She tapped her watch. 'We said we'd start early so people wouldn't be traipsing home too late. There's work to get to in the morning for most of them.'

'In a minute. I need to eat something, and I can just sling that dress of Mum's on, you know, the woollen one. The children have planted the flags.'

April entered. 'Yes, I know, on pea sticks. I hope you get them back for planting up the peas. You know how these things get forgotten.' Over her arm she had a dress, deep blue satin.

Bryony finished the toast, and wiped the crumbs from around her mouth. 'I'll try to remember to pull them out before I leave, but if not . . .'

April nodded. 'I will. Now, forget your mother's old dress, this is for you. Catherine and Anne knocked it up between them, using a ball gown I found in my wardrobe. I'd forgotten I had it.'

Bryony looked from the dress to April. 'Hey, what's wrong with you? I don't need a special dress.'

April shook her head. 'Indeed you do, it's your farewell party. You must pack it and take it with you. After all, you'll probably be dashing into the London clubs night after night like the rest of the ATA girls who seem to burn the candle at both ends.'

Bryony reached for the dress, sighing. 'Oh I can't be bothered, you know me, April. Leave it and wear it yourself, I'll just drag the woollen one on. But thank them, please.'

April kept the dress well clear of her grasp. 'Wash those hands, if you don't mind, and go upstairs. I'd like to see you as a smarty pants, just for once in your young, and my old, life. We have the same size feet, so here are some blue shoes. They're not the same shade, but close enough. Come on, the girls have worked hard on this. It's their gift to you, so accept with good grace, if you don't mind. We might find that Cissie thinks you're just as much a princess as Wendy.' She grinned.

Eddie, who had arrived at three in the afternoon, now walked into the kitchen. 'What's up, why aren't you two changed? The children have helped me open the doors between the dining and sitting rooms, the long table is set up on the south wall, the gramophone opposite. Eric is going to operate that. Chairs are ranged around the room so we just need the food on tables. Chop chop, get changed, for heaven's sake. Bee, before I forget, I double-checked your billet before I left and Pearl has you on the floor below mine. I suggest we get the train at about midday.'

Bryony dried her hands. She didn't want to think of leaving here. But she would be back, of course she would. She said, 'What if I don't pass the training? What if it's been too long since I've flown?'

Eddie was standing by the door into the hall, gesturing again and again, waving her through. 'Don't be absurd, you can fly in your sleep, so none of that. Will you please, please go and change and I'll organise the team. But actually, before you go, just check the children, would you, and make a fuss. They're upstairs with clean nails, brushed hair, and their best clothes, courtesy of the vicar's trunk, where he keeps a million "could be useful" things. He will be here this evening at six o'clock prompt. You know how he hates it when people are late for church, and he thinks we all feel the same.'

By the time Bryony had talked to the children in their attic room, and admired their outfits, and retied Cissie's bows because the child felt they were not quite right, it was almost 5.45.

Eddie appeared, panting, in the doorway. 'Bee, what are you doing? Look in, I said, not faff about. I'm not having you wearing those overalls. Look at that dress you've just slung on Cissie's bed, it's probably creased to buggery and looking as though it's been dragged through a hedge backwards.'

The children gasped and Frankie said, 'You swore.'

Eddie picked up the dress. 'Sorry about that, gang, but just look at it. What do you think? Should we iron it again?'

Cissie cocked her head, and crossed her arms, examining it. 'Hang it up, run your hairdryer over it, Bee. The creases will drop out . . . And hurry up, or—'

Eddie hushed her. She coloured, and put her hand to her mouth. She said, 'Or the others will be here. Wendy blows away creases with the 'air dryer.' Frankie looked bored, Betty was interested. Sol was picking his nose.

'Use your handkerchief,' Bryony said. He sighed and did.

Eddie checked his watch. Bryony realised he'd been doing it for the last few hours.

'Calm down, it's just a party.'

Eric was in the doorway now, checking his watch too. 'Come on, Bee, do as the man says.'

As she went down the stairs, April was starting up them, and stopped, retracing her steps. 'It's bad luck to cross on the stairs. I don't want anything to go wrong.'

Bryony said, 'You're not to worry. I will be fine, as Eddie said, I'm experienced, and haven't had many accidents.'

April looked confused, then her face cleared. 'Oh that. Yes, of course.'

She too checked her watch. 'Hurry up, Bee, this is ridiculous. Your guests will be here long before you appear.'

Bryony slipped into the bath, regretting that she could only run it to the depth of the two inches suggested in aid of the war effort. A wallow would be a good thing with all this tension around the place. But if it was Cissie who was going off to the ATA she'd probably be as jumpy. She washed her hair and as she emerged from the bathroom in her dressing gown, the music began downstairs as the doorbell rang. It was the vicar, so it must be six o' clock exactly. She shrugged; the others would cope.

In the bedroom she pulled down the blackout blind and drew the curtains, before turning on the light. She had hung the dress on a hanger, and hooked it over the wardrobe door and now ran the hairdryer up and down it, almost drowning out the music and the arrival of the villagers. She was grateful for the pause, for being left alone to say goodbye to her room, and, in her heart, to her family – all of them. But not Adam, of course, not the one she missed so badly that her heart felt pummelled most of the time.

He must have forgotten she was leaving tomorrow, for there had been no telephone call, but perhaps he was still at sea. He could have written before he embarked, though. Didn't he care that accidents did happen? That the weather just might close down and the aircraft fly into a hill, or the pilot become lost, or run out of petrol or make an error, or run into a Nazi bomber, because the ATA aircraft were not armed, and neither did they have radios.

She turned the hairdryer on to her hair now until it was dry. There was a knock on the door. It was April. 'I'll put your hair up,' she told her.

'I can do it.' April looked strange, perhaps because she and Eddie would both now be flying. 'I'll be there to keep an eye on Eddie,' she said, as April brushed and put up her hair, taking the hairpins from her mouth and tucking in the pleat.

'I know you will, but you need to be downstairs.' She put in the final pin, and fetched the dress. 'Come on, put this on. Climb into it or you'll muss your hair, let's have you like a princess, Bee, just for me.'

'Calm down. What's the matter with everyone?'

She heard a motorbike coming up the drive, but

April was pulling up her zip and talking about how she'd keep an eye on Cissie, and wouldn't it be wonderful if Wendy came in the spring? Bee thought about the motorbike. The only person she knew with one, was Sid. Surely not, not tonight.

'You haven't ordered anything from Sid, have you? Is that what everyone's so nervous about? Because if you have, I don't want it.'

April said, 'Don't be absurd, we have more sense. There, look at yourself in the mirror.'

Bryony did, and just stared. The woman in the reflection didn't look like her. She was too pretty and elegant. April insisted, 'On with the shoes and no moaning. Pretty shoes are always uncomfortable. Let's give our friends a really good vision to keep with them when you clamber back into flying boots and Lord knows what.'

The shoes were indeed uncomfortable. She tried walking in them, and she could, no trouble. April sighed with relief. 'Perfect. Now, I'm going down, so you follow in two minutes.'

'Oh no, you don't. If you get everyone to sing some daft song, I will never forgive you.'

April laughed. 'Oh come, give us a bit of fun. Two minutes, remember.' She left.

Bryony moved to the dressing table. She opened the top drawer and her hand closed over her father's watch. She picked it up, and held it against her cheek remembering her father, his kindness, his strength, his confidence in her, his pride in his pretty

Hannah. 'I love you, Daddy. I'll go and fetch Hannah, I promise. I haven't forgotten.'

She replaced it, and closed the drawer. She checked her own watch. Thirty seconds to go. She waited, and then opened the door on to the landing, and there was Adam standing at the top of the stairs, in a weary-looking uniform. He looked at her, and his colour rose. She stared, and at last found her voice. 'You? How?'

'The motorbike.' He said. 'We came into Pompey. Geordie Gilchrist has a friend who owns one. I was pillion. The blokes on *High Ground* pooled their petrol ration. It was a bit bloody cold but worth it. I telephoned here a while ago, when we nipped into a port, and cooked this up with Mum, though I expect the whole shower came in on the act.'

She came to him, wiped a smear of dirt from his cheek, and the goggle marks. 'Cold and dirty,' she said.

He grabbed her hand. 'That doesn't matter. What does is you. Am I too late? Have you and Eric . . .' He stopped. 'Well, I don't care, because I'm telling you it would be a mistake. I don't think you'd be happy, and I know I wouldn't.'

Bee tried to pull her hand free. 'What on earth are you talking about? If you mean, have we fetched Hannah, well, of course not. That's for you and me, if you can bear the thought.'

He kept a hold of her hand. His was freezing. 'Oh, leave the wretched girl out of it. You. You and Eric,

I mean. I'm such a fool. I shrugged you off. You fell. I would have taken you to play darts when you came home from hospital, not to Frank's restaurant.'

She listened, weaving through the chaos of his words, wanting to believe what she thought he was saying, but was he?

Eddie's shout came from the bottom of the stairs, 'For goodness' sake, get it out, boy.'

Another shout reached them: 'I didn't drive you this far, in this weather, with a hangover, for this messing about and neither did the blokes pool their— '

Adam shook his head. 'Oh shut up,' he bawled at them. He turned back to Bryony, and now he grabbed her other hand. 'Oh God, Bee, can't you see how much I love you? I couldn't see it, not really, but then you were so hurt, and I knew you were my everything. Can't you see that?'

She watched his face, the anxiety, the tiredness, the love which she had longed to see for so long, and felt a great peace – not creep over her, but deluge her in one great shower. At last. It was there in his eyes, in his beautiful face, in the tightening of his hands. 'I can see it,' she whispered. 'Can you see that you are *my* everything?'

He pulled her to him, enfolding her in his arms, kissing her hair, her eyes, her mouth, saying against it, 'I love you. I always have, and I always will.' He smelt of the sea and his uniform was cold from the ride over.

'At last,' she heard April say, from her bedroom door.

Cissie stood with her, warning, 'Mind her bloody dress, you'll crease it and she'll 'ave to 'air-dry it again.'

April, Bee and Adam shouted, 'Language!'

Frankie, Sol and Betty laughed, crowding out from April's bedroom too. 'We had to keep the secret, it wasn't 'alf hard,' shouted Sol. Eric stood on the bend of the stairs. 'Do come on, you two. The gramophone's set up for a waltz, a smoochie one, just to embarrass us all. She's my mate, Adam, and I love her, but not like that. She's good for a darts match is all.'

Adam's mouth was on hers again, and then they were both laughing, and she pulled away, whispering, 'We just have to stay safe, to make it worth all their efforts.'

'Indeed we do.' He turned, his arm still around her, pressing her to him, and together they went down the stairs to meet their friends, who were waiting there, singing 'Here comes the bride'.

She groaned. He said, turning and whispering, 'You will marry me, won't you? It will make Old Davy so happy.'

She leaned further into him, if that was possible. 'Oh yes, I most certainly will, and we can call our business Adam and Eve's Apple. Do you remember?'

He did, but no one else knew what they found so amusing. They danced together and it was as she had known it would be. He kissed her hair, and tightened his grip on her hand. 'All the time I've wasted,' he murmured.

She shook her head and pressed close. 'No, it's not been wasted, we've been together all these years, and know all there is to know about one another. It means I can trust you with my life, because I know that you will always catch me if I fall, and you know I will catch you.'

He nodded. 'And that you're a good darts player, so you can always be on my team.'

She slapped him, just as Eddie cut in on their dance. 'A twirl round the floor, Bee, if you please, before those shoes of yours become agony and you have to put your boots back on – but not the overalls, please. Not tonight.'

She felt almost as safe in Eddie's arms as she had in Adam's and said, 'You've always caught me too, Eddie.'

Somehow he knew what she meant, and smiled down at her. 'You've done your fair share of catching, my love.'

It made her think of Hannah. She'd dropped her sister, but would gather her up, one day soon, and then she'd be free to live her life. Well, for as long as anyone had one in this day and age.

Chapter Seventeen

Bryony and Eddie took the bus to the station the next morning, 2 January. Dan looked tired, and rattled the gears a few times, but that was not to be wondered at. He and Myrtle had danced until the bitter end of a party that should have finished at ten so the children could get to bed. It had in fact wound up with 'Auld Lang Syne' as the clock struck two and by rights they should all have turned into pumpkins.

As they trundled around a bend, Bryony removed her flying gauntlets and examined her engagement ring, which was in fact a curtain ring April had found on the spur of the moment. On it, Cissie had stuck a lump of plasticine for a jewel. Eddie nudged her. 'Are you happy?'

She nudged him back. 'Do you have to ask?'

He slipped his arm around her shoulder. 'Dearest Bee.'

She leaned into him, her head aching, wishing that she had not had so much of the scrumpy cider Barry Maudsley had liberated from the back room of his barn, the rest still stored until they achieved victory. She said, 'So, we can end this nonsense about you and April? She'll move into your room, and you'll marry the woman.'

He laughed, then winced. 'In that order? The scrumpy was not a good idea, it really wasn't.'

She shook her head. 'In whatever order you wish.'

'But there are the children, so it should be done properly, surely?'

'Then get on and marry her but until you do, remember that they're up in the attic and you're one floor down. Don't be so stodgy.'

Eddie groaned as they screeched to a halt at the station. They had to run for the train, giving their hangovers no quarter.

Once they arrived at Hatfield they caught a taxi to Number 12, Harlow Street. Mrs Bates, the plump landlady, met them at the door. She was wearing a floral pinny, her white hair curled into a tight perm. 'Just in time, my dears, I have a soft cheese and sage casserole ready. I'm so pleased to meet you at last, young Bryony. Your Uncle Eddie seems to mention you at least once in every conversation. Leave your bags there, the two of you. Eat first, sleep next. It's nine o'clock and time all good men and women were thinking of bed.

'Ah,' Eddie said. 'But there aren't many of those Goody Two-Shoes here, are there, Pearl?'

She slapped his arm and led the way into the dining room. Two young women sat opposite one another in silence, as though waiting in a state of animated grace, thought Bryony.

Mrs Bates clapped her hands. The two girls jumped, Bryony winced, and beside her Eddie groaned. 'Now, Bryony dear, these two are here for the training course too. Joyce and Trixie, here we have Miss Bryony Miller, and First Officer Eddie Standing. The girls stood.

Eddie laughed. 'No, no, sit down, it's not like that in the ATA.'

Bryony slipped on to a seat next to Joyce. Eddie sat alongside Trixie. Mrs Bates dished up. The talk was stilted. Trixie's hands trembled as she held her knife and fork. 'I'm nervous,' she whispered as she climbed the stairs behind Bryony.

'My stomach is inhabited by butterflies,' Bryony replied, and it was. She had hardly been able to eat. They took turns in the freezing bathroom, but then, everywhere was freezing. It was winter, after all. She shared a room with Trixie, who tossed and turned as Bryony crept into bed, having had a brisk and shallow bath.

'You're engaged?' Trixie murmured from the depths of the eiderdown she had pulled up around her ears.

'Yes.'

'Interesting ring.'

'Yes, spur of the moment, but I've waited a long time and it was all we could rustle up.'

'The plasticine might detach. You must keep it if it does, or your luck will ebb. Someone has obviously made it with love.'

Mrs Bates had put a hot-water bottle into her bed but Bryony wore socks as well, and burrowed down. 'Goodnight, I'll tell you the story as we cycle to the aerodrome tomorrow.'

Alone at last with her memories of Adam, her fiancé, her love, she walked down the stairs of Combe Lodge again, his arm around her, her friends grouped in the hall, his friend Geordie Gilchrist grinning up at her.

After she and Adam had danced their third waltz Geordie had broken in, sweeping her off into some sort of jig which had nothing to do with the rhythm being played. He had told her of Adam's misery, of the crews plotting because of it, the bets being taken. He had won a tenner, and thanked her kindly for accepting the daft lump. Then he'd twirled her round, laughing.

He told of the phone calls the 'pirates' had scripted when Adam had still not been able to speak his heart, of Adam's suspicion of Eric, whom he thought the better man, until finally they had received orders to head for Portsmouth, and even Cobham, the skipper, had said, 'If we had bunting, we would be flying it, so don't muck it up this time, or Lord knows what we'll do with you.'

Bryony lay in bed, feeling his arms around her as they danced, kissing him farewell at her bedroom door, wishing that, for once, the house was not full of children, for how could they spend time alone while Cissie and the other three lay in their beds above them?

She remembered he had held her so tight in her doorway that she had wished they need never be apart again. They had made promises to be careful, to live, to meet when they could. He had left, riding pillion behind Geordie at five in the morning, after three hours' kip. As the motorbike skidded down the frost-rimed drive, Adam had turned and waved, his face alive with joy.

He had telephoned on his arrival in Portsmouth, just before embarkation, to wish her well, to make her promise to take no risks, to swear that on their next mutual leave, even if it was only two days, they would use the winter weather to fetch Hannah. It would clear the decks, he said, and added that Eric had sworn that the *Sunflower* would eat up the nautical miles and that he would also come in order to stay with the *Sunflower*, at anchor, while they rowed to the cove.

Her love knew no bounds.

The girls cycled on Mrs Bates's bicycles to the aerodrome. The other two were also experienced pilots, but nonetheless they were put through their paces day after day, extracting themselves from a spin, exploring the mysteries of meteorology, and how pressure in the Arctic could transform the sky in Britain from blue equanimity to a dark tantrum, and of the counterpressure that would restore equilibrium.

'Sounds like someone's mum,' Bryony murmured.

The instructor smiled. 'Indeed.'

They tapped out Morse code, but quite why they never knew. The stars became signposts to safety, rather than merely things of beauty. The sun and moon followed a logical sequence and Bryony thought of the woman on the train who had sung 'By the light of the silvery moon'.

He, her beloved, would be under the same sky, navigating by the stars, checking the position of the sun and moon. She had thought she had known all about him, but no, she realised she would never know all. But at least they were gaining similar skills.

The trainees showed their ability to make tight, or loose and whatever you like turns, freezing in the open Tiger Moth cockpits, basting their faces with goose grease in the mornings and evenings to minimise the dryness. They were sent on cross-country flights, following maps torn from school atlases, and taking fixes from the contours of the countryside, always returning safely, even through, or over, weather that descended as though at the click of a switch. It always made Bryony think of the Arctic misbehaving like a naughty child and sending the consequences their way.

On the last cross-country, as she followed the contours of the Cotswold hills, Cissie's plasticine came off, nudging her palm inside her gauntlet. Once back at Mrs Bates's she placed it on cotton wool, inside a matchbox, and never flew without it in her pocket.

Towards the end of the six weeks they were to train to fly Harvards, it was announced in the last of their briefing sessions in the classroom. The Harvard was a single-engine trainer, which they knew they would like because of the covered cockpit. The instructor said, however, with the familiar touch of sadism that the women felt lurked beneath his surface, that he preferred the Tiger Moth, 'Because it needs a positive and sure hand and weeds out the inept.'

'Kills them, you mean,' Bryony muttered.

He looked past Trixie, Joyce, Barbara and Gloria, the other girls who had survived the rigours of the training, and the men who were part of the contingent. 'Ah, yes, you again, Cadet Miller, so, into the Harvard, if you will. Let's see you put it through its paces.' He paused. 'No, on second thoughts, into the Tiger Moth with you, Cadet Miller, just so that I am totally convinced that you are not inept. I feel it's suitably freezing and we'll have a series of tight turns, then gain height, fall into a spin, get yourself out, and land.'

'I did that three weeks ago, sir.'

'And now you'll do it again.'

She made her way to the Tiger, did the preflight checks, climbed into the cockpit, dragging on her helmet, taking out the pot of cream from her pocket, and lathering her face.

The instructor bellowed, 'What in God's name are you doing?'

'Goose grease. I know you didn't mention it in your list of instructions, but I am on the way to looking like a wrinkled walnut, and if I forget, no one will want to kiss me.' She knew that would shut him up. It did, but the mechanic laughed as he swung the propeller, and said, 'That'll teach him, but he's one of the best, Bee.'

She knew he was, and that he was determined he would give the pupils on his watch their best chance of survival. She stopped at right angles to the take-off path, completed the cockpit drill, checked the sky, the runway, left and right. She turned into the wind, opened the throttle, easing the control column forward to lift the tail. She climbed gently, loving the solitude, determined to bring Cissie into this world one day, knowing the girl's heart would soar as hers did. Who knew, perhaps she would become a pilot for Adam and Eve's Apple. She laughed out loud, climbing, always climbing, looking for bombers because you never knew, looking for other trainers, because you never knew.

She spun, flew out of it, did all that he who must be obeyed had demanded, and before landing, she buzzed the runway. The instructor was the only one who didn't duck. He would make her pay for it, but it was worth it.

That evening, her punishment was to buy a round in the pub for all the trainees, and for the instructor, who had a beer and a chaser. The chaser was brought forth by the publican as though it was gold dust, which in these days of rationing it probably was. Barbara, Trixie, Joyce and Bryony shared a table. As Barbara tutted at the rings of beer on the table, Trixie said, 'Tiger Moths are as cold as Hades.'

'Wrong geographical area,' Joyce said, in her dry voice. 'But at least it's hot down there. I vote we take a picnic and head down for a while, shall we?'

Barbara threw her arm around Joyce. 'Let's wait for summer. I'm not ready to choose between heaven and hell quite yet awhile and, besides, I haven't the energy to be naughty enough to earn Hades.'

The instructor came up behind Bryony and said quietly, 'No one talks about death in my hearing, because I forbid all accidents, all errors, all mechanical failures. Is that quite clear?' He moved back to his group of Ancient and Tattered Airmen which tonight included Eddie, who raised his tankard to Bryony. Cards tonight at Mrs Bates's, he mouthed. She nodded, glancing at the blackboard tucked in the corner near the fireplace. On it was a list of names. RAF and ATA pilots who would never go home. There were three new names written in glistening white chalk on the black of the board. Yes, she thought, it was quite clear.

In two days they had qualified to fly Class 1 aircraft, which meant that the single-engine trainers, Magisters, Harvards and the old warhorse, the Tiger Moth, were to be their world, until they were ready for their Class 2 training. The next day they took the train into London, where Austin Reed measured them for their uniforms. While the others returned to their billet to sleep, Bryony took the Tube through a battered and bruised London, towards the East End. She kept Wendy's address in her hand, following the *A–Z* map.

She found the flat in a street of converted terraced houses. One end had been bombed, but not Number 6. She followed a man up the steps. He knocked. The door was opened by a slim woman smoking a Woodbine. He said, 'I'm here for Sandra.'

She nodded him in, then stared at Bryony, who said, 'I'm Celia's foster mother. I thought perhaps I would take her sister Wendy out for tea to bring her up to date. I didn't know if I could speak—'

The woman raised her hand. 'She's working. You can find her at the end of the street, on the corner. She won't have time for tea.'

Bryony tried to smile, but failed. 'Thank you.'

She hurried down the steps and on to the street, then along to the left, looking ahead, not to either side where young women loitered, leaning back against the walls in short skirts and no coat, some picking at their nails, some just staring into space when the pedestrian was a woman. She dug her hands into her pockets. At the end of the road she saw Wendy, also leaning back against the brick wall, her skirt short, her knees red with cold. Her top was low cut, her skin mottled. Smoke from her cigarette trailed up past her face. There was a dark bruise on her neck.

Bryony approached. Around Wendy's left ankle was a gold chain. It might just as well have been a manacle, Bryony thought. A man approached from the opposite direction. Wendy eased from the wall, 'Hello darling,' she said. The man brushed past. Wendy shrugged, and looked to her right, at Bryony, who smiled. 'Thought I'd take you for tea. I've just been measured for my uniform.'

'Bee.' Wendy coloured. She threw her cigarette to the pavement, ground it to nothing, and crossed her arms. She shivered. Bryony went right up to her, hugged her, held her close, anything to keep this woman warm even if it was only for a moment.

A man in a camel overcoat, the collar turned up, a woollen scarf floating in the breeze, came out of a doorway a few houses along. He strolled to them, and stood, waiting. Wendy stiffened, and stepped free of Bryony's arms. The man said, 'If you want women, you go to Osmond Street. Wendy is for respectable folk.'

Bryony stared at him. 'Timmo?'

He shot a look at Wendy and then back at Bryony, looking her up and down. 'Says who?'

'Says me,' said Bryony. 'I'm Celia's foster mother. I've come to take Wendy for tea.'

Wendy was shaking her head. 'Not going, Timmo, course I'm not.'

Timmo took Wendy by the arm and pulled her to stand by him, smiling at Bryony. 'No, 'course she ain't.'

Bryony wanted to barge him, stamp on him, do whatever she could to him, then rip off his coat and put it around Wendy, and drag her back to Devon. She did none of these things, because it was not her decision to make, and if she challenged this load of rubbish it was not she who would suffer, but Wendy. She dug her hands deep into her pockets, feeling the one-pound note that would have paid for a slap up tea, and more. She palmed it, and held out her hand to Wendy. 'I'll tell Celia you are well. I'll see her soon, when I have leave. She's growing. She and the other three have painted the attic corridor with palm trees and blue pools. She thinks of you every day. Shake on it, Wendy. I promise we'll see you again soon.'

Wendy did, and smiled when she felt the one-pound note. She pocketed it while Bryony held Timmo's gaze, saying, 'I'm sorry to disrupt your working day, Timmo.'

She turned on her heel, and walked back down the street, and just before she turned right she snatched a look back. Timmo was wrenching the pound note from Wendy's pocket, before cuffing her. Bryony swallowed, and pushed it out of her mind, bringing Adam in, seeing his wholesome smile, the strength of his arms, the goodness in his eyes. There was nothing she could do here. Not yet, anyway.

The next morning the cadets, now qualified, entered the common room in which ATA men and women lounged. Some played cards, some read the paper, some wrote letters. A male Second Officer was standing on his head. 'Yoga,' whispered Joyce.

Bryony smiled at Eddie as he sauntered across to the hatch, which was opening. She, Joyce and Trixie followed. Their chits were to take Tiger Moths to Lossiemouth from a factory near Cowley. Eddie was the taxi pilot for today. They'd get the train back from Lossiemouth.

They clambered aboard the Anson taxi, with five others. Eddie landed at Cowley. 'Break a leg,' he called. 'See you this evening.'

Four of them disembarked: the terrible trio, which is what Eddie had named Bryony, Trixie and Joyce, plus Second Officer Melvin Morton who had come from South Africa to help the war effort. 'I'm leading today, then you'll know the way. Use these maps to follow the route as well.'

He gave them the familiar school atlas pages.

'It's a well-oiled machine, I don't think, honey pie, when school atlas maps are the best they can do,' Trixie said, heading towards the Tigers, pocketing her map.

'Sarcasm doesn't become you,' Joyce muttered.

Bryony laughed, happy to be doing her job, and even happier to be flying to Scotland because, once there, she would telephone April to see if Adam had also telephoned home, which was the plan they had arrived at. She would meet him at the time and place he gave April, if only for a few minutes, or perhaps even an hour. Every second was precious, because who knew if . . .

She shut her mind to 'if'. It's what Eddie had advised. Tomorrow was a mystery, the next hour too, he'd told her last night. 'You are breathing at this moment. Make it enough.'

In the cockpit she lathered her face with goose grease and they took off, one after the other, like goslings following Mother Morton, clawing for height, up into the grey. Visibility was just enough, the cold intense. Melvin was ahead, driving through the industrial haze over the Midlands and on and on northwards.

Keeping the map folded at the right section on her lap, Bryony followed their route, leaning over, seeing moorland. The gaggle closed up as the rain began, and she peered ahead and around as visibility decreased. Her fingers ached with the cold, her face was numb, Adam's ring dug into her finger. It made him feel close, just as the matchbox did. Where was Wendy? Still standing out in the rain?

She had telephoned Cissie at Combe Lodge, and lied, saying they had met for tea and Wendy was so looking forward to the spring, when she would come. Even here in the cold and damp, Bryony's shoulders tensed, because she had decided that somehow she would bring this woman out of the world in which she existed, away from Timmo and the streets. She forced herself to relax, and wiped her goggles free of precipitation.

The land disappeared as they flew on through cloud. She could only see Joyce's Tiger now. Her petrol gauge was low, so it would be the same for everyone. They needed to land, but where? And were there hills ahead of them? Her mind began to race. She leaned over and looked below – nothing but mist, or was it cloud? What should she do? She stared ahead, but Trixie had gone, sucked up by the mist. She was alone, she was lost, she was going to die and never see Adam again.

She needed to think, but couldn't.

She looked below again, and there as the mist rolled and tumbled a window opened, and moorland reappeared. She peered ahead again, searching for Trixie, then down at the window again, and decided she had to take it, whether the others had or not, as the petrol gauge had sunk to the bottom of the glass. Steadily and slowly she took the window, knowing what was below, but not ahead. She was through the window and there were the others, leading down to an RAF airfield. Her hands in her gauntlets were slippery with sweat. She landed after Trixie and, stiff with cold, taxied to the parking ramp.

She marked the airfield on the map, and clambered out, almost staggering to the mess for tea, alongside Trixie and Joyce, while Melvin whistled, his hands in his pockets, his goggles on his forehead. 'I do so hate cloud and mist,' he said. 'Such a bloody nuisance. One wonders if one is going to have to wriggle down to terra firma more by touch than anything else, only to find oneself staring up the backside of a rampant stag, when one would so much rather have a civilised cuppa. Heigh-ho.'

His hands were rock steady as he drank his tea and swapped news with an RAF pilot officer. Bryony shook so much she slopped her tea into her saucer, and so did the other two. They smiled at one another. 'Heigh-ho,' muttered Bryony.

They took off again within seconds, it seemed, up into the mist, flying over it this time, having been assured by the pilot officer that according to the forecast it would clear any minute now. It did and eventually Melvin slackened speed, dropped his nose, and they landed at Lossiemouth.

She begged the use of a telephone, as did the others, letting boyfriends and Melvin's wife know that all was well. April had not heard from Adam, but somehow it didn't matter too much. 'How was it, darling?' April asked.

'Wonderful,' Bryony said. 'No problems, straightforward, the heather was a lovely sight. Bit cold, perhaps.' She mentioned nothing of her fear, her panic, her indecision. As she replaced the receiver and listened to Trixie telling her fiancé, Brian, another pilot officer in the RAF, that it had been a breeze, not a thing to worry about, she smiled tiredly. One didn't plant distress on relatives; it would be bad enough for them if one day they received the call that told them it had not actually been a breeze, and no one was coming home again.

Until then, everything was fine, no problem, easy-peasy.

Melvin was ferrying a Tiger on to another destination but would get the train down tomorrow. The girls, however, took the overnight train to London. There were no seats. They sat on the corridor floor, leaning against one another, cold, hungry and thirsty.

They arrived in London in the early morning, and took the train to Hatfield. As they queued for their chits, which decreed Scotland again, they were told that they must rely on their map reading, because Melvin had flown into a hill. Bryony nodded when told she would lead the goslings, beating aside the shock and the sadness, just as they were all doing. They left the common room, meeting no one's eyes. Bryony used the map from the atlas. The weather was clear all the way and she wept for Melvin, and his wife, and she thought that probably the others did the same, but when they landed to refuel, again no one said a word. Just shook out their hair as they removed their helmets and sniffed the wind. 'An easterly,' said Trixie. 'Lossiemouth might be clear too, you never know.'

The others nodded, their parachutes heavy as they lugged them on their shoulders. Somewhere a sheep was baaing. In the mess they watched the pilot officer strolling towards them as they sipped their cups of tea with rock-steady hands. He said, 'Bad show, he was a good sort.' He swung away.

They, too, nodded, and this time on the train they

found seats, but not together, and slept like the dead because there was nothing more to be said, though there was a heaviness in their hearts, which Bryony felt would never go.

At the end of the week, Melvin's name was on the pub blackboard. Eddie put his arm around her. 'It happens. We go on. It's war.'

She said. 'You must be careful.' That was all, and then she joined the girls in a game of dominoes, thinking of Cissie, whose reading and sums were in line with everyone else's now. It was all you could do, in wartime.

Chapter Eighteen

Late February 1941
Jersey

Hannah cycled to the nursing home, checking her watch as she seemed to soar over the bridge and then took the left-hand turn. She pushed harder on the pedals, because she'd be late, and that would set off Mrs Amos again, and perhaps Sister Maria would hear. It could mean the sack this time.

The wind was behind her as she turned the corner, and she pushed harder on the pedals, tearing past walls and bare hedges careful to keep on the right-hand side of the road, as the German authorities dictated. She checked her watch again as she swept into the drive, powering for the back door. She parked her bike in the shed. Well, she was almost on time. It was twelve minutes past six, and why the patients had to have breakfast at that ungodly hour, no one could tell her, beyond the fact that there were babies who needed feeding. Well, why couldn't they be trained to wait?

It was warm and steamy in the kitchen and Mrs Amos was stirring milk into the porridge. The milk was a gift from Uncle Thomas's farm. The cook, her hair in a net, laid the huge spoon on a plate at the side of the range and snatched a look at Hannah. 'Are those stockings I see beneath your socks, girl? It's as well your mother . . .' She stopped, tutted and shook her head. 'You're late, again.'

Hannah pulled a face as she hung her mackintosh on the peg on the back of the door, and the scarf she had inherited from her mother. Silly old fool, what did she know about anything? Yes, she was wearing stockings, and that was because Hans liked to watch her put them on, and why shouldn't a girl-friend accept a gift from the man she loved? A man who was worth twice as much as any of the men she had so far known, and what the hell did it matter if he had been born in Munich and had different beliefs? And how dare this mere cook bring up her mother.

'Hurry up then, Hannah, and help me plate up the porridge. You can see I've set the trays ready, though that should be your job. You'll need to hurry, we've a lot to do because the scullery girl is down with this chest that's going round. We had two new babies last night and I'm popping up to see them soon, why not come?'

Hannah put on the shoes she kept in her locker, picked up one of the huge trays and stood at the range while Mrs Amos ladled in the porridge. There was not even one lump, and Hannah wondered how she managed it. Back at the cottage the only one who produced lumpless porridge was Sylvia, but now she had gone it was up to Hannah, and she just couldn't get it right. Hans didn't mind but Cheryl just picked out the best bits.

At least Rosie, being a dog, made no complaints and gobbled anything that was put in her bowl, as long as it wasn't Hans who gave it to her. The dog would have to go, because her hackles rose whenever he came near and it was embarrassing.

Mrs Amos said, 'Come on, what are you staring at, it's only porridge and won't bite. It'll be cold before you get it upstairs at this rate.'

Hannah's focus returned to the kitchen, and she backed out through the swing doors and up the stairs, straining under the weight of the tray. Her back ached, the chilblains on her big toes itched and she didn't feel well. What's more, she hated having to serve these women who looked at her as though she was something they'd found under their shoe.

She lugged the tray into Rose Ward and placed it on the end of the long table that stretched down the centre of the room. Some women had not yet had their children, and two in the corner were in early labour, judging from the way they were wincing, and bending over the beds. One of the women who had born twins two days ago called, 'How are you doing, Hannah? I was so sorry to hear about your mother. Not much of a welcome to your New Year.'

Hannah swallowed.

Sandra, lying like Lady Muck in the bed by the

window, said loud enough for Hannah to hear, 'I expect the poor woman was stressed out by her daughter's carrying on.'

Hannah continued to lay out the porridge bowls, with a spoon at the side of each. She heard Sylvia's voice, loud and clear from the ward entrance. 'Sandra, that's quite enough of that. Have some compassion. We don't choose who we love.'

Hannah kept her eyes on the table until she had finished laying up. Sylvia was working hard to become a fully fledged nurse, though whether the wartime training, under occupation, would ever be validated was another matter. Hannah whispered as she left, 'Thank you.'

Sylvia just said, 'Tulip Ward is waiting for their food, Hannah.' Her voice was totally neutral as it always was now, as though Hannah was a stranger. It had been like that since Hans had moved into the cottage full-time to share Hannah's bedroom, and Sigmund had moved in to share Cheryl's. Sylvia had moved out on Christmas Day night after the doctor had knocked on the door. 'Hannah, your mother has had a stroke. She left written instructions that if she became ill she was to remain at Haven Farm and not be hospitalised. Sylvia – Thomas and Olive Charlton have asked if it would it be possible for you to move in to help with the nursing?'

'What about me?' Hannah had asked, dragging on her coat. 'I should come.'

The doctor had looked at her, with a look that

was close to Sylvia's neutral expression. 'Would you like to nurse your mother, then?'

'Well, not nurse. I don't know enough. But I want to see her, of course I do.'

Doctor Clements had merely nodded and returned to his car, taking the two girls to Haven Farm.

When her mother had died a few days later, Sylvia had not returned. Now she lodged in Hannah's empty bedroom at the farmhouse.

Hannah leaned the tray against the wall by the double doors of Rose Ward, and hurried down to collect the other breakfasts. The routine was always the same, and she could do it in her sleep. They had more old people in an annexe now, and the matron, Sister Maria, had suggested last week that Hannah might like to introduce a painting class. She hadn't been sure, but Sister Maria had hinted that perhaps there would be a bit of money in it. The elderly weren't sure either, it transpired, after she had visited them one afternoon. Sister Maria had said it would help if she didn't wear lipstick, and face powder, because no one but Jerry-bags could acquire it.

She had also suggested she take it off for her mother's funeral, too, which she had done, because the term Jerry-bag had hurt. Couldn't people see that she was a girl who had lost her mother and was now an orphan? It wasn't her fault that other people didn't know how kind Hans was, how well he kissed, how much he liked her pictures, how he had held her when she returned from Haven Farm with the image of her mother, who no longer looked alive, filling her mind.

He had insisted he would come with her the next day to visit, but her uncle had refused him admittance, on her mother's express orders when she had briefly regained consciousness. That was the trouble with people, they only saw the uniform, not the man.

Mrs Amos called from the kitchen as Hannah hurried down the stairs, 'Come along, Hannah. The breakfasts are getting cold.'

'We need someone else to help,' Hannah said, running down the corridor, and lifting the tray.

'No we don't, you just need to get a move on,' Mrs Amos snapped, and Hannah parroted her words to the cook's back.

Mrs Amos was scraping the bottom of the pan and Hannah grimaced. 'It's not burnt is it, Mrs Amos? You know I hate burnt porridge.'

'Get a move on, Hannah, or there will be none for you, burnt or not. I'll take the last tray, and follow you up.'

Hannah turned on her heel and led the way, with Mrs Amos too close behind. As they turned the corner the older woman's tray nudged her. 'Hey,' Hannah called.

'Well, hurry up, girl.' Mrs Amos was panting, but she'd had the cold that was going round, and her chest was still bad. Hannah put on a spurt and almost ran into Tulip Ward, slapping down the tray and then placing the bowls of porridge on the table, thinking of Hans's hands on her this morning as she had slipped on her stockings and eased the loop of the suspenders over the button. That's why she had been late; the thought made her smile, and she brushed aside the contempt on the faces of the women in the ward.

On her way back to the kitchen she paused outside the nursery, looking through the glass at the crying babies who would not be fed until breakfast was finished. Hans had been a baby once, like these. He was a human being, and he was going to win the war and give her a good life, so what the hell did she care about what this lot thought?

She spent the rest of the morning washing dishes and preparing vegetables. The carrots made her fingers orange, the swede was woody and past its best. Mrs Amos sat on the stool, and had Hannah running about like a servant. Hans had said yesterday evening that he felt she was made for better things. Well, of course she was, but as she had said to him, there was no art college here.

She had told him of Sister Maria's suggestion that she should teach some of the elderly but they hadn't liked her make-up, and how ridiculous was that?

He had nodded, and pulled her onto his knee in front of the fire that roared in the grate. Roared, because he could acquire logs. 'When I write to my family of us, which I intend to do when Britain is defeated, it would be good to say that you teach art. Do you see, *Liebchen*? That would be admired, whereas orange fingers might not.' He had kissed those fingers and then her mouth.

She started to pull off the outer leaves of the sprouts. Mrs Amos shouted, 'No, wash them, how often do I have to tell you. We need every tiny bit of vitamin C for our charges.'

She carried them through to the scullery, nervous at the thought of Hans's family. What if they thought of her as these people did. What if in Germany she was called a – well, what? There must be a name.

The water was icy as she ran it into the colander and she gasped as it splashed her apron and soaked through to her skin. She turned off the tap, and shook the colander before tipping the first of the washed sprouts into the huge pan. Again and again Hannah washed and drained, and tipped.

Even his superiors on the island did not want their men fraternising with the locals. This was why his official billet was still the house next door. But how long could they keep it a secret, because there were men in suits and macs now, walking around the place in pairs. They were called the Gestapo, and were secret police. They were said to listen at windows, because although wirelesses had been allowed again they were spotting houses that had them, for when there was a new round of confiscations. Or so Cheryl said.

This morning, after Hans had dragged her back to bed, she had finished dressing and reached for her make-up but he had laid his hand on hers. 'You are pretty enough without, for those at the nursing home. When you have finished your chores, see Sister Maria again, and make your suggestion that you will enlighten the hours of the old. Perhaps this time you will be welcome. Hannah, my lovely Hannah, you waste your talent, when you could be improving your standing.'

She heaved the pan from the draining board into the kitchen. 'Let me check,' Mrs Amos insisted. She carried the pan to the cook, who peered into it. 'Yes, good girl. Pop them down the end of the table for later, and Hannah, I like the new look.' Her voice was gentle. 'Perhaps you should see if Sister Maria would like you to show the ladies how to sketch, now?'

Hannah smiled. 'Hans will be pleased. He wants his parents to like me, even though I'm British. He thinks it will help if I'm an artist, not a cook.'

Mrs Amos flushed. 'That is so rude, on many levels, and the worst thing is, Hannah Miller, you don't see why, do you? Just go and see Sister Maria, for heaven's sake. And Hannah.' The cook took a deep breath. 'Why not try doing something *you* aspire to, never bloody mind anyone else.'

Mrs Amos slammed the pastry she was making for the rabbit pies on to the marble slab. 'Go now, out of my sight, and see Sister Maria.'

That afternoon she entered the annexe common room, where the residents sat in high armchairs, with shawls around their shoulders, and blankets over their knees. Sister Maria, in her habit as always, walked by her side. She led Hannah to the two ladies who had before rejected her help.

Sister Maria said, 'Ah, ladies. I have a treat today. You will remember that I asked our dear Miss Miller to use her expertise to help you with your sketching and it didn't go quite as well as I had planned. Well, we thought we would try again, and she has looked at your work and admires it enormously but has one or two ideas that will perhaps improve it.'

The women looked at one another, and then up at Hannah. One of the them said, 'This is the girl to whom you said we had to give another chance?' The old woman had short hair, a bit like a man's, and large hands and feet. She wore old brogue shoes and heavily darned lisle stockings. Her voice was large too, and boomed across the room.

Sister Maria sighed, and smiled gently, but everything about the woman was gentle, thought Hannah, except for reminding her that she, Hannah Miller, was thought of as a Jerry-bag. 'Well, I wasn't sure I put it quite like that, Marjorie, but I certainly think that we can use Miss Miller's skills, and be thankful for her willingness to use them on our behalf. I find it rather wonderful that she chops vegetables and carries trays, when she is in fact an artist, don't you? She's clearly not afraid of hard work, and doing what is necessary to earn a living in these parlous times.'

The other woman, Miss Helena Sinclair, put her hand on Marjorie's arm. 'Hush now, Marjorie. Whatever you were about to say, and say loudly, I for one think it is commendable, and we will not mention anything else about the choice of friends, will we, Marjorie.' It was not a question. 'Why not sit down, Miss Miller. Sister Maria says you have examined our sketches, so shall we get to work. Have you charcoal or should we use our own?'

Sister Maria gestured Hannah to the third chair, and left the common room, gliding as though on wheels, her habit swishing the floor. Marjorie Webster boomed, 'No need for a brush to sweep our floors when we have our dear Sister Maria. So, young lady, tell us the worst. Will we eventually produce a masterpiece, or are we just dabblers, doomed to flounder in the deepest depths of mediocrity?'

Miss Sinclair smiled at Hannah. 'Our dear Miss Webster taught Classics. She is burdened with a tendency to alliterate, for whatever reason. I blame the Greeks – so very wordy, one feels. But it does us good to think of the past, because when all is said and done, time passes, and people accept.'

She reached over and patted Hannah's hand. 'You must remember that, my dear.'

The two old women listened as Hannah explained the art of representing three-dimensional objects on a two-dimensional surface so as to give the right impression. She guided their hands and talked of Brunelleschi and found she could remember more than she thought from all that her art teacher had taught her. Miss Webster and Miss Sinclair's cups of tea arrived at three, brought by Sylvia and Mrs Amos. The two elderly women sat back, their hands black from the charcoal, their cups and saucers in their hands, talking of a trip they had made to Italy when they were in their twenties.

Hannah didn't mention that Italy was an ally of Germany, and no one brought up the fact that the Italians and Germans interned on the island at the start of the war had been released once the invasion occurred.

The two women split their biscuits in half, and hesitated, before each offering to share with Hannah. She accepted. Two halves made a whole, and she was young and needed it while they were so old they didn't, so half each was enough for them. She saw the disappointment in their faces. Well, if they hadn't meant it, they shouldn't have offered. Anyway, it was too late, she had fingered them now so she ate, and felt slightly sick. Well, it was probably the charcoal, or divine retribution, as Bee would say.

She stared out of the window at the tops of the leafless oak trees, which almost enclosed the nursing home from the rest of the world. All she could hear through the glass was the slight knocking of the panes in the wind. There were no bombs, no aeroplanes fighting, no ack-ack, as Bobby said the BBC reported was the fate of Britain. Thank heavens she had not returned.

When her shift ended, Hannah rolled up their sketches carefully. 'Shall I take them home and note ways in which they could be improved?'

They smiled. Miss Sinclair said, 'That would be most kind. Have you any Brunelleschi pictures we can copy, or perhaps Sister Maria has here?'

Miss Webster boomed, 'That'll be the thing. We'll ask.'

Hannah headed for the door of the common room, and Miss Sinclair called after her, 'We're so sorry about your mother, Hannah.'

She stopped, sickness rolling over her again. Her mother. She tried not to even think about it. She headed for the door again. 'Thank you,' she called, without looking back.

She knocked on Sister Maria's door.

'Come in.'

She did, and stood just inside the doorway. 'I think I helped.'

'I'm so glad, Hannah.'

Hannah waited, then said, 'Do I get the extra money you mentioned for doing this?'

Sister Maria's smiled faltered. She said, 'Perhaps we could say that today your payment was the biscuit you gained from two elderly patients, leaving them with only half each.'

Hannah rolled her eyes, then shrugged. 'I'm going to be working on their work at home too, which I'll bring back tomorrow. We can talk about the money later.'

She cycled home, the sketches in her bicycle basket, her scarf wrapped up around her throat. A patrol flagged her down. 'You need your bicycle?'

She was used to this, as requisitioning was increasing. 'Yes, I work at the nursing home.' She reached for her exemption slip. He nodded. The soldier's eyes were cold, and he was nothing like Hans.

She continued home. Cheryl was in her bedroom, but came downstairs in her dressing gown, calling, 'Who's that?'

'Me, who do you think?'

Cheryl called, 'It's all right, Bobby.' She was tucking some money into the pocket of her dressing gown. Hannah did wish she wouldn't, because Sigmund might come home early but she said nothing. Bobby had stolen her uncle's wine, knowing she could be blamed, but not caring. When she had bearded him he had just smiled. 'Let me know what else he gets up to, there will be something in it for you. Otherwise never cross me.' He was frightening.

She unrolled the old women's sketches on the kitchen table, and used charcoal to alter the figures with dotted lines, changing the organisation of the scale and distance in the drawing to make a better visual sense. Cheryl came to stand beside her. Her cigarette ash dropped on the paper. Hannah tutted, and blew it off.

Cheryl laughed. 'This is the work of the old trouts, is it? Not the ones who didn't like your make-up, for heaven's sake? Hannah, get Hans to give you money, then you won't have to work.'

Hannah rolled up the sketches, and took them up to her room. Hans had never offered, but one day he would. This evening she would show him the sketches, and he could write to his parents and soon her life would become much easier.

She lay down on the bed, tired. She held up her charcoal-smudged fingers. The last time they had looked like this she'd been sketching with Peter, and had shown her mother the result on her return and her mother had been so impressed. The sketches must be at the farm, but it didn't matter, because she could do more now, and this time she'd show them to Hans. She brushed aside the ache. She'd get used to her mother's death, she just needed to ignore it for now and concentrate on herself for a change, because being an orphan was hard.

Chapter Nineteen

March 1941

It was a cold, damp day in Scotland when Bryony and Adam managed to get to the head of the queue to make a telephone call to Combe Lodge, where Eric had said he'd be waiting to hear from them. It was ten in the morning, and Eric confirmed he had brought the *Sunflower* out of dry dock and round to the nearby cove, having removed the cabin in its entirety. 'Adam said we needed to be low lying in order to meld in with the sea. Less chance of being spotted,' he almost whispered.

She said, 'Why are you whispering, April's the only one there, surely? The children are at school.'

'Eddie's here, and April doesn't want him to know, or he'll come too, and she says the ATA can't afford to lose two bloody idiots. She wanted you to know her exact words, Bryony. She's not amused.'

'Keep whispering, then.' She tilted the receiver to share the conversation with Adam, who had one arm round her and had been trying to listen, his head resting on hers. They were waiting at the aerodrome for the lift they were hitching with Andrew

Burcott, an RAF transport pilot on his way to Taunton. They were making the call from the village, because they didn't want anyone at all to hear their Jersey plans. From Taunton, a friend of Andrew's would drive them on to Exmouth where he had business, in the form of a blonde beauty he had met at a dance.

Bryony's two days' leave started at 6 a.m. the next morning, when she would normally arrive back at Hatfield by train. She wouldn't be expected to report until Monday morning. Adam had two more days than she did. It should be enough to get to and from Jersey.

Eric whispered, 'I've the map, and balaclavas as Adam suggested. I managed to get camo-cream, felt-soled boots and dark clothes, just don't ask me how. They'll be on the *Sunflower*. Meet me at the cove – don't go to the Lodge, because Eddie could be pottering about. I have a Goatley collapsible boat for getting into the Jersey bay, and again, don't ask how I "released" it. My contact doesn't want to be named, and he does want it back into stores. He was once on the trawlers and is now into something more interesting. The forecast was right. The weather is appalling, the visibility low, and will be for at least two days. Perfect for us.'

Adam said, 'You're a pal, but maybe not "us" after all. I've been thinking, and we could be blasted out of the water, or shot as spies once we hit Jersey.'

'Shut up,' Eric muttered. 'The home front has a

limited appeal, you know. I've got to do something worthwhile.'

'You already have, and are,' Bryony insisted. 'What was Dunkirk if not worthwhile, and the Home Guard? Adam's right, we can manage, no need to risk three of us. Your dad would never forgive us.'

'Don't be patronising, Bee. I can't keep up on land, so I'll stay with the *Sunflower*, and make ready for when you bring Hannah back.' The line went dead. They had not run out of money, but Eric had run out of patience.

They sat as close to each other as they possibly could on the floor of the transport plane, each second together too precious to waste in sleep. Adam's arm was around her, and their hands clenched tightly together. It was only the second time they had met up since the party. The last time they had shared a room in a damp Scottish hotel which had been utter heaven, and Bryony thought of the feel of his body on hers, his lips, his hands. It wasn't just now she thought of it, but most of the time.

Trixie had raised her eyebrows at Joyce on her return that time. 'Uh-oh, look at that face. Something's happened that's going to keep her nice and warm as she bats through the sky in the Maggie.'

Ah, the Maggie. Yes, they'd been busy delivering Miles Magisters, the two-seater monoplane being used as a basic trainer, and very necessary it was too as the rate of destruction of both planes and pilots increased. Bryony buried her head in Adam's shoulder, and sped the images of the poor young beggars away. Nothing mattered but these minutes and hours until they were separated again.

He murmured into her hair, so that no one else in the aircraft could hear, including the burly marine who sat alongside them, supposedly asleep. 'I won't mind if we're blown out of the water, as long as we're together.' It was what she had been thinking ever since speaking to Eric.

Finally, having changed the aircraft for a well-used Austin motorcar, they were driven to Exmouth by Tony Bertram, and waved him goodbye on the coast road. While he roared off to his blonde, they headed across the fields to the cove, slithering down the path on to the sand, which was so far not mined and had no coiled barbed wire.

By three, they had changed into their dark clothes, and their uniforms were stowed in a bag which Eric stuffed into a cleft of rocks, swapping it for the black haversack Bryony had asked him to bring. Into this she put the tobacco and soap that she had managed to acquire. Eric shoved the *Sunflower* out into the water, and heaved himself over the side on to the deck. The drizzle created visibility so reduced that Adam navigated by compass, which he'd done many times. They had two boathooks with them, and while Adam steered, Eric and Bryony each took a side, their eyes straining through the dense mist, seeking mines.

'The seas have probably been swept, but magnetic mines are on timers, and will bob up when you least expect it.' Adam was whispering because sound carried more easily in the damp air. He was driving the *Sunflower* hard, and she was smashing her way through the waves like a battering ram; time wasn't on their side. In the distance, a foghorn wailed. It was the sort of weather Bryony hated flying in. Eric came to her side, saying into her ear, 'Change over, Bee. After a while I can't see anything. It might jerk me back into action.'

She had been feeling the same, and as the *Sunflower* juddered through a cresting sea she lost her footing. Eric grabbed her. 'Steady the Buffs.' His voice was little more than a whisper.

Adam swung round, 'Don't get hurt again, darling. Do you hear me? I won't have it. It's enough that we're . . .'

He stopped, their eyes met. She nodded. 'I won't.' He had been about to say, it's enough that we're going to get the wretched girl, and risk our lives for her without that. He whispered, 'Getting blown out of the water is one thing, putting up with your bad temper while you heal is quite another.'

They all laughed, but quietly.

Eric muttered, 'Don't forget there'll be a curfew, so you've got to stay alert once you land, and the cove might be mined. Stick to the rocks. They'll have built gun emplacements along the coast.'

She nudged Eric. 'We've been through all this.

Don't worry, just keep your eyes on the sea, your ears peeled. Let's at least try to get there. How's the Home Guard, by the way?'

Eric smiled. 'Makes me feel better about myself, and they're a grand bunch of grandfathers who'll go down fighting, you can bet on that.'

By the time Bryony heard the alteration in the sound of the sea, it was 8.30 at night. It meant they were close to shore. Adam reduced speed, puttering towards the roaring of the waves crashing against the cliffs. All around, the mist swirled in the darkness. Were they at the right cove? They strained to see, and there, in a brief window, they saw the outline of the soaring folly that someone had built above the cove. He chugged almost silently into the lee of the cliff, setting down the sea anchor and saying quietly, 'Spot on. Who's a clever boy then?'

Wearing their felt shoes and balaclavas, they made no sound as they erected the Goatley, the collapsible, wooden-bottomed rowing-boat-cum-canoe with canvas sides. 'Just room for four, if your mother wants to come too,' Eric breathed. 'I'll stay, guard the boat, and be ready to take off the moment you're back.'

Adam lowered the Goatley from the stern, holding it tight in with a paddle as the *Sunflower* rose and fell in the choppy sea. Bryony hitched on the black rucksack, and hurried down the ladder, the spray catching and drenching her. 'Watch for mines,' she whispered to Eric. 'Mind your own business,' he muttered. 'You watch for the damn things, and the Nazis, and everything else that's likely to bite you in the bum.'

Adam was in the Goatley now, and they paddled towards the shore, straining over the waves as the roaring and crashing became louder. Now they were almost on Jersey soil, Bryony felt the danger in a way she had not allowed in her imagination. Was the cove guarded? Or would the Boche think it was impassable as the path was little known? In fact it wasn't really a path, just a narrow ridge that they had skipped down as children, heedless of danger. Would she find it again? The surf was running fiercely and she could hear the suck and surge of the sand.

Adam turned, and pointed to the rocks to the left. She dug in the paddle, and they headed for them. Adam leapt on to the rocks, holding the hitching rope. She joined him. Together they hauled the Goatley close and lifted it on to the rocks, lodging it high up, then she led him in a circular direction towards the path, staying on the rocks to avoid any mines, picking her way, sometimes on all fours. The wind plucked at her saturated clothes. She could hear Adam's teeth chattering above the sound of her own. She peered ahead. There was the ledge. She pointed, and hearing him behind her she headed onwards and upwards.

As Bryony approached the top she paused, only her head visible over the cliff edge. She waited for

Adam. They breathed through their mouths, listening, and looking. Nothing. But then a German voice barked out something. There was a laugh, a cough, over to the left about fifty yards from the folly. Adam squeezed her shoulder. Was it a patrol or a gun emplacement? They waited for the sound of men moving. There was nothing.

Bryony adjusted her balaclava and scrambled over the edge, dislodging a stone. It tumbled to the base of the cliff. She froze. Nothing. She lay on her stomach and waited for Adam. When he joined her she led them forward, almost sure of the way to Haven Farm in the dark. They had decided they'd head for it first because that would surely not have been requisitioned, as houses could have been.

She used the fields, sometimes upsetting the sheep, but couldn't find the stile. In the heavy mist she stood still for a moment, trying to think. She tracked back along the hedge, and found a gate where the stile used to be. They climbed over, the sheep gathered and baaed. She set off across the field, ankle deep in mud, and found the farm. There were no lights showing in the blackout; perhaps everyone was in bed. Thomas kept nature's hours.

Bryony crept around the farmyard, listening. No dog barked, so no Rosie. Were Olive and Thomas still here or had they had to leave after all? There was a spare key under the flowerpot, as always. She eased it into the back door, turning it, and entered the passageway. Light was showing beneath the kitchen door. Bryony listened. There was someone moving. Crockery crashed, Aunt Olive swore. 'Damn.' Bryony smiled, and opened the door. Aunt Olive spun round, a broken cup at her feet. She screamed, and backed against the dresser.

Bryony and Adam snatched off their balaclavas. 'It's us, Aunt Olive.'

Adam said, 'We've come for Mrs Miller and Hannah, at last. Better late than never, eh?'

Bryony almost ran to her aunt: she had lost weight, and had dark sunken eyes. She hugged her, murmuring, 'Will you come too, both of you? We can make two trips in the Goatley, but we have to hurry.'

Aunt Olive, who still smelt of lavender, enfolded her in a hug, almost squeezing the air from her lungs. 'Oh darling girl, you're too late. Your mother died before New Year.' She was weeping now, her sobs shaking her body, as Bryony's arms fell to her sides. Her mother, dead?

Adam was just behind her, rubbing her back. 'I'm so sorry, darling, but we need to get Hannah. We've got to get back to Devon before the darkness lifts, and the mist.'

Uncle Thomas's voice reached them now, from the passageway. 'Who's that? What the hell is going on?'

He entered, and saw them both. 'Bloody hell.'

Bryony smiled at him, over her aunt's shoulder.

'Yes, we've come for anyone who needs to escape. What about you, Uncle Thomas? Is Hannah in bed, or still at the cottage?'

He held out his arms, 'Come and give your old uncle a kiss and then get yourselves back to the cove. I 'spect that's where you came in?'

She did, feeling his strong arms around her, the smell of a strange tobacco. 'What on earth are you smoking these days?'

He grimaced. 'This and that. Nettles at the moment.'

Bryony pulled back, removing her backpack and taking out a tin of pipe tobacco, and soap for her aunt. 'I thought you and Mum – well, you – would enjoy the soap. Was it TB?' She felt strange, detached, almost as though a burden had been lifted.

Aunt Olive shook her head. 'A stroke. Perhaps for the best.'

There was a silence. 'Why? Where's Hannah?' Bryony asked.

A girl's voice spoke from the doorway. 'I'll take you.'

She was blonde and slight, and carried a book she'd been reading. Aunt Olive explained that Sylvia had moved in to look after Bryony's mother, and stayed on. Hannah was at the cottage, with her German beau.

Adam hung his head, then dragged his hands through his hair. 'All this way?' Suddenly he sounded exhausted.

Aunt Olive said, 'She might just be looking for a chance to get away, you never know. But let Sylvia go with you. If you really wouldn't mind, Sylvia my dear? You'll be breaking the curfew but how will they find it, without a guide? Bee darling, let Sylvia enter the house first because you don't want to come face to face with trouble. Thomas would go, but . . .'

Thomas was shaking his head. 'No, never, not even for Bee.'

Soon they were heading down the track in Sylvia's wake. Bryony saw that the young woman carried a large haversack on her back. Adam tugged at Bryony's arm. 'What's that all about?' he whispered. Bryony caught up with Sylvia. 'Are you going somewhere, Sylvia?' she breathed.

'Back with you, and Hannah, if you'll have me. I want to nurse, I want to get away from all of this. I'd rather have the bombs, and even if the Germans invade I'll be with my own kind. My mum and dad are gone, but I'm English not a Channel Islander, so who is to say what they'll do with us eventually. They could send the Brits to Germany, or so some of us think.'

'Sssh,' Adam whispered. 'Keep your voices down or none of us will be going anywhere but a cell.'

At last, as they crept along the back lanes, Sylvia pointed through the mist. 'There. I'll go in, and get her to come to the door, then I'll nip out to the gate and wait for you. I don't trust . . .' she paused. 'I'll wait by the gate. Be careful, be prepared to run.'

Adam and Bryony stepped into the shadows as Sylvia tried the door. It was unlocked. She whispered over her shoulder to them, 'Hans might not be here but if he isn't, keep an eye out for him coming in.'

She entered. Bee and Adam pressed back into the shadows, listening for the sound of this German called Hans coming along the path, as they waited for Hannah. Somewhere within the house, a dog barked. Bee leaned into Adam. It was Rosie. At least *she* had survived. Still she felt nothing about her mother.

The back door opened, and Sylvia slipped out. 'She's coming, but Hans is here. His unit had an exercise and he's washing.' She was whispering.

She vanished into the darkness, and then Rosie was there, barking, whining and licking, her paws up on Bryony's shoulders. Bryony hugged and stroked her, murmuring, 'Sssh, sssh.' Adam dragged the dog over to him, as Hannah came to the door. Bryony couldn't see her face, as everywhere was in darkness but she heard her sister's petulant voice. 'Why've you come? Mum's dead, and that's your fault. If you'd persuaded her to leave she'd be all right. Anyway, I don't want to come. I'm happy. I've got someone who loves me.'

Bryony's eyes had become adjusted to the gloom and she held out her arms to her sister, but Hannah crossed hers and stepped back into the house. A dim strip of light showed beneath a door at the end of the hall. 'You've got to go. If Hans knows you're here, you'll be in trouble.'

'Come with us,' Bryony whispered. 'We've been missing you, we love you, we want you back with us. You don't know how long Hans will be here. He could be posted, then what? We can't come again. Oh Hannah, please come. I promised, and here I am.' She heard the urgency in her own voice.

'He's telling his parents about me, now I'm teaching the old dears how to draw, so I'll be part of the family. Besides, we'll be over in England soon enough when they invade, and I'll come and visit. I might even bring you something nice. Just don't spoil it, for once.'

Bryony reached for her. 'What happens if *we* win, Hannah? Will you be safe, what do people think about those who live with Germans? What can he do for you then? Oh, Hannah, be sensible. Come home.'

Hannah slapped her away. 'We won't win. Look at all the bombing and England's so small and alone, against all that Germany has. Why don't you all just give in, and what's so wrong about loving him, anyway? Under the uniform he's a man, just like Adam, or Eddie.'

Bryony grabbed her. 'Come on, now, I'm not leaving you, you talk such utter . . .'

She stopped and pulled her sister, and Hannah fought her off, screaming, 'Get away!'

A German shouted from upstairs, 'Hannah, what is it?'

Hannah looked at Bryony, hesitated, then shouted, 'I need help. Quickly.'

Bryony let her go, stunned. She heard the clatter of feet on the stairs, and Adam was pulling her away from the door. They tore down the path, grabbing Sylvia as they passed. 'Run, run,' Bryony hissed.

They ran through the fields, the mist still as heavy, and now Rosie was with them. There was a shot from behind. They ducked at the noise, but as they couldn't be seen it was panic-shooting. Sylvia was labouring, and Adam grabbed the straps of the rucksack and heaved it off her. 'Now go,' he urged. 'We'll follow.'

He took up the rear position as Rosie bounded ahead. Bryony held Sylvia's hand as another shot rang out. Germans called from the cliff. Oh God, it was the gun emplacement. They tore on, over the gate, scattering the sheep. On they ran in the darkness and mist, following Sylvia, who only stopped when they reached gorse bushes. 'Here,' Sylvia panted. 'We must be close to the cliffs.'

Rosie was quiet, and waited. Bryony led now, almost feeling her way forward until at last there they were there, with a great nothingness at their feet. She edged her way along, looking for the ledge, but Rosie bounded past her and down it, scattering stones in her wake. Germans shouted to the right. Some shots were fired, but at what?

Bryony took a deep breath and followed Rosie,

forcing herself not to rush, hearing the others behind. At the bottom the dog bounded across the sand and Bryony held her breath, but there were no explosions, so no mines. They followed in Rosie's footsteps, collected the Goatley and eased it into the water. Adam held it while Sylvia and Bryony clambered in, finally easing himself in too. Rosie launched herself on top of him. He shoved her down between his legs. 'For goodness' sake, dog.' But he was laughing quietly.

Why the hell was he laughing? Bryony thought as they paddled. Shots sounded, but hit no targets, and distantly a searchlight stabbed at the mist, but way off to the left. They paddled as though the furies of hell were at their backs, which they were. Ahead, they heard the *Sunflower*'s engine powering up. Thank God for Eric. They steered towards her, then hurried up the ladder. Adam hurled Rosie up, then followed, rope in hand. Together he and Bryony hauled up the Goatley. Bryony could hardly get her breath. Eric powered off, not looking behind, saying in a hushed voice, 'Well, Hannah, at last.'

Sylvia said. 'She wouldn't come.'

Eric spun round, looking from her to Bryony. 'A long story.' Bryony could say nothing else, because her sister had betrayed her, and how can you explain that?

Adam put his arms around her. 'She'll regret it. I'm so sorry, darling, but we've done all we can, for now. After all, she's just lost her mother, she's in a strange situation, all we can do is wait until the end of the war, whichever way it goes.'

She loved this man so much, for he wasn't berating the girl, he was thinking of a solution. Was this the love Hannah felt? Was it true love at last? But nevertheless would Bryony have . . .? She stopped. It was pointless. They had to get home, Adam had convoys to guard, and she had planes to fly. That's all that she must think about.

Rosie was nudging her. Bryony sat on the bench, pulling Rosie's ears gently, leaning back against Adam, watching Sylvia as she stood by Eric. They would have time to call in on Combe Lodge and leave Rosie there. Cissie would love that, and what about Sylvia? Where would she live? This was what she must concentrate on, this world, her world and the people in it. But all the time her heart felt bruised, and now she thought of her mother. She tried to concentrate on the better days but still all she felt was relief that she was dead, for what would she have said about Hannah? If it had been her usual nonsense, then Bryony could not have borne it, and if her mother's heart had been broken, neither could she have borne that.

Adam whispered, 'Are you all right?'

'I think so. Are you?'

'I think so, but it does take the bloody biscuit.' His arm tightened around her. 'All you can do is laugh.'

She smiled. 'Ah, that's why? Yes, that just about sums it up.'

Chapter Twenty

1ˢᵗ June 1941
Combe Lodge

Cissie was shrieking in Bryony's ear, 'Bee, Bee, wake up, it's morning. April will be Mrs Standing by the end of the day, it's so exciting.' She felt the child's hot breath on her neck, and her warm hands shaking her shoulders.

Bryony groaned, turned, forcing her eyes open, snapping them shut again and wincing at the light that streamed through her bedroom window. 'Oh, Cissie, have mercy.' She remembered through her headache that it was the morning of April and Eddie's wedding, something that had been sprung on them a few weeks before, to everyone's great delight.

Cissie laughed, shaking her again. 'Uncle Eddie said you'd say something like that. He said I had to say, "Serves you right for drinking so much. It's supposed to be the men who have the stag party." Why is it called a stag party, Bee?'

Bryony felt the child sit on the side of the bed. Clearly there was to be no mercy so Bryony eased herself into a sitting position, peering towards the window. 'Did you open the blind, and the curtains? You must have been very quiet.'

She saw the other three then, ranged at the foot of the bed, staring at her, jiggling with impatience. Frankie said, 'We shouldn't have been, I told you, Cissie. We should have shouted and poured water on her.'

Betty objected, 'Then she'd have looked worse than she does. That eye stuff's smudged all over her cheeks. It looks like shoe polish.' Sol stared, horrified. 'Will it ever come off? She looks like something horrid.'

Bryony looked back at the four children who were eyeing her much as if she was a specimen in a glass jar. She remembered, then, that she'd worn some of Sylvia's mascara for the 'few drinks' on the terrace with April while Eddie had gone to the pub with Eric and the darts team. Well, not the whole team. She swallowed. Adam hadn't been there. They had thought they would marry at the same time as Eddie and April, but leave had been changed, and the *High Ground* was to be 'elsewhere'.

She flung back the bedclothes and checked the clock. 'What?' This time it was she who shrieked. It was 8 a.m. and the wedding was at eleven. There was the food to lay out, the children's clothes to prepare, Wendy to meet from the bus. 'Have you woken Trixie and Joyce?'

She snatched up her overalls from the chair next

to the bed, and dragged on her pants under her nightie. She threw the nightie on the bed and hauled on a shirt, then overalls and socks. The children were watching, as though she was a circus turn.

Cissie muttered, 'Trixie and Joyce have locked their door, and one of them sort of groaned, 'Go away, and let me die.'

Betty looked serious. 'It was Trixie. She didn't sound well. Do you think she'll really die? Will they still have the wedding if she does?'

April entered now, with the bridesmaids' dresses over her arm. 'Well, the bride-to-be is feeling fresh and perky this bright June morning, thank you all very much for asking. How are you doing, Bryony Miller, supposedly my mainstay and support? Isn't that what you called yourself yesterday as you opened another bottle of Eddie's home-made elderberry wine? Our little gang' – she indicated the children – 'have been up and at 'em since six. Catherine, Anne and Sylvia are downstairs, beavering away in the kitchen. Eddie is prone in his room, with Eric snoring on the sofa downstairs. Am I making you feel a sufficient failure? Or are you still too excited about the remote but real chance of flying a Spitfire on your return? You'd better pass the test, my girl.'

'Shut your noise, woman. I need coffee. And no, Betty, no one will really die today.' Bryony fled into the bathroom: teeth, face, quick look in the mirror. 'Oh God.' She scrubbed at the mascara. 'What was I thinking of?

'I don't know,' said Frankie who stood in the doorway.

'Is there no such thing as privacy?' Bryony groaned.

Frankie shrugged and remained, with Sol. Cissie brought goose grease. 'Sylvia said to use this.' Betty had cotton wool, which she handed her. They all watched as she wiped the blackness away. Frankie said, 'You still look awful, sort of extra tired.'

'You don't say that to a woman, my lad. Just remember that as you grow older, if I let you live that long.'

As she headed out of the bathroom she heard Frankie say to Cissie, 'She's a funny old thing and, what's more, she's Bee, not a woman.'

'Mouths of babes and sucklings come to mind,' April sang as she passed on her way to Eddie's room, calling back, 'Do have a go at Trixie and Joyce again. I don't know, you'd think you flyers were a bunch of wilting violets the way you've all collapsed. How do you cope at the clubs in London?'

'They don't serve elderberry wine.' Bryony called the children to her. 'Go and knock on the girls' door, and keep knocking, do not stop until you hear the key turning in the lock. I am going to find coffee. April promised me some of the real stuff and no one, including you, Frankie, is to ask where she found it. Then I'll be in the garden, picking flowers for the lunch tables.'

She ran down the stairs, not even thinking about her headache. It would go. It must.

319

In the hall the telephone was ringing. She picked up the receiver. 'Hello.'

'And hello to you, beautiful woman.' She sagged. It was Adam. Oh, Adam.

'Adam. I thought you'd have gone.'

'Any minute now. The skipper felt the no-show bridegroom deserved a last call. Have you managed to call everyone to let them know? Did you give them my apologies, my sincere, sincere regrets? Just remember that it doesn't matter whether we're married or not, I will love you for ever, just as Mum and Eddie have loved one another. You and I just have to stay alive, do what needs to be done, and somehow, somewhere it will happen. You are my everything. Got to go.'

'I love you so much,' she said, wanting to weep but he was gone. 'Be safe,' she murmured.

'He will be.' It was Cissie peering over the banisters. 'April said he wouldn't dare not, because she'd have something to say about it. I love you, Bee. I really do, and I'm sorry you're not getting married today as well, but it means we'll have another wedding, and we four can be pageboys and bridesmaids again. Will we have to wear the same dresses?'

She was skipping down the stairs – when did she ever not? Together, hand in hand, they hurried to the kitchen, to be met by the aroma of coffee. Over by the back door the babies, Bryony and Eric junior, were beating at some sort of drum in their playpen. At the table, Catherine and Anne were mashing hard-boiled eggs for the sandwiches, and the smell sat heavily on the air. At the far end of the table Sylvia sliced home-made bread. Catherine raised an eyebrow, and said to Anne, 'These fly girls are lightweights. We were on the terrace as well, keeping pace, and look at us in comparison to the state of her.'

Sylvia sniggered, then came and hugged Bryony. 'Take no notice. I couldn't do what you lot do. You're all exhausted, that's what's wrong with you. Eddie, too.'

Anne muttered, 'Well, he will be after tonight.'

The three women laughed. Cissie looked at Bryony, who was pouring coffee. 'What's happening tonight?'

Bryony muttered, 'Sylvia, my dear girl, I will leave you to answer that.'

She sat at the table, removed a slice of bread and ate it, without butter. She was home. Adam wasn't here, not actually here, but he was all around.

The church was within walking distance, which was as well, because by 10.20 Wendy had still not arrived. She had said that she and Timmo would be finding their own way from the station, not catching the bus. Apparently, Timmo knew a friend in the locality who had said he'd pick them up from the station and bring them to Combe Lodge. This friend knew it well.

Cissie, standing next to Bryony, fidgeted on the front steps of the Lodge. 'We can't miss it, Bee. I'm head bridesmaid. Where are they?'

Bryony checked her watch. She was wearing uncomfortable grey high heels to match her outfit, and taking the short cut across the fields didn't bear considering. She made a decision. 'Come along, we'll walk to the end of the drive, and wait another five minutes. It's wartime, a bomb could have damaged the train line.'

She began walking on tiptoes, but on the grass, not the gravel. Cissie held back, 'Bomb? They'll be hurt.'

Bryony cursed herself. 'No, they won't, we would have heard. Hurry up, now.'

She hurried on, pulling Cissie behind her, waiting for the question that would inevitably come. 'How could they tell us?'

'Cissie, there are ways,' she snapped, then regretted it. She adjusted her hat. 'The police would have told us. They always do. You're next of kin, so never worry until you see them standing on our front doorstep, and they're not, darling.

She snatched a look behind. Cissie was quickening her pace, her face lightening as a car swept into the drive and screeched to a halt in a shower of gravel beside them. Wendy called through the opening rear door, 'Quick, quick, Sid will take us to the church. So sorry to be late, the train was held up. There was a raid as we were leaving London, or so they said. Probably just late.'

Cissie ran to her sister and jumped in through the open door. Sid leaned out of the driver's window. 'We meet again, Bryony Miller.'

She forced herself to smile. 'We do indeed, Sid.' She followed Cissie into the back seat. Timmo sat in the front passenger seat, in a navy blue suit. The smell of cigarette smoke was heavy. Sid turned the car and set off down the drive. 'Me and Timmo was just doing a bit of business, Bryony, as yer do.'

She smiled at Wendy, who sat with her arm around Cissie, telling her she looked like a princess in her pale pink bridesmaid outfit. Bryony replied to Sid, 'Yes, I'm sure it's as you do, Sid.'

His laugh was hard. 'Me and Bryony Miller has history, you see, Timmo. Dated her sister, I did . . .' He raised his voice. 'I heard tell you tried again, and she still preferred to keep 'er distance.'

Bryony stared into the rear-view mirror. 'I don't know where you hear such rubbish, Sid. But then I expect you have a finger in so many pies you don't know which way is up as you swim through the slime.'

'You gave her my present then, when you went over first?'

'I told you back then I had.' Beside her Cissie was laughing with Wendy. Timmo turned round and looked. 'You tell the kid we can't stay, Wendy. I know you missed the spring, but there's a war on, and things happen. We're off after a bit of nosh, kid. I don't want no messing about.'

'Why?' Bryony shouted before she could stop herself, leaning forward, wanting to put the pimp in a stranglehold and choke the life out of him. She forced herself to soften her voice. 'Why? Cissie thought Wendy was coming now instead of spring. She's got so much planned.'

Sid tutted. 'Naughty naughty Bryony Miller, don't do to cross our Timmo. Makes him all riled.'

Bryony banged her fist on Sid's shoulder, wishing it was his face. 'It doesn't do any good to get me riled up, either, you little . . .' She forced herself to stop, take a breath. 'Just get us there, and then disappear. You're bad news, and you too, Timmo. The least you could do is to give your girl some time off.' The last was said in a whisper.

They were drawing up at the church as Timmo said into the silence that had settled on the car, twisting right round, 'We've got a lot of business on, ain't we, babe? We got 'ere, didn't we, when we ain't got time, not really. So Cissie will understand. Tell you what, when she's a bit older, say twelve or so, she could come and stay, couldn't she, long-term. We'd like that, wouldn't we?'

The look he gave Bryony was cold and full of venom. She leaned closer and whispered, 'That will never happen. I'll drop a bloody bomb on you first.'

She opened the door. Eddie and April had broken convention and arrived together, though Eddie would wait in the front pew with his best man, Eric, while April and her retinue sorted themselves out in the vicar's little room off to the side. Bryony clambered out of the car, followed by Cissie, who was still chattering and had heard nothing. But there was fear in Wendy's eyes, and Bryony wished she'd remained silent. As they walked towards the church, she knew that something had happened to her when Hannah had chosen the Nazi over them. It had left Bryony full of – well, what? It wasn't anger, it was – indignation, and more, it was strength. Yes, strength.

After all, she flew replacements for the RAF in all conditions, some of her friends had been hurt, some killed. The man she loved was out there doing his bit. She had looked after her sister so much of her life, and look at the result. What's more, her mother was dead and couldn't be hurt by Bryony's behaviour ever again. These men were reptiles, squirming around in the filth making money out of the seamen in the convoys Adam was trying to protect. Why shouldn't she defend those worth defending?

She stopped, and sent Wendy and Cissie on. 'I'll talk to Timmo,' she said. She returned to the car. 'If you're coming, come, Timmo. If you're not, bugger off and never come back.'

He came, slouching into the church behind her. She pointed to the rear pew. 'Wait for us there, if you would.' She smiled, and leaned forward, hating the smell of his Brylcreem. 'If you touch one hair of Wendy's head from now on, you won't live, let me tell you that. Do I make myself quite clear? I have friends as well as you and you might think you're tough, but take a look at this lot. See the merchant seamen, the pilots.' She turned, and he scanned the guests. 'They'll cut you into pieces and feed you to the pigs, especially when they know you deal in the goods they risk their lives to bring to England. See that bloke over there: he's a fighter pilot. The other is on the fighting trawlers. They're not good at obeying rules, but they're good at killing. There are others, in London, friends of our local policeman. You will not be safe if you hurt that woman. Wendy will be staying tonight. You will not. Stay with Sid, for all I care. You will fetch her at ten in the morning, ready to catch the eleven o'clock train and not a moment sooner.'

She joined April in the vestibule, kissing Cissie and then drawing Wendy to one side. 'I've had a word with Timmo. He will be staying with Sid overnight, and you'll be up in the attic, alongside the children, but in your own room. Then you can catch the eleven o'clock train tomorrow with him. A fair compromise, I believe.'

Wendy looked nervous. 'Is 'e mad at me?'

'Why ever should he be? He's got business with Sid so they can sort that out, probably over many illicit pints of beer.'

She waited until the wedding march began, and then sidled into the pew next to Constable Heath, whispering to him as he stood with his wife. As they turned to see the bride moving down the aisle, she pointed out Timmo, who watched her do so. He also saw Constable Heath, who was on duty, so still in his uniform, nod in his direction.

Gerry Heath said to Bryony, his eyes still fixed on Timmo, 'Can't be doing with that sort of bloody nonsense. You were right to say I know people in the big smoke. They're on the shady side of nasty and they owe me a few favours from my days there. There's always Tommy Templer, you know, the uncle of Stan Jones, the lad who wrote down Ben Rowan's telephone number at Dunkirk. I know for a fact he has interesting contacts. Between 'em all, they'll keep an eye, and make it known they are too, then it's up to the sister whether she stays or not. In the meantime she should be safe. But, Bee, don't get your hopes up. A lot of these lasses are tied to their pimps, sort of love 'em, it seems.'

The music had stopped. Gerry Heath looked to the front. Bryony did not. Her gaze held Timmo's and his was the first to fall. It was only then that she concentrated on the service. Now it was up to Wendy, and there was nothing at all she could do about that.

Later on the terrace she stood with her uncle. His arm over her shoulder, he said, 'It will be all right. He'll come home.'

She leaned into him. 'I'm not a child. You can't

say that, any more than I can, as Cissie would say. It will be what it will be, Eddie. Everyone here knows that even in the West Country they're not safe. How many bombs fell on Exeter just a few days ago? Nine, wasn't it? So who knows who's safe, who isn't? Enjoy your marriage, Eddie. I'm sure Mum knew all along, and would approve.'

He sighed, and tightened his grip. 'If she did, she never spoke out, which is not something we can ever now accuse you of. Gerry Heath told me of the slight to-do with that less than delightful pimp of Wendy's.'

She laughed slightly. 'I wouldn't have said any of it if I hadn't been sure I could keep him under surveillance. Gerry said he'd be given the warning when he was back in London. I gather it's a conversation that involves concrete.' She shuddered.

Eddie laughed. 'Well, it will keep him within what rules that world works by. Your father would be so proud of you, Bee. Not just for the ATA, but for who you are.'

Behind them the gramophone was playing Glenn Miller, and earlier Wendy had been showing the children how to Charleston to a jazz number. Bryony replied, 'He'd be proud and grateful to you, Uncle Eddie.'

'I didn't do a good job with Hannah, though.' They both looked out into the darkening day. Soon the blackout would be drawn and the lights flicked on.

'It's up to her,' she said. 'It has been for a long while and I've only just realised.'

April called to them, 'First Officer Standing, and our newly promoted Third Officer Miller, time to join the party for the toasts, and then you youngsters can party on, Bee, while Barry Maudsley runs us to the Bear Inn. However, do not, if you don't mind, add to that hangover as you're on duty tomorrow. You'll need all your wits about you. I've had a word with the other two girls too. And now, we're off, Eddie Standing, because you need to be on the milk train with the girls.'

Chapter Twenty-One

Bryony, Trixie and Joyce arrived at the ferry pool at 8 a.m. the next day, having only just caught the milk train, and as they leaned their bikes against the brick wall, the girls promised themselves they would never drink home-made wine ever again.

Trixie groaned, and nodded, 'The after-effects hang about so. You have my permission to shoot me if I ever dare so much as moot the idea.'

'You're on,' Bryony laughed. Joyce was beavering ahead of them, clutching her cap, which threatened to blow into worlds unknown. One of the reasons Joyce had loathed flying the Tiger Moths was the damage the open cockpits did to her hair, because some always escaped their helmets and the ends dried and split.

They headed for the common room. As always, some of the pilots were smoking, some reading, some playing cards. Joyce grabbed the remaining armchair, offering an arm each to Trixie and Bryony. 'So generous,' Trixie muttered, nudging Joyce. 'Don't worry, you're not bald yet. It will come though with all the primping and preening you do. Leave it alone, for pity's sake.'

Bryony drew from the pocket the folded sheet of paper and pencil. She finished off her note to Adam, then sauntered to the table, whispering to Katherine, one of the card players, as she played an ace.

'Pen?' Katherine nodded towards the pen lying next to her mug of coffee. Now Bryony pulled out an equally folded and crumpled envelope, and wrote his service number and address. Somehow her letters always found him, and his found her. She always flew with his last one in her pocket, as well as the plasticine in the matchbox. It kept him close.

Over at the end of the room, the hatch on the counter flew open and they were called to pick up their ferry-chits. 'Come and get 'em.'

The queue formed quickly, and dispersed as quickly, with Eddie arriving in the nick of time, having cadged a lift from a friend of Barry Maudsley who was doing a delivery to the area. At the counter Bryony whispered, 'After you missed the train, I didn't think you'd make it, and you could have had an extra day.'

He grinned. 'Maybe, but we need everyone at the moment. April understands.' Bryony dropped her envelope into the box on the hatch. Someone would deliver it to the mailbox. She wasn't sure who, just a someone who should be given a medal for making life easier for them all. She checked her chits, grabbed her parachute, helmet, and a small holdall with cash, knickers and a book, just in case there was any hanging around.

She joined the others as they half ran out to one of the milk-run taxis. She was destined for Katherine's whilst Eddie hurried to David's Anson. Bryony had three flights. The first was a twin-engine Oxford to pick up in South Wales, bound for an aerodrome near Kidlington, or in other words, from A to B, a Hurricane from B to C and a Maggie from C to D, which was in Scotland. Sometimes there was an air taxi back from D, but today Bryony would have to take the train and there was no point in trying to meet Adam because he wouldn't be back off convoy yet.

Her thoughts jogged along with the parachute that banged against her side as she ran to the Anson, scrambling up and shoving in close to Trixie.

'Welcome, Bee's big bum,' Trixie muttered.

'Go and wash your mouth out with soap.' Bee drew out Adam's letter. She was word perfect but loved his chaotic handwriting. Part of the joy was deciphering it. 'Each read an adventure,' she said. Trixie nodded, reading her letter from Brian.

They were taxiing for take-off as Joyce lamented, 'Just when are we going to ferry operational aircraft?'

Bernice, sitting on the other side of the aisle, laughed, 'Lust is a maiden's downfall. You must wait, my dear, and who knows, the Spitfire might come to us if we stop chasing.'

'Mighty big might,' grumbled Penny as they flew in rain to South Wales, with the cloud descending all the time.

Bryony and Penny, who had also got on the plane with Bee and Trixie, disembarked and Katherine called, 'Remember, there's a safety minimum, girls. No showing off today, the visibility is becoming increasingly iffy.'

Penny protested, 'It's June, for goodness' sake.'

'It's Britain,' replied everyone in the plane, and then continued with crosswords, gossip, books or letters.

Bryony checked the meteorology report before she took off in the Oxford, and though drizzle and low cloud were forecast for most of the route to the Oxfordshire airfield, there was a promise of improvement. The journey wouldn't take long. She and Penny traipsed out to their aircraft, with Penny taking off five minutes ahead of her, while a mechanic tweaked one of Bryony's Oxford engines, 'Just a tad,' he said as she paced slowly backwards and forwards, her parachute dragging at her shoulder.

Bryony had learned patience, or a vestige of it anyway, and the destination aerodrome wasn't going anywhere. The drizzle became heavier and cloaked the hills, making them look half the size but she knew there were some bloody high summits tucked away, just aching to spring a surprise. Soaked, she climbed on board into the dry, slinging her parachute on the seat and sitting on it. It gave her extra height and stopped the need to strain to see forward. She dug her maps and notes on the route from her pocket, laid them on her lap, and checked through, again.

Finally the mechanic signalled the all-clear. The trundle to the runway across the grass felt soggy but the Oxford otherwise handled well. At least it was the aircraft's wheels wading through it, not her boots. Was it raining on *High Ground* as Adam surged through the waves? Probably; it always seemed to be, according to him. She turned into the wind, checked the instruments, then the sky above and all around. All clear. She opened the throttles, checking, checking, increasing speed until she was airborne, and then she headed into the curtain of rain, which was growing denser by the second. She gained another one hundred feet, then another. Denser still. Bloody Wales.

She peered ahead. The end of the narrow valley was hidden by cloud. Was it up and over, then? Or should she return? All right, it was iffy, but they had a schedule to keep. She opened up the throttles, pulling back the control column, forcing the old dear to climb steeply. 'Come on, ducky, stop showing your age. If it was the hokey-cokey being played by a tall, dark and handsome, you'd have your knees up in a shot.'

She was now in dense cloud, which always frightened her. Well, she'd be irresponsible if it didn't. She kept her eyes on her instruments, forcing her mind into neutral. She repeated the route in her mind, and the height of the hills. 'Constancy, Mrs Oxford, that's what we need. Just let's fly at a constant. That's what Hannah doesn't understand.' She was surprised at herself. What was Hannah doing in here with her?

She checked her rate of climb. Again she thought of Hannah. Was she happy with her German? Was she happy on an island where she had chosen the enemy above her own family? Were people treating her well? What about Uncle Thomas and Aunt Olive, did they ever interfere? Had her mother approved? Perhaps; one never knew with her mother. Was the German kind to Hannah? Something twisted in Bryony's heart. Well, Hannah, I hope he is, and that it's all worth it.

She continued to pull back, and back, on the control column, feeling the Oxford beginning to protest but then she burst out into the sun, with the Oxford's shadow darting along the top of the cloud. She checked her watch, working out the ETA, and knew that soon she should be landing. But if not at the exact airfield, there would be somewhere else, as long as she had fuel, and she had plenty.

Heading south-west, away from the hills and the barrage balloons, she throttled back and put the nose down, descending steadily through the cloud. She kept one eye on her instruments, the other on her path through the density. The visibility should have improved, or perhaps she should have headed for the Bristol Channel? No hills on the sea. It always made Adam laugh when she said that. She wondered if Eddie was on her route today, or heading north.

He could have had another day with his wife but no one took an extra day if it could possibly be helped. Poor April.

One thousand. Seven hundred. The cloud would end soon, and at five hundred it did. She was spot on, coming into the airfield from the south. There was another plane, a Hudson, coming down out of the clouds ahead and to the north of her. As she looked, it waggled its wings. 'It's Eddie, you dear old Oxford. He must have been on a different taxi.'

She patted her control column, laughing. He always waggled his wings when he came out of cloud. She waggled back. They sometimes met like this, but not often. He was ahead of her so she pulled her nose up, to indicate he was to land first. He waggled again. She smiled, and circled round, and came in behind him. As she did, she saw a Maggie turning on to the runway preparatory to take-off, just as Eddie came round into the wind. She snatched a look back at the Maggie. It seemed to be holding hard, and giving way, as it should, because any incoming had the runway. 'That's right,' she said aloud, 'hold hard.'

Instead, out of nowhere, the Maggie suddenly gained speed, roaring along the runway and she screamed a warning, glancing from the Maggie to Eddie, who had already committed to the landing. As she watched, Eddie took evasive action but too late. Surely it was all too late. She didn't breathe as he hauled the Hudson around, trying to find lift. 'Go on, for God's sake, go on,' she urged.

She throttled back, held her course, seeing – as clear as day – Cissie running across in front of her lovely Dragonette. She shook her head, and there was the bloody Maggie pulling away, gaining height, while Eddie, in the Hudson, was left clawing, clawing, then, as she watched, one of the Hudson's engines sputtered and died. A wing dipped, and the Hudson slowly, so slowly fell from the sky, cartwheeled, and crashed on to the airfield. 'No!' she shrieked. 'No. No.'

The Maggie flew on. It should be rammed. Instead she brought the Oxford into the wind, descending, descending, copybook, through the oily smoke, Eddie's smoke. Her legs were trembling, her hands shaking. The fire engines were racing, the ambulance too. She shouldn't be landing. She should abort and find somewhere else but there was nowhere else when Eddie was down. She landed, taxied off the runway on to the grass, out of everyone's way. The mud caught and threatened to tip the aircraft. She released the brake, and then applied it gently, and with the help of the mud the plane stopped. She threw open the cockpit, ripping off her helmet and racing across the grass, running faster than she'd ever run in her life.

The ambulance was there before her, and the fire engine.

She pushed, shoved and kicked her way through

the gathering crews. Someone grabbed her. 'Hey, what's your game?' She wrenched free and carved her way to the front. Eddie was on the grass. He'd been thrown yards from the Hudson, which was a crumpled mess on the grass, the muddy, soggy, wonderful bloody grass. He stood a chance because the ground would have absorbed some of the impact. She was beside him. Someone pulled her away. She shrieked, 'He's my Uncle Eddie! He's my uncle, let me bloody well go!'

They saw her uniform and let her go. She screamed at the squadron leader who was leaning over Eddie. 'You should train your bloody pilots. That Maggie didn't look before take-off. You're a bunch of bloody incompetents, Neanderthals, and bloody murderers.'

She sank down beside Eddie, taking his hand. The medic working on him looked up and grinned. 'Tough old bugger then, your uncle, bit like you, I reckon. He damn well bounced, and then near drowned in the mud. Ask him how he is, why don't you, and give the boss a break?' She looked at him, astonished, and then down at Eddie, who lay mud-covered but with eyes half open. 'Do stop shouting, Bee. I've the worst hangover ever,' he murmured.

She burst into tears, and the medic took the opportunity to tell her that Eddie'd live, that he had a broken arm, a broken wrist, probably a pelvic injury and she should let her uncle's hand go so they could get the old bugger onto a stretcher. 'It's time he retired.'

Bryony nodded, wiping her face on her sleeve. 'He got married yesterday. He will retire, or if he doesn't one of us will drive a stake through his heart, which should just about bring him to his senses.'

The medic roared with laughter. 'Is it worth me sending him to hospital, or shall I just give you a hammer, and there are several stakes in that fence over there. It'd save us all a lot of bother.' He nodded towards the perimeter fence.

Eddie said, 'Can I interrupt the pair of you? Would you get me to a hospital, Oxford would be good, anywhere quick. I swear I will retire, so you can leave the stakes and the hammer where they are. Come on, Bee, you have your day to finish but before you go, telephone April. Perhaps they can stay at Pearl's.' As she watched, he passed out.

The medic nodded at the ambulance. They carried over the stretcher. 'As I said, tough old bugger. I'll get him to Oxford. Catch up with him there. He's not out of the woods, but I'd place a firm bet on him surviving.'

The squadron leader pulled her up. 'Pilot Officer John Folkes, who caused this spot of bother, will be spoken to when he returns but he probably heard you and is on his way to Kathmandu. Bad show. Apologies. Pilot Officer Folkes will be at your service: his petrol, his car, whatever you need in recompense. Will you stay for a cuppa?'

At the back of the crowd she saw Katherine, beckoning. Bryony shook her head, shaking all over, mud soaking through her uniform. 'I need to make a quick telephone call because my other taxi is waiting.'

He led her through the dispersing rescue services and pilots into his office, which was warm and dry. She telephoned April, who said, 'Bee?' She paused. 'It's Eddie, isn't it? Is he dead, or dying?' She sounded extraordinarily calm.

Bryony said, 'I'll kill him again if he is. He's pranged. I was there. He has a hangover, he says, and therefore his head hurts.' She heard a half sob, and continued. 'The medic said he was a tough old bugger, and has some breaks, but nothing life threatening. What's more, he's promised to retire. Call this number.' She read it off the telephone, as the squadron leader nodded. 'There will be a lift from the station available, probably a certain Pilot Officer John Folkes. He will take you to the hospital, the name of which the lad will have discovered by then.'

Again the squadron leader nodded. She continued, 'I have to catch my own taxi now, and get back to work, but I will see you at the hospital later this evening. I love you, April. Bring Cissie or she'll never forgive you. Perhaps Sylvia is off duty and will look after the other three. I have to go, time and tide, the same old thing. Don't worry.'

She replaced the receiver, unable to bear April's crying.

The squadron leader was scribbling his telephone number on a scrap of paper. 'Telephone any time for a chastened, bloody lucky taxi driver: this is the best lesson he will ever have. Again, apologies, and fly safe, whoever you are.'

'Bryony Miller,' she said, shaking his hand then hurrying out of the door.

The squadron leader called. 'Yes, fly very safe, Third Officer Miller, my regards go with you, and all the Attagirls like you.'

That evening, Bryony hitched a lift from Scotland to the Oxfordshire airfield on a Maggie. As they landed she saw that the runway and grass surround had been cleared. John Folkes should have been given a roasting, leaving him red-faced, and with a memory that would haunt him all his life. When she knocked and walked into his office, the squadron leader smiled, his face drawn with tiredness. John Folkes met her outside, at the passenger door of his car, nervous and distraught. He started to apologise. She just shook her head. 'Mistakes are how we learn. We all make them. Just get me there, please.' He said nothing more, and dropped her at the hospital.

Still carrying her parachute she made for the post-operative care ward, where Folkes said Cissie and April would be waiting. She should be tired, but all she felt was a running anxiety. Was Eddie really a tough old bugger? Had he relapsed since her last call, this time from Scotland?

She was still caked in mud, but as in so many close-knit organisations no one had asked why. They didn't need to because they had heard over the grapevine and merely got on with the job. It's what they did, no matter what awfulness occurred in their lives.

The corridor shone, the nurses' shoes squeaked, the lights cast a strange, almost green light. Bryony saw April and Cissie sitting on chairs, waiting. She called, 'Is he dead?'

'No, and hopefully not likely to be.'

'Then I will find a stake.'

'Join the queue,' April said.

Cissie ran full pelt along the corridor and threw herself at Bryony. 'He's had an operation and has an arm and leg in plaster. There's something wrong with his pelpic, or something.' Her arms came around Bryony, who lifted her up, heavy though she was, so she could keep walking towards April, who remained seated, smiling as she approached.

April said, 'Sylvia has moved into Combe Lodge from her digs and is looking after the other children. Catherine, Anne and Eric are in support. We've found a boarding house round the corner from the hospital.'

Bryony sat next to her and settled Cissie on her lap, clasping April's hand. 'How's he really doing?'

'Fine, but he's too old and too crumpled, the doc says, for this sort of shenanigans. That young pilot who drove us has been in. He left him some roses. He said it was his fault. He told me how. I said that we all make mistakes. He said it was a bloody big one. I said, we all make those too. They're not allowed roses in post-op, so I've got them under my seat. How was your day, Bee?'

Cissie said, 'You said all that in one breath.'

'I have big lungs. So, again, how was your day, Bee?'

Bryony sighed. 'Oh you know, this and that, and there was some old bugger who cluttered up the runway for a while. No sense of tidiness.' They laughed quietly together, even Cissie.

Bryony said, 'I thought he'd broken his neck like Dad.'

April waited a moment and then said, 'If he had, it would have killed him immediately.'

Bryony nodded.

April insisted, 'Do you realise what I'm saying? Your father could not have spoken to Hannah, especially with the additional head injury.'

Bryony nodded again. 'I do realise that. I've known for a while, perhaps underneath I've known it always. But she is what she is, and that's nothing to do with me. Not any more, though perhaps I helped create her.'

'Or perhaps your mother did?'

'Well, what's done is done. And it's now that's important, for all of us.'

They stayed there until the nurse came out at four in the morning, and said Eddie was doing better than expected, and within a day or two would be an impossible patient. Perhaps they should go and

343

find their beds. Bryony checked the number the squadron leader had given her. He'd told her to ring any time, and so she did.

John Folkes arrived to pick them up within half an hour, dropping off April, who clutched the roses, and Cissie. He drove Bryony to Hatfield. They spoke little until they drew up outside Pearl Bates' Edwardian house. He was out of the car almost before it stopped, sprinting to open her door. She smiled as she got out. 'John, thank you. You've done enough now. The deal is that I just want to hear that you get home to your mum in one piece at the end of this damnable war, do you hear me?'

John Folkes nodded, saluted. She knew he was watching her as she set off up the path, and tried to stride out, but quite suddenly exhaustion pulled at her and she almost tripped on a non-existent something. He ran after her, and took her arm. 'Are you flying tomorrow, Miss Miller?' he asked, as she slid her key into the lock and opened the door.

'Of course,' she said. 'You lads have got to have replacement aircraft.'

He saluted again, then paused. She waited, wondering what he wanted to say, but all he did was to wrap her in his arms and hug her. For a moment she rested her head on his broad young shoulder. Then pulled away. 'Thank you,' she said, and entered.

He called, 'Be safe.'

'You too.' She shut the door, leaning back against

it, and didn't have to try to climb the stairs on her own, because there was a rustling of clothes, the sound of steps on the stairs, and Trixie and Joyce helped her to her bed. She told them Eddie was battered but all right. They said, 'We'll wake you, don't worry.'

As she fell fully clothed on top of the eiderdown, Trixie said, 'There'll be dirt on the counterpane.' Joyce yawned. 'We can shake it out of the window in the morning. Pearl won't mind. I'll slip a note under her door, she's worried about Eddie.'

They covered her with a spare blanket. At last Bryony slept.

Chapter Twenty-Two

July 1941

Hannah stood by the sink at the back of the cottage, staring at the potted geranium on the window sill, gasping, unable to draw a deep breath, hating its acrid scent. The baby kicked and she could still feel Hans's hand on her belly even though he'd been posted to France, and beyond, with his unit. She opened the window and threw the pot out on to the patch of neglected garden. Some faded crinkly brown leaves still lay on the cracked white tiles of the window sill. She tried to pick these up, but they disintegrated beneath her fingers.

Above she heard Cheryl and one of her 'friends', a corporal in the replacement infantry unit. It was how Cheryl earned her money now Sigmund was also gone, and it was how she had her fun.

Hannah moved to the back door to escape the steam of the tea cloths she was boiling. They smelt. She couldn't bear smells any more. She leaned against the doorpost. The day was merging into evening but there was no change in the heat. Her feet throbbed. The earth was cracked, the flowers and lettuce were wilting even as she looked at them. The tomatoes in pots against the wall were pungent. Once she had liked the scent of tomatoes growing. So had Bee, and her mother. Did they still? She should water them but the smell was too strong.

She heard the door open, the one that led from the hall into the kitchen. Cheryl called, 'Nice boy, good payer. How long is your money from Hans going to last?'

'I don't know.'

'You should give this sort of work a bit of a go when the baby's born, which is any minute, isn't it? When you get back into shape you can get cracking. Bobby will help with customers. You'll have to do something, what with the bloody old nun saying you were too preggers to work there any more. Who knows if she'll take you back afterwards: too much of a scandal probably. Good of her to have you there for the birth, though.'

'Hans will send more money. Or come back or send for me. I know he will.'

Cheryl came over then. Hannah heard and smelt her cheap rose scent that the French merchant ships bought in for Bobby, amongst other black-market stuff. Perhaps they'd bring in bread now that it was also rationed, that thin sort of bread the French ate. Or medicine? The island needed medicine.

Down at the end of the garden she had planted potatoes. They needed watering. She'd do that tonight in the cool, because potatoes didn't smell.

The French sailors must be glad of that when they shipped the harvest over to France, though her Uncle Thomas and the other farmers were growing much more wheat now, for the islanders. Was he still hiding a pig? She'd never told, just like she hadn't told about the wine. Or had she? Yes, she remembered that Bobby must have overheard her but that wasn't her fault.

Cheryl was so close now the smell was overpowering, roses and sweat, his and hers. She almost retched. Cheryl stood beside her. 'I've got to tell you something, Hannah, and you must be brave. Hans will not be coming back. Bobby told me when he brought the scent that Hans has been killed, in Russia. You remember Bobby telling us that the Nazis had invaded to the east, don't you? So forget him, he isn't coming back. There'll be no more money, so you've got to be sensible and make plans. You're spoilt goods, aren't you? You have a Boche brat, no one will help, so you got to help yourself.'

Hannah clutched at the door frame as the heat shimmered and the tomatoes oozed their scent and all the while the smell of sweat and roses beat against her.

'Bobby said he needs another girl.' Cheryl's hand was on her shoulder.

The garden was shimmering, the whole garden was shimmering, the potatoes were lifting and falling. The air was so heavy that though she gasped she couldn't drag any more into her lungs. She felt Cheryl's hand fall, heard the scrape of a chair on kitchen tiles behind her, felt the hard edge of the pine seat against her legs. Cheryl dragged her backwards on to the seat. 'I didn't know how to tell you, love.'

In a moment Hannah heard the tap gushing. It sounded cool. The shed was moving, bigger, smaller, bigger, smaller, and in her head was the sound of waves crashing on the shore. She should have gone home. Bee would have looked after her, she would have made all this go away, she would have helped her breathe. There was a glass of cool water in her hand. Cheryl's hand was around hers, guiding the glass to her mouth. Hannah sipped but only once, because she had to keep breathing, trying to force in air. The baby kicked. It was Hans's baby. Of course Hans wasn't dead, how could he be, when they were having a baby? Cheryl was wrong.

She looked out into the garden again and the vegetables steadied, the shed too. She stayed in the doorway, feeling what slight breeze there was, as the sun dimmed and a semi-darkness fell. The glass of water became warm, the house silent. Cheryl had gone to Bobby's, laughing, kissing Hannah's hair. 'It will be all right, love, trust me, everything will be all right. We'll have some fun, you'll see, and at least there are no bombs, and with Bobby and the blokes we won't go hungry.'

At midnight, well after curfew, the backache that

had been deepening and stretching all evening suddenly ripped and tore at her but then passed. She looked out at the garden, at the shadow of her bicycle in the moonlight. An owl hooted. She must go to Sister Maria, because she was in labour, she knew that, and as another pain came she groaned. It passed. She rose and walked to her bicycle. She pushed it round the cottage and out on to the road. She must remember to cycle on the right now they were part of Hitler's Reich. Part of Hans's Reich. She bent over as a pain came, dropping the bike. The wheel whirred as though it too were gasping.

She would walk. She waited until she could breathe again, until the water which had suddenly poured from her stopped. She walked. She had no shoes. It didn't matter. At the bridge she stopped as another pain roared. Flowing beneath was the cool river that Bee would follow as she brought the Dragonette to her uncle's. She placed her hand on the parapet. The lichen was dry and rough and holding the heat from the day. Everywhere held the heat from the day. She groaned and sank to her knees as another, longer pain grew, deepened, and seemed to stretch until she could not bear it any longer, but then it stretched and tore further and she must bear it, because there was nothing else to do. Finally it too faded.

She struggled to her feet, and staggered on as the pains came, thick and fast. It was by the left-hand bend that she was challenged by a foot patrol. 'Halt. Curfew.' A shape loomed out of the gloom towards her. She sank to her knees, knowing that she really could not go another step. She heard boots hammering as the patrol ran towards her, and the shouts. Was it Hans? She felt the hands that lifted her, the clink of metal on rifle, the orders in German. Yes, it was Hans.

The stars shook as they carried her, then the stars were gone and instead there were overhanging trees. She had given the name of the nursing home. She heard the gravel of the drive beneath their boots. They tugged the bell pull. There was always someone on duty. The door opened. They carried her in, their boots crashing on the tiled hallway. The midwife said, 'Please, help her to sit on the chair, if you would.'

They did. Hannah looked down. Blood from her cut feet stained the tiles. She looked for Hans, but he was leaving, clattering down the steps. Another pain swept her. Sister Maria was gliding along the corridor, adjusting her wimple. It was all right, Sister Maria was like Bee. She'd look after her just like her father would have done if he hadn't died.

In mid-August Hannah took Elizabeth from Sister Maria's arms on the steps of the nursing home. 'Thank you,' Hannah said. 'For everything.'

'Are you quite certain that you won't consider adoption? I know a couple who would be very pleased to give your daughter a home, in spite of her parentage.'

Hannah looked down at her daughter. Her hair was blonde, or certainly wasn't dark anyway. Was she like Hans? She wasn't sure. 'You told them then, I was a Jerry-bag?' She heard her voice shake.

Sister Maria touched the baby's head. 'They asked for confirmation of the story they had heard. I think they were scared that he might return for her if they did adopt her.'

'Well, he might.' Hannah stuck out her chin. 'He could be alive, armies get things wrong.'

It was her arm Sister Maria touched now. 'When your money runs out, you can always work here. I was wrong to send you away, but you should have told me Hans had gone, and you had no means of survival.'

'He left money.'

Sister Maria nodded. 'Then when that is running low, return to us. We will find you work, and we'll manage the care of Elizabeth somehow. Miss Webster and Miss Sinclair have missed you. I think we'll have you in the kitchen, though, as before. You can then pop into the sitting room of the annexe and help with their sketching. Best not to put you in the wards.' There was a slight hesitation as though she was going to continue. Eventually she said, 'Keep well, Hannah. Don't forget that your aunt and uncle are not far from you.'

Hannah walked down the drive, with Elizabeth

wrapped in a 'granny blanket' made of knitted squares of wool, a present from Mrs Amos. She called back to Sister Maria. 'My aunt and uncle haven't bothered to visit, so why should I put myself out. I know they left flowers, but they've got lots at this time of year. It's not fair, you know, she's their family.'

There was no reply from Sister Maria, just the sound of a closing door.

She walked along the verge, and though Elizabeth was only eight pounds her arms were soon aching and her shoulders strained. Her shoulder bag, which was full of nappies given to her by the nursing home, felt as though it weighed a ton. Her belly ached, her feet too. The cuts on them had not yet healed, and Sister Maria had given her bandages with which to bind them to keep them clean. By the time she reached the cottage Elizabeth was crying and she carried her round the side of the house, into the kitchen. She sat, undid her blouse and fed her, wanting to sleep. Above her she could hear Cheryl, and a man's voice. Another customer? Then all went quiet.

Elizabeth started to cry again as Hannah lifted her to her shoulder, patting her back. Above her, a man shouted something. She carried Elizabeth into the garden, but still she cried. She walked to the end by the potatoes, hushing her, praying she'd bring up her wind and settle. She did, and dirtied her nappy. Not another one?

She walked back down the path, glancing up at the window. A German soldier stood there, shaking his head and shrugging into his braces. She entered the kitchen and grabbed her bag. She laid out a nappy on the kitchen table because she daren't take Elizabeth to the bathroom upstairs. The front door slammed, Cheryl barged into the kitchen in her silk lookalike dressing gown. She threw open her arms. 'Well, doesn't this just get better and better? That's disgusting. Get her off the table, Hannah, for God's sake. And you owe me two Reich Credit Marks. All that fiddling about with the fat idiot, who not only stinks but doesn't know his arse from his elbow, and you come home to put him off further. The bastard wouldn't pay, and I don't blame him.'

She stormed across to the sink, grabbing the stubbed-out cigarette from the ashtray, and relit it. She leaned back against the sink, her arms crossed, smoke rising in a straight line as Hannah sat down, exhausted. She lifted Elizabeth from the table and held her in her arms, like a barrier. Cheryl sighed. 'The bloke knew it was a German's. You need to get rid of her, because they could come and take her back to Germany, or that's what Bobby told me they did sometimes, in some of the other countries.'

Hannah clutched Elizabeth tighter, staring. 'No, she's mine.'

Cheryl inhaled so strongly that her cheeks sank. She lifted her head and exhaled up into the air. 'Hannah, she's a bloody Boche.'

'That's not fair.'

Cheryl inhaled again, twisted, and dropped the stub in the sink. It hissed. She came to the table, leaned on it, shoving her face into Hannah's. 'Why the hell don't you grow up? Life isn't bloody fair, but you have to deal with it. You didn't have to open your legs, you didn't have to be so damned stupid as to have a child. It might not be fair, but it's your fault. Yours, Hannah Miller. No one kept you here when you could have left, no one buggered up your relationship with your family. That, my girl, is all down to you.'

Hannah reeled back. 'That's not fair.'

Cheryl drew back her hand and slapped her across her face. 'That is *all* totally fair, and so is the slap. Now get the kid out of here, and get over it.' She stalked to the kitchen door, yelling over her shoulder, 'And get that disgusting nappy out of the house.'

It was mid-afternoon as Hannah arrived at Haven Farm. Uncle Thomas would be out at work, but Aunt Olive would be in the kitchen, or not far from it; either that, or in the vegetable patch. But what if she'd gone into town? Hannah carried the painting she had done after Cheryl had left. It was a watercolour because she couldn't wait for oils to dry. She was going to leave it when she left Elizabeth on the doorstep with the nappies.

In the wrapping paper around the watercolour

was an envelope containing the remains of the money Hans had left, and every bit of jewellery Hannah possessed. It could be sold for Elizabeth's keep. Hannah's breasts ached, but there was milk at the farm, which Aunt Olive could use if she could find a bottle. But what if she couldn't?

Hannah hesitated on the path. Elizabeth stirred. She would bring one from the nursing home. Yes, that's what she'd do. But dare she just leave her child? What if Elizabeth was found by a fox? She wanted to cry, but bit down on her swollen lip. Not now.

She had written an unsigned note with her left hand, because there must be no way to identify this child. The painting should be identification enough for her aunt, who had requested a painting of the view so often. So, at last, she thought, Hannah Miller had done something for her aunt, but it had also been for herself, as usual. She felt disgust at the girl she had been, and probably still was. But then paused. Well, she had created the painting not quite for herself, but for her child, because Elizabeth mustn't be taken. Perhaps that made things slightly better.

She started to walk down the path towards the house, the lavender scent heavy as it always was at this time of year. In her note she'd written that if her uncle could hide a pig, he could hide a child when it was necessary. She'd admitted that she'd done nothing to deserve their kindness, but she was begging for their help. She'd told them to destroy the note immediately.

'Hannah, what are you doing here?' There was surprise, but not censure, in her aunt's voice. Aunt Olive was on her knees over by the wall, weeding. For a moment she looked like Bee.

Her aunt pushed herself to her feet. 'I heard you'd had the baby and so I often wondered how you were. Did you receive our flowers?'

Hannah looked all around, then hurried to her aunt. She thrust the painting at her. Aunt Olive took it, looking from it to Hannah. 'Are you all right?'

Hannah whispered, 'I have brought you Elizabeth. Cheryl told me that Bobby said the Boche could come for her and take her to Germany because she's half German. She also told me I had to leave the cottage when I said I wouldn't work for Bobby. Please take her. I will work at the nursing home. People think we are not friends, and Uncle can hide her if they come looking.'

She placed the bag at Aunt Olive's feet. Elizabeth stirred. Her aunt stared from her to Hannah, dropping the weeds and hand fork she still held. The fork fell with a clunk to the hard ground. 'Hannah, no, I'm sure that's not the case.'

Hannah shook her head. 'But how *do* we know? Several people have said this, and how do we really know what the Germans will do? Hans is dead, you see, and this is a child of the Fatherland.'

Aunt Olive reached out, tugging Hannah to one side. 'No, no, we need a cool drink, and to talk about this. It can't be right.'

Hannah resisted. 'But who do we ask?'

Aunt Olive just shook her head. Hannah whispered, 'I have painted the path, for you, but because I want you to have her. So I am still selfish.'

'No, I think perhaps you're not.'

'Please, will you take her?'

Elizabeth started to cry, it was that high-pitched wavering cry, with fists that shook. Hannah's milk started to come in. She touched the skin of her child's cheek. 'It's so soft. Please just look after her for now, and I'll stay away until somehow she is forgotten. I will come back for her, Aunt Olive. I promise.'

She pushed Elizabeth into her aunt's arms, and left, looking left and right, half running down the road but even at the cottage, as she packed her clothes and the sketch she had made of Elizabeth, she could hear the cries of her child. She packed her skirts, and could feel her in her arms, and smell her skin. She clicked shut the lid of the case and thought that perhaps it would be better to die than to endure even the remains of this day without her, let alone all those to come.

Olive Charlton looked at Elizabeth. She didn't have a baby bottle but she did have one that they used for lambs, with a selection of new teats. She always sterilised well after the lambing season, but they'd need doing again. 'You'll have to wait, little Betty.'

She carried her niece, well, her great-niece, round

to the kitchen, and put the pan on to boil, while Betty settled and slept on the seat of the armchair. Olive unwrapped the painting. It was excellent. There was money and jewellery in the envelope, with a note, written in a strange, almost childish hand, in which Hannah said she would be earning more and would leave it under a stone at the back door. She also said that Bobby had overheard her talking about the wine, so perhaps it was her fault, but she hadn't meant it to be stolen. Olive looked across at the baby. 'I just don't know, just as I know so little any more. Would they really take you now your daddy's dead? Have they taken anyone's baby?'

She had heard whispered rumours about what was supposed to be happening in occupied countries, especially Poland, so could they dare to ignore it, or even ask about it? The answer was no. All they could do was to wait and see. But for how long? She had no idea, but for as long as it seemed wise. Aunt Olive had her nieces' old pram in the loft. She had kept one for when they came across from Combe Lodge, all those years ago.

Betty was whimpering, and just then Thomas arrived at the back door, easing off his wellington boots. Olive sighed. 'Thomas, sit down, please. We have something we need to talk about, and you might know the answer.'

Betty woke them in the night, and Olive slipped from bed, leaving Thomas to groan and turn over.

She heated the milk, thinking about Thomas, who had said, 'Who knows how they think, but surely they've better things to do than take away babies. On the other hand, there's talk of them bringing workers over to the islands to build some sort of fortifications while they're up to their eyes in fighting a war on two fronts. So perhaps they would take children to reinforce their country. The Nazis are mad, remember. Did I tell you the doc had asked a Nazi private how many children he had, just because he couldn't think of anything else to say to him while they waited for a convoy to pass? The lad said he had none, but his cousin in the SS had the Lord knows how many, because he was in this insemination scheme to boost the Aryan race. It chills the blood, so we'll keep her safe until we know different.'

Olive soothed Betty. 'I wish you'd told me earlier.'

'Why, so you could lie awake at night wondering what hell was stalking the earth?'

Now, in the light of the kitchen, she tested the milk. 'For now, I'm your mummy, Elizabeth, but we must remember that you have a real one. Every day I will remind myself of that, and we must pray that no German ever asks whose child you are, because I won't know what to say.'

Chapter Twenty-Three

November 1941

Adam and Mick stood on the well-deck forrard watching the morning mist lift over the east coast harbour. The replacement skipper, Lieutenant Neston, came out of his cabin. 'Let's not stand about watching the gulls poo, Number 1.' Gilchrist followed him out. 'Get 'em up, coxswain.'

Mick put his head down the mess deck hatchway, shouting, 'Tumble up. Stand by wires and fenders.'

The *High Ground* came to life, hands almost pouring to their stations. Adam, as Number 2, was in charge of a party of ratings and moved off aft as they stood by to cast off the wires and ropes. The helmsman was on his way to the wheelhouse. Neston, megaphone in hand, stood on the wing of the bridge and looked at everyone, and everything.

Adam nodded to himself, as the gulls clustered, then soared, some gliding on the wind as though in sheer joy. He was tired, they were all tired. Cobham was dead, so too, Tom, Mick's mate, both caught in the same burst of Luftwaffe gunfire. Hitler had almost reached the gates of Moscow, and had taken the city of Kharkhov in the Ukraine. Still there was no British advance, except in the Western Desert, around Tobruk, where the Eighth Army was nibbling at the Nazis. 'But we're still holding,' he muttered. 'Threadbare, but holding.'

It was better than being in Norway anyway, which was being threatened by the Germans with starvation if anti-Nazi unrest continued. How was the agent they'd rowed in to the shore near Oslo getting on? What was happening on Jersey and the other islands?

The bow of the *High Ground* swung round into the convoy stream.

On the telephone yesterday evening he and Bee had spoken of it. Darling Bee, so worried though she never actually said, but so was he. Were Olive and Thomas all right, and Hannah? Collaboration was a risky business, almost more so than resistance, because you could lose some of your soul, and be taken behind the bike sheds, or something similar if someone took exception. But did young Hannah have a soul?

The engine-room telegraph jangled 'Midships'.

The helmsman repeated, and then reported, 'Helm amidships, sir.'

Three hoots sounded on the siren, and *High Ground* slipped through the mist. There was another trawler ahead of them, and several behind. They were heading towards a merchant convoy. How many had survived on this trip? How much produce would find its way into the hands of the spivs? How many of these would be rich men by the end of the war? How many of the merchantmen would be dead? Adam beat down the hate. Love and hate: when one wasn't consuming him, the other was.

The breeze was dispersing the mist when they finally cleared the harbour boom: the cloud was low, ideal for enemy attack, the weather mild. 'Nice and warm for a dip, then,' he murmured, head up into the breeze.

'Let's not,' Mick ground out as he passed.

Visibility was good. Adam looked again at the sky. He hoped the cloud layer was higher for his darling love, but he tried not to think of it because it was Britain, and therefore there was invariably cloud of some sort. Would they go somewhere hot when this was over and live beneath a hot sun and blue sky? It was bloody tempting.

He shrugged beneath his duffel coat, his binoculars scanning the sea. The channel had been cleared but magnetic mines could bob up the moment the minesweeper had cleared the decks. He spotted the masts of two shipwrecked boats sunk by mines earlier in the war. They reminded him of the denuded stalks of Bryony's sprouts after harvest. He swung the binoculars back again, and there was the convoy of small merchantmen, each flying its own small barrage balloon just below cloud level. He wasn't sure it provided an iota of protection against dive bombers but it just might.

As they hove into sight he felt the usual stirring of love for the dirty little smokestacked beggars, heroes all. He snatched a look at Gilchrist, whose face reflected his own thoughts. He shrugged again. Rabbie Burns was rearing his head again, or were they getting too bloody soft.

A signal lamp winked from the bridge of the destroyer at the head of the convoy. The *High Ground* took her place as did the other trawlers, and they herded their ducklings on until midday. Lunch was taken, a tot too, talk was desultory, tasks fulfilled, and eyes always searching, ears always listening. The cloud hadn't lifted, and as the afternoon wore on, and dusk approached, conditions for the enemy could not have become more ideal. On the merchantmen the tension would be rising. Or would it? Had they become so used to ever-present danger that they had achieved a state of acceptance?

As dusk fell, gunfire was heard. Gilchrist set the alarm bell ringing throughout the ship, the men tore to action stations. Adam joined his gun crew. The lookout shouted, 'Aircraft on starboard bow, sir.'

The Nazi dived out of the cloud, and escort and merchantmen alike opened fire. A collier was hit, the scene hidden by a deluge of spray. A nearby merchantman's master was still letting fly with his guns. Acceptance, my Aunt Fanny, Adam thought. Dozey's gun was rattling, the barrel would be hot. The raid ended. One loss. Another trawler was sent in to pick up survivors. There were none. *High Ground*'s crew were stood down for now.

Darkness fell. It was Adam's watch and he stared out into the darkness ahead. To port he saw the vague outlines of two merchant ships. He heard the swish of the bows, the muffled beat of *High Ground*'s engines, the distant thump of the propellers of a merchant ship, which seemed to be in ballast and riding high.

The alarm bells rang again. The men tumbled up from below. 'The buggers,' moaned Derek. 'I were having a dream about the wife and for once she wasn't bellyaching.'

'Take it up with them up there, sailor,' Adam called as Derek joined Dozey on the gun.

'We should give 'em a bunch of roses. They've stopped your snoring,' Dozey called, searching the sky, and the sea.

Mick came past. 'Give 'em a blast instead, lads. Keep your 'eads down. You too, Adam.'

'And you.' Adam was scanning with the binoculars, to be joined by Geordie. Out of the darkness a destroyer was racing towards them, hailing *High Ground*. 'Fall back, pick up survivors. Another collier's gone. Torpedo.'

The skipper headed towards the stern of the convoy. An aircraft dived down, bombs fell, U-boats targeted more merchantmen, the destroyer let fly. To the west two trawlers were depth-charging. It was a scene from hell. Dozey opened fire with the four-inch, as the German flew over. They had reached the area of the survivors; the collier was on fire, illuminating the scene, before it upended and slipped, steaming, beneath the waves.

Men were picked up and hauled on board, coughing and spitting, before being dragged down below. And so the night crawled on. The skipper received orders to peel off for Portsmouth. Why? God knew, but they'd drop off the men there, and at last he could see her, his love, his world.

Bryony was based at Hamble, near Southampton, in the all-female ferry pool, but for how long? Who knew and what did it matter? Trixie was with her, sharing the same billet, but Joyce had been posted to the Midlands.

She collected her ferry chit and ran for the taxi, clambering on board. She was dropped off at Cowley to fly a Spitfire to Tern Hill. She adored these aircraft, and there it was, waiting for her outside the hangar as a biting wind bore across the runway. She climbed into the cockpit, gazing at the instruments. Adam was coming this evening. It was two months since they'd met. Adam. Adam. She saw his face, not the controls, not the clouds scudding across the sky.

The *High Ground* had come into Portsmouth to offload some survivors and he'd be there with her overnight. The landlady, Mrs Windsor, turned a blind eye to visiting boyfriends, because life was 'too bloody short', she would say, patting her hair, a twinkle in her eye.

Bryony laughed in the cockpit. 'You're my kind of girl,' she muttered, meaning both the landlady and the aeroplane, for how could anyone think this beauty was anything but a woman? The seat was made for a female; the cockpit fitted like a glove.

She started her up, feeling the power coursing through the frame. The Merlin engine had its own throb, one that seemed to say, for goodness' sake release me from this hidebound earth.

Quite, Bryony thought.

She taxied to the downwind end of the field, using the brakes sparingly because they were touchy. 'As befits a woman,' she murmured. Within seconds, it seemed, she was airborne and had to restrain herself from making the plane dance, roll and spiral as it was begging her to do. The ground fell away at a fantastic speed, the Spitfire responding almost before she asked anything of it. Finally clear of Cowley she gave it its head, spiralling, twisting, climbing and diving, in love with its power, its elegance, its joie de vivre.

Within seconds of regaining course it seemed she was at Tern Hill. From there she took the taxi to the airfield near Kidlington. John Folkes met her on his way to his plane, his parachute slung over his shoulder, she with hers. They smiled at each other.

'Still alive, then?' he shouted against the rising wind.

'No, I'm a ghost. Adam's coming this evening.'

Neither stopped. They just turned, backing as they continued the conversation. 'One day I'll meet him, when this is all over.'

Bryony laughed, turning back the way she was going. 'In a hundred years, then.'

'Probably.'

She took a Hurricane to a Kent airfield, then a Maggie from there to Scotland. There'd better be a taxi, or she'd hitch a lift somehow. The taxi was a Rapide and Joyce was flying it. Bryony clambered in, lugging her parachute, and taking the front seat. Three others were already seated, reading or sleeping, all men. 'Don't spare the horses, Joycey. Adam's at Portsmouth and on his way to my billet.' She checked her watch. 'He'll be arriving in two hours.'

Joyce just nodded. There was no smile on her face. Bryony stood, and leaned over. 'Who?' she asked.

'Trixie.'

The breath went from Bryony's body. The two women exchanged a glance but then Joyce fired up the engine. Bryony slumped in her seat, strapping herself in. She leaned forward again as Joyce brought the Rapide round into the wind. 'Weather?'

'Mist on the bloody sodding hills.' Joyce was thundering the Rapide down the runway. Bryony leaned back and closed her eyes. She was so tired. Before they were airborne she was asleep.

She woke, and checked her watch. She'd only

ducked out of life for ten minutes. It was what she seemed to do now when people died. She slept, and when she woke her brain had processed the loss. There were so many now, what with the navy, the air force, the ATA, the bombing, that they were like leaves scattered beneath trees in autumn. She stared ahead, feeling the Rapide's purring, hearing Eddie calling it an infernal drumming, seeing Jersey, her aunt and uncle, then Hannah and her mother and lastly Trixie, her smile, her hangovers. She stopped and slept again.

She cycled to her south-coast billet through the darkness. She didn't need the slit in the bicycle lamp, it was as though the rackety old bike knew the way, and besides, the stars were sufficient. The door was unlocked. She slipped into the dark hall. It would break the blackout if the light was on. Mrs Windsor would wait until she heard the door shut behind her, and then pop her head out of her sitting room. The girls had the back room.

The door opened. Suzy Windsor said, 'Your friend is here. He arrived twenty minutes ago. I sent him up. Tonight you will need him.'

Bryony smiled, slipping out of her mac. So Suzy had heard. Suzy said, 'Trixie was doing what she loves, remember. Her mother might like a letter from her best friend. I will need to send back her ration book. Perhaps you could include it in your letter, rather than me leave it with her stuff? Will you write to Brian, too? She did love him so very much, and he is such a nice lad. They were to be married at Christmas, leave permitting.'

'Of course.' Their voices were quite steady but their eyes were not. Bryony said, 'Her parents'll come for her stuff, I think. Should I try to be here? It will be hard for you.'

'Dearest Bee. It will not be the first time. Up you go now. In half an hour there will be a meal on the table for you both.'

Bryony climbed the stairs. Adam waited at the top. He held her and together they walked into the bedroom.

Adam said, 'Suzy told me. I understand.' Of course he did, he was on the armed trawlers. John Folkes would, too, everyone who was living now would. He soothed her as she wept for her lovely friend who had a taste for home-made wine. After this evening, she would not cry for Trixie again, but neither would she forget, ever.

After they had eaten they returned to the bedroom, and they lay naked, and talked of life, and love, and marriage, and children. It would all come, probably. But for now, they were together, and love like theirs could not be destroyed as long as one of them lived. It gave them a sort of peace.

Chapter Twenty-Four

April 1942

Wendy, Cissie's sister, spent Easter at Combe Lodge together with the mothers of Sol, Betty and Frankie. Bryony managed to snatch Saturday with them and found that Eddie had at last moved on to one walking stick and his frustration at being out of the war following his accident had eased, which was a blessing for all concerned. He used his walking stick to poke the children into hysterical giggles until they begged for mercy, and when he stopped they asked for more.

Timmo was down, but staying with Sid, doing a 'bit of business', or so Wendy explained in the sitting room, after a lunch of cold chicken. Eddie held Bryony's gaze, making her keep her mouth shut about the merchantmen being sunk to facilitate that 'bit of business'.

He should have included Cissie, who said, 'Adam says black marketeers are bad. The ships are being sunk while they bring in the coal, fuel and food which keeps us fed and warm.'

Wendy stubbed out her cigarette in the ashtray

she balanced on the arm of her easy chair, as the mothers of the other children shifted uncomfortably. April bustled to the coffee table, and handed around the honey biscuits.

Eddie struggled off the sofa. 'Come along, let me show you children how to wash up the dishes.' There were groans from the children, and laughs from the mothers, who sprang into action to join the kitchen 'party'.

Ten days later, Suzy took a telephone call from April at six in the evening. Bryony had heard the ring, and waited. Not for her, please, not for her. Suzy shouted, 'It's April, Bee.'

She was down the stairs almost before her landlady had stopped talking. She knew that behind the bedroom doors of the other girls there would be sighs of relief.

'Yes?' Bryony said.

There was no preamble. 'It's Wendy, she was killed by a car in the blackout yesterday evening. Her solicitor just telephoned. If you remember, he is one of her "customers" but we needn't mention that. I think you should come, so that you can tell Cissie.'

'I'll be there when I can.'

She put down the receiver, then lifted it again, making calls, finally rousing the squadron leader at the Oxfordshire airfield. He listened. She could picture him nodding. 'Let me make some calls. I'll get back to you.'

She replaced the receiver, tore upstairs, and

dressed. The telephone rang again. He gave her instructions. She was on her bike, and cycling at a punishing speed within ten minutes, heading for a small RAF aerodrome where the squadron leader had found a transport that was flying to an airfield beyond Exeter. She in turn telephoned April with the details and was told that Eddie would be waiting to drive her to Combe Lodge.

Bryony sat in the rear of the transport aircraft with a few RAF personnel, the drumming precluding conversation but she was glad because – death by car? Was it really? Or was it Timmo? Had she brought this about? She'd threatened him, after all. All the way these thoughts tormented and wriggled, and when they landed she ran to Eddie's car, wrenched open the door and shrieked, 'Was it me? Did I kill her?'

Eddie raised an eyebrow as he started the car. 'Well, hello to you too, Bryony Miller. I'm very well, thank you, and I hope that you are too?'

She stared at him. 'But I threatened him.'

Eddie nodded, as he drove towards the sentry at the gate. 'Manners, Bee.' His voice was sharp. She stared as though she didn't understand. He slowed and waved a sort of thank-you salute at the sentry. She came to herself, and did the same. Had she thanked the pilot, or even the navigator? She knew she had not, but had headed for the car without a backward glance.

She threw herself back in the seat. 'How could I be so rude?'

'Quite, but when you come back for the return flight, you make it up to them.'

He turned on to the Exmouth road as the evening closed down into darkness, the slits of his headlights piercing the gloom in an inadequate fashion. 'You can see, can you not, Bee, that it is quite possible that, indeed, poor Wendy was killed in this way. One can barely see a hand in front of one's face – and imagine the London smog, and fog.'

They didn't turn down the road leading to Combe Lodge but continued on. She turned to him. 'Where are we going?'

'Good old Constable Heath has been making enquiries of his contacts in London, so we are going there first. I can't be putting up with you tearing yourself apart all evening when we need to have all our thoughts on Cissie.'

They drew up in front of the police house. The blue light was no longer lit because of the blackout, but it still existed, which was more than could be said of the railings, which had stood outside for decades. 'Have the Scouts been round?' Bryony murmured.

'Indeed. April had to beat them away from the saucepans and direct them to the pile of scrap at the back of the hangar. That kept the little devils busy for quite a few days. In fact they had to get the Guides involved, and the girls did it a damn sight quicker, let me tell you.' He was easing himself out of the car, and the tightening of his voice told the story of his pain.

She waited, knowing better than to offer help. Together they walked along the path and tapped lightly on the door. The police station was also where Constable Heath and his wife, Andrea, lived.

It was she who answered the door. 'Just come in, it's not locked. Be a daft thief that stole from a cop shop.'

Constable Heath came to meet them in the reception room of the police house, his braces looped down his thighs, a newspaper in his hand. He beckoned them through into the back room. Andrea had brewed tea. 'Weak,' she said. 'It's its third brew of the day, but hot and wet.'

They sat. Andrea disappeared into the kitchen.

'Bad business, sad, a young lass like that. I 'ad a word in Templer's pearly ear, and he 'ad a word in a few others. Seems kosher. Poor young thing was crossing the road, and bang. 'Appens a lot, they sez, in the blackout. They'd know the truth of it, Bee. Why would a pimp cut his schnoz off to spite his face, if you think about it? Good little earner, his Wendy was, and just think on: even if it weren't kosher, you gonna be the one to tell our Cissie her sister's been murdered? Not the thing to go through life picturing, I should say.'

They sipped their tea, which was appalling, but they were so used to it they barely registered the fact.

The clock on the mantelpiece chimed. Constable Heath looked across at them. 'You going to tell our

Cissie tonight, or give her some sleep, and tell 'er at the start of the day?'

They didn't know, but drove to Combe Lodge ten minutes later, motoring around the back of the house and into the large barn. Bryony walked to the terrace with Eddie limping at her side. She said, 'I suppose she's in bed at this hour?'

Eddie nodded, and they stood together. The Anderson shelter was unrecognisable in the darkness, and anyway, it had never been used, except by the children. April had planted snowdrops in the turfs on the roof, and forget-me-nots had seeded themselves just as they had done last year. Catherine and Anne had become box hedge monitors, whilst Bryony weeded the herbs and the herbaceous border every time she was here. Deadheading the roses was anyone and everyone's task, as long as they replaced the secateurs afterwards. The moment they forgot, they forfeited the privilege. Catherine had snorted, 'Not sure about privilege – ruddy nuisance, I'd say.'

She hadn't meant it, for she was religious about returning all and any tools.

Eddie said, 'Eric and Sylvia are engaged.'

She smiled. 'Of course they are.'

'He's promoted to sergeant in the Home Guard and Sylvia is doing well as a student nurse.'

'Of course they both are.'

Eddie slipped his arm through hers. 'And you are

alive, and so too Adam, and Combe Lodge survives, and the children within it.'

'I love Cissie,' she sighed, leaning against him and pulling her leather jacket around her against the chill of the breeze.

'We all do. She's ours, especially now.'

'Quite. So do we tell her now, or in the morning?'

They still couldn't decide, but they entered the house through the back door, and then the softly lit kitchen where Rosie barked her joy, her tail wagging itself into a frenzy, sitting in her bed until invited forward. It was only then that Bee crouched and held her. 'I love you, darling Rosie, my big girl. What shall we do, do you think? Tell her?'

April entered, pale and anxious. 'I'm so glad you're back. I don't know whether we tell her now or in the morning. What would I want? I keep asking myself, but I simply don't know because I'm not a child.'

Cissie said from the hall doorway, 'But I am, so who do you need to tell what to?'

She stood there in her pyjamas, coming to Bryony, who scrambled to her feet. 'What are you doing home, Bee? What's wrong?' Rosie licked Cissie's face. Cissie stroked her. 'I don't like you licking my mouth. I'll get worms.'

'Then I won't,' said Bryony.

Cissie laughed. 'Don't be silly, Bee. I heard the car, and woke. The others haven't.'

Bryony lifted the child and held her close, smelling the shampoo in her hair. 'Has April been rinsing your hair in lavender again? It should make you sleep.' She carried her to the kitchen table. 'I'm home because I have something to tell a child, and that child is you. We just didn't know whether to tell you now, or in the morning, because it is something that will upset you very much, and make you really terribly sad.'

She sat on the kitchen chair, holding Cissie tightly. Cissie wriggled free, and put her hands on either side of Bryony's face, turning her head so that Bryony looked straight at her. 'Is it Adam?'

Bryony shook her head. The pressure of Cissie's hands increased, and her nails dug into Bryony's face. The child whispered, 'Is it Wendy?'

Cissie waited, her eyes unwavering. Bryony swallowed. 'Yes, darling, it's Wendy. We've just heard that she was hit in the blackout by a car, and died. We didn't know how, or when to tell you.'

The pain of the child's nails was sharp, but didn't distract Bryony from seeing the tears pooling in Cissie's eyes, her lips trembling, her face becoming pale. Without a sound Cissie dropped her hands and leaned into Bryony, who held her as though she would never let her go, and that was because she wouldn't. This child was theirs, she would grow up within their love. Most of all, she would survive this news.

Cissie said, her voice almost a wail, 'You didn't

know how to tell me, but you came back so you could. I do love you, Bee. You're so brave.'

Bryony rested her chin on the child's head and looked across at April, who was crying. So was Eddie. But she wouldn't. The tears were streaming down her face but no, she wasn't crying.

Cissie came into Bee's bed that night, and slept. In the morning she woke, and remembered, but said, 'I thought she'd die in the bombing. Then I thought it would be some other way. I don't have to worry now, because it's happened and it was sort of clean. I thought it might be Timmo, hurting her so badly she died. Now I know I won't have to hear this news again.'

The children went to school together, as usual. Betty held Cissie's hand as they set off down the drive, their socks held up by garters, their satchels slapping against their backs, their gas masks hanging over their shoulders.

At lunchtime Mrs Sanderson, who was still billeting officer, dug her brogues into the gravel of the drive, and powered her way to the door. She had a man in tow. He wore a suit, and carried a mackintosh over his arm. He held a brown briefcase up against his chest, as though to protect himself against the vicissitudes of life, or was it just Mrs Sanderson? April and Bryony watched from the steps leading to the front door of the lodge, where they had been talking to Stubby Baines the milkman about the cow he had doubts about. 'Poor milker, she be, but she's a dear old girl,' he now said, lifting his hat and scratching his head. His horse chewed the carrot that April had given him, rattling his bit and tossing his head.

Mrs Sanderson mounted the steps as though heading a charge, but then, when didn't she? Stubby said, 'Which is more than I can say about this one.'

Mrs Sanderson ignored him, and directed her words at April and Bryony. 'Celia's headmistress telephoned me this morning with the news of Wendy Jenkins's death, so sad. It should, of course, have been you who told me.' She blasted on. 'I informed the local authorities, as I must, because Miss Jenkins was Celia's next of kin, and only living relative. Mr Torrence from the authorities has been to see me.'

Mr Torrence held up his hand. 'If I may?'

Clearly he might not, because barely drawing breath Mrs Sanderson crossed her arms. 'He is here, of course, to relieve you of Celia's presence. She must be taken to a children's home, where the next stage of her care will be decided.'

Stubby Baines looked from Mrs Sanderson to April and Bryony. He had stopped scratching his head, but his hand remained beneath his hat. His horse had dropped bits of carrot on the steps. Stubby said, 'Sounds bang out of order to me, you daft old baggage, and yon bloke should be ashamed of hisself, standing there, clutching that damned bag as though it holds the crown jewels.'

The horse neighed and Mrs Sanderson took a step backwards, into Mr Torrence, who yelped as her weight sank on to his foot. It seemed to galvanise him, and he shoved her off with great force. Mrs Sanderson tumbled down the steps. Bryony had sight of pink bloomers meeting brown lisle stockings as Mrs Sanderson sat on the drive, her skirt up round her backside, trying to get her bearings.

The horse nosed her. She shrieked. Mr Torrence shouted, 'If you wouldn't mind, all of you.' It brought silence. Mrs Sanderson got to her knees, and then her feet, as he stepped closer to April and Bryony, saying, 'I am merely here on a reconnaissance visit. Do not be alarmed. We were indeed alerted to the sad state of affairs, but it is not our intention in any way to hurt the child further.'

At last Bryony found her voice. 'Why not fetch Eddie, April, if he is up and at it yet?' She held out her hand to Mr Torrence. 'Would you like to come in?' He freed his hand from around his briefcase and shook hers. She had expected a clammy, weak handshake but it was surprisingly firm, warm and hearty.

Mrs Sanderson had regained her position at his side. He said, 'Thank you, Mrs Sanderson. Your presence will not be required now that you have delivered me safely. I will order a taxi, or take the bus back to my office.' He turned his attention back to Bryony. 'I hope that you can spare the time to discuss the matter forthwith. I think that would be best for all concerned.'

'Indeed it would.' Bryony's voice was firm, and grim.

Stubby Baines yanked Mrs Sanderson's arm, pulling her with him as he began to lead his milk cart away from the steps. 'You'd best be chuntering your big arse on back to your little cottage too, Dilly Sanderson. You always did have a beak to match your buttocks, and loved poking it in where it wasn't wanted. You best get yonself back and tend that poor old boy of a husband of yours. Unless the darned old devil 'as made a break for it while you're 'ere flashing yon knickers. Could send 'em for parachutes, you could.'

The wheels of the milk cart crunched their way down the drive, drowning out Mrs Sanderson's reply as she walked alongside. Mr Torrence sighed as he looked after them. 'One does meet all sorts . . .'

'Indeed one does.' Bryony led him into the kitchen, to be met by Eddie, wagging his walking stick at Mr Torrence. 'That child's not setting one foot in any children's home.'

Mr Torrence placed his briefcase on the table, and undid the straps. 'Probably not,' he said. 'May I sit?'

'You may,' said April, taking a place at the table. The others followed. April removed Eddie's walking stick from his hand and passed it to Bryony, who felt she would use it herself if Mr Torrence even suggested that Cissie should be removed from their care.

He withdrew a file from his briefcase, and from this he extracted an envelope. 'We received this in the first post. Clearly Miss Jenkins's solicitor was informed immediately of the accident, and managed to catch the evening post. This—' He waved the documents he had removed from the envelope. 'This makes clear Miss Jenkins's wishes, which are that Cissie is to remain in your care, Miss Miller. In effect, that you adopt her, and I see from the notes that you have a copy of this same letter.'

He placed the other documents on the table and waved the letter. He coughed. 'May I trouble you for a glass of water?'

April shook her head. 'The kettle's simmering. I'm sure you'd like to share our first brew of the day – fresh tea leaves, in other words.'

Mr Torrence's face cleared. 'How very kind. Mrs Sanderson was diligent enough to telephone our office the moment it opened, so I had to scamper here. She means well.'

'No, she doesn't,' Eddie muttered.

Mr Torrence seemed to nod, but perhaps it was a trick of the light.

'At this present time, regretfully I cannot rubber-stamp your adoption, Miss Miller.'

He steepled his hands beneath his chin, and looked from one to the other. April brought the tea to the table. Bryony leaned forward. 'Why the hell not?'

April warned, 'Bryony.'

Eddie slapped the table. 'Why?'

'Miss Miller is unmarried.'

'But engaged.' April poured the tea, putting the tea leaves caught by the strainer back in the pot when she had finished. Mr Torrence nodded at her offer of milk. 'But presently unmarried.'

'Adam's at sea, we haven't managed to combine our leave yet. This can't be happening, I will not let you take our Cissie. It's not what her mother wanted.'

Mr Torrence was reading the documents again. April sipped her tea, her eyes on Bryony. Does she think I'm going to rip his throat out with my bare hands? Bryony wondered. She reached for Eddie's walking stick. April shook her head. Bryony almost laughed. She was only going to rest her hand on it, wasn't she? Suddenly she wasn't sure, because no piece of paper would separate her from that child. A child who wanted to fly, and Bryony was going to teach her. And what about her three friends, who made up an indissoluble gang?

Mr Torrence pulled at his lower lip, and replaced the papers on the table. 'My thoughts are that Miss Miller, together with Mr and Mrs Standing, act as foster parents to Celia Jenkins until such time as Miss Miller ties the knot, as it were. So, there will be no hurry to do so. We don't want to rush anything through. Rather too much of that going on in the world today, and too many people will look at one another over the breakfast table when peace arrives, wondering quite how they will manage to stagger on together until they die.'

He looked round at the three of them, and grinned, widely. 'I suspect that Mr Sanderson had much the same feeling when he returned from the trenches, don't you?'

That afternoon, when the children returned from school, they all trooped into the kitchen, their faces down to their knees because Agnes had asked Cissie where she'd be living now that her sister was dead.

Bryony blessed Mr Torrence when she explained the situation and the children rushed out to the cottage to tell Catherine and Anne, who they knew would have been worried. Bryony hadn't even cast a thought in the direction of the two women, but to the children, Combe Lodge and its inhabitants were their world. 'Thank God for Combe,' she murmured.

April brought biscuits over to the table. 'Yes, we are so lucky that we have somewhere to come home to. Do you find it makes a difference, dearest Bee?'

Bee looked around the kitchen, the dresser with its chipped plates and paintwork, the children's drawings on the wall, just as once there had been hers and Hannah's. 'It keeps me sane. It, and all of us, is why I go on. I can't bear the thought of jackboots tramping through our garden, our house. We're so damned lucky, so far, and I'll go down fighting for it.'

April put her arms around her. 'No one is going down on my watch, so no need for the dramatics.'

Bryony thought of Jersey. 'What's happening to them, d'you think, April? Will they survive and how will they be, if they do?'

'I don't know, and what about Hannah? She betrayed you and my son when you went to fetch her. I'm not sure I can ever forgive her, can you?'

'I can't afford to think about it.'

Chapter Twenty-Five

September 1942
Jersey

Hannah adjusted her face mask, watching Sister Maria as she palpated the extended abdomen of the woman who was ten days overdue, before listening to the heartbeat through the fetoscope.

'Well, Mrs Myers, you have a baby in a hurry at last, my dear. It won't be long until you meet one another. Now, I wonder if you will allow student nurse Hannah Miller to feel your abdomen and listen to the heartbeat. She's starting her nursing course, with the ultimate aim of being a midwife. We'll just hope that it's accredited at the end of the war. Either way, we need her. There does seem to be a rise in the birth rate, but what else is there to do, I suppose, of an evening?'

Mrs Myers and Hannah laughed in surprise. Sister Maria said, 'I wasn't always a nun, you know. So can our Hannah learn a little today?'

Mrs Myers nodded. 'She can do what she likes, as long as the little devil gets on and comes out. Lazy, like his dad, seems to me.'

Sister Maria and Staff Nurse Williams laughed while Hannah took the wooden fetoscope and listened. Sure enough, there was a steady heartbeat. Sister Maria then examined Mrs Myers 'down below' and announced to Staff Nurse Williams, 'Ah, two fingers dilated.'

Hannah looked at the clock. It was almost midday. 'By teatime?'

'I think so,' Sister Maria agreed. She took her patient by the hand. 'Our Miss Miller has a knack for picking the right delivery time. If I weren't who I was I'd have a bet on it, but I dare say Staff Nurse Williams will be chalking it up on the board.'

Again there was laughter, but another contraction began and Mrs Myers grimaced, twisting and turning. Hannah said, 'Try to concentrate on breathing. It helps.'

Mrs Myers gripped Sister Maria's hand tightly, and gasped, 'Easy enough to say when you're not going through it, isn't it, Sister? You wait until you're married with a brood of your own, young lady.'

Hannah looked down at the hand that squeezed Sister Maria's, and the wedding ring. How lucky. She stopped herself. No, not lucky – how sensible, how wise. Staff Nurse Williams called from the doorway. 'Time for your break, Hannah. I'm chalking the time up on the common-room board, so, Mrs Myers, be a good girl and produce at five, and I'll share my winnings with you.'

'How much?'

'A couple of eggs from the henhouse at the back.'

'Ah, and there I was thinking it would change my life. So an egg each, eh?'

Again there was laughter.

Hannah patted Mrs Myers's leg. 'I'll be back soon.'

She slipped downstairs to the kitchen. Mrs Amos was drinking tea. When she saw Hannah she waved her to a seat. 'Have a cuppa, and then get off and send little Elizabeth a big kiss from me. How is the little soul?'

'Very well, and trying to walk.' She forced herself to smile. 'I'm knitting a cardigan which I'll leave on the wall as usual.'

The tea was weak, but it didn't matter. Mrs Amos pushed across one of the biscuits she'd baked.

'I think Sister Maria wants to talk to you. It's been a year, and there have been no children taken by the Germans.' Mrs Amos put up a hand. 'I know the poor wretched prisoners they're bringing to build the fortifications say that the Germans have taken children from their areas into Germany, but this has not happened here. Elizabeth needs you, your aunt too.'

Hannah finished her tea. 'I'm still frightened.'

Mrs Amos sighed. 'I know, my dear, but how brave you've been, and how you have changed. But you cannot be as frightened as those poor prisoners who are made to work so hard. Like skeletons, they are. I put food out again last night as Sister Maria said I should. It's all gone, and some of the lettuce was pulled in the night. I think they must come out to eat, and then go back. Poor beggars – there seems little point in trying to escape, because where can they go? We're surrounded by water. But they do go on trying, and a very few are not recaptured. Presumably some islanders hide them?'

She looked at Hannah, who shook her head saying, 'If so, how brave.'

Hannah took her cup and plate across to the sink and washed them. 'The Germans are foul. On top of all that cruelty they've confiscated the radios again. They've shipped out Jews from Guernsey. They've deported most of those who aren't islanders to camps on the Continent – the British, in other words. Thank heavens I'm an islander, so my daughter is too. I hate the Germans for all that they are doing.' Not for the first time was she glad that Hans had gone. What if she had begun to feel like this when he was here? How could she and Elizabeth have escaped from that world?

Hannah put away the crockery, and wondered where the girl of old had gone, the one who thought of nothing but herself. Gone back into a time that knew no Elizabeth, the child she would die for and would protect with her last breath. A child who had taught her the value of others, and the shame of being the person she was.

She removed her white starched hat and cycled in the warmth of the mellow September. It was such a beautiful time of year. At Combe Lodge the perennials would be in the last stages of blooming, and had Bee's box hedge survived? Had they been bombed? Was Bee flying? Were they even alive? There was so much she didn't know, so much she didn't deserve to know.

She kept to the right as a patrol guarding skeletal prisoners marched past. Had one of those prisoners come to the nursing home last night, was there a sort of sign that said where food could be found? Was it enough help to give them? Should they be doing more, should they be trying to hide them if they escaped?

But she was now a mother so . . .

The road curved left, then right, and sloped slightly downhill. She liked this bit, because she could soar towards Haven Farm, just as her heart felt it was doing. Hannah slowed as the farm came into sight. Her brakes screeched. She dismounted and pushed her bike down the track leading to the sties. She rested it against the wall. As she did so she heard a crash from one of the sties, a flash of movement where she knew no pig was housed. She turned away, retracing her steps. There had been patrols out, searching for escaped prisoners, prisoners with nowhere to go. She did not look back.

She walked along the road in front of the farm. Aunt Olive was weeding in the front garden, cutting down the lavender. Elizabeth was sitting on a rug, pulling at a hobby horse made out of one of Uncle Thomas's old socks stuck on the end of a cut-down broom handle, with reins made of plaited wool. Hannah leaned on the gate and called across. 'Hello there! Such a lovely morning.'

Aunt Olive heaved herself off her knees, and waved. 'Elizabeth, it's someone to see you.' She whispered, 'It's Mummy.'

Hannah's daughter crawled across the lawn. Hannah said, 'It's a gee-gee.' Elizabeth sat up, and said, 'Mama.'

Aunt Olive handed Hannah a paper bag. 'Lavender heads. They will be nice in the delivery room, and your own bedroom. But please come and live here now, with us, this has gone on too long. No one has taken any notice, no child has been removed.'

Hannah took the lavender, her eyes on Elizabeth. She shrugged. 'I heard a noise from a sty. It's dangerous, Aunt Olive, to give sanctuary to anyone. The Boche will take revenge on everyone living at the farm, including my child.'

Aunt Olive looked behind her, as though searching, but for whom? She picked up Elizabeth and brought her to Hannah. 'You go to your mummy, because we have something to show her, haven't we, but we mustn't tell Uncle Thomas.'

Elizabeth put her finger to her lips and nodded, then nestled against Hannah, who pulled her close, rubbing her cheek against her hair. Together they walked through the farmyard to the sties, approaching quietly. Aunt Olive called, 'It's just us, no need to worry.'

Again Hannah felt a surge of alarm, and fury. How could her aunt jeopardise Elizabeth in this way? She stopped, turning back. But then she heard a bark. She swung back. Vicky, Uncle Thomas's sheepdog had died three months ago.

Aunt Olive laughed. 'Did you really think I'd put Elizabeth in danger, silly girl? It's your uncle's birthday present, a replacement for Vicky – well, two replacements. Brother and sister, they'll be good working dogs.' They approached, and peered in the doorway. Four eyes looked back, two sheepdog puppies tumbled out of the straw.

Hannah laughed, then fell quiet. 'I was just wondering, you see, if those of us at the nursing home should do more. What if we took in an escapee and the Germans tracked him down? How many of us would be sent to a camp? We have children, what would happen to them?

Aunt Olive slipped her arm through Hannah's and walked back. 'I think that's a problem too far, let's concentrate on our own. You see, I was talking to Sister Maria the other day. I met her in St Helier, she thought I was looking tired, and I had to admit that I find a baby just too much. Old Davy does what he can to help Tommy and Clive, who has so far avoided deportation, but I really do need you here. More to the point, Elizabeth needs you. Come back here, Hannah, because we can and should establish a family, and yes, let's prepare a fiction about her father for the authorities, should they ever ask. We could say he's married to someone else, or some such.'

'But . . .'

Aunt Olive carried on, 'The German personnel is changing all the time, and I'm sure none remember you and Hans. The islanders are too tired, too hungry to care really, or most are and will have forgotten the relationship you had with him. The Jerry-bags they object to are those who flaunt their perfume, their "gains" like that silly Cheryl. Anyone who matters knows you have turned a corner. You can still nurse, in fact we want you to, to provide for your own future. We think it's marvellous and you've already been at it for nine months, so to leave would be a waste.'

Hannah moved Elizabeth to her other hip as they moved into the farmyard, and then the kitchen. 'What about Uncle Thomas?' She sat down at the table; the oilcloth was torn and faded.

'He'd rather the family was together, now he's seeing you really turning things around.'

Elizabeth clambered down to the floor and crawled to the playpen, hauling herself up on the bars. Aunt Olive said, 'See, she's really trying to walk. Soon nowhere will be safe.' They laughed.

Hannah lifted Elizabeth into the playpen, where she played with bricks her uncle had carved out of wooden block ends and sanded smooth. The words 'the family' rang in her mind. The family. After all that had happened, he wanted the family together.

She could have wept, but didn't. Grown-ups didn't weep at the drop of a hat.

She leaned forward, her elbows on her knees, watching her daughter. There was such a look of Hans about her, but that didn't mean that she was a Nazi, it meant she was a Miller, with an Aunt Bee who was as straight as a die, and a great-aunt who was a saint, as, too, was her great-uncle.

She stood, and said, 'I'll talk about it to Sister Maria. Now, I must go, I have a patient in labour.'

Hannah cycled back. Parking her bike at the rear of the home, she saw that the tool-shed door was ajar. As she watched, it slowly shut. She knew that beneath the shed there was a food store, for potatoes, carrots, and now sugar beet which was being grown to help out in the sugar shortage. She turned on her heel, realisation dawning. Doors didn't close on their own, and the cellar was almost empty – or was it? So why was she was pontificating when others were actually doing something?

The September shadows were long, and lay across the vegetables. Trugs were piled up outside the back door. Nappies were waving in the breeze. She must bring them in before the dampness came down but she needed to see if Mrs Myers would produce at five, and there was Sarah Wallace who she thought would give birth at 3.22. She was to be in attendance.

She shook off her wellington boots, which leaked, but a bit of rain never hurt anyone, and besides, there were no new ones available. She'd left her sensible lace-ups in the hallway. If she returned to Haven Farm the puppies would be kept outside, so at least her shoes wouldn't be chewed. She closed the back door, but flashed a look at the tool-shed. Was there room in the cellar for one man, or two? Those harbouring escaped prisoners, and possibly their families, suffered deportation to God knows where. There was talk of appalling concentration camps.

Hannah entered the kitchen. 'A bit windy out there,' she said to Mrs Amos, who was talking to Sister Maria. 'The tool-shed door closed on its own. Might be an idea to sort that out in case someone thinks to have a look.'

Sister Maria waved her goodbye, and headed outside.

Mrs Amos hesitated in her preparation of salad for lunch, but then continued with the finishing touches, saying, 'Strange gusts we get sometimes. Sister Maria was just saying she needs to talk to you, in about ten minutes, I would think. She'd like your room for some of the mothers. As we've said, all this isolation is upping the birth rate. Just put the potatoes for baking into the oven for me, there's a pet.'

Hannah checked the clock: it was midday. She put the potatoes in the oven and checked the clock again, just as Mrs Amos was doing. It was five minutes past twelve. Mrs Amos nodded towards the plates on the dresser. 'Just pile them on the trays for me. Mavis is busy stock-taking in the back pantry. You don't mind, do you?'

At ten minutes past twelve, Mrs Amos nodded. 'Up you go then, or she'll wonder where you are.'

Upstairs, she tapped on Sister Maria's door. 'Enter,' Sister Maria called, panting. She must have rushed in from the garden and up the back stairs.

Hannah opened the door and entered. Behind Sister Maria was a crucifix, and on the side wall a print of Holman Hunt's *Light of the World*. She found it comforting. Sister Maria, her wimple as gleaming as ever, indicated the chair on the other side of her desk. 'Hannah, sit down.'

Sister Maria explained that as her aunt would by now have talked to her about living at Haven Farm, she did hope Hannah would consider such a move. She would be provided with curfew exemption certificates in order to continue to work at the nursing home. Hannah nodded. 'A shed door swings shut, my aunt talks of a discussion with you about me moving to Haven Farm, and here we are, in your study, having very much the same conversation. Do you ever feel manipulated?' she asked.

'Always. I call it doing God's work for him. We have enjoyed your presence here, dearest Hannah, but I have come to believe, very recently, that it is best for you to live elsewhere. You are a mother and should not be too closely associated with us.'

There was a silence. She must indeed leave and

it was for her own good, or at least the good of her child. She looked again at the *Light of the World* and then at Sister Maria, and was humbled. 'I understand, and though I don't pray, tonight I will, for the safety of you all.'

At 3.22, Sarah gave birth to a healthy son, and at five o'clock Mrs Myers was delivered of a daughter. Staff and mother each had an egg.

Chapter Twenty-Six

September 1942
Combe Lodge

Bryony met April and Cissie at the British Restaurant at St Luke in Exeter. The train journey had been trouble-free though there had not been a seat. As she hugged April, she knew that it would have been difficult to sit still even had there been. There was a table available and the food was good.

'So, my girl, no doubts about marrying my son tomorrow?' April sat back, patting her mouth with the serviette.

Cissie looked with alarm from one to the other. 'Oh, Bee, no, you can't have.'

Bryony laughed. 'Cissie, don't worry. I've never been so excited in the whole of my life.'

They walked around Exeter, waiting for the bus. The city smelt of brick dust and sulphur, courtesy of the May blitz they had endured, and many of the houses looked like broken teeth, replicas of areas of London. Well, she thought, like so many cities around the world. How could one madman and his followers cause so much misery and disaster?

Cissie was skipping along ahead of them, but dropped back to hold Bryony's hand. 'The Luftwaffe bombers go one way over Combe Lodge, and our bombers go the other. Do you really fly the Wellingtons to the bases, Bee, or the maintenance units, anyway?'

'Yes, I really do. It's not a problem, but looking back the tail seems miles away.'

They passed St Luke's School, minus its windows and roof, and all the houses opposite were gone. They toiled to the bus stop. 'I hope the weather holds until tomorrow,' April muttered. 'It's hot for all this tramping around, but we need it like this for the bridesmaids' dresses.'

Bryony laughed. 'Forget about the bride, then?'

April put her arm around her and pulled her to her side. 'My dear, anyone who goes from an open cockpit Tiger Moth trainer to a Wellington in one easy movement can cope with a bit of changeable weather, but we mere mortals fuss about such things.'

All three of them were laughing, though Cissie looked back at the school. 'I suppose they don't have to go any more? You should have heard Miss Evans fuss when I asked if I could come to meet you today, instead of going to school.'

'It's her job to fuss, just like it's ours,' April muttered, sharing a glance with Bryony. Bryony said, 'I expect she'll have forgotten about it by tomorrow, when she sees her pupils walking down the aisle behind the prettiest bride in the country.'

'Oh, you show-off, Bee. I'll tell Adam on you, and then he won't want to marry you, so there. And besides, Sylvia will be a bride too, and she's pretty. But not as pretty as you.'

Cissie was skipping ahead. The two women watched her. 'Just where is my intended right this minute?' Bryony asked April.

'Don't even think about it.' April shook her head. 'I gather Barry Maudsley has produced some of his infamous scrumpy so they've trooped off . . . Well, run off, I should perhaps say. I think Jean Maudsley is putting on some sort of lunch to sop up the worst of it, but the Maudsleys are so thrilled at the double wedding. They love Sylvia and it's quite right that they do. It's just such a shame that Adam's mother doesn't feel the same about her daughter-in-law.'

The women roared with laughter again. Cissie skipped back to them. 'But April, you are Bee's mother-in-law.'

April ruffled her hair. 'Exactly.'

They walked on, arriving at the bus stop just as Dan hove into sight. The talk on the bus was all about the bombing of Torquay, and the buses set on fire by bombs in Bristol, and then what about those E-boats seen off Seaton? April told Bryony, 'Eric's Home Guard were alerted but the permission to fire didn't come through from London until they'd gone. He was so upset. I think he wants notches on his gun.'

Dan called, 'Four of the big bombers came over yesterday but our boys took one down. Don't want them going over when old Bert's whacking out the wedding march on the organ, eh, Bee? That'd let the air out of his buffers, that it would.'

The bus almost rocked itself off the road with the laughter. People did laugh more these days, Bee thought, looking around. Perhaps they were grabbing at the chance. April had fallen silent. 'I don't want you up in those planes with all this going on. You're not armed, they could shoot you down.'

'But they haven't.' Bryony pointed to a windsock blowing almost horizontally over to the east. 'I flew into there on Thursday. John Folkes was there, on secondment. He said to remind you, Cissie, that he's bringing the shell that you can hold to your ear and hear the sea. He'll make sure to give it to you at the wedding.'

Cissie was sitting across the aisle, and her face lit up. She told Mrs Smith, whose leeks, piled high in her basket, were stinking out the bus. 'It's a conch shell, but Bee can never remember the name. Pilot Officer Folkes told me it was given to him by a dancer on a tropical island wearing a grass skirt.'

Mrs Smith laughed. 'I'm sure she was.' She winked at Bryony. 'Sounds like my old dad and his fishing stories. To hear him tell them, you couldn't have squeezed the fish in through the back door.'

They trundled on, and at last drew up at the gates to Combe Lodge. 'Thanks, Dan,' Bryony said. 'You could have dropped us back at the bus stop.'

'I'll back up then, shall I, lass?'

April tapped the top of his cap. 'See you and Myrtle at the church tomorrow.'

Bryony said the same to everyone on the bus. 'See you at the church tomorrow and then for eats at Combe Lodge afterwards. Don't be late, because I won't be. I've been waiting long enough to get a combined leave.'

She hadn't seen Adam since they had met up at Hamble six weeks ago and for tonight he was staying with Eric, while Sylvia was at the Lodge.

The next day dawned clear and warm. Bryony rose early and slipped out to the garden. She gathered up the spade from the shed, and her gloves. Catherine and Anne had given them a ceanothus and two brooms for a wedding present, and she wanted to plant them before their roots dried out.

As she dug in the herbaceous bed the breeze was fresh, the earth friable, the clink of stone on spade satisfying. With each spadeful she felt the sense of needing to rush fade, and the need to be alert diminish. After all, America was in now, Russia had not been defeated, so Germany was stretched, and she might even live to see the end of it.

She tested the broom in the hole. Yes, that would be just right. She slit the sack from the roots, spread them, and then refilled the hole, tamping it down. She moved to the other side and began to dig the second hole. Joyce would be down in time for the wedding, having had a night at the clubs in London, though she had said it wouldn't be the same without Bee. Did they go because they needed to live every second, was this what everyone everywhere was doing, just squashing in as much as they could because there might not be any more time? What were they doing in Jersey?

She blanked the thought because she did not know how she felt, but somehow the image of Hannah with her soldier was embedded in her consciousness.

Bryony and Sylvia arrived at the church at eleven, on the dot. The same torn parachute had been used for both their dresses, though Sylvia's was full with long sleeves whilst Myrtle, Dan's wife, had created a long, fitted dress with a rear train for Bryony, with short sleeves. The bouquets were from the garden, and comprised the last of the roses with myrtle, for constancy. They had given a bouquet to Myrtle, too. Eddie drove, having polished his MG until it shone.

He no longer used his cane, 'Which is as well, girls, as I will have you on each of my arms, and I don't want to be falling flat on my face, again.'

Bryony leaned forward in the back seat. 'Quite. Just how many glasses of scrumpy did you have?'

He started to shake his head, and then thought better of it. 'Please, do not mention the word scrumpy in the presence of anyone who was at Barry's yesterday. It would amount to unendurable cruelty.'

The girls laughed. Sylvia suggested, 'Just drink water for the rest of the day. That is what Eric will be doing if he wants the marriage to succeed beyond this evening.' They were approaching the church as the women laughed again. He held up his hand. 'No, not so loud, if you don't mind, girls.'

They did mind, and laughed again. He drew up at the lychgate, the white ribbons on the front of the car shimmering in the breeze.

Eddie walked the two girls up the path. Cissie and Betty met them in the porch, with Sol and Frankie, all four in new clothes, because they had grown. For a moment, as she looked at these children, Bryony found her lips trembling. She loved them all, but Cissie especially, and they must go on growing, go on living. The organ was playing the wedding march. April kissed both Sylvia and Bryony. 'Beautiful, quite beautiful, my dears.' She slipped into the church. Bryony looked over her shoulder at the children. Cissie and Betty led the boys. Cissie's steady grey eyes met Bryony's. 'I love you so much, Bee. Wendy did too, you know. That's why she wanted me to stay with you.'

Eddie squeezed Bryony's arm and whispered, 'We are blessed with these children. Cissie reminds me of you, dearest Bee. Now come along, or Bert and his infernal machine will run out of puff halfway down the aisle, and we'll have to hum.'

He released both girls, leaned forward and eased open the double doors. They squeaked. He stood, arms akimbo. The girls captured him. He said, 'All right, troops, on the count of three.' Bryony glanced back. Betty and Cissie nodded. The boys were kicking one another. Cissie slapped them. 'One, two, three.'

They were off.

The church was full. Mr Torrence and his wife, who had become regular visitors, were sitting with Catherine and Anne, whose husbands were now in North Africa, and otherwise occupied. Their babies, or rather toddlers, were clambering along the pew. Stubby Baines was sitting alongside Dan and Myrtle. The usual bus passengers were scattered around. Joyce, and others of the ATA girls, were there in their uniforms, alongside their landlady, Suzy Windsor, and Pearl from Hatfield. Mick plus a few others of the *High Ground* crew who could be spared had raced to arrive on time. Clearly they weren't used to scrumpy, from the sweat and paleness of their skin, but Bryony doubted they would stick to water. They weren't trawlermen for nothing.

Cissie's teacher, Miss Evans, was near the front, wearing a very odd hat. She seemed to have found some pheasant feathers and popped them in, willy-nilly, along with sprigs of honesty, some rather too high. Eddie had noticed too, but Cissie whispered, 'We helped her make her hat, isn't it lovely?'

Eddie whispered back, 'It's the best hat I've ever seen, and I think your teacher is one in a million.' His voice was quite serious. Bee nodded, because any teacher who wore a hat like that in a public place because it had been created by her class was indeed a special woman.

Constable Gerry Heath, his wife and their neigh-bouring farmer, Mr Simes, sat behind Ben Rowan, a lieutenant now. He had been in charge of the queue at Dunkirk and sat alongside Mr Templer, the uncle of Stan Jones, who had remembered Ben Rowan's tele-phone number. Stan had been killed in North Africa.

Interspersed with these guests were friends of Sylvia's from Exeter Hospital, but no family. Bryony had said last night as they chatted in the shared bedroom, 'You're part of the Combe Lodge lot, now, you know. Whether you like it or not.'

Sylvia had said, 'And Hannah?'

'Ah, Hannah. I rather think she made her decision.'

As she looked ahead she saw April in the front pew, looking at her family walking towards her. Bryony grinned. Beside Eric was his friend, Bob. At Adam's side was Geordie; all four men were in uniform, all four had the scrumpy pallor. She and Sylvia sighed at the same time.

'Bear up, girls,' Eddie encouraged. 'Just like your men are doing.'

'Self-inflicted injuries are not clever, funny or nice,' Bryony murmured. They were the words her Aunt Olive used to use. Did she still?

They each took aim at their man, and stood beside him, and the best men stepped back. Adam smiled, and his heart was in his eyes. He murmured, 'I love you, Bryony Miller.'

The service began.

*

At Combe Lodge, as the last of the guests straggled down the drive long after the sun had gone down, and the food, drink and music had disappeared, Adam stood behind her on the terrace. 'Where did you plant the broom?'

She told him as he kissed her neck.

'And where's the ceanothus?'

She told him. He kissed her again, saying, 'It all continues, darling. Whatever happens, the plants will come up, the seasons will ease one into the other, Cissie will become a young woman, and probably we will survive. If not, we've been here, we've been enclosed by Combe Lodge, we've loved one another. It's enough.'

She turned round, into his arms. 'Do you have some alchemy whereby you can read my mind?'

He shook his head, and said against her mouth, 'No, I just have a good memory. I remember what you say to me as we lie together talking of life and love.'

She laughed, as did he. Above them the stars shone, the moon was bright. She remembered the woman in the train, and began to sing 'By the light of the silvery moon'.

Cissie called from the French windows. 'It's a bomber's moon.'

Adam gestured her over, and hauled her up, one arm still around Bryony. 'It is indeed, but that's war for you, and it won't last for ever. You should remember that, young Cissie. You are loved, and you have been born at a difficult time, but you will gain from living through this. You will know what it is to survive, and you will value those lessons.'

Cissie looked at him. 'Stop being so serious, you sound like the vicar. Today is a happy day because now I can be your real child. Mr Torrence promised, didn't he?'

They walked inside, drew the blackout, and then the curtains. Only then did they switch on the light. All three sat on the sofa, Cissie in the middle. Bryony said, 'Yes, it's quite true. We signed the papers today, after the ceremony, little madam. It should all be fine. Just a bit of rubber-stamping to come.'

Cissie leapt to her feet, her eyes shining. 'April said you would, she did, you know. Wendy would be pleased, she really really would, and I expect she's up there, looking down, feeling happy.'

She flew from the room. Adam slipped along the sofa. 'Quite how did we become parents to a ten-year-old?'

Bryony shook her head. 'The mind boggles. I think it was just a flanking movement, through the long grass.' They held one another. It was then she shared with him that Betty's mother, who still lived in Poplar, in the East End, because she was a valiant and brave woman, had asked if Bryony would stand as parent, in the event . . .

She'd said when she telephoned. 'You see, how

can we ever split the girls, Bee? So, if I cop it, with 'er dad already gone west...?'

Adam shrugged. 'Come one, come all. Eddie's handed me a share of Combe Lodge, did you know?' She did. 'So between us, we can keep the girls safe, and Mum and Eddie aren't going anywhere. It will sort itself out.'

She leaned against him. It was her wedding day and she didn't want to think of Hannah, but she shared Bryony's half of Combe Lodge. What if Hannah and her German wanted to sell her half at war's end? Would she and Adam have the money to buy her out?

He kissed her now, then held her tightly. He said, 'Don't worry, darling. Eddie and I have talked about Hannah. We can buy her out, somehow.'

She half laughed. 'There you are, you are a magician.'

Adam whispered, 'No, but I'm not daft. I under-stand about the inheritance issues. We'll handle it, as and when. Together, all of us at Combe Lodge will handle it but we have to finish the war first, and we're by no means there yet.'

Bryony slept against him, the worry which had nagged at her for so long, and which she had tried to block, fled into the ether. Together they could handle anything.

Chapter Twenty-Seven

Jersey 1944

They heard about D-Day at Haven Farm via Uncle Thomas's wireless, which had remained safely in the chimney, withstanding all efforts at confiscation. The Allies made no attempt to liberate the islands, because their priority was to subdue and defeat Germany in Europe; then, the islanders supposed, they'd finish off Japan.

Food distribution was down to an absolute minimum, the electricity works, gasworks, water supply and harbour all had extra occupation guards posted. Very few soldiers were seen on the streets, which was a blessing, because discipline was fracturing beneath the knowledge of inevitable defeat. In November relief arrived in the shape of the Red Cross vessel *Vega* with supplies, saving the population from starvation.

At the nursing home they were ordered to take in some of the injured German troops who were shipped from France to the Channel Islands for care, and by now Hannah was complicit in sheltering the very few escapees who had made the break.

They were housed beneath the shed in the root vegetable cellar, until they could be moved on to other homes.

When she had finally asked to be involved in mid-1943, she had said to Sister Maria, 'One has to make a choice. I have made far too many stupid ones. Perhaps this is another, but it feels right, it feels as though my family would approve, but Olive and Thomas must not know.'

At her desk, Sister Maria had smiled gently. 'But my dear friend, they are already involved, they are part of the chain.'

As D-Day became a memory, and the war appeared to be drawing to a close, the bombing of targets on the island by British planes became more frequent. Gun emplacements, and boats in the harbour or offshore were attacked. There were rumours of an underground hospital for Nazi troops. Perhaps there were more injured than appeared, and the underground hospital was full. Or perhaps it wasn't finished. Who knew anything any more? Who had known anything much about their island over the last few years?

Alderney was evacuated, bringing Jews, Russians, Poles and a few German political prisoners from their appalling concentration camp to Jersey. They were moved on to God knew where, but two Russians slipped away and found their way to the nursing home. Hannah's role was to take food before lunch in a basket, a basket that contained vegetables when she re-emerged, in case any wounded soldier peered from the ward windows. While there she spent twenty minutes teaching some English, which Sister Maria deemed would be useful to the escapees, should the war end and a life in Britain become a possibility. A third escapee arrived, a Pole, who already had some English.

As well as feeding them, Hannah piled more blankets high in the cellar to keep the underground chill at bay. When it was deemed safe by one of their guardians, the men would sneak out into the sunshine through a back entrance in the shed. The men laughed at the smell of manure, which Staff Nurse Williams, Mrs Amos, Hannah or even Sister Maria spread over the vegetable beds to distract the German patrol dogs, should they come. In addition, the nursing home inherited one of Uncle Thomas's young dogs, which raised the alarm whenever a patrol approached, and the escapees would slip back into their cellar until the barking stopped.

As 1944 became 1945 and a cold winter grew colder, they moved the men into the attic, because the home had thus far never been searched. If it was, then there was a gap in the eaves into which they could squeeze, and Hannah spread Aunt Olive's lavender across the floor to confuse the dogs. In the spring the men returned to the cellar, as there was no other home able to take them, and they were scared to move at all in the attic.

As 1945 moved into early May, the people grew

thinner, even with the Red Cross ship making two return trips. In addition the troops became even less disciplined, and more dangerous. Uncle Thomas daily expected that the islands would be relieved by the British, but they weren't. He shrugged and said to Hannah in the farmhouse kitchen, as he jiggled Elizabeth on his knee, 'I have learned patience.'

Aunt Olive had said, 'Your nose is growing, because that is a fib, isn't it, Elizabeth?'

Elizabeth had looked closely at Uncle Thomas's nose. 'Yes, it's longer.'

Clive, who had somehow survived all the deportations and was part of the escape chain, found a tape measure in the drawer, and measured Thomas's nose, pretending it had indeed grown longer. He showed the child the tape.

Hannah laughed, and looked at this family sitting around the kitchen table, a family that was thinner, but happier, though content might have been a better word. Clive nodded to her, as if reading her mind. Clive lived in hope of peace, he had told her many times, but perhaps it was already here, he had taken to saying recently.

Later that day, 4 May, he invited her to his room above the small barn. She saw that he had a sketch of her and Elizabeth on his wall. Calmly he said that one day he hoped she would love him.

Hannah looked from the sketches to him, seeing for the first time his strength, his calmness, his containment. She said, 'One day, perhaps I will allow myself such luxury, but it would depend on Elizabeth. She comes first.'

He nodded. 'Of course, I have known that for a long time, but is there hope?'

She looked from him to the sketches again. She still taught the booming Miss Webster and the gentler Miss Sinclair, and the others who had joined their small class. One day she hoped to have time to return to her own painting. Clive's were better than hers, much better. 'I didn't know you were an artist,' she said.

His smile was tired. 'I have a small studio on the north coast of Somerset. I lived and painted there before all this. It is still mine. I teach too, as do you.' He showed her his portfolio of sketches of the island at war.

She nodded. 'I have a lot to learn.'

He said, 'Perhaps I could teach you.'

She left his loft. 'Perhaps,' she said. She paused. 'There is room at Combe Lodge for a studio. One each, in fact.'

They looked at one another, but said no more.

On 8 May at 10 a.m., the islanders were informed by the German authorities that the war was over. At 3 p.m. a message from Churchill was broadcast proclaiming that a ceasefire had begun yesterday, and the Channel Islands were to be liberated today.

Hannah and Sister Maria felt quietly relieved, but

that was all, because they were too tired and hungry to feel anything else. They walked into St Helier with Elizabeth in the pushchair and said hello to everyone they passed.

'Now,' Sister Maria said, 'what do we do with our three men? They don't want to return to their homelands, especially the Russians.'

They turned the corner. There were people in a group, shouting and cursing. Sister Maria put up her hand to Hannah. 'Wait,' she said.

She glided as she always did, and the people parted for her, just as they always did. It was Cheryl. The group had cut her hair, and daubed her with something black, on to which feathers stuck. Hannah watched as Sister Maria held up her hands, her habit falling from her wrists. 'This really will not do. Perhaps you are angry, but start your freedom with something more worthy to commemorate this moment.'

Cheryl ran out of the melee past Sister Maria, stopping for a moment when she saw Hannah, her face twisted by fear and rage. But then she ran on down the street, her dress, once so smart and brought from Paris by her latest German protector, ripped and torn. Her officer had left two weeks ago, or so the gossip had it, and the calls following Cheryl were asking where her pimp and racketeer, Bobby, was hiding because he had milked them for too long.

The next day HMS *Beagle* arrived to accept the German surrender. They raised the Union Flag at the Pomme D'Or Hotel but Hannah, Aunt Olive and Uncle Thomas were too busy to be there, because they were trying to think of a way that the escapees could be saved from repatriation. It was then that Bobby knocked on the front door of Haven Farm. His hat was pulled down, but they could see his black eyes, and bloodied nose. He needed to be hidden, just for a day, until he could get Cheryl and himself off the island.

Hannah shook her head. 'Why would I, or would we?' She indicated Aunt Olive, who was standing behind her.

'Because I have papers that would let your Russians stay. Can't help with the Pole but he should be all right cos no one's going to send him back to have his throat slit, or that's what they're saying is going to happen to the Ruskies. How you get them to Britain is up to you, but you've got to get their English up to scratch. You see, I still have my ear to the ground. It would just be me and Cheryl.'

Aunt Olive eased herself beside Hannah. 'Bring the papers, and make it for our Pole as well. If Sister Maria thinks they're good enough, you can stay in the cellar from which you stole the wine. You'll be safe from your own people and I imagine it is from them that you are hiding.' Bobby said nothing, just nodded and said, 'You drive a hard deal.'

'It's the only one there is,' Hannah insisted. Bobby hurried away, looking to left and right, pulling his hat even further down.

He brought Cheryl and the papers after dark. Sister Maria had come to the farmhouse kitchen, and she pored over the papers, until finally nodding.

Uncle Thomas took the two to the wine cellar, which was, of course, empty of all alcohol. He climbed down with them. Hannah followed with some food and water. She placed the food on the small table she and Aunt Olive had set up earlier.

'You two will be gone in the morning.' It wasn't a question from Uncle Thomas.

Cheryl touched her short, uneven hair. It was still stiff with tar. How on earth would it ever come out? Hannah wondered. Bobby said, 'You're right about that. We'll be long gone.'

Uncle Thomas hadn't finished. 'You will not return.' This was not a question either.

Cheryl shook her head. 'Who needs a dump like this?'

Bobby put out his hand towards her, as though to stop the words. He said, 'We're grateful.'

'Indeed,' Hannah said, making for the ladder up into the barn.

Cheryl called after her, 'We was friends once.'

Hannah nodded. 'Yes, once, but we were different people then and you sent me away, with a new baby. But, Cheryl, you also told me some home truths, and for that you have my absolute thanks. That's why we're doing this, well, partly. We need those papers too. I wish you good luck, Cheryl, and a good life.'

She didn't look back. Cheryl's voice had been full of fear and desperation, and that could so easily have been her.

Once back in the farmyard her uncle said, 'It's as well you've been working on the escapees' English. We just need to get them off the island and into Britain, but that's tomorrow's problem. Come on, lass, just think, soon we'll have food and can stop cutting down what's left of the trees for firewood. Sick, I am, of sitting in a thousand sweaters of an evening. Clive's brought in some salad this morning, and I asked him to dispatch one of the chickens, which he did. Your aunt's roasting it. We'll bring some down for Cheryl and Bobby. They need a warmer, don't they, silly sods that they are.'

Chapter Twenty-Eight

July 1945
Combe Lodge

At Combe Lodge, John Folkes arrived at eleven in the morning and banged on the front door. Cissie opened it, but Bryony, six months pregnant, and out of the ATA for three months, was close behind. John grinned at Cissie, and then said to Bryony, 'I did as you said, and survived, and now, again as you said last week, I have arrived to work for you.'

She smiled. 'Indeed you have, and one day when rationing is finished, you may have a sweetie for surviving. You are such a good boy.' They laughed. She pointed up the stairs. 'You'll have Adam's bedroom for now but the cottage is yours once it's redecorated. Eddie's at the hangar. The beautiful Dragonette is almost ready, but he could do with some help – a final service, just to be sure. I took her out for a spin yesterday, but Eddie just wanted to tighten this and that. I warn you, she's been out of action a fair old while so he'll make you work.'

John slipped past, and followed Cissie up the stairs. Betty came rushing from the kitchen to join them, and the two girls chattered with John all the way to the landing. Betty's mother hadn't survived the V2 rockets, so now there were two girls, and Sol. Frankie had returned to his parents, both of whom were fit and well. Sol's mum had lost her mind after being buried in rubble for two nights. She might recover, but for now, as Adam and she had explained to Sol, his mum needed a bit of looking after and they needed a boy in the family to balance the girls.

April came from the kitchen, wiping her hands on the towel. 'I'm glad young John's going to be your second pilot. He and Eddie get on like a house on fire, in spite of John trying to kill him.' She raised her voice just to make sure that John heard as he bounded down the stairs. His laugh pealed out. 'Failed, though, didn't I? Where's Adam?' His overalls were suitably stained with oil, Bryony was pleased to see.

'On the terrace.'

'Still making progress?'

'Of course he is,' Cissie replied. John muttered to Bryony as they walked around the house together, 'Well, I never saw your lips move.'

Bryony laughed. It would be good to have John around. Adam was on the terrace with Eric, who was adjusting his friend's wheelchair. She bent over and kissed her husband. 'Hello, peg-leg.'

'Hello, beautiful girl.'

He shook John's hand. 'Fitted the tin one yet?' John asked, nodding at Adam's mid-thigh stump.

'Any day now, lad,' Adam said, 'then I can strike my matches on it.'

John laughed, and then set off down the path, waving. 'Give us half an hour, Bee, then come and take her up. Am I coming to Jersey with you?'

'Why not, and you can help load the Dragonette with provisions.'

Cissie, Betty and Sol followed in his footsteps, Sol copying John's walk, which was more a swagger.

Bryony sat on the wall, next to the wheelchair. 'I thought he could move into the cottage once it's decorated. Those toddlers of Catherine and Anne took their toll but thank heavens their men survived, and they've found their houses in good shape now they've returned to Jersey. I miss them, though.'

Eric tightened the final nut on the wheel. 'There, that'll have you spinning round corners on one wheel, lad.' He patted Adam's shoulder. Adam laughed at Bryony. 'Not sure about spinning, a gentle trundle will do.'

Eric joined her on the wall. 'I gather Olive telephoned, hence the flight today. Is there any news of Hannah? Is she still on Jersey or has she gone somewhere with Hans?'

'She didn't say a lot.' Bryony was watching Adam manoeuvre his wheelchair, puffing and panting as he brought it round to face them, knowing better than to offer to help. Geordie had also survived the magnetic mine which had bobbed up after the mine-sweepers had been through, but not Mick, nor several others of the crew. When Bryony had visited them in hospital, Geordie had laughed because, he said, he and Adam made a pigeon pair: they had each lost a leg, Adam the left, he the right. Between them, they made a whole.

Eric was waiting, and now she remembered the question. 'Olive just said that all was well, that Hannah was quite the girl she could always have been, and Hans was long dead. She said that everyone on the island was very hungry. Apparently Hannah is a staff nurse and on the way to becoming a midwife. Sister Maria has had the exams accredited. We're taking produce today, and perhaps I will see her.'

Adam was nodding. 'I still think I should come.'

'You're expected at Exeter, to get the stump dressed. John will come. It might be as well if I go anyway, you are still too angry.'

Adam and Eric shared one of their looks. 'You're not, then, Bee?'

'I don't know what I am, but she owns half my share of Combe Lodge. I need to sort that out because we can't buy her out yet, in spite of Eddie's brave words.'

'A bird, I should have been a bird,' Bryony Miller whispered to herself. High above the white-capped sea her smile was one of pure joy, as she sat at the controls of Combe Airline's de Havilland Dragon Rapide. 'What do you think, Cissie? And Sol, and Betty? How are they doing, John?'

John was sitting behind her, next to Adam, who had put his remaining foot down and insisted on coming, especially after he'd bribed Sylvia into dressing his stump. The rest of the aircraft was jammed full of what meat they'd been able to obtain, and fish from Barry Maudsley, butter from Mr Simes, clothes, firewood, a few bags of coal, and medicines from anyone and everyone. Apparently the nursing home had need of it all.

Bryony's leather jacket was undone, her overalls stained with engine oil just as peacetime demanded. She loved the sense of escaping earth, as always, and the soft purr of the engine. She laughed aloud at the thought of Eddie's voice as they left. 'It's an infernal drumming and don't be such a silly sod.'

It was what he had always said.

She patted the control panel. 'Purr away, my little Dragonette, Uncle's a nasty horrid man.' It's what she had dreamed of saying once more, if they survived. She patted her belly. Well, they had and soon there'd be a baby at Combe Lodge. She searched the autumn sky wondering if the few remaining Air Transport Auxiliary pilots were delivering any aircraft to the Continent, though everything was being wound down so quickly she rather doubted it. Still, there were a few aircraft powering through the sky, and one heading north, probably bound for Exeter Airport.

She peered down, seeing what looked like toy boats heading to and from the Channel Islands as though there had not been an absence of years. They would be carrying supplies, and returning evacuees. There were some fishing smacks too that would return to harbour at day's end.

She continued towards Jersey and before long land was in sight. Behind her she heard Adam and John discussing the plans they had all put together for the airline. They would run the business in tandem with Eric and Adam's fishing smacks, which could double as pleasure boats. They weren't going to call it Adam and Eve's Apple, as Old Davy had suggested, though Eddie had tormented her with the idea for some months before he had stopped the game.

From behind, a hand shifted her leather helmet, moving her earpiece, and Adam leaned forward and said, 'I love you. Don't worry, she could have really changed and now be the sister she could always have been.'

How did he know what she was thinking, beneath all the fluttering her mind was doing? 'I know,' she muttered. 'Besides, nothing matters. We can buy her out now that John's confessed he wants a share of the business. What's the betting it's the first thing she asks for, because I'm not sure I believe April's talk of the new Hannah.'

All the time she was talking, she was alert to the wind, to the engine sounds, to the Dragonette's feel. She looked around, up, and down as they flew over Jersey. How few trees there were now. But Olive had said they'd been needed for firewood. Damaged gun emplacements and fortifications were evident. Busy below were British troops, and boats flitted in and out of the harbour. She glanced down at the control panel. All was well.

Gradually she eased back on her speed and height as they passed over Haven Farm Bridge. She called, 'Make sure you're all strapped in, please, children, as we'll be landing very shortly. Adam, when we land, don't you dare move until John takes your weight – one knock on that stump and we're back to square one. I'll have to cut off the other one as punishment.'

Adam groaned, 'She never changes, ever the lady.'

The Dragonette's shadow flashed over fields as Bryony called, 'Please, it's important to tighten those straps. John will have a quick look around to check.'

Adam squeezed her shoulder once more before settling back. She straightened her helmet, descending into the wind, checking and rechecking her instruments, her height, her speed, easing the yoke, gently, gently. She saw Uncle Thomas and Aunt Olive arrive at the field, and her heart actually fluttered and the baby kicked. 'Yes, little one, it's your aunt and uncle,' she murmured.

To her relief, Hannah was not there.

She landed the Dragon Rapide, feather-light, holding the aircraft steady as it rumbled along the mown grass, slowing with no yawing, until she drew it to a halt. Bryony switched off, and eased her shoulders in the silence. She stretched, then removed her helmet, her hair falling free. She returned the waves of the welcoming committee, hung up her helmet, then slipped back through the cabin where the passengers were undoing their straps. It was almost as it had always been, but in other ways, nothing was as it had been.

John had the cabin door open. He slipped on to the wing with the footstool, jumped to the ground and settled it firmly. Bryony led the way out on to the wing, carrying Adam's crutches, and then to the ground. She held up a hand to Adam who had eased on to the wing, and was sitting on his backside. Uncle Thomas was running across the grass. He hesitated when he saw Adam's stump, but then came on at a rush. He grabbed her husband as Adam eased himself from the wing, hugging him and looking up at Bryony. 'A sight for sore eyes,' he said. She had never seen her uncle cry, never seen him so thin. She stood, unsure suddenly, but then Aunt Olive reached her, enfolding her in her arms. She too was too thin, and too old.

Cissie was on the wing, with Betty and Sol. John held out his arms. 'Cissie first, then Betty, finally Sol.' They jumped in turn into his arms, and he swung each child around before he set them down. They came to stand next to Bryony, and for once Cissie was quiet, and pressed against Bryony's side, staring up at the aunt she had heard so much about.

Bryony said, 'Aunt Olive, these are our children.'

Aunt Olive kissed each one as though they were the most precious things in all the world, which they were.

The pony and trap entered the field, with Clive flicking the reins. Bryony waved. He was very thin too. John was unloading the aircraft, and Clive brought the trap close, and helped, hauling the goods straight into the trap.

Aunt Olive pulled at Bryony's sleeve. 'Come, all of you. I have made biscuits, not very sweet, but we'll drizzle honey on them as the rest of the cooks are doing. Or, children, perhaps first I'll take you through to have a look at our piglets, shall I, while Bee goes to say hello to her sister? She will be in the kitchen. They can put water on the tea leaves, the first brew of the day.'

Bryony checked that Adam was all right. He was, having taken Clive's place on the trap while Uncle Thomas chocked the Dragonette. The wind was keen, just as it so often was, here on the island. The women and children walked out on to the road towards the farm. Cissie was telling Sol that he couldn't have pork because he was a Jew, but he could at least look at the piglets. He would think they were sweet. Betty said, 'But I don't want to think they're sweet because I won't want to eat bacon again.'

Aunt Olive and Bryony exchanged a smile. Aunt Olive took her hand. 'You look well, and it's such joy to see you pregnant. Poor dear Adam looks well, in spite of . . . Well, in spite of everything. Now, I just want you to listen to Hannah. She has changed, I swear to you, she has, and we love her in a way we did not before. She has stuck to her nursing, she has been part of our escape chain, in spite of having a child. She has cared for the wretched slave labourers at risk to herself, and her work is not yet quite done.'

Bryony said quietly, 'Yes, you told me of Elizabeth, and I'm glad for Hannah's sake, but she betrayed us. We could have died.'

Aunt Olive nodded. 'She knows that, and the realisation is something she has had to live with. I believe that, along with other things, it has guided her onwards.'

They were at the farmyard. Aunt Olive gathered up the children, to take them to the sties. She nodded to the back door, but before Bryony could enter a child of about four flew out of the door. 'Can I come, Aunt Olive?'

She was the image of Hannah, but blonde, but then Germans were.

Bryony instinctively looked away, then back as she heard Hannah say, 'Put on your boots, Elizabeth. Come along now, you know the rules.'

Hannah was now standing at the back door, watching as her daughter did so, and then ran in pursuit of the others. 'Hello, Bee,' she said.

Bryony nodded. This was the woman who had . . . She stopped herself and said, 'We're to put the kettle on.'

Hannah disappeared into the kitchen. As Bryony prepared to follow she saw three men at the barn, watching. They were skeletal, thinner than anyone should be. When they saw her watching they fled inside.

In the kitchen Hannah waited; the kettle was on the range hob. She indicated a chair. Bryony sat. The kitchen looked almost the same, but shabby, and smaller. Her sister was similarly diminished and too thin, but held herself differently. Her shoulders were back, her head up, her gaze steady.

Hannah stood in front of the dresser. 'I lied for years. Dad did not ask you to look after me. He was dead when I arrived. I didn't want to be alone, I didn't trust Mum to look after me, only you. I used you.'

Her gaze was still steady but Bryony avoided it, and instead looked out of the window, studying the clouds spinning across the sky.

'I betrayed you when you came to fetch me. I was stupid, selfish and I could have had you killed. I can't forgive myself, so I don't expect you to. But I want you to know I'm sorry. Elizabeth is Hans's child. Hans is dead. I'm sorry because I did love him, after a fashion, I think, but I hope he never told his parents of me, because I don't want them coming to claim her. But if they do, I alone will deal with it.'

She stopped. Bryony had nothing to say, there had been too many years of Hannah. She waited as the kettle simmered, building up steam, bubbling now.

Hannah said, 'But, as always, I need something from you. I need to sell my share of my inheritance.'

Bryony relaxed back in her chair. She felt relieved because they were now on familiar ground. So, nothing had really changed. She waited, still saying nothing.

The kettle was whistling. Hannah picked up the oven cloth, grasped the handle and moved it from the hob, pouring water into the huge teapot. She shook the cloth out and hung it on the bar in front of the ovens.

She turned. 'You see, we have three escapees here. Two are Russian. They cannot go home, because we understand, from things Sister Maria has heard via the mother house, that on their return they will be killed or imprisoned by Stalin's regime. We have false papers for them, but they have no means of earning a living and we have no money. If, however, I sell my share of Combe Lodge, then it will set them up, to some extent. I don't want to sell it all, just some.'

Bryony was listening closely. 'You don't want this for you, or your child, but for two strangers?'

Hannah shrugged. 'Well, perhaps three. Not what you're used to, is it?'

They could hear the sound of men's voices, the shrill chatter of the children, and then they were all bundling into the kitchen, Adam swinging in on his crutches. He nodded to Hannah as he lowered himself on to a chair pulled back by John. Cissie was being led into the hall by Elizabeth; the other two followed. Aunt Olive carried the cake April had made. 'John remembered this. Tea and cakes, what could be better. We'll save mine until another day.'

Adam took Bryony's hand under cover of the table. She squeezed back, and smiled. The conversation strayed into safer waters while beneath the surface Bryony tugged and delved into the truth or not of her sister's request.

After an hour, John tapped his watch. He was right, they needed to return. Was anyone coming with them?'

She asked the question. There was a silence. Aunt Olive looked at Hannah, and then Uncle Thomas. Uncle Thomas suggested Bryony should come to take a last look at the false wall in the barn, which should come down soon, though it had served well enough throughout the war. Once in the barn, full of the scent of hay, he supported all that Hannah had said. He waited, before opening the door into the sty. Inside were the skeletal young men, sitting on camp beds, their arms resting on their knees. 'They need to continue to hide, because now we have British authorities on the island and the agreement with Russia is that these lads must return to their home-land and Stalin's regime. It is a fate they fear,' he said. 'We have procured papers, do not ask how, and they appear to be good enough. They need work, or money. We can provide neither. Hannah has the potential for some money, though, to give them a start.' He nodded at the men, and led Bryony back into the barn, closing the door behind him.

Bryony gripped his arm as they walked into the farmyard. 'So this is real? Not just a scheme, or more of her manipulation?'

Uncle Thomas shook his head. 'Don't be a daft sod, of course it's a manipulation, but not for herself. One day she'll tell you of her war. It began as not something to be proud of, but it became different.'

For a while she said nothing. Adam came then, swinging on his crutches through farmyard muck.

'You could have gone round the edge,' she yelled.

'I'm in too much of a hurry to see you,' he said, winking at Uncle Thomas, who laughed and left them to it. She told him. He leaned against the barn wall, unsure, and so they stayed until John came to see if they had taken root.

John flew them back, while Bryony sat beside Adam, holding his hand. 'How good are good false papers?' she whispered.

'I wish I knew.'

'I will telephone Mr Templer. He knows all sorts of people in London and was the one who put the word out about Timmo. It seems the best thing to do, but we'll feed them up first. They can go in the cottage for now. I checked with John that it was all right with him.'

'Hannah's done a good job with their English.'

She looked at him, and grinned. 'She's done a good job on us.'

'Yet again,' Adam groaned. 'But this time it is something that you, my girl, would have done.'

She looked around the aircraft. Cissie, Sol and Betty were chatting to the three men, who had each taken hold of Bryony's hand when she had told them her plan, and held it to their lips. 'We can never thank you.'

She had said, 'It's my sister you should thank.'

Hannah and Elizabeth had seen them off, happy to remain in Jersey with Aunt Olive and Uncle Thomas, but more happy that Bryony would not buy Hannah out. Instead a share of Combe Lodge would remain hers, and the rest of the family would make sure these young men were secure, with a financial safety net, though probably the Millers would never know where they were. It was better that way.

Hannah had called out just before Bryony shut the Dragonette's door. 'We'll be home for Christmas, and then Easter, if that's all right with you, Bryony?'

'Combe Lodge isn't going anywhere, Hannah. It will always be waiting for you, and there are enough buildings to create a studio.'

Clive had walked across the field towards them at that point, and stood beside Hannah. Elizabeth had taken his hand, after he had lifted the child to his shoulders. Somehow Hannah and he looked a couple. Hannah had smiled, and at last met, and held her sister's eyes. They had nodded at one another. Bryony said, 'Or two studios, come to think of it.'

John was bringing the Dragonette in to land. Bryony leaned across to Cissie. 'One day you'll be flying the Dragonette, so listen to everything that John tells you. The war is over, the peace is beginning.'

Find out more about

Milly Adams

Read on for an insight into *Sisters at War*,
an interview with Milly, plus the chance to sign up to find
out more about Milly and our other saga authors...

Dear Reader,

I hope you enjoyed *Sisters at War*. I was looking for an era which would allow sibling tensions to exist but to be overridden by changes beyond the girls' control. Changes which meant the girls could develop independently, and perhaps reach a point at which they could find common ground. But what changes? Well, how about the occupation of the Channel Islands for one and the precarious world of the Air Transport Auxiliary for the other?

I am old enough to have grown up with my parents' memories of their experiences during the Second World War. I'm sure that this will be greeted with the chorus, 'Surely not, you look far too young.'

Well, nonetheless I did. My dad was a pilot in the RAF, and served start to finish. He was one of the lucky survivors. My cousin, Maureen, also flew but within the Air Transport Auxiliary. I have always found it a fascinating and courageous world. So why not use this as the backdrop for the eldest sister?

And as for the other sister, the intensely irritating Hannah? Life on Jersey in the war was another scenario which was suitably precarious and courageous, and what's more, Hannah would be unable to rely on her big sister.

What about life on the armed trawlers for one of the romantic 'leads'? It is a little known area of the war, but desperately hard, and the loss of life was high. It deserved to be written about. I was on my way.

As for Combe Lodge in Devon: I lived in Somerset and then Dorset before moving nearer London, and am familiar with Devon's rolling hills, its glorious climate, but I have never seen 'Combe Lodge'. If I ever win the lottery I will hunt it down.

I confess I loved Bryony, but not so Hannah, though I could understand her because I was a middle child. Was I this irritating? Probably. Was I this good as an older sister? Probably not. But Hannah 'got it together' in the end. So now there is a way forward for them, as sisters at peace.

Lots of love   Milly

Interview with Milly

1. What made you want to become a writer?
I wanted to be a star, actually, but have had to accept I have no talent. But I can talk for England and tend to embellish, though my family say I fib. Clearly I was destined to be a writer.

2. Describe your writing routine and where you like to write.
Generally, I get the germ of an idea, then I research, after which I plan in detail, chapter by chapter. Throughout this stage I am out and about, having fun. Then I settle down to write at the dining room table, with the television on for company. And for as long as it takes, even breathing is a nuisance. Though I love the phone going, and emails pinging in, as I do believe in distraction.

3. What themes are you interested in when you're writing?
I like to write about the balance of power in relationships, set in a social and political context.

4. Where do you get your inspiration from?
That's the million-dollar question. It just comes. I suppose I'm naturally curious and notice things. Though others would say I'm nosy. I can live with that.

5. How do you manage to get inside the heads of your characters in order to portray them truthfully?
Research. I need to understand their world, actually swim amongst it, until I have captured the essence of it, then I can *be* them.

6. Do you base your characters on real people? And if not, where does the inspiration come from?
No, I don't base my characters on real people. On the whole I try to empathise. For me, I can imagine myself as a person in any given situation. This is why I felt I should be a star.

7. What aspect of writing do you enjoy most (e.g. plot, character development)?

Character development and plot creation go hand in hand for me. Creating a plausible character living a plausible life is challenging and enjoyable. I feel it is because usually it is the only thing I can control. Perhaps I'm a megalomaniac or a dictator in the making?

8. What advice would you give aspiring writers?

To learn the ropes. So attend a reputable class, and, in addition, support literary festivals, and conferences like the Winchester Writers' Conference. At these you can hear established writers talking about their work. You also need powers of endurance and a hide like a rhino to endure the rejections.

9. What is your favourite book of all time and why?

I think *Little Women* possibly. *Little Women* showed me that I'd rather be Jo, the independent soul, than any of the other sisters. But there are so many wonderful books out there.

10. If you could be a character in a book, or live in the world of a book, who or where would you be?

Oh crikey. Would I be a pole dancer? No, on balance I think I'd be a lady who lunches in expensive but casual restaurants in Florence, New York and London, whilst being deep into espionage – she'd save the world on a daily basis. Importantly, she'd be someone who never ever puts on a pound in weight, has her hair done every morning, and is utterly adored by George Clooney.

To find out more about Milly and her books, you can join our mailing list by sending in your name and contact details (address and email) to:

Saga books, Penguin Random House,
20 Vauxhall Bridge Road,
London, SW1V 2SA